MIDN

A soft sound at the [door made her turn] around. She drew in [her breath with a] hard thump. Ryan stood [in the doorway.]
"What are you doing here?" she asked.

He leaned against the door frame, that familiar, mocking smile on his face. He wore a dark dressing gown, tied with a sash. "I might ask you the same thing."

"It *does* happen to be my home," she said coolly. "I may go where I wish." She gave him a cool stare. "I don't know why you followed me, but I don't want you here. Please leave."

Instead, Ryan moved closer until only a foot separated them. She could feel his heat, smell his masculine scent of soap and spice. He reached out his hand to lazily touch her cheek.

"What *do* you want, Calista?" he asked.

"I want you to leave me alone," she told him, but her voice trembled, betraying the lie.

Ryan's gaze held hers for an eternity before finally dropping to her mouth. Slowly, he lowered his face to hers. She felt the whisper of his breath teasing her lips, then his mouth was covering hers, devouring hers. Calista could no more keep from returning his kiss than she could stop breathing.

PUT SOME PASSION INTO YOUR LIFE... WITH THIS STEAMY SELECTION OF ZEBRA *LOVEGRAMS!*

SEA FIRES (3899, $4.50/$5.50)
by Christine Dorsey
Spirited, impetuous Miranda Chadwick arrives in the untamed New World prepared for any peril. But when the notorious pirate Gentleman Jack Blackstone kidnaps her in order to fulfill his secret plans, she can't help but surrender—to the shameless desires and raging hunger that his bronzed, lean body and demanding caresses ignite within her!

TEXAS MAGIC (3898, $4.50/$5.50)
by Wanda Owen
After being ambushed by bandits and saved by a ranchhand, headstrong Texas belle Bianca Moreno hires her gorgeous rescuer as a protective escort. But Rick Larkin does more than guard her body—he kisses away her maidenly inhibitions, and teaches her the secrets of wild, reckless love!

SEDUCTIVE CARESS (3767, $4.50/$5.50)
by Carla Simpson
Determined to find her missing sister, brave beauty Jessamyn Forsythe disguises herself as a simple working girl and follows her only clues to Whitechapel's darkest alleys... and the disturbingly handsome Inspector Devlin Burke. Burke, on the trail of a killer, becomes intrigued with the ebon-haired lass and discovers the secrets of her silken lips and the hidden promise of her sweet flesh.

SILVER SURRENDER (3769, $4.50/$5.50)
by Vivian Vaughan
When Mexican beauty Aurelia Mazón saves a handsome stranger from death, she finds herself on the run from the Federales with the most dangerous man she's ever met. And when Texas Ranger Carson Jarrett steals her heart with his intimate kisses and seductive caresses, she yields to an all-consuming passion from which she hopes to never escape!

ENDLESS SEDUCTION (3793, $4.50/$5.50)
by Rosalyn Alsobrook
Caught in the middle of a dangerous shoot-out, lovely Leona Stegall falls unconscious and awakens to the gentle touch of a handsome doctor. When her rescuer's caresses turn passionate, Leona surrenders to his fiery embrace and savors a night of soaring ecstasy!

Available wherever paperbacks are sold, or order direct from the Publisher. Send cover price plus 50¢ per copy for mailing and handling to Penguin USA, P.O. Box 999, c/o Dept. 17109, Bergenfield, NJ 07621. Residents of New York and Tennessee must include sales tax. DO NOT SEND CASH.

SWEET ENCHANTMENT

ELIZABETH GRAHAM

PINNACLE BOOKS
KENSINGTON PUBLISHING CORP.

*For my friends, Cathy, Marti, Gloria, Frances,
Gerry, Dolores, Hortense, Sandra, Dencie, and Sharron.
For my editor, John Scognamiglio.
And for Barbara J. Brett, my first editor.
My heartfelt thanks for your belief in me,
help and support.*

ZEBRA BOOKS are published by

Kensington Publishing Corp.
850 Third Avenue
New York, NY 10022

Copyright © 1995 by Elizabeth Graham

All rights reserved. No part of this book may be reproduced in any form or by any means without the prior written consent of the Publisher, excepting brief quotes used in reviews.

If you purchased this book without a cover, you should be aware that this book is stolen property. It was reported as "unsold and destroyed" to the Publisher and neither the Author nor the Publisher has received any payment for this "stripped book."

Zebra, the Z logo Reg. U.S. Pat. & TM Off. The Lovegram logo is a trademark of Kensington Publishing Corp.

First Printing: August, 1995

Printed in the United States of America

Chapter One

South Carolina, 1835

"I've put you in the best guest bedroom," Estelle Howard fluttered, leading the way up the wide, curving stairs. "And of course Baxter can't *wait* to see you!" She gave her niece a coquettish sideways glance.

Alarm shot through Calista Shelby. She glanced at Lucinda, to find her other aunt's eyes on her, a reassuring message in them. *Don't worry,* Lucinda mouthed silently.

"Of course, we were all surprised at poor Isabelle's will," Estelle chattered on. Gaining the top of the stairs, she turned right and moved down the wide hallway, the other two women following.

She paused before a white-painted door and opened it with a flourish. "But we soon realized your mother was very wise. She knew every woman needs a husband, and what better choice than your own dear cousin?"

Calista, who'd been surveying the large, beautifully furnished bedroom, jerked her head around at her aunt's words to stare at her. Surely she didn't mean what her words implied. She felt Lucinda's fingers grasp her hand, squeezing it in warning.

"I see you've redecorated, Estelle," Lucinda said, her voice calm and pleasant as she looked at the mahogany four-postered bed, draped with mosquito netting, and the twin armoires flanking it.

A pleased, smug smile spread over Estelle's face. "Since Farley's business has done so well, we simply had to refurbish the old place. We must keep up appearances, you know."

"That's very important," Lucinda agreed solemnly, her fingers still holding tightly to Calista's hand.

Calista barely heard Estelle prattle on. Finally, she left, after showing Lucinda her smaller, plainer room.

A few minutes later Lucinda came back inside Calista's room and closed the door. Calista turned to her aunt, her green eyes stricken. "Aunt Lucie," she pleaded, "tell me I misunderstood."

Lucinda reached out a gentle hand to stroke her niece's cheek. "I'm afraid we overlooked one thing. Naturally, the Howards will push a marriage between you and Baxter—to keep you from marrying someone else and doing them out of Meadowmarsh. We should have realized they'd jump to the conclusion your mother wanted you to marry Baxter and that's why she left such a peculiar will. Obviously, Baxter also thinks it a splendid idea."

Calista walked to the window and swept back the lace curtains covering the panes. The window looked down on a secluded courtyard, screened from the street by a low brick wall, with trees and shrubs forming a higher barrier. The courtyard was laid out with formal gardens containing many exotic flowers. Fruit-bearing citrus trees were arranged gracefully at intervals.

It was tasteful and beautiful, but already she missed Meadowmarsh's woods and beaches. She took deep breaths until she'd calmed down, then turned and faced her aunt again, pushing back a springy black curl that had strayed onto her temple.

"I know we've gone over this a dozen times, but I still can't understand why Mama did this to me! Why would she say I must marry by the time I'm twenty-one or Meadowmarsh goes to Baxter?"

"I don't know. But I'm certain she had your best interests at heart."

"But *Baxter?* After what he did to me?"

"What he *tried* to do to you, dear. As I recall, even though you were only fourteen, you managed to defend your virtue quite successfully." Lucinda chuckled. "When he came in the house that day, you could see the imprint of all five of your fingers on his face."

Calista's face relaxed into a smile. "So this makes it a little harder, but also more challenging."

"That's my girl!" Lucinda clapped her hands. "If you can make Baxter think you're interested in him, no one will be watching you as closely."

Calista shuddered. "And that is going to be the hardest part of this whole business. I guess I'd better start thinking of what to say."

"Most definitely. I'll be your coach." Lucinda moved to a rosewood settee on the wall facing the bed and motioned to the empty space beside her. "We'd better get started."

Seating herself beside her aunt, Calista pulled up the skirts of her black traveling dress to be more comfortable. "I suppose the proper attitude is reserved warmth, with a slight remoteness, signifying all is forgiven, but not quite yet forgotten. What do you think?"

"Yes, that should do nicely. Of course, I'll be there to serve as chaperon every moment."

"Thank God! Now, let us hope and pray the dinner

guests will also include an amiable, not too bright, eligible young man!"

"You certainly don't have your sights set high," Lucinda said dryly.

Calista nodded. "Mama and I ran Meadowmarsh for years by ourselves. I don't need or want a man to tell me what to do—just one who'll go about his own affairs and let me do the same."

"You couldn't have turned out any differently since both your parents were such strong-willed people." Lucinda waggled a finger at her niece. "But if you're not careful, my girl, someday you'll meet your match."

Calista looked around the well-appointed table in the Howards' opulently furnished dining room. If this were her aunt's idea of a small dinner party, she wondered what a large one would be like.

So far her luck was holding. Baxter had come in late from his office, barely in time for dinner, and she'd managed to avoid a confrontation with him. Now he sat several seats down from her, where she didn't have to try to avoid his glance. She was safe—at least until dinner was over.

And there were *two* unattached males here. One was much better looking than the other—his black hair contrasted with deep-blue eyes, fringed with thick, dark lashes. His mustache was as black as his hair, and his beautifully tailored frock coat displayed a well-muscled body precisely as it was intended to. He'd been introduced as Ryan Burke, a member of one of Charleston's most prestigious law firms, the one the Howards employed.

He didn't look like a lawyer, she thought. No, he seemed much too vital to spend his days shut up in a musty office dealing with legal affairs.

SWEET ENCHANTMENT

The man in question glanced across the table and caught her staring at him. His thin, yet somehow sensual mouth curved upward slightly, as if he knew exactly what she was up to, and the cleft in his firm chin seemed more pronounced.

"And how are you enjoying your visit to Charleston, Miss Shelby?" he asked, interrupting her thoughts.

His rich voice was as attractive as the rest of him. "I've only just gotten here," she said coolly. He and his partner, Jerome Kingsley, had also arrived late, full of apologies, with barely time for Estelle to introduce them before dinner was announced.

"Then we'll have to make sure it's enjoyable." Ryan Burke's gaze lingered on her mouth for a moment, then traveled down to her smooth throat, revealed by the rounded neckline of the plain, black mourning gown she wore.

"Charleston is an interesting city. I'd be delighted to show you some of the sights."

Calista swallowed, her throat feeling dry at his thorough appraisal. "That's kind of you," she said noncommittally, still keeping her voice cool.

This was no man she could control. She'd do well to ignore him and concentrate on the other single man at the table, a few places down from Ryan. Timothy Gardner also looked at her, but with a very different expression on his rather rabbity face.

Admiration shone from his light-brown eyes, which almost exactly matched his hair color. But his look was not the kind that would make a girl blush. She gave Timothy a radiant smile. He smiled back, looking both pleased and surprised. Timothy, like her Uncle Farley, was a factor. His father was a friend of the Howards.

Relieved, Calista turned her attention to her dinner.

The food was well cooked and plentiful, but a trifle heavy, what with both beef and pork roasts, along with turkey and ham, as well as several vegetables and hot bread.

She missed the seafood that appeared at almost every Meadowmarsh meal. She could almost taste the delicately flavored oysters, the succulent shrimp and clams. Her mouth watered at the thought, and she grimaced at herself. This was only her first day here. She had to forget her longings and concentrate on the business at hand.

Which, and she'd better not forget it, was finding a malleable man who'd take her to wife. And then let her continue with the life she found so fulfilling. She glanced at Timothy, gratified to find him once more staring at her, the admiration in his eyes stronger.

Calista gave him another warm smile, even fluttering her eyelashes a bit, and reached for her glass of wine. As she lifted it to her mouth, her glance crossed Ryan's. The small smile curved his well-shaped mouth again.

Unexpectedly, shame for what she was trying to do went through her. She felt red creeping up her throat into her face. She'd deliberately set out to trap a man into marrying her—for her own, selfish reasons.

Three places down from Calista, Lucinda Shelby also blushed like a schoolgirl.

"I do hope I'll have the opportunity to show you the sights of Charleston, Miss Shelby." Jerome Kingsley's voice was deferential, his faded-blue eyes admiring, as his glance met Lucinda's.

"That would be very nice, Mr. Kingsley," Lucinda murmured, willing her hot cheeks to cool. Her heart was fluttering, too, she realized, her astonishment growing. It had been so long since a man had paid her this kind of attention she'd forgotten the physical manifestations that came with attraction between the sexes.

Jerome Kingsley was a senior partner in a law firm—

the same firm as the good-looking young man who was having such an effect on Calista, she'd discovered a moment ago.

"Excuse me," Dacia, Estelle's serving girl, who spoke flawless English, murmured. She deftly removed the soiled dinner plates, replacing them with a dessert made from the oranges growing in the walled courtyard.

Jerome Kingsley tasted the sweet concoction with appreciation. "The Howards certainly know how to set a table, don't they? But I imagine your plantation does, too. We summer on Sullivan's Island, and the seafood is bountiful and wonderful."

"Yes," Lucinda answered, picking up her own dessert spoon. "Our table is plainer, not given to these exotic fancies, but we make up for it with our fish and seafood delicacies."

She glanced quickly down the table and sighed. Calista looked as if she'd like to be anywhere but here, and young Burke seemed to know exactly what she was up to and was amused by it.

However, there was the other young man down from Burke. He'd made sheep's eyes at Calista ever since they'd sat down to dinner. And he was exactly the kind of man her niece wanted. She'd found out from Jerome that both of the men were extremely eligible. She sighed again. Pity Calista would have to settle for young Gardner.

"Calista, dear," Estelle's voice floated down the length of the table, "whom did you find to oversee Meadowmarsh while you're away? If you're not satisfied, Farley will be glad to locate someone for you."

Calista managed a smile, despite her new and unwanted doubts about her mission here. "I don't think that will be necessary, Aunt Estelle," she said, thankful her voice sounded calm and unruffled. "Zeke has done a fine job for us for ten years."

"Zeke?" her cousin Baxter asked. "You don't mean to say you left a darkie in charge?"

Her smile faded as she glanced at him. Every hair of his blond head was in place, his handsome face flushed with wine, his black eyes, so like his mother's, lingering on her mouth, her throat.

Out of the corner of her eye, she saw Ryan Burke looking at her intently. She nodded, lifting her chin. "Yes, I did. I have every confidence in Zeke."

From the other end of the table, her uncle's loud voice boomed out, "My girl, that won't do at all."

She gave him a quick glance. Farley Howard's beefy face had darkened, his mouth hung slightly open as he stared at her. He reached for his wine glass and took a hearty swallow, then put it down.

"No, won't do at all," he repeated, his voice allowing no argument. "Why, those darkies could take over your place while you're gone! Burn it to the ground." He shook his massive head of graying hair.

"I'd feel more uneasy with some stranger in charge," Calista said, annoyance rising. "We've always been good to our people. They wouldn't harm Meadowmarsh. It's their home, too."

"I'll send someone out there first thing tomorrow," Farley went on as if she hadn't spoken. "I know several good men who'll take no nonsense. That's what Meadowmarsh needs. Your parents were always far too lenient. It surprises me that you haven't had trouble long before now."

Calista felt the eyes of everyone at the table on her. Her uncle's loud voice could be heard in the next room, she had no doubt. She pressed her lips together mutinously. She *wouldn't* let him force this on her! Then, she noticed her aunt Lucie giving her discreet signals.

Don't say anything back, Lucinda's eyes warned.

Calista forced herself to calm down. Aunt Lucie was right. She couldn't make a scene here at the dinner table, not if she wanted to keep on being a welcome guest in this house. And the stakes were too high to jeopardize her plan. It wouldn't be for long, and she could make a trip out to Meadowmarsh in a week or so to see how things were going.

"You're right, Uncle Farley," she said stiffly. "I'd be much obliged if you'd handle it for me."

Her uncle nodded, pleased with her assent, his high color fading a little. "That's being a sensible girl, my dear. I knew you'd see it my way." He returned his attention to his dessert.

Calista made her expression neutral as she glanced at Baxter again, reminding herself he was the one she had to placate. He looked as self-satisfied as his father at her decision, and also as if he'd like to undress her right here in the dining room. She repressed a disgusted shudder. She suddenly hated all this.

Ryan Burke was surprised at the stab of annoyance that shot through him as he observed the greedy expression in Baxter Howard's eyes. It was nothing to him at how many men the beautiful young flirt made eyes. But she wasn't flirting with Baxter, he realized. No, she looked as if she might faint or lose her dinner. So, it seemed she was at least a little selective. She'd narrowed it down to Timid Timothy.

Finally, Calista tore her stricken gaze from Baxter and returned it to her dessert dish. She picked up her spoon and daintily dug out a portion, then lifted it toward her mouth.

That brilliant green gaze met his again, and Ryan felt an all-gone feeling in the pit of his stomach and the tightening of his groin. Damn! What was it about the baggage? She was beautiful, granted, but Charleston was full of beautiful women.

Ryan looked at her downcast eyes, the delicate tracery of veins in her eyelids. A tear glistened on the tip of her dark lashes, and she quickly blinked it away. He wanted to reach across the table and pull her into his arms and comfort her, he realized, amazed.

He shook his head to clear it of these crazy fancies, but the amazement lingered. In the space of one dinner party, she'd filled him with lust, then an unfamiliar tenderness. He hadn't felt the last emotion for a woman except his younger sister, Gabrielle, since his mother's death five years ago. He'd felt desire, of course. But lately, even that seemed to be deserting him.

He was tired of Charleston social life, tired of the long days spent in the Kingsley law firm. He was beginning to feel as if he were drying up, becoming an old man like Jerome.

However, tonight Jerome didn't seem so dried up. Ryan glanced down the table to where his friend and partner talked animatedly with the elderly woman who had been introduced as Calista's aunt. Jerome had been a widower for ten years, and as far as Ryan knew, he'd never so much as looked at another woman since his Lydia died. Until tonight.

Ryan's thoughts came back to Calista again. The girl had been furious when her uncle insisted on sending an overseer out to her plantation. Obviously, she was used to running things herself; but for some reason, she'd decided to give in tonight and let Howard have his way. Ryan's gaze returned to her still-lowered head.

Now, why had she done that? To avoid making a scene in public? Possibly, although she looked spirited enough not to care too much about that. No, he decided, there was another reason why she'd given in. He didn't know what it was, but he intended to find out. He'd drop a few hints to Jerome, who came here often for dinner or late suppers, that he wouldn't at all mind coming along, too. Which should be enough to get him invited.

The girl had aroused his curiosity, and he planned to scratch the itch. Another thought inched its way into his mind. Maybe, sometime in the next few weeks, he'd be able to scratch another itch she'd kindled in him. The thought of her soft pink lips pressed to his, her full breasts against his chest, tightened his loins again.

As if drawn by a magnet, his gaze strayed across the table once more. Calista's clear, green eyes looked straight at him as if she could read his mind. She compressed her tempting lips and turned her head quickly away, but not before he saw red suffuse her cheeks.

Ryan narrowed his eyes, his own mouth tightening. Don't be a fool, he told himself. You'll do no such thing. You won't get involved with that little minx.

Chapter Two

"Don't you worry 'bout dat old white overseer. He soon be eatin' outta my hand." Lotus smiled at Zeke across the rough wood of his eating table, her black eyes gleaming.

Zeke frowned at her as his hands picked a crab apart to get at the luscious meat inside. "Maybe I oughta worry 'bout you. What you gonna do to get him like that?"

His glance raked her supple body, which, now that she'd been promoted to housekeeper, on his recommendation, was clad in a pink-sprigged cotton gown not unlike what the young mistress wore. In fact, he wasn't at all sure it wasn't one of Miz Calista's gowns. She hadn't borrowed any petticoats, though, he noticed, his body stirring as his eyes followed the garment's clinging lines.

He hadn't cared to bring it up with Lotus. If he said something to displease her, likely as not she'd stay away from his cabin for a week to punish him. Often he wished he hadn't gotten mixed up with her, but then he'd think of the long, humid nights when she lay in his arms and those thoughts were quickly banished.

Lotus's slim dark hand moved across the table and picked up a chunk of crab meat. She popped it into her mouth. "You want him to treat you like dirt in de fields?" she demanded, her black brows drawing together in an answering frown.

Zeke quickly backed down. He decided it was better he didn't know what Lotus had to do to keep Ira Atwood from making his life a living hell. Ever since the white overseer had arrived a week ago, things had been bad. All the field hands complained about his treatment of them, and more than one had felt the unfamiliar lash of the whip.

Zeke hated to believe Miz Calista had sent the man here; but he had to, he thought, resentfully. After all, she owned the plantation now. At least for a while. Rumors had been going around the quarters about her having to find a husband soon or lose Meadowmarsh because her mama had left that in her will, but none of them knew this to be true for a fact.

"All right," he agreed, gathering up the remnants of the crabs and standing. "But this pallet gonna be lonesome without you."

Lotus gave him a sly smile and got up from the table. "I'll be back in here before you knows I'm gone."

She moved across the few feet separating them, her hips and rounded bottom swaying enticingly. Her bare feet slapped on the hard-packed earth of the cabin, the two wide silver anklets on her legs jingling.

When she reached Zeke, she placed her hands on her hips, tipping her head to stare at him from black, almond-shaped eyes. "It's too early yet to go to dat white man's house." She moved closer and reached out a hand to caress his dark, gleaming midriff, bare of shirt and ridged with hard muscle.

Lotus felt the muscles contract beneath her touch. Her hand slid under the waist of his homespun trousers, then farther downward.

Zeke's big, work-worn hand suddenly clamped down on hers, pressing it closer against his body, moving it even lower. Sweat beaded his forehead, and he felt a trembling begin in his lower regions. Lotus was a witch. He'd been with several of the slave women over the years, but he'd never found another who affected him as this one did.

He reached out with his free hand and pulled her against the rapidly hardening length of his strong body. Her full breasts under the cotton dress pushed against his bare chest, and he could feel the nipples contracting, firming into hard nubs. "Come on, woman," he muttered hoarsely into her ear. "That pallet's waitin' for us."

Lotus followed him to the pallet rolled against one of the chinked cabin's walls, content for the moment to let him lead, to let him pull her roughly down under his fully aroused body. Even while she followed his movements with her own, her mind strayed to what lay ahead this evening. She hadn't been with a white man for a long time—not since she'd left the other plantation six months ago.

The young master there had slipped into her cabin many a night. He'd been eager to pleasure her, and she'd taught him all the ways she liked best. He'd let her get out of work by playing sick, given her gifts—including the silver anklets which she'd hidden in her kerchief until she'd reached here.

And he'd loved the light-skinned baby boy she'd birthed, because his wife couldn't give him any sons. Oh, but then the stupid mistress had found out about the baby.

Lotus's face tightened as an image of the hated woman filled her mind's eye. Black silky hair and green eyes, pearly white skin....

Her face stiffened even more. Just like the young mistress here. *Miz Calista*. Every time Lotus looked at her, it was all she could do to keep from scratching her eyes out.

Lotus had been sold before she could catch her breath, the baby sold separately out of spite. Not that she cared that much, but the baby was *hers*. She hated the power the despised mistress had had over her.

The same kind of power Miz Calista had here.

But not for long. An evil smile twisted her full lips. Not for long.

Meadowmarsh was far different than her old plantation. The fool of an old mistress—and now the young one—let the blacks alone. As long as the work got done, no one bothered them. She couldn't believe there wasn't even a white overseer. Just Zeke.

Until Ira Atwood arrived a few days ago. But she'd taken his measure at once. She was confident she could handle him. And she'd let Zeke think it was all for his benefit. Her smile in the dark was contemptuous.

Men were all the same. She'd easily talked Zeke into persuading Miz Calista to let her take over as temporary housekeeper.

She had plans for Zeke he didn't know about yet. Some he wouldn't like, so she'd wait until later to tell him. But one of them he'd like fine....

Her tongue came out and ran over her full lips, her mind wandering to the hours ahead. Ira Atwood was middle-aged and none too clean, but he had a look about him she'd come to recognize. The look that said he knew how to satisfy a woman.

Zeke groaned and covered her mouth with his own,

urgently seeking her response. Lotus forgot what else the night might hold for her and concentrated on the moment at hand.

"Miss Calista, you are without doubt the most beautiful woman I've ever seen," Timothy Gardner said earnestly, his pale-brown eyes giving her a worshipful stare.

Calista smiled at him sweetly. Or at least she hoped the look was sweet. Her mouth ached from all the smiles she'd given him during the evening.

"You are too kind, sir," she said, mouthing the conventional words. Oh, how she wished she were home! A vision of Meadowmarsh's fertile green fields, the lagoon, the white dunes dotted with sea oats, filled her mind's eye. Stifling a sigh, she edged closer to Timothy on the brocaded settee in a secluded corner of the large salon.

A tall potted palm screened them from the rest of the room. Aunt Lucie, in her role as chaperon, along with Jerome Kingsley, had sat opposite them on a matching settee until a few minutes ago.

The older couple had slipped out through a side door, saying they needed the fresh air of the courtyard. Judging from her aunt's heightened color, Calista thought there was another reason for their withdrawal besides giving her and Timothy a chance to be truly alone. Thank God for Aunt Lucie.

Estelle seemed unworried that Calista spent so much time with Timothy, even thanking him for his attentions to her niece while Baxter was in bed with the ague he'd so conveniently come down with the night of the first dinner party. Gritting her teeth, Calista kept the illusion of her interest in Baxter alive by putting little notes her aunt dictated on one of the trays Dacia took up to him each day.

And as Lucinda pointed out, why *should* Estelle worry? Baxter was handsome and well-to-do, fully as eligible as either Ryan Burke or Timothy. And he obviously wanted Calista. Most people would assume Calista would be happy to marry him.

Timothy's hand suddenly covered hers where it lay beside her on the seat. Covered it, then squeezed a bit. Calista swallowed. Things were moving along as she'd hoped and planned. This was only her second week here, and her instincts told her soon he'd be ready to propose marriage.

So why didn't she feel better about it? The shame she'd felt at the first dinner party had faded. Aunt Lucie had reminded her that Timothy wouldn't be cheated by marrying her. Meadowmarsh was prosperous, and Timothy obviously thought Calista a prize to be greatly desired. Why couldn't she feel the same about him?

Something alerted her and she glanced up to see Ryan Burke leaning against a column beside the palm, the sardonic smile which always seemed to be on his well-shaped mouth firmly in place.

Calista felt red creeping up her throat, and tightened her lips. She tried to release her hand, but Timothy, emboldened by her earlier response, held fast.

The blush traveled to her cheeks. She gave Ryan a tiny, frosty smile. "Good evening, Mr. Burke."

Timothy gave a small start and glanced at the other man. "Evening, Burke," he said politely.

Ryan acknowledged their greetings with a small bow, which also managed to seem mocking. "I hope I'm not intruding." He sat down on the settee opposite theirs.

"No, certainly not." Timothy released Calista's hand and moved away from her a little.

Calista frowned, annoyed by his meekness. If she sat here with Ryan and another man intruded, she felt certain

Ryan wouldn't mince words in telling him to be on his way. But, she reminded herself, that was one of the reasons the man beside her wasn't Ryan. She didn't want such a forceful man—she wanted one like Timothy.

Also, Ryan wasn't in the least interested in her. True, like Timothy, he came here for dinner or supper often. And he usually seemed to be somewhere in the vicinity whenever she managed to be relatively alone with Timothy, but it was strictly in the role of interested observer. Although this struck Calista as odd, she tried to dismiss it and keep her mind on her mission.

"Are you planning to remain in Charleston during the holiday season?" Calista asked Ryan when the silence stretched out awkwardly.

"No, I'll go back to Ainsley Hall for Christmas." Ryan struggled to keep from showing his amusement at her obvious wish to be rid of him. For the past two weeks, he'd watched her maneuver Timothy.

After the first dinner party, he had realized she wasn't merely flirting, but going after Timothy with single-minded persistence. This added to the intriguing puzzle she presented, further whetting his curiosity.

He'd heard Miss Shelby's plantation prospered. She couldn't be trying to snare Timothy merely because his family had money. And he couldn't believe she loved him. Tonight he'd discovered the truth.

A few minutes ago he'd overheard Estelle Howard telling a friend Calista would lose Meadowmarsh unless she married before her twenty-first birthday, only a few months away. Furthermore, Estelle had said, her own Baxter was going to marry dear Calista. They'd been childhood sweethearts. Such a shame Baxter's illness kept them from being together now. As soon as he recovered, they would announce their engagement.

The pieces of the puzzle fell into place, and Ryan found

himself rooting for Calista's success before her slimy cousin regained his health. The other feelings he'd had that first evening he'd tried to keep firmly in check, which hadn't been easy. Still wasn't, he thought, glancing at the beautiful woman across from him.

Calista let her own gaze settle on the wall an inch from Ryan's face. She guessed she'd have to carry on a polite conversation since Timothy was apparently going to sit there like a slug and contribute nothing.

"Why did you become an attorney, Mr. Burke? Plantation life doesn't interest you?" Since that first evening she'd discovered Ryan had a younger sister and brother and his father owned a large plantation nearby.

Ryan shrugged, pretending total indifference. "I got tired of it. Decided I wanted the city life."

When he went back for visits, he felt like an outsider. His father and Andrew didn't need him. His father, as always, made it plain Ryan wasn't even wanted at Ainsley Hall. His mouth twisted. Not until he needed another loan from Ryan, that was. If it weren't for Gabrielle, he probably wouldn't even go home for Christmas.

He liked the way Calista had arranged her black hair, pulled smoothly to the back of her neck in a twist. A sudden vision of her shining hair spread on a snowy pillow, her lithe body gleaming and bare, filled his mind. He quickly blanked it out. His interest in her was strictly curiosity, he reminded himself firmly.

"Oh? And have you changed your mind since then?" Calista liked the way his mustache moved when he talked; she liked the deep cleft in his strong chin. No she didn't, she hastily told herself. She wasn't interested in him at all.

Ryan tried to ignore Calista's full, pink mouth; her black-fringed green eyes; the way the plain, black dress she wore only accentuated her beauty. "I'm not—"

"Oh, *there* you are, Ryan!" a light, feminine voice

said. Around the edge of the potted palm appeared Leora Howard. She smiled radiantly at all three of them and then sat down beside Ryan, her blonde curls bobbing on her shoulders, her brown eyes sparkling. "I've been looking all over for you." Her rosebud lips pouted.

Hell and damnation! Ryan had been trying to avoid Leora ever since he'd arrived tonight and seen she was back home, afraid she'd renew her campaign. He'd stopped coming to the house a few months ago because the girl had developed a yen for him. "I've been in plain sight," he told her, smiling in spite of himself at her fresh, young beauty.

Calista felt a stabbing sensation in her chest as she watched Baxter's sister flirt with Ryan. The silly little twit! Then her sense of fairness took over and Calista had to admit Leora wasn't doing anything she herself hadn't done the last two weeks with Timothy. And maybe with Leora pursuing him, Ryan would stop shadowing her and Timothy. He certainly didn't seem to be trying to get rid of the girl.

Just the same, she wouldn't sit here all evening and watch them, she decided, getting to her feet. "I think we should mingle with Aunt Estelle's guests." She gave Ryan and Leora a prim smile.

Leora returned the smile, openly pleased at being left alone with Ryan. Ryan, on the other hand, gave her a look she couldn't fathom. With Timothy at her side, Calista walked back into the main part of the huge room.

Aunt Lucie and Jerome were nowhere in sight. Still in the courtyard, she guessed. Calista had a sudden urge to get away from these people milling around, making small talk and laughing. She was tired of Timothy, tired of all of this. She longed to be alone, outside in the fresh air.

"Timothy, I've developed a headache," she said. "I believe I must bid you good night and go upstairs."

He looked disappointed but concerned. "Yes, do go on, Calista," he said. He took her hand in his and brought it to his mouth.

The feel of Timothy's soft mouth was unpleasant. Calista forced herself not to snatch her hand back. You'll soon have to put up with a lot more than hand-kissing from him, she reminded herself.

He released her hand, looking pleased with himself. "I'll see you two days from now, then," he told her. "At the Reynolds' house."

Calista nodded, so eager to get away she could hardly stand still. "Yes. Goodnight, Timothy."

She walked up the wide stairs without anyone else seeing her, stopping her. At the top, she breathed a sigh of relief. The wide floral-carpeted hallway was clear, too, she saw, walking quickly toward her room. When she reached Baxter's door, she checked her rapid walk. His door was ajar—what did that mean?

The door suddenly opened all the way. Baxter stood there, in his dressing gown. His handsome face looked pale, she noted, his blond hair mussed. He leaned on the door frame. "Well, hello, little Cousin." His full bottom lip turned down in a smirk. "What brings you upstairs so early in the evening?"

"I'm not feeling well," Calista answered cautiously. Alarm filled her as Baxter stepped out of the doorway toward her, but she forced herself to smile at him and not move away.

He moved even closer. "I hope you're not coming down with the ague, too. That would be such a shame. Mama is planning to announce our engagement as soon as I'm up and about, which won't be too much longer."

Calista forced the smile to remain on her frozen mouth. Baxter smelled strongly of liquor and an over-sweet cologne. It made her almost gag to be this close to him. Thank God things were coming along so well with Timothy. "I trust not," she said evenly. "And I'd better go to bed and get my rest to ensure that."

Baxter reached out and gripped her upper arm.

His palm felt slightly damp and very soft. Calista repressed a shudder of distaste.

"Just think, little Cousin, in a few months we'll be sharing the same bed. I can't wait." His hand moved caressingly up her arm.

"If I catch the ague from you, we'll be apart even longer," Calista warned. Oh, how she wanted to jerk her arm from his grasp, run down the hall to her room, and slam the door and lock it!

A frown wrinkled his forehead, and he reluctantly dropped her arm and stepped back. "Go ahead, then; I wouldn't want that to happen. Would you?"

Calista stepped back. "No, of course not," she said, despising all the lies. "Good night, Baxter." She turned and walked rapidly down the hall, half-expecting him to follow and touch her again. If he did, this time she would scream and slap him. She wouldn't be able to help it.

But he didn't. She reached the door of her room and turned the knob, darting a glance back down the hall. Baxter had retreated to his doorway again and was watching her, the lustful look on his face making the hairs on her arms stand up and a cold chill race down her back. She hurried inside and closed the door.

She stood leaning against it for a moment, shaken to the core. "Maybe Aunt Lucie and I should move into a hotel," she muttered, knowing that wasn't possible. If Timothy and Jerome visited them there, the gossip would be so bad that Timothy would probably cut and run and her plan to save her home would be lost.

When she heard Baxter's door close, relief filled her. After a few minutes, she'd steal downstairs to the garden. She *had* to get some fresh air away from this awful house.

Five minutes later, a black shawl over her shoulders, Calista slipped down the kitchen stairs and into the walled courtyard, taking deep breaths of the citrus- and flower-scented air. Blissfully alone, she walked down the landscaped paths, which were illuminated by the bright half-moon, and came to a decision.

She would go back to Meadowmarsh tomorrow instead of waiting until next week. Baxter might be up and about by then, and she'd have no more time to bring her plans to fruition. She *had* to get away from here, walk on the earth of her own beloved plantation again.

"Do you mind if I join you?"

Ryan's voice sounded so close to her shoulder that Calista jumped and whirled to face him. The moon cast shadows across his face, emphasizing his cleft chin, his deep-set eyes. She could smell the soap he'd used, a clean, masculine scent. She moved back a step.

"As a matter of fact, I do. I want to be alone." After the encounter with Baxter, she meant that with all her heart.

Ryan gave her an amused glance. "My, my. What happened to all the sweet little nothings you were whispering to Timothy?"

"You're not Timothy," Calista returned. "And you seemed to be fully occupied with Leora a few minutes ago."

He threw back his head and laughed. "She's only a child, even though she thinks she's a woman. Don't tell me you're jealous."

She stared at him, feeling her heart beating faster. *"Jealous?"* she asked. "What an absurd idea, Mr. Burke. I hardly know you—and I assure you, what you do is none of my concern." She turned and began walking rapidly down one of the paths.

Ryan fell into step with her. "You're right," he agreed. "What I do *is* none of your concern. Especially since you have poor old Timothy so befuddled he doesn't know which way is up. Tell me, Miss Shelby, when do you plan to have him propose?"

Calista sucked in her breath. "That's none of *your* business." She tilted her chin up and started walking even faster. Ryan easily kept up with her.

He reached out and placed a firm hand on her slender forearm. Her skin was warm and smooth to his touch. A sudden urge to stroke his hand down the full length of her arm swept over him. "Wait a minute, Calista," he said, all the mockery gone from his voice.

She could feel the imprint of each of his fingers on her arm, burning into her skin. She wanted to fling off his hand and run back into the house; yet at the same time, something else inside her wanted him to touch her bare throat, to kiss her.

She turned to face him again, forcing herself to look merely affronted. But the expression in his blue eyes made her forget that.

"I'm sorry. You're right. I was out of line." Damn, but she was lovely. Her skin looked like ivory in the shadowy moonlight. It was all he could do to keep from pulling her into his arms.

Don't be a fool, he told himself. She'd chased Timothy ever since she'd come here, and she was well on the way to landing him. Love was a game to most of the men he knew. Marriage was for other purposes—the ones for which Calista planned to marry Timid Timothy. To keep control of her plantation. To run it herself.

The situation was chillingly similar to the mess his own parents had called a marriage.

His hand dropped from Calista's soft arm. "You'd better go inside," he told her, the mocking intonation back in his voice. "You wouldn't want Timothy to see us out here alone together."

Calista drew her arms under her light wool shawl, pulling it snugly around her. "Good night, Mr. Burke," she said frostily. She turned and walked back to the house, knowing he still stood watching her.

She made it to her room without encountering anyone else, her head aching in all truth now. She poured cool water from the enameled pitcher and bathed her face and hands, then slipped into her nightdress.

A knock sounded on her door, and Calista stiffened. Surely Ryan hadn't followed her upstairs. Baxter? Her stomach tightened at that thought. She went to the door and cautiously opened it a few inches. Lucinda stood there, her cheeks flushed rosy, looking fifteen years younger than her true age.

Calista stepped back and Lucinda came inside, closing the door behind her. "I missed you, child," her aunt said. "Are you all right?"

Calista forced herself to smile. "Yes. Only a headache. But we have to go home to Meadowmarsh tomorrow—just for a day or two." She decided not to tell her aunt about her encounter with Baxter—or with Ryan.

Lucinda's brow knitted with concern as she looked at the girl she'd loved like her own child for many years. Finally, she reached out and patted her shoulder.

"All right. It would be a good idea to see how everything's going anyway. I've been concerned ever since Farley hired the overseer."

Calista let out her breath in relief at her aunt's understanding. "So have I. I don't know how Zeke and the others will feel. They've never had an overseer before."

"I'd like to get away myself," Lucinda admitted. "This city life isn't for me, either."

"Even with Jerome Kingsley in it?" Calista asked, not able to resist teasing her aunt. She was rewarded when Lucinda reddened under her scrutiny.

"Sometimes I feel like a ninny," Lucinda said, smiling ruefully. "And then other times I feel as if I'm sixteen again!" She laughed, and shook her head. "No fool like an old fool, they say."

It was Calista's turn to gently squeeze her aunt's thin shoulder. "Don't talk like that, Aunt Lucie. If you and Jerome—" Calista hesitated, not knowing exactly how far things had gone between the two.

"I think Jerome is a very nice man, and we get along with each other excellently," Lucinda said primly. "Other than that, it's much too soon to say."

Relief filled her at the older woman's words. She wouldn't have to face the prospect of her aunt's leaving Meadowmarsh any time soon. "That's true. There's no hurry for you as there is for me."

Her soft lips tightened, then she forced herself to smile. "I think Timothy will ask me to marry him very soon."

"Are you sure you're doing the right thing, child?"

Calista's smile faded. She began taking down her hair to brush. "Of course I am."

Her voice came out firm and steady, but the image in her mind's eye wasn't Timothy's weak face. It was Ryan's dark and mocking visage.

Chapter Three

Lotus opened the door of the wooden frame house where Ira Atwood was staying, a satisfied smile on her face as she pulled it closed behind her and walked onto the porch. My, that man was frisky tonight. He'd more than satisfied her. She smoothed down the skirt of her blue dress and went down the steps.

The almost-full moon lit her way back to the cabin where she knew Zeke waited impatiently. She smiled again. Zeke would have to wait awhile longer. Tonight they had other things to do. She slipped like a wraith down the path. No one was stirring, which didn't surprise her. All these darkies were superstitious fools who didn't venture out at night for fear of 'haints.

She had them convinced she could put hexes on them. She threw back her head, her long, graceful neck shining in the moonlight, and laughed silently. She'd soon had those uppity house servants, Junie and Delphinia, who thought they owned the plantation, doing everything she said.

Zeke was awake, a candle flickering by his pallet. She stood poised in the doorway, knowing the moonlight outlined her body in the dress she'd taken from Calista's wardrobe.

"Come here, woman, and git in this bed with me." Zeke's voice sounded half-angry and half-desirous. She knew he hated her going to Ira's house at night. He didn't hate the way the white overseer had started treating him since Lotus's visits had begun, though. Ira left Zeke alone now. But he seemed to be even harder on the field hands to make up for it.

For the first time since Owen Shelby had built Meadowmarsh, fear had come to the island. And that was fine, too, Lotus thought. It kept the others from bothering her and Zeke.

"Why you standin' in the doorway?" Zeke demanded. "This pallet gittin' mighty cold."

Lotus laughed, a sound that sent a chill down Zeke's spine. "Git up from dere, old man. We got things to do tonight besides lay up in bed."

"What you talkin' about?" Zeke leaned up on his elbow to look at her. His bare chest gleamed like polished mahogany in the moonlight shining through the open doorway and, for a moment, tempted Lotus to forget her plans and crawl into the pallet with him.

No, she wouldn't. This was the perfect night for them to begin. The moon gave enough light so they wouldn't have to use any of their lantern oil.

"You'll find out if you come with me," she said, her rich voice firm. "We needs to stop in de work shed and git us some shovels." Meadowmarsh's practice of not locking the shed at night would make things easier.

Zeke grumbled under his breath but rolled out of the pallet and pulled on his breeches. "You one crazy woman, you know that?" he asked her, moving across the floor to where she still stood outlined in the moonlight. He pulled her up against his hard body.

Lotus leaned against him for a moment and let him kiss her, then pushed him away and headed outside. "When you finds out what we gonna do, maybe you change yo' mind," she told him as he followed her, closing the cabin door behind him.

Calista stood beside Zeke, Ira Atwood on the other side, all three of them looking over the fields nearest the house. Bolls of the silky Sea Island cotton still clung to the low-growing plants. It was almost time for another picking.

She'd arrived on a butchering day, the weather cool and crisp. A few minutes ago she'd walked among the hands who were rendering lard, making sausage, and preparing hams and shoulders for smoking, everyone bustling around at his or her job.

Calista smiled at Zeke, trying to put down the uneasy feeling that had hit her the moment she and Lucinda had stepped off the flatboat at Meadowmarsh's dock. "Everything looks fine, Zeke," she told him. And it did. Even though she'd noticed some of the Negroes seemed sullen and wouldn't meet her eyes.

"Yes'm, Miz Calista," Zeke answered. "We been busy, but we ain't had no trouble."

Something in Zeke's voice bothered her, but she couldn't decide what it was. She turned to Ira Atwood, knowing he was probably the cause of the discontent. The hands wouldn't like having a white overseer for the first time in their lives, even if he treated them fairly and kindly. And she wasn't at all sure about Ira Atwood's attitude toward the plantation workers.

"Mr. Atwood, everything looks in order," she told him, her voice reserved.

The white overseer nodded confidently. "It is, Miss Shelby; it is. I take pride in makin' sure any plantation I oversee is run properly. Even if it is only a temporary job."

There was more than a hint in his gravelly voice that he'd be glad to be here on a permanent basis. That would never happen. She hadn't liked him on sight. He was neatly enough dressed, but not very clean. He didn't smell good, either. But at least he and Zeke seemed to get along, so she'd decided against trying to find someone else. She couldn't offend Baxter and his father, and she fully expected to be back here to stay soon.

"I'm going up to the house now. You men can get back to your work," she dismissed them. She watched the two walk away together, as far apart as the path to the hog-slaughtering area allowed.

They didn't like each other, but they could work together, which would have to do. And before she went to the house, she was going to visit her favorite spot on the island.

At the lagoon, a great blue heron flew away at her approach, his huge wings flapping lazily. Calista threw her arms in the air, flinging aside the black shawl draped over her shoulders. She stood on the firm white sand and breathed deeply. "Oh, it feels so good to be home!" she said out loud, her voice exultant.

Sitting on the grassy bank, she pulled her legs up under her and waited, as still as the glassy, blue water. In a few moments, several egrets glided over the lagoon, then landed at the shallow edge. More than a dozen wood ducks followed, settling in the deeper water. In the winter the water fowl were thick here.

After a half hour, she sighed and regretfully got to her feet. The old, familiar air of contentment that used to surround her everywhere on her island was missing. She tried to dismiss it. "You're imagining all this because you like to think Meadowmarsh can't get along without you," she told herself.

She smiled as she came out onto the oyster-shell road and saw the black Arab mare tied to a tree. Zeke knew her habits well. He'd brought Sable for her. As the plantation house came in sight, Calista reined in her mount, and a smile curved her mouth as she looked at the only home she'd ever known.

The sea air rotted wood so fast, her father had used brick for the beautifully proportioned Georgian-style structure. It was a wonderful choice, its mellow rose color set off by white Corinthian columns and black shutters.

The wide front veranda was echoed in a second-story gallery surrounded by a gracefully styled railing. How many times had she stood on the gallery watching the night sky with its diamonds of stars and the full southern moon, which everyone said was bigger and brighter than anywhere else?

Calista let herself into the spacious front hall. All seemed in perfect order. A smell of lemon oil hung in the still air. No dust lay on the polished hardwood floors or the rosewood table by the front entrance. She walked down the hall, glancing into rooms. Everything looked fine, but the sense of uneasiness was still with her.

Suddenly, she stopped, listening to the silence around her. It was too quiet. She'd grown up listening to the good-natured chatter and snatches of song of the house Negroes as they went about their work. Now there was no sound, and no one seemed to be about. The hairs on her arms rose. It felt eerie and unnatural.

Frowning, she headed for the wide stairs. Aunt Lucie must be up in her room. She'd go talk to her. She heard a noise and glanced up to see Lotus coming down the stairs.

The newly-appointed housekeeper wore a loose-fitting dress of blue wool which didn't hide the slim grace of her body. She smiled at Calista, but the smile didn't reach her eyes. They looked as cold as ice.

Calista repressed a shudder and smiled back. "Good afternoon, Lotus. The house looks good," she complimented the other woman. "You're doing a good job."

Lotus stopped on the step above, her hands clenched tightly at her sides. "Yes'm, I tries to."

Her tone was civil and polite, but something wasn't right there, either. Lotus didn't appear gratified at the praise she'd received. No, Calista and Lucinda's unexpected trip home seemed to have surprised and unsettled her.

Well, that was to be expected. No doubt everyone had slacked off a little during their absence. She smiled again. "Where are Junie and Delphinia and the others?"

Lotus gave her a level look from her dark, onyx eyes. "Dey in the cookhouse helpin' with dinnah."

Calista refrained from remarking that it was early. It was a small thing and since she had to return to Charleston tomorrow, she'd leave Lotus alone. She did, in all truth, seem to be doing a fine job. She'd done the right thing in accepting Zeke's recommendation of her for the temporary position. "Is Miss Lucinda upstairs?"

Lotus nodded. "Yes'm, Miss Calista."

"Thank you, Lotus." Calista continued up the stairs, determined to forget her worries and enjoy the rest of the day and evening.

The staircase led directly onto the hallway to the second-floor bedrooms, unlike some larger and more elaborate plantation houses with branching staircases and galleries. But the house more than filled her needs, Calista thought, walking down the hall to her aunt's room.

It would be adequate for several children, too, she

mused, trying to picture the offspring resulting from her union with Timothy. All she could come up with were pale, slightly rabbity-looking babies. She quickly chased those images away.

She paused outside Lucinda's door, wondering if her aunt were asleep. "Is that you, Calista?" Lucinda's voice asked. "Come on in, dear."

The white, crocheted counterpane had been drawn back. Lucinda lay on the quilt covering the sheets on the big four-postered bed.

"Well, did you get reacquainted with everything on Meadowmarsh?" She pushed herself upright and arranged a pillow behind her back.

Calista nodded. "Aunt Lucie, does everything feel all right to you?"

Her aunt gave her an inquiring look. "What do you mean? Everything seems to be in order."

Calista nodded again. "Yes, but it's so *quiet*. Lotus said Delphinia and Junie and the others were out in the kitchen, but still. . . ." Her voice trailed off, and she gave her aunt a sheepish smile. "I guess I'm being silly."

Lucinda tilted her head, considering. "Everything *does* seem very quiet. But after Estelle's house, no wonder."

Calista sat down in a slipper chair upholstered in pale-green brocade. "You're probably right, Aunt Lucie. How do people stand living like that all their lives? Timothy has never even been on a plantation. He asks the silliest questions about Meadowmarsh."

The poor child, Lucinda thought. She doesn't love Timothy Gardner. What a bind she'd been put in by her mother. Again, she wondered at Isabelle's motive in leaving such a will, and again she felt there had been one. Her sister-in-law had been a kind, intelligent woman. And she'd known how much her daughter loved Meadowmarsh.

Lucinda patted the bed beside her. "Come and lie down for a while. Everything's going to be all right." Even as her niece obliged, Lucinda knew repeating the comforting words she'd used since Calista's childhood wouldn't change the fact that the girl planned to enter a loveless marriage to save her beloved home.

What a pity she hadn't gone after Ryan Burke. Now, *there* was a man. Lucinda had noticed plenty of sparks between the two, but nothing had come of it. Of course, Calista couldn't manage Ryan as she could Timothy. It wouldn't have been a placid marriage—but too much placidity could be dull.

Thinking of Jerome, Lucinda smiled. When he was young, she imagined he'd been a great deal like Ryan Burke. And even at sixty-six, he had plenty of spark left. Her smile faded, and she sighed. Her heart ached for Calista, but there was nothing she could do to help.

As she placed the steaming platter of fresh oysters on the mahogany dining table, Delphinia's eyes avoided Calista's, her dark face expressionless. Calista drew in a deep breath. "Oh, that smells heavenly! Thank you, Delphinia." She smiled at her favorite of the house servants.

The other woman didn't smile back. Her eyes looked flat and black and remote. "Dis suit you, Miz Calista?" she asked, straightening up.

Calista gave her a puzzled look. "Of course it does. You know oysters are my favorite food." She smiled, then went on. "Of course, so are shrimp and clams and bream...." Her voice trailed off, inviting the black girl to share the joke, but Delphinia's face remained stiff and remote.

"What on earth ails her?" Calista asked Lucinda. "Do

you suppose she's angry because I didn't leave her in charge of the house?"

The other woman helped herself to several oysters, then looked at Calista, across the long table from her. "Maybe. I imagine Lotus is a hard taskmaster."

Calista put oysters on her own English bone china plate, but her pleasure in the food had lessened. "Delphinia's a good worker, but she's a follower, not a leader." She took in a breath, then let it out in a sigh. "I'll soon be home to stay, and things will get back to normal."

Lucinda toyed with an oyster, then glanced over at her niece. "Maybe you should think about keeping Lotus on as housekeeper."

Calista knew what her aunt hinted at. In the event something serious developed between Lucinda and Jerome, the older woman wouldn't be returning to Meadowmarsh.

She shook her head. "No. If I should need another housekeeper, I'll train Junie."

Listening inside the door of the warming room, Lotus narrowed her eyes, her mouth tightening. So the young mistress planned to send her back to the washroom, did she? Junie walked by her, carrying a heaped-up dish of cornbread, and gave her a half-frightened, half-defiant glance as she passed.

"Go on, git outta here," Lotus hissed at her. Her eyes narrowed even more.

Junie straightened and stared her in the eye. "You not gonna be in dis house much longer," she said softly. "When Miz Calista come home to stay, you be bendin' your back over de washtubs again."

"Hush your mouth or I hush it fo' you," Lotus said, her voice venomous. "And I knows how to do it."

Junie backed off, her hands trembling on the plate, her face terrified. She whirled and left the room quickly.

Lotus's slim shoulders shook with laughter as she watched her go. The laughter changed to a satisfied smile. She might have to go back to her laundress job, but not for long. Soon, soon now, she and Zeke would be gone from here. They'd be up north and free. And rich. *Rich.* She rolled the word over in her mind, then let her tongue roll over it, too, in a vibrating whisper.

Zeke didn't really want to leave here, but she'd talk him into it. She knew how to talk him into *anything*.

Her smile widened, became evil. But before they left, she'd make sure the mistress knew how much she hated her.

Her mental image of Calista's face changed, merged with that other white woman's face she hated so much. Her hands formed into claws as she imagined them raking down Calista's smooth, white cheeks.

Oh, yes, before they left, Miz Calista would be very sorry she'd treated Lotus this way!

Chapter Four

Her black cloak pulled around her, Calista slipped out the side door into the courtyard. Peering up into the night sky, she felt the last few almost-sleepless nights catching up with her. Her appetite had deserted her, too.

Ever since Timothy had proposed three days ago.

The big southern moon was full and no clouds were in sight to dim its radiance. She'd have liked to have waited for a dark night, but she didn't dare after her encounter with Baxter the evening before she'd gone to Meadowmarsh. Fortunately, he'd had a slight relapse and this morning was again running a fever, but she knew he'd soon be up and about.

Her stomach fluttered nervously, and she wondered if she'd done the right thing in having Timothy come for her while the house was still full of guests.

To wait until they all left and the house was quiet would have been even worse, though. This way the sound of the carriage wouldn't be noticed over the talking and laughter going on inside. At least she hoped not.

She walked to the side gate and opened it, her palms damp and clammy even though a chilly wind blew. She slipped through it, then waited, partly hidden by the branches of a red cedar. She threw an uneasy glance back at the lighted house. All the doors remained closed and no silhouette showed at any of the windows.

Closing her eyes, she prayed for Timothy to hurry. At last she heard the sound of carriage wheels, and her pulse accelerated. She stepped out from under the branches. A dark carriage approached on the otherwise-deserted street.

The driver pulled up and stopped before the gate, as she'd told Timothy to do. It *had* to be he. The carriage door opened and Timothy leaned out, his face pale and anxious as he beckoned to her.

"Calista, hurry!" he said, his voice low and trembling slightly.

She felt a stab of disappointment because he wasn't coming to get her, but then told herself he was right; they couldn't waste any time. Strangely reluctant, she walked the few feet to the carriage.

Timothy, still looking anxious, reached out for her hand to help her inside. It was almost over; soon she'd be Mrs. Timothy Gardner, and then she could go back to Meadowmarsh and live in peace and safety forever.

Behind her a door banged and a loud male voice shouted, "Stop at once!" She heard the sound of running feet. Her heart slammed against her ribs.

Timothy's hand jerked away from hers. He shrank back inside the carriage, leaving Calista outside.

The courtyard gate opened, then crashed shut. Calista turned to see Baxter bearing down on them, a ferocious scowl on his face. His blond hair was disheveled and his coat unbuttoned. Her stomach tightened in shock as she stared at him.

"It's a good thing Mother saw you slipping out and got me out of bed, isn't it?" he asked grimly.

Oh, God, this couldn't be happening. Not now. Not with her plans so close to being realized. Calista whirled toward the carriage. She felt Baxter's hand clamp down on her arm, pulling her back.

"Help me, Timothy," she begged, but instead Timothy shrank even further into the seat cushions.

She stared at him in disbelief. "You, you *rabbit!* Aren't you even going to fight for me?"

Timothy's face paled as if the mere thought of fighting was more than he could handle. He looked away from Calista, toward Baxter.

Baxter gave Timothy a menacing glare, then turned his attention to the driver. "Get out of here," he ordered. The old man nodded quickly, his whip coming down on the horse's back. The carriage jerked into movement.

She watched it move rapidly down the street, then turn a corner and disappear from view. The cold knot in her stomach felt like lead. She spun to face Baxter. "Let go of my arm," she told him between clenched teeth. "You're hurting me."

Instead, Baxter tightened his grip, a smirk on his face. "Surely, you didn't suppose I'd let you and Meadowmarsh get away from me that easily."

Calista glared at him, her green eyes brilliant with anger. "If you don't let go of me, I'll scream so loud everyone in the house will hear," she threatened.

Baxter laughed unpleasantly, his handsome face menacing in the shifting shadows. "I don't think so." He pulled her closer to him. "Come here, little Calista, and give me a kiss. You've grown up to be a ravishing woman."

She could almost hear the deep thuds in her chest as her heart began pounding, and her breath came with difficulty. Calista tried to pull away from him, but he was too strong.

Baxter laughed again and drew her against his chest. His hand reached for her chin and tilted her head up toward his.

Then he was suddenly jerked backward, his hands dropping from Calista, and she staggered and nearly fell. She righted herself and stared at the dark-haired man standing just outside the courtyard gate.

"The lady asked you to let her go," Ryan said, his voice low and almost casual. He dropped his hand from Baxter's shoulder, but Calista saw his powerful muscles bunching under his coat.

Baxter saw them, too. He stepped back, his face pallid in the moonlight. "What are you doing here, Burke? This is none of your business."

Ryan straightened to his full height. "I'm making it my business." The sardonic smile she'd come to expect on his face was gone. He looked serious and very sure of himself.

"I wasn't hurting her," Baxter said, his voice sullen. "Women like to play these games. They don't mean what they say."

"I think Miss Shelby meant exactly what she said." Calista heard the steel in Ryan's even voice and shivered. "I would suggest you go inside and leave her alone."

Baxter glared at Ryan but made no move toward him. "You can't tell me what to do on my own property."

"I'm telling you." Ryan stared into Baxter's black eyes, holding his gaze.

The other man blinked and looked away. "Burke, you're no longer welcome in this house. I'll make sure you're never invited again." He turned and walked to the gate, opened it and stepped through. Calista and Ryan watched as he hurried to the house.

The silence stretched between them. Finally, Calista cleared her throat, looking at Ryan. "Thank you very much for what you did," she said stiffly.

Ryan's blue eyes stared into hers. The mocking smile she'd grown so familiar with tilted the corners of his mouth upward. He made her a sweeping bow.

"At your service, ma'am. I'm sorry your, ah, elopement was unsuccessful." He'd seen Calista slip out of the house and followed her. He'd stood just inside the gate, watching Baxter chase Timothy away, not trying to prevent him. Why had he done that? Why had he interceded only when Baxter tried to kiss Calista?

The reminder of her failed plans hit Calista like a blow. What was she going to do now? "I'm sorry, too," she told him, her voice shaking. A wave of faintness swept over her. She staggered and put out a hand to the nearest object to steady herself.

That object happened to be Ryan's hard chest. He caught her hand in his, steadying her. Her hand felt so soft under his own. He studied her drawn face. She looked as if she couldn't take much more. While he watched, a tear starred her thick, black lashes, then dropped to her cheek, followed by another, then another.

Ryan drew in his breath. His free hand gently wiped away the tears. "It's all right," he said, his voice as gentle as his hand had been.

Calista sniffed, giving him a woe-filled look. "No, it's not all right," she told him, her voice low and trembly. "I'm going to lose my home."

He moved further under the shelter of the cedar tree, taking her unresisting form with him. "Hush, hush," he told her soothingly, as he might talk to a small child. He was filled with a tenderness he hadn't known he possessed as he stroked her silky black hair away from her tear-stained face.

"What can I do?" Calista asked him, her voice sounding like a child's, too. She gulped and sniffed again. "I—if I don't marry by my twenty-first birthday, I'll lose my plantation."

Ryan nodded. "I know."

Calista blinked. "You know?"

"Yes, I overheard Estelle telling someone. She also mentioned that you were going to marry Baxter."

She shivered. "I'd rather die!"

His hands were still on her face, and she didn't even seem to notice, so preoccupied was she with her troubles. He stroked her satiny cheek, then his hand slipped farther down to her throat.

A shudder went through him. God, she was so soft, so beautiful. He'd wanted to do this ever since that first night at the dinner table. Her eyes had a dazed, unfocused look, and he knew he was taking advantage of her despairing mood.

Knew it and couldn't stop. He tilted her head up and the moon shone full across her white face. "Calista," he said. He bent his head, his mouth searching for hers, then hungrily covering it.

Her full pink lips were even softer than her cheek, Ryan discovered as the kiss deepened. He felt as if he were drowning in her sweetness. He breathed in her intoxicating scent, a blend of flowers and citrus. Calista's arms encircled his neck and she blindly held on to him, as to a lifeline.

Silently cursing himself for a fool, Ryan's hand slipped to her hips, molding her slender form to his rapidly hardening body. She didn't resist., only moved closer into the shelter of his arms, opening her mouth to the forays of his tongue.

She shouldn't be letting Ryan kiss her like this, Calista told herself. She shouldn't be kissing him back. But too much had happened in the last few minutes, and nothing seemed quite real anymore. And his strong arms felt so good, his hard mouth softened against hers. Oh, she'd never dreamed a kiss could be like this.

Hardly realizing what he was doing, Ryan guided her completely under the tree. He sank down on the grass, pulling her with him, their mouths still pressed together.

Soon kissing was no longer enough. Ryan's impatient hand swept her cloak aside, then fumbled with the buttons down the front of her dress. He cursed under his breath. The buttons were tiny, impossible to unfasten.

This was very wrong, Calista told herself, but the dream-like feeling intensified. She should push Ryan away, get up from the ground . . . but his hands on her neck felt so good. . . . He smelled so clean and his touch made shivers of pleasure run up and down her back. . . . She was glad Baxter had stopped her from marrying Timothy. . . . Timothy could never make her feel like this. . . .

Ryan's mouth left Calista's, and he drew back to concentrate on his task. At last he had the top two buttons undone. He glanced down, and his eyes met her wide green, slightly unfocused ones.

Her mouth curved in a warm smile. Ryan's kisses, mixed with her fatigue and anger and disappointment, had affected her like potent wine.

This was the man she wanted—needed. And he must care for her or he couldn't have kissed her as he had. Hadn't he told her everything would be all right? There was only one way that could happen—if she married. Ryan knew it, too. Calista reached her hand up to his face and outlined his mustache, his mouth, the cleft in his chin.

A deep, indrawn breath sounded close by. "What is the meaning of this? Sir, unhand my son's fiancée at once!" Estelle's shrill voice demanded from behind him.

Calista looked out into what seemed a sea of faces, some hostile, some shocked, some merely amused. Horrible embarrassment swept over her. She made out Aunt Lucie hurrying from the back of the group. Oh, thank God for her.

But before Lucinda could reach her, Ryan's strong arm pulled her up to stand beside him. He took her unresisting hand in his. Her dress gaped open at the neck and she fumbled to fasten the buttons.

Ryan's mouth tightened. He couldn't stand the stricken expression on her face. He couldn't bear to see her humiliated before this crowd of vultures. And it was all his fault, he had to admit. If he'd left her alone, none of this would be happening.

Lucinda stepped forward, her gray eyes steady on his. "Mr. Burke, you have compromised the honor of my niece," she said quietly.

Ryan stared back at her, frustration and anger on his hard features. Damn it all to hell! What kind of a mess had he gotten himself into?

A new voice spoke up. "My son has already demanded you leave our property, Burke," Farley Howard blustered. "Do so at once."

Jerome stepped up beside Lucinda. "Ryan, I expect you to do the right thing by this girl."

Ryan shook his head to clear it. This situation was becoming more farcical every second. The Howards wanted to get rid of him so they could try to patch things up between Calista and Baxter. On the other hand, Calista's aunt apparently expected him to marry the girl. His partner Jerome seemed to be siding with Lucinda.

Because he and Calista had exchanged a few kisses? Anger swelled inside him. Well, by damn, he wouldn't do it! They couldn't force him. He had no intention of marrying, ever.

Calista's hand moved inside his own. It felt so small and cold. She shivered against his side. Compunction smote him again. He had to admit he'd taken advantage of her momentary weakness. And if these people hadn't interrupted, what had passed between them could easily have turned into much more than a few kisses. He knew the code of honor as well as anyone, and what he must do. He took a deep, frustrated breath, then let it out.

He was well and truly trapped.

"Mr. Howard, I have every intention of leaving your property. But not without Miss Shelby. She's just done me the honor of agreeing to become my wife."

He heard Calista's small gasp and drew her more firmly against his side. He didn't look at her, but kept his gaze on Farley. That gentleman's eyes widened, and he seemed to be at a loss for words.

Estelle worked her mouth as if trying to find something to say. Finally, she raised her head, haughtily. "Humph. It's just as well. I never did think you were good enough for my Baxter. Come, Farley." She crooked her arm in her husband's and marched him back to the house, most of the group following her.

Lucinda and Jerome stayed behind. Lucinda hurried forward. "Child, are you all right?"

"Yes, of course, Aunt Lucie." Calista's heart sang inside her chest. Ryan did care for her. Those kisses had meant something to him, as they had to her. He wouldn't have so readily agreed to marry her otherwise.

"Don't worry, Miss Shelby. I will take care of everything," Ryan said stiffly.

Lucinda gave him a long, searching glance. Then, apparently satisfied, she nodded and smiled. "I believe you will, young man."

She looked at Jerome, a question in her eyes. He nodded, then turned to Calista. "You and Lucinda will come to my house," he told her. "Of course, you'll be properly chaperoned by my housekeeper."

Calista felt like laughing. After tonight's events, a chaperon was the least of her worries. But none of this was her aunt's fault, and she'd made it impossible for Lucinda to stay in the Howard's household any longer. "All right," she agreed.

Lucinda looked at Ryan, who still held Calista firmly pressed to his side. "Come, Jerome," she said, and took him by the arm. "I'll see you in the house in a moment," she told her niece.

Calista watched her leave. She turned to Ryan, the smile she'd been holding back spreading over her face, making it radiant. "You'll love Meadowmarsh. It's so beautiful. It's like nowhere else on earth."

Ryan stared at her as shock washed over him. Her fragile, vulnerable air had vanished. The little minx stood there looking completely satisfied with herself. His hand dropped from hers. He stepped back, his blue eyes hard and cold. So all the helpless despair—all the passion— had been feigned. Only an act to get him to propose. She probably even expected someone to find them, helping things along.

She was the one who'd trapped him into marriage, not all those other people.

"Your trick worked, Madam, but surely you don't think I'm fool enough to move out to your plantation?" he asked her, his voice as cold as his gaze. "You've saved your reputation and your precious Meadowmarsh, and that's all you can expect from me."

He gave her a mocking bow. "I will come to Jerome's house tomorrow, and we will make arrangements for the marriage. Good night, Miss Shelby."

His back very straight, he turned and walked away,

down the deserted street. Calista watched him go, the shock of his words vibrating through her body.

How could she have been so wrong in her estimation of Ryan's motives? He'd only been trying to seduce her. And he'd been caught and forced into marriage. He had no real feelings for her. No real honor, even, only that forced upon him. And then he had the gall to accuse her of tricking him!

She took a deep breath and let it out. All right, she'd have to accept that he'd fooled her, made her believe he really cared for her. She squared her slim shoulders. But he was right about one thing. She *had* saved Meadowmarsh. After she and Ryan were married, she could go back to her plantation with no further worries about losing it.

She had a husband who not only would leave her alone to run Meadowmarsh as she pleased, but one who didn't even plan to live there at all. Everything she'd come here for she'd accomplished.

So why did she feel as if she'd lost everything in the world that mattered?

Chapter Five

Calista found her abandoned cloak under the cedar tree and draped it around her shoulders, her face flaming as those moments in Ryan's arms came alive for her again. Damn him! She let out her breath. No, she couldn't do that. She owed him too much. She smoothed her dress and straightened her spine, dreading going back inside.

She breathed a sigh of relief as she let herself in the side door. No one seemed to be about. Talk and laughter—probably at her expense—came from the salon. She made her way toward the stairs, still throwing glances behind her. She didn't think Baxter would try anything else, but she couldn't be sure.

Her hand on the curving banister, she looked up, surprised to see Leora standing a few steps up. She didn't know if the girl had witnessed the humiliating scene outside; but if not, she'd surely have heard about it by now.

Stopping below Leora, she forced a smile. "I hope you'll come out to Meadowmarsh to visit," she told the younger girl. Her invitation was sincere. She'd always liked Baxter's sister, who was unassuming and friendly, so she was startled to receive a fierce glare in return.

"I'm certain you do hope that," Leora said, her voice trembling. "So that you can display your new husband. You are a *worm*, Calista! And I always thought you were my friend."

Calista swallowed. She'd watched Leora flirt outrageously with Ryan, but she'd never dreamed the girl fancied herself in love with him. Calista reached out her hand to touch her cousin's shoulder. "I'm sorry, but you don't understand everything that went on tonight."

Leora flinched away from her touch as if Calista had some deadly, communicable disease. "I understand enough to know you stole the man I love. And you don't even *want* him! All you care about is your plantation." Her voice broke and she whirled, her skirts rustling as she ran up the stairs. A few moments later, a door opened, then slammed.

Calista stood as still as a tree, Leora's bitter accusations washing over her. First Ryan, now her cousin, denouncing her for having no feelings for anything but Meadowmarsh. Did everyone else here have the same opinion? That she'd deliberately set out to snare Ryan after Baxter foiled her elopement with Timothy?

Color flooded her face again, and her lips thinned. Probably. And there was nothing she could do about it. She walked on up the stairs and into her room and found Lucinda sitting on her bed.

"My word, child, you look like death! Come here." The older woman held out her arms, and Calista stumbled into them, fighting back tears.

"There, there, it's all right," Lucinda soothed, patting Calista's shoulder. "Things are going to work out fine. Just wait and see." She looked down at Calista's glossy, black hair, feeling an enormous sense of satisfaction. Her dearly loved niece was going to marry the right man, after all.

Calista lost the battle against tears. Ryan had said almost those exact words to her. She sniffed and blinked furiously, then moved back. She'd done enough crying. No more.

"No, they're not, Aunt Lucie," she said. "Ryan hates me; he thinks I tricked him into marrying me. He's not going to come to Meadowmarsh. He's staying in Charleston."

Lucinda's mouth fell open in dismay. What on earth had happened to cause this after she and Jerome had left the two young people? If she'd ever seen a man and woman mad for each other, it had been Ryan and Calista a few minutes ago. "The circumstances have him upset, but he'll come around. He does love you, I'm sure."

"No, he doesn't. He only lusted after me," she said bitterly. "And got caught and has to marry me." She walked away and began to gather up her possessions which were scattered around the room.

There was no use trying to talk to her now, Lucinda decided. Maybe by tomorrow, she and Ryan would have calmed down, be in more reasonable frames of mind. She got up from the bed and started helping Calista.

Her mouth firmed. This might be a hasty, forced marriage, but one thing she'd see to: Even though Calista was in mourning, she wouldn't marry in black.

"Well, well, and what do you two think you're doin'?"

Ira Atwood's heavy voice exploded into the night. Lotus jerked around, the spade she held swinging wildly in the air.

The overseer jumped back, barely escaping its sharp edge. "What in hell are you tryin' to do, you bitch?" he asked viciously, grabbing for the spade.

She held on, but felt her grasp weakening. He was stronger and soon wrenched it out of her hands. She fell back against Zeke, who stood frozen, his own spade still buried to the handle in the hole they were digging. Her movements jiggled a lantern sitting near the edge. It tilted, and Zeke grabbed for it as he dropped the spade and steadied her.

Ira leaned on the spade he'd taken from Lotus, his small, piglike eyes gleaming. "So you two don't get enough work durin' the day, you have to come out and dig holes at night for more exercise?"

Lotus righted herself. She gave him a defiant look and tossed her head. There was no way she and Zeke could explain this. Ira was no fool. But she had to try. "We ain't hurtin' nothin' diggin' an ole hole."

"Is that right?" Ira laughed unpleasantly. "I wonder what Miz Shelby will make of this when I tell her?" He carelessly dropped the spade, turned his back, and started to walk away.

"You go after him and change his mind," Zeke whispered urgently into her ear.

Her eyes narrowed as she watched the overseer swagger off, the night soon swallowing him up. Pleasuring him wasn't going to work this time. He'd already had that from her. She drew in her breath, then let it out in a hiss and turned to give Zeke a cold look. "What you think I can do?" she demanded. "We gotta let him in on dis."

Zeke's eyes grew frightened. He shook his head vigorously. "No! We cain't do that!" Oh, lordy. He knew he shouldn't have got mixed up in this. Why had he let this crazy woman talk him into it?

Without another word, Lotus shook his hand loose and

hurried after the overseer. She could just make out the gleam of his white shirt ahead of her in the blackness. Not a sound came from the cabins. She wasn't worried about *them*. Her bare feet slapped on the earth, and her long legs soon caught up to him. She slid her hand around his arm. "Why you in sech a hurry? We didn't say we wouldn't tell you."

In a few moments Ira's heavy steps slowed. Finally, he stopped and faced her, a sly, satisfied smile on his thick lips. "I thought you'd see it my way."

Still trying to see if she could bluff her way out of this, Lotus shrugged. "We just foolin' 'roun. Ain't doin' nothin'. If you wants to dig holes, come on back. I'll give you my spade."

Ira's hand shot out and grabbed her by her upper arm. "I'm not a fool like Zeke. You better tell me the truth." His hand tightened on her arm, his smile widening as he saw her wince.

There was no way out. Either she told him or no doubt he would send word to the mistress, and then there was no telling what would happen. They'd be punished for sure. Might even be sold. Her nostrils flared at that thought. She moved back a step and gave Ira a beguiling smile. He dropped his hand from her arm.

"Ever since I come here, I been hearin' tales 'bout buried treasure on dese islands," she said. "Zeke and me is lookin' fo' some of it." Her smile widened. "If you wants to help us, dat's fine."

Ira blinked, surprise spreading over his face. "I've heard them stories myself, but I wouldn't have given you credit for that much brains. How long's this been goin' on?"

She shrugged. "Jus' a little while."

He gave her a nasty grin. "You're probably lyin'."

Lotus looked sullen. "I ain't lyin'. One of de field hands say dere even was a map somewheres."

His gaze sharpened. "A map? Did you see it?"

She quickly shook her head. "Nobody know where it got to."

Ira gave her a disgusted look. "He's probably lyin', too, and none of you could read it anyway. Come on, my beauty, let's get to work." He started walking back to where Zeke still leaned on his spade.

He had them now, Lotus thought, glaring at his swaggering, fat back; but the mistress would be coming back soon, and Zeke was sure she'd get rid of Ira. The overseer was too conceited to believe that.

She caught up with him and let her lithe body sway against his as they walked. "After we gits done diggin', we can do other things."

Ira slid his arm around her and squeezed her rounded buttock. "Now, that's the way I like my women. Ready to do anything I want, when I want it."

She hid her contemptuous smile and leaned closer to him. Things would work out the way she'd planned. She'd see to that.

Lucinda stood on the piazza of Jerome's town house. She took deep breaths of the fresh morning air, wishing she could stop worrying about Calista long enough to appreciate her surroundings. Made of red Philadelphia brick, in itself unusual for Charleston, the house had a gabled pavilion on its garden side which greatly appealed to her. She could be very happy living in this house.

She pressed her lips together. It was much too soon to be having such thoughts. And if her niece didn't come down in five more minutes, she'd go up and get her. When she'd left her half an hour ago, Calista had looked pale enough to keel over in a dead faint. Her gown of pearly gray silk fit her to perfection and enhanced her vivid coloring. She was beautiful, as every bride deserved to be. Even in such unfortunate circumstances as these.

And where was Ryan? What if he didn't honor his agreement to marry Calista? Last night, he and Jerome had discussed the arrangements in Jerome's library. After Ryan had left, Jerome had come to the sitting room, where Lucinda waited for him.

"I love that boy like my own son," he told her, "but right now I'd like to shake him. He can be the most stubborn jackass in the world when he sets his mind to it." He suddenly became aware of his language and gave Lucinda an apologetic glance. "I beg your pardon, Lucie."

She smiled, moving over to give him room on the brocaded settee. "I don't shock easily, Jerome. I've lived too long on a plantation for that." Her face grew serious. "Does Ryan regret his decision to marry Calista? Does he want to be released from his promise?"

Jerome sat down, sighing gustily. "He regrets it all right, but he's prepared to go through with it. But he's adamant about not living on Meadowmarsh. Of course, no one expects him to give up his law practice, but he says he won't set foot on the place."

She sighed, her brows drawing together. So nothing had changed for the better. Calista was cloistered in her room upstairs, refusing even to come down to speak to Ryan. Not that he'd asked to speak to her. "He doesn't plan to sell the plantation, does he?" she ventured, voicing her worst fear.

"No, no." He shook his mane of white hair. "Quite the opposite. He had me draw up an agreement giving Calista complete control of the property. He wants nothing to do with it in any shape, form, or fashion. Very noble of him, too, considering that his father has drained him dry of cash over the years." His eyes met Lucinda's and lingered.

Lucinda blushed. He still made her feel like a young

girl with her first love every time he looked at her. Well, she supposed that was natural. She wasn't a young girl, but he was her first love. She sat up straighter and cleared her throat. "That will surely please Calista," she said primly. "She was so worried about losing her home."

"If you ask me," Jerome had answered, "they're *both* acting like stubborn jackasses, begging your pardon again, Lucie."

Lucinda had laid her hand on Jerome's frock-coated arm. "Give them time. They're angry with each other now, but they're young. Their feelings may change over time."

Today, she felt much as Jerome had last night. Calista shut in her bedroom, Ryan not here, even though the ceremony was to begin in fifteen minutes, and the minister due any second. She'd like to shake somebody!

"I'm not going to wait any longer," she said and marched across the piazza and into the house.

Jerome came out of the library as she passed it, his brows raised quizzically when he saw she was alone. "Is Calista—"

"Still upstairs," Lucinda said, her face set in uncharacteristic lines of irritation. "And Ryan hasn't arrived yet. Perhaps you'd better send someone to inquire."

"That won't be necessary, ma'am. I'm here to do my duty, however distasteful it may be," Ryan's stiff, ironic voice said.

Calista, halfway down the stairs, stopped dead as Ryan's clear tones reached her. *Distasteful duty!* Her face and neck flooded with color. What a fool she'd been to think his attitude might have softened by now. That he might even be happy to marry her.

She lifted her head. She wouldn't give him the satisfaction of knowing how much he'd hurt her. Head held high, she walked to where the group still stood outside the library.

"I do hope I'm not late for my own wedding," she said coolly. Her eyes found Ryan's surprised blue ones.

Ryan felt his mouth go dry as he looked at her. He'd forgotten how beautiful she was, how desirable. The pearly gown made her fair skin luminous; her black hair gleamed. In spite of the anger and resentment he'd harbored for two days and nights, he felt his body hardening. Damn, but he'd like to take her to bed! And in a few minutes, when this travesty of a wedding ceremony had joined them, he'd have every legal right to do just that.

Legal right. In spite of her cool control, he knew she was as angry as he. Her stiff carriage gave her away, that and the glint in her green eyes. Why should she be angry? She'd gotten exactly what she wanted!

However, he supposed she'd expected him, like meek Timothy, to let her call the shots. She'd probably thought he'd move out to her plantation and live like a kept man. His mouth curled at that thought. He'd watched his father and mother exist like two caged animals for years—until he'd finally gotten the hell away from his childhood home.

Unlike his own, Calista's anger wasn't mixed with desire. And he'd never forced a woman in his life. He didn't intend to start on his wedding night. No, he'd do just as he'd planned—marry the conniving jade and then leave. Forget the heat she kindled in his loins. If he could.

He inclined his head in a mocking bow. "Not at all," he said, his voice as aloof as hers.

The knocker sounded at the front door. Lucinda turned in relief at the sound.

"That must be the minister." She turned back and forced a smile as she looked at her niece, lovely in her wedding gown, but miserably unhappy. Her glance traveled to the handsome groom-to-be, grim-jawed and angry.

What a pity these two attractive young people were so obstinate. But in spite of everything, she hadn't given up hope for the eventual success of this forced marriage. She'd seen the way Ryan looked at Calista, seen Calista's attempts to ignore him.

Maybe only passion was between them now, but that was something to build on. Yet how could they build on it when they wouldn't even be living together? She'd have to think of something.

The maid brought the somberly garbed, serious-faced minister back to them. "Let's all go into the front sitting room," Lucinda said, leading the way.

The sitting room was shabby for lack of a woman's touch. Jerome's wife had been dead for ten years and he, like most men, hadn't changed anything in his house since, Lucinda thought. She'd put some flowers around, done all she could to brighten up the room for Calista's wedding, but it hadn't helped much.

The glum, unsmiling minister was aware this marriage wasn't the usual kind, Calista decided. He gave both her and Ryan disapproving glances as they stood stiffly before him, carefully not touching each other.

It was not until Reverend Watson asked Ryan if he took this woman to have and to hold until death did them part that Calista fully realized the enormity of what was taking place. They were legally joining themselves together for the rest of their lives. Her heart lurched as she listened to Ryan's flat, clipped responses; and then it was her turn.

She swallowed and nodded, then felt herself redden as the minister raised his eyebrows. "Yes," she said hoarsely, "I will."

To her shock, Ryan took her hand and slipped a wide gold band onto her finger. She'd forgotten about the wedding ring! How could she wear his ring when he detested her? His touch sent shivers down her spine, and the ring felt far too heavy. She glanced at him from under her lashes, tensing, wondering if he would kiss her.

He hesitated, but then stepped back. She fought down the wave of disappointment that flowed through her. No! She didn't want his kiss. She didn't want anything more from him since he'd made it so plain he couldn't stand the sight of her.

"Mrs. Burke." Ryan bowed, his face cold and hard. "I bid you goodbye. Jerome has all the necessary documents you will need."

Documents? What was he talking about? "Goodbye," she answered, her voice equally cold, her features as hard as his. But she didn't feel that way inside. No, she felt raw and wounded.

Lucinda stepped forward, her face distressed. "Oh, won't you stay for some refreshments, Ryan? They're all prepared."

Ryan's face softened as he looked at her. "No, Miss Shelby. I must be going."

Then go! Calista told him silently. She never wanted to see him again as long as she lived. All she wanted to do was go home, back to Meadowmarsh, and forget the events of these last few horrible days.

She watched as he walked out of the room, out of her life, without a backward glance.

Outside on the street, a figure wearing a dark-blue, hooded cape watched as first Ryan, then the minister entered the house. So, it was really going to happen. Ryan was actually going to marry Calista—just because he'd been caught kissing her!

He shouldn't have to marry her when they didn't love each other. All Calista loved was her plantation. Calista could never make Ryan happy. Not like *she* could. Through the half-drawn draperies Leora watched the shadowy figures in the sitting room. In a few minutes, the front door opened, and the minister descended the steps.

Leora slid behind the trunk of a big live oak as the door opened again and Ryan came down the steps. Alone. She drew in her breath as she watched him walk off down the street, looking straight ahead, his face set in grim lines.

She came out from behind the tree trunk, staring after him. She knew where Ryan lived, and he appeared to be going in that direction. Why wasn't his new wife with him?

Jerome's carriage with its pair of matched bays came up the street and stopped before the house. Once more the house door opened, and Leora quickly hid herself again. Lucinda and Calista came down the steps, dressed for traveling. They got into the carriage, and the driver went in the opposite direction from that which Ryan had taken.

Hope sprang up in Leora's breast as she watched the carriage disappear. Ryan going in one direction and his new bride in another could mean only one thing. They weren't going to live together. He'd only married Calista because his honor forced him to, not because he loved her.

A rush of adoration surged through Leora's veins. A marriage like this didn't have to last. There were such things as annulments. She didn't know the details, but she had a vague idea it had something to do with never living together.

SWEET ENCHANTMENT

Ryan could still be hers. He must care for her or he wouldn't have decided not to live with a woman as beautiful as Calista. Of course he couldn't admit it openly, honor forbade it now that he was a married man—at least temporarily.

She would have to go to him. Her brown eyes sparkled as she drew her cloak closer around her neck. Yes, that was what she would do. She would go to him in his lonely house and comfort him for the wrongs her cousin had perpetrated on him. But not today, of course. She'd bide her time, plan this out carefully.

"Miss Leora! What are you doin' here by yourself?"

Her maid Summer's horrified voice made her jump guiltily. She couldn't let anyone find out her plans. She turned to Summer and gave her a sweet smile. "Why, I'm just taking a walk. It's such a nice day."

Summer shook her head. "Your mama sent me lookin' for you. Now you come on home with me before anyone your family knows sees you."

"All right," Leora agreed amiably, falling into step with the black girl she'd known all her life, that she'd played with as a child. She wished there were someone to talk this over with. She certainly couldn't tell her parents or Baxter—but what about Summer?

She looked at the black girl's profile for a moment. It was set and firm. No, Leora decided, regretfully. Summer's loyalty was to Leora's parents. If she dared to tell her anything, she'd go straight to the elder Howards.

Leora sighed, then brightened. She wouldn't have to wait very long. A man like Ryan needed the love of a woman like her. He'd be lonely and ready for her soon. She smiled as she pictured his surprised, then happy face when she came to him. He'd take her inside and give her a glass of wine . . . and then he'd kiss her passionately.

After that she wasn't sure what would happen. She'd only kissed two other young men and that hadn't been exciting at all.

Of course, Ryan wouldn't take her to his bedroom.... Would he? Leora shivered at that naughty, delicious thought and walked sedately beside Summer down the street toward home.

Chapter Six

Lotus folded and stroked Calista's pink silk gown. The mistress and her aunt were due back home today. A scowl hardened her jaw as she thought of how she'd have to smile and scrape, pretend devotion. Picturing Calista's face, her hand clenched on the gown, wishing it were her mistress's white neck. The image blurred and faded, replaced with that of her former mistress.

It didn't matter. She hated them both! She wished them both dead!

Zeke had gone to Beaufort in the flatboat to fetch Miz Calista and Miz Lucinda. The hand who'd brought the message had seen a brand new wedding ring on Miz Calista's finger, but no husband was with her, and he'd heard tales that she and her man would live apart. But no one at Meadowmarsh had believed that.

How could anyone not want to live with Miz Calista? Zeke had asked. She was so beautiful and good. A man would have to be crazy to stay in Charleston with her here on Meadowmarsh.

"You think dat white gal purty?" Lotus had demanded, her eyes narrowed. "Dem white folks look like grubs and maggots dat need some sunshine." She'd posed seductively for him.

Zeke had pulled her down on his lap, his big hands holding her tightly against him. "You right," he'd whispered in her ear. "Ain't none of them white peoples who look good as you."

Recalling that moment, Lotus's face relaxed in a satisfied smile and her hands unclenched on the gown. She smoothed out the wrinkles and replaced it on the armoire shelf. Soon she'd be wearing silk gowns all the time, and she had Zeke right where she wanted him. Ira Atwood, too. Both of them resented sharing her favors, but they couldn't do anything about it.

Zeke was sullen and gloomy because he'd begun to fear Miz Calista would keep Ira on after she returned, the way Ira was bragging she'd do. Lotus wanted him gone, too. She had no intention of splitting the pirate gold three ways. In spite of the nightly digging, they'd found no trace of treasure—but they would. After Ira left, she'd keep Zeke at it until they did.

But Calista would send her back to the quarters.

No matter that she'd kept this big house better than it had ever been kept before, the old aunt would take over again. Her smile faded, the scowl returning. She closed the armoire door with a vicious slam.

A sound made her whirl. Junie stood in the open doorway, hands on her hips, a knowing smirk on her face. "How you gonna stand dat cotton dress after gittin' used to Miz Calista's silk gowns?"

Lotus's nostrils flared. She advanced on the other woman. "You bettah be careful what you says. I got a long memory," she said softly.

Junie glared defiantly, but gave ground, backing out of

the doorway into the hall. "What difference dat gonna make? You be back in de washroom. And we'll still be heah in de Big House."

Lotus stopped only two feet away from Junie. "Maybe you ain't gonna be here long." She laughed unpleasantly. "Maybe nobody is."

Junie gaped at her. "What dat s'posed to mean?" Her voice was weaker now, and she backed further away.

"You'll know when de time comes. Till den, you can worry 'bout it."

Junie gave in to her fear and loathing of the other woman and turned and ran for the stairs, Lotus's chilling laughter following her all the way down.

Ryan's vision blurred as he picked up yet another legal document, exhaustion from the previous two almost-sleepless nights finally catching up with him. He'd worked in his office all day and now it was past time to leave. Time to go home.

Home? His mind mocked him. *You don't consider that house home and never have.* Despite all his attempts to shut it out, he thought of the other choice he'd had—and rejected. He could be in a far different place now if he'd chosen. An island he'd never seen but had heard was lovely. He could be bedded down tonight with a beautiful woman—his wife.

His hand clenched the paper he held, crumpling it. Damn! Now it would have to be copied over. Why was he letting that conniving female torment him like this? No other woman ever had. Of course, no other woman had enticed him into marriage, either.

His jaw tightened as he remembered that scene under the tree. Calista had clung to him, met his kisses with her own warm mouth and body. He'd have sworn she was as eager as he. But then, she was a good actress. He'd had proof of that, watching her skillful maneuvering of Timothy. And she'd taken him in just as adeptly.

But yesterday, during the ceremony that linked them together, she hadn't seemed to be acting at all. He'd felt a moment of blinding tenderness when she'd forgotten to say her responses aloud. She'd looked so vulnerable and defenseless, as she had that night. He'd wanted to gather her into his arms, to comfort her....

"Well, Burke, are you planning to stay here until morning?"

Jerome's voice boomed in the quiet office. Ryan's eyes met those of the older man, and he saw the disapproval in their depths. He knew what it meant, too. Jerome thought he'd behaved badly.

Ryan turned back to gather his papers into a neat stack. "No, I was just finishing up." He waited for the other man to leave, but instead heard a sigh.

"Why don't you come home with me for supper? I miss Lucinda already. I don't feel like being alone. You'd be doing me a favor."

"Go on home, Jerome. You don't have to flutter around me like a mother hen. I'll be all right."

Jerome let out his breath in a whoosh of exasperation. "You haven't got the sense God gave a goose! Here you are married to a sweet, lovely girl and you let her go off alone to her plantation."

Ryan genuinely liked his partner. He was closer to him than he'd ever been to his own father. But tonight, he was getting irritated with him. He got up from his desk and pushed the heavy chair in, then faced the older man.

"Why am I the one doing the wrong thing?" he demanded. "You know I didn't want this. I was forced into it. Why do you and Lucinda expect me to behave as if this were a normal marriage?"

Jerome took a deep breath and let it out. He'd tried to see this situation from Ryan's point of view, but he found it hard to be sympathetic. "You cared enough for the girl to half-undress her only a few nights ago," he said bluntly.

"She led me on," Ryan said, feeling his temper rising. "All she wanted was a husband, *any* husband. When she lost Timothy, she latched onto me."

Jerome's temper wasn't at its best, either. He stared Ryan down. "And I suppose next you're going to tell me she unbuttoned her own dress and dragged you under that cedar tree."

Ryan glared at his partner, his eyes narrowing. "No, she didn't. I admit the girl tempted me. As you just said, she's beautiful. She's no doubt tempted every man she's come into contact with—probably even you, if you'd be honest. But that didn't mean I wanted to marry her!"

"No, just seduce her. Wasn't that what you had in mind? I pity you if you think lust is all there is to a relationship between a man and a woman. True, I've admired Calista's beauty, but I love Lucinda. An emotion you seem to know nothing about."

To his amazement a wave of shame washed over Ryan. Until this moment, he hadn't believed he'd behaved badly. Damn it, he still didn't! "I did the honorable thing," he said stiffly. "I married the wench. And now, Jerome, I'm very tired. I want to go home and go to sleep."

The other man moved back to let him go by, watching his erect back and shoulders with chagrin. By damn, he'd never seen a more stubborn young man in his life. It was going to take more than Lucinda's machinations to get those two together.

He didn't know if he'd helped matters with his blunt

words. But he didn't see how they could be worse. He heard the front door close as Ryan left and sighed as he picked up his umbrella and walked out after him.

When he'd said he already missed Lucinda, he'd spoken the truth. Why wouldn't she agree to marry him? What difference did it make that they'd only known each other a few weeks? At their ages, they couldn't afford to waste time.

His carriage and driver were waiting on the street outside the office. He'd planned to give Ryan a ride home, since his partner didn't keep a carriage, but he was nowhere in sight. Jerome decided he wasn't going to sit back and give up. Not on his desire to wed Lucinda or his wish to see Ryan happy and settled down with his pretty wife.

Fortunately, both plans would work together. Since Lucinda also greatly desired to see Calista and Ryan together, why then, of necessity he'd have to keep in close contact with her to try to work things out.

The rain that had held off all day began just as his driver started toward home. Halfway there, he overtook Ryan, soaked to the skin. He had the driver stop, and he opened the door and leaned out. "Get in here, you young fool; you'll catch your death."

Ryan shook his head. "I'll spoil your seat cushions," he said and kept on walking.

Jerome closed the carriage door, his face relaxing into a wry smile. He'd probably been that obstinate himself when he was young, hard as that was to believe. But his partner would be a damn good husband once he got used to the idea. Between him and Lucinda, one way or the other, he and Calista would have their chance.

Calista woke instantly, as always, at the sound of Zeke blowing the conch shell announcing "day clean," even though she'd slept little the last few nights. She stretched, wishing she could regain the old simple joy in living she'd had before she went to Charleston.

Before she met Ryan Burke. Before she married him. Before she spent her wedding night alone, trying to fight down the longing to have Ryan beside her. Calista Burke. Mrs. Ryan Burke. She tried out the new name again.

A knock sounded on her bedroom door. That would be Delphinia with her morning tea. "Come in," she called, smiling at the girl who entered with a tray.

She *could* regain that joy, she told herself firmly. Meadowmarsh was safe now; she could live here the rest of her life as its mistress. That was what she'd wanted, *all* she'd wanted.

"Good morning, Delphinia. My, but that looks good." In addition to the pot of tea, the tray held a small dish of fried oysters. Delphinia had remembered she liked to munch them with her tea. Well, of course she remembered, she told herself crossly. After all, she'd only been gone a few weeks. It seemed like years.

Delphinia smiled back widely as she carefully arranged the tray across her mistress's lap. "Yes'm, I fixed dis just de way you like it. We all so happy you back, Miz Calista. Now things'll be like before."

Her voice held a question and Calista, pouring tea into the delicate porcelain cup, knew what it was. She sighed inwardly. Today, she'd pick up the reins of Meadowmarsh again, and she didn't look forward to two things on that agenda.

First, she had to pay Ira Atwood his wages and send him on his way. The man wouldn't be happy about that. Yesterday, when she and Lucinda had arrived, he'd proudly shown her around as if he owned the place, broadly hinting that he'd greatly improved conditions here since he'd taken over. Calista didn't agree. True, all was in good order. The cotton was due for one last picking in the next few days. Everything was neat and the work done. But the blacks looked sullen and unhappy—and sent fearful, hating glances Ira's way.

But Delphinia, who still stood by the bed, wasn't concerned about Ira. Calista lifted her cup to her mouth and took a long, grateful swallow. She put it back on the tray and glanced at Delphinia.

"How do you and Junie get along with Lotus?" she asked carefully. "Now that Miss Lucinda's back, of course she'll take over as housekeeper again; but I was thinking maybe Lotus could stay on here in the house."

The black girl's face changed. Hope and happiness left it, replaced by fear and alarm. She quickly shook her head. "We don't need Lotus. Ain't we always done a good job?"

Calista nodded, giving Delphinia a reassuring smile. "Of course you have. It was just an idea."

Delphinia's face looked hopeful again. "Den you gonna send Lotus back to de washroom?" she asked eagerly.

"No, I don't think I can do that. But I won't let her remain here in the house," Calista promised.

Delphinia's black eyes shone. Her smile beamed. "Dat's good, Miss Calista. Can I git you anythin' else?"

"No, this is fine. Thank you, Delphinia. It's wonderful to be home."

"It sho' good to have you home," Delphinia said fervently as she headed for the door and closed it behind her.

Well, she'd backed herself into a corner. Calista's sense of fairness wouldn't let her demote Lotus to the laundress position after she'd done an excellent job of managing the house. And she couldn't make her a field hand, either.

But she couldn't let her remain in the house. Delphinia's reaction to that suggestion had only confirmed her own feelings of uneasiness when Lotus was around her.

Calista picked up a crisp oyster between her fingers and closed her eyes as she savored the delicate taste. She finished the oysters and her tea, flung the covers back, and carefully lowered herself to the floor from the high bed.

Of course, she could always sell Lotus. But her parents had seldom sold any of their Negroes, and then only for extreme insubordination. That policy had been passed down to her in full measure. What could she do?

The children! Why hadn't she thought of that before? Maum Fronie was getting too old to have the sole responsibility for minding the children of the field workers. Lotus was strong and agile. It was the perfect job for her. Calista smiled in satisfaction as she drew her nightdress over her head.

Oh, it was so good to be home! But something was missing, fight it as she would. She frowned, dismissing those weak thoughts. She'd never needed a man before. She didn't need one now. Especially one like Ryan Burke, who wanted nothing to do with her or Meadowmarsh.

"Yes, I understand," Ira Atwood said stiffly, his pale brown eyes hard and cold. "As you said, you never told me this position was anythin' but temporary."

Calista felt a wave of relief that he was taking his dismissal so well. She handed him a leather pouch. "I'm giving you an extra month's pay as a bonus for doing your job so well during my absence."

His expression didn't change. His heavy-featured face looked bland and unconcerned, but she knew he didn't feel that way inside.

"Thank you, Mrs. Burke. That's very generous of you." He carelessly stuffed the pouch into the front pocket of his dirty wool trousers without glancing at it.

Calista felt a small shock go through her as he called her by her married title. Her relief faded, replaced with the uneasiness that had gripped her since her arrival yesterday. No, longer than that. Since the visit home she'd made before her failed attempt to elope with Timothy.

"I'll be goin' now, ma'am." Ira turned and walked away, toward the flatboat that waited, Zeke at the pole, to take him to Beaufort.

Her troubled glance followed his swaggering walk. He reached the boat, got aboard, then said something to Zeke in a low tone. Zeke looked startled, then darted Calista a furtive glance before just as quickly turning his attention back to navigating the boat away from the dock.

She didn't like that little exchange. Zeke and Ira looked like—she searched for the term that eluded her. They looked like conspirators—partners in some unsavory scheme. Her uneasiness increased.

Don't be ridiculous, she told herself crossly. She was just tired from lack of sleep and these two ordeals today. She trusted Zeke completely. Besides, he didn't even *like* the overseer. He certainly wouldn't be involved in any nefarious plan with him.

She turned away and walked briskly toward the lagoon. She hadn't had time to visit it yesterday, and she sorely needed its comforting serenity. That's why she'd come down here to pay Ira off instead of summoning him to the house.

A flock of marsh birds took startled flight at her approach, and she heard the sliding plop that meant the ancient alligator had just entered the water. Calista settled down on the banks, pulling her skirts up under her. She sat motionless, and soon the wildlife began returning.

Calista closed her eyes, trying to relax, to let the lagoon work its magic. But the rigid tenseness in her spine remained. She felt as if someone watched her from the underbrush. Opening her eyes, she glanced around. Nothing but an egret landing at the edge of the blue water, fish jumping. She sat stubbornly there for several more minutes, even though itching to flee. No! She wouldn't let this somehow wrong atmosphere spoil her special, wonderful place.

But in the end, she got up and left, pulling her shawl around her, feeling chilled to the bone and worse than when she'd sat down. Coming back out onto the path leading to the plantation house, she looked around carefully. Still no sign of anyone. Or anything but Sable, patiently waiting. It had probably been one of the hands. They considered it odd that she loved the lagoon so much. It really wasn't quite proper for the young mistress of the plantation to sit on the banks as she did. That's who it had to be.

Lucinda, looking out the long window from the front sitting room, saw Calista coming, saw her drooping shoulders, her air of exhaustion. Lucinda frowned and pressed her lips together. She longed to see the old Calista, carefree and young and joyous.

But that girl was gone forever, she feared. A woman had taken her place when Calista and Ryan exchanged vows. An unhappy, troubled woman. Zeke had brought a letter from St. Helena today—from Jerome. He said Ryan was miserable, too. He also told her some disturbing news about Ryan's father.

She'd pondered whether to tell Calista, finally deciding not to. Lucinda left the window for the rosewood settee by the fire. The early December day was chilly.

Calista reached the house and came inside. She paused in the sitting room doorway, giving her aunt a wan smile.

"Come and sit down and have your tea." Lucinda patted

the space beside her, indicating the silver tea service on the pie-crust table.

Instead, Calista moved to the window and stood, gazing out much as Lucinda had done. In a few moments she left the window and paced a few feet, then went back to the window. Finally, she turned, her black skirts whirling around her. "What's wrong with Meadowmarsh, Aunt Lucie? There's something in the air now, some kind of discontent. But I can't put my finger on it."

Lucinda smiled at her niece. "You're just tired and overwrought. How did your interviews with Lotus and Mr. Atwood go?"

Calista took off her shawl and laid it across a chair, then came to sit beside her aunt. She wouldn't mention the interchange between Ira and Zeke. It was no doubt just her imagination.

"All right, I suppose. I'm glad to see the last of Mr. Atwood. I think he was too harsh, but that's all over now. Lotus surprised me. She didn't seem to mind leaving the house. I guess she was relieved not to have to go back to the laundry. I couldn't see that, and besides, she's intelligent. No use wasting her talents."

"So you think she has a talent for minding children?" Lucinda asked carefully.

Calista shrugged and sighed. "I don't have the slightest idea. But it's about the only other job available, except field work."

A few feet outside the open sitting room door, Lotus listened. Her eyes narrowed at the mention of field work. The mistress couldn't do that! But she knew better, and her anger grew. Her detested mistress could do anything to her she wanted! But not for long!

"Somehow I can't see Lotus as a loving caretaker of children," Lucinda mused, thoughtfully steepling her fingers under her chin.

Calista sighed again. "Neither can I. But Maum Fronie will be there, too, you know. Even if she is getting old, she's still alert. She won't let Lotus do anything harsh to the children."

Lotus curled her lip in disgust. That's what they thought. She'd have that old woman so scared of her in a week, she'd never dare say a word against her. And she'd have those children the same way.

Lucinda got up and poured tea for them both. "Yes," she said, after a moment. "I suppose you're right. You don't have any other choice—except selling her."

"And it may well come to that," Calista answered, her voice firming. "Meadowmarsh has always been peaceful and happy. I won't let one bad Negro ruin everything. Mama taught me that."

Adding sugar to her tea, Lucinda gave her an inquiring look. "So you think Lotus is the source of the bad feeling you sense here on our island?" she asked, trying to make her voice light. Maybe, after all, she should tell her niece what Jerome had said about Ryan's father. Was it her duty to tell?

Calista sighed, gratefully sipping the hot brew. She lowered the cup and saucer to her lap. "I guess I do, and I just didn't want to face it before. I thought it was Mr. Atwood, but he's gone and I still feel it. Lotus hasn't done anything, as far as I know, but. . . ."

Out in the hallway, Lotus sucked in her breath in anger and outrage. No! She wouldn't be sold away from here. She intended to stay until they found the treasure. So, it looked as if she'd have to put up with the squalling children.

But not much longer.

She threw a look that should have scorched the wooden panels of the door and silently made her way to the back of the house and down to the quarters.

No, not much longer, she repeated to herself as she reached the large cabin used as a communal day care center. She looked with distaste at the dozen or so children, the older ones playing outside on the sandy earth, the younger ones in. Old Maum Fronie bounced a fretting infant in her lap while an older child held on to her skirts, whining.

Miz High and Mighty Calista would wish she hadn't treated her like this before Lotus was finished with Meadowmarsh. Oh, yes, she would.

Chapter Seven

"Damn it, boy, you call this a house?" Emory Burke roared, looking around the small sitting room. "Why, my overseer had a bigger place than this."

Ryan bit his tongue to keep from answering his father in kind. He knew the older man was distraught over losing his plantation to bankruptcy. Damn, he'd been upset, too, that his childhood home was gone forever. But not as upset as he should have been. It hadn't been home to him for a long time now. He'd also smelled liquor on his father's breath, even though it was only mid-morning. Hell, who could blame him? He'd lost everything he'd worked for, what had been his whole life.

"Why, I think it's a darling little place!" Gabrielle said brightly. She took her father's arm and smiled beguilingly up at him, her blue eyes sparkling, her dark brown ringlets bobbing around her pretty face.

Emory's lined face softened for a moment as he looked at her. But only for a moment. He gave his older son another glare. "You should be able to manage something better than this." He snorted. "What's wrong, boy? Can't you get any good cases?"

Ryan's temper, which had been on edge for days, flared. Nothing had changed since he had left the family plantation ten years ago. His father still treated him like an incompetent, small boy.

And also conveniently forgot that Ryan had given him sums of money numerous times when Ainsley Hall had been in financial straits. The last occasion had occurred recently, but his help hadn't saved the plantation, which was one reason Ryan lived in this small, rented house.

He forgot that Emory was his father and that he owed him filial respect. "I don't think you're in any position to quibble over your living quarters, Father," he said coldly. "If I hadn't taken you in, you'd have no place to live."

His father's gray eyebrows drew together. His florid face darkened. He shook off his daughter's hand impatiently and took a step forward. "Why, you disrespectful young whelp! How dare you talk to me in that manner?"

Gabrielle's eyes widened in fright. "Papa," she said, timidly. "Please, don't . . ."

Her father ignored her. He took another step toward his son.

Ryan stood his ground. He stared icily at Emory. "It isn't difficult. You gave me many lessons in disregard for a person's feelings before I left home."

Andrew, a younger version of Ryan, moved between the two angry men. "We won't be here long, Papa," he said, his voice confident. "We'll have another plantation before you know it. Why, with all your business contacts, you'll be able to get a loan to buy more land with no trouble."

The older man stared at him belligerently for a moment. Then, he lowered his hand and stepped back. He nodded stiffly. "You're right, Andrew. This is only a temporary setback. Ainsley Hall was a grand place. We'll soon have another like it."

Slipping up beside him again, Gabrielle took his arm. "Of course, we will, Papa," she said softly. "We have faith in you." She gave Ryan an imploring look.

This was only the first day. Ryan took a deep breath and let it out. How on earth were the four of them going to exist in this cramped house until other arrangements could be made? What other arrangements? his mind asked him. Your father is bankrupt, penniless. No one will lend him money. He's too old. He has nothing to back up a loan. And he's drained you. You can't give him any more.

The knocker sounded at the front door. Thank God! Any interruption was welcome now until all their tempers cooled. He walked out into the hall and swung open the front door. Leora Howard stood on the step.

She gave Ryan a warm smile, even though her stomach was a mass of fluttering butterflies. She knew this was daring, that proper young ladies of her social position shouldn't do this. But she'd never see Ryan again if she didn't do something.

And he was obviously miserable—his face drawn, as if he hadn't been sleeping well—and he appeared to have lost weight. Oh, yes, he needed her!

"May I come in?" she asked him. "I was just in the neighborhood, and . . ."

Ryan stared at Leora in surprise. This girl had no business here. If anyone saw her enter his bachelor household alone, her reputation would be ruined. He looked around. But he saw no one on the street, and she would certainly be well-chaperoned once inside. Her presence might be just the thing to calm everyone down.

He stepped back, giving her a slight bow. "Of course."

Relief spreading through her, Leora entered the narrow

hall and looked around. Dull and drab, it needed a woman's touch. *She* could have it cheerful and bright in no time.

Ryan led her to the sitting room. Leora stopped just inside the door. An older man stared out the front window; a young, worried-looking man stood behind him, and a pretty girl was straightening a slightly askew picture of a full-masted schooner.

"Oh, I'm sorry. I didn't know you had company," she stammered. Who was the girl? Had she waited too long? Had Ryan already found another woman?

The young woman moved across the room, smiling. "Hello, I'm Ryan's sister, Gabrielle."

His sister! Relief made Leora's knees weak. The younger man also turned toward her, and she drew in her breath. Why, he looked just like Ryan! No, he didn't, she decided. He was younger and even better looking, and he was giving her a glance of frank admiration.

"This is my brother, Andrew, and my father, Emory," Ryan said from behind her. "Miss Howard, a cousin of my wife's."

Emory turned from the window, the amazement on his face reflected on his son's and daughter's visages. "You're married? When did this happen? Didn't you think that your father might want to know about it?"

Ryan sighed wearily and ran a hand through his black hair. "I didn't think you'd be interested."

"Not interested?" Emory asked incredulously.

"Never mind." Ryan shook his head. "It doesn't matter. My wife and I aren't living together."

Gabrielle looked from one to another. Leora saw she was distressed, torn between the drama of what her brother had just revealed and the lack of courtesy they were exhibiting toward a guest. Manners finally won out. She crossed the room to Leora's side.

"I'm so happy to meet you, Miss Howard," she said sweetly. "Won't you sit down? I—I think we were about to have tea." She flung a beseeching glance at Ryan.

He let out his breath. "Yes, tea. What an excellent idea. I'll go see if Arva has it ready." He quickly made his escape to the kitchen.

Leora sat down on the drab settee, carefully arranging her skirts, acutely conscious of Andrew's eyes still on her. Gabrielle sat down beside her. Andrew found a chair directly across from her. His father still stood by the window, anger and surprise mingling on his face.

"Married! I can't believe it," Emory muttered. He moved away from the window and sat heavily in a chair beside his younger son. "And what does he mean they're not living together?"

Leora moistened her lips. Should she tell what she knew of the situation? Or pretend ignorance? No, she couldn't tell, she decided. It would sound too much like tattling nasty gossip.

"My cousin has a plantation on one of the Sea Islands," she finally said, her voice prim. "I believe Mr. Burke can't leave his law practice at present to join her."

She was pleased with her reply, especially so since Ryan entered the room again in time to hear it. There, he'd see she wasn't spiteful or hateful toward Calista, the way her family were. Confusion filled her. Why, when she had come here, she'd *hated* Calista. She brushed it aside. Of course she did, but she couldn't let Ryan know that. Men didn't like spiteful women, Summer always said.

Ryan gave her a surprised, grateful look; and she gloated over it, smiling sweetly back. Oh, yes, this was the tack to take now that her plans to have him all to herself had been spoiled. This way might take longer, but it would work out in the long run.

Arva, Ryan's servant, followed close behind with a tea tray which she deposited on a small table, then left. Gabrielle gracefully arose and started pouring tea for everyone.

Ryan's father stared hard at Ryan, who stared back at him blandly. Once or twice the older man started to say something, then stopped. Gabrielle handed around the tea and small cakes.

Daintily taking a bite of cake, Leora glanced across at Andrew. He gave her a wide smile which, to her surprise, made a warm tingle move down her back. It was just because he reminded her so much of Ryan, she told herself, quickly looking down at her teacup.

Forcing himself to sit in his chair and sip his tea, Ryan wanted nothing so much as to grab his coat and hat and leave, go to his office, go anywhere. But at least Leora's tactful remark about why he and Calista were living apart seemed to have calmed his father down.

He shouldn't have given in to his momentary impulse to goad his father further by revealing his marriage. But damn it all, he'd told the truth. Emory hadn't shown any interest in Ryan's life, personal or professional, for years.

And why in hell had Leora come here, unescorted? A sinking feeling hit the pit of his stomach as he realized the most obvious reason. But surely the girl didn't still think he was interested in her?

Why not? Like everyone else, she knew he didn't plan to live with his wife. He'd certainly have to get any ideas like that out of Leora's head. And in a hurry.

A sudden vision of Calista filled his mind. Her emerald eyes, her shining black hair. Her ripe body. He felt his own body hardening and was furious that she still affected him this way. Ryan turned those thoughts off and swallowed a sip of tea.

* * *

Ira Atwood looked furtively around to see if any of the blacks stirred in the dark night. No, all the cabin doors were tightly closed. He slipped out from the shelter of a big live oak and hurried over to Lotus's cabin and rapped.

The door swung open and Lotus stood there, stunned amazement on her face at the sight of him. She started to close the door in his face, but he stuck a large, booted foot in the crack and pushed his way inside.

"Is that any way to welcome me back to Meadowmarsh?" he asked her, smirking.

"What you doin' here?" Lotus demanded, scowling. "Miz Calista done paid you off last week and tole you to git."

Ira pulled up one of the two crude, wooden chairs in the small cabin and sat down, tilting it against the wall. He folded his hands across his chest. "You thought I'd leave for good before we found the pirate gold?"

Lotus felt anger building up from deep inside her. She glanced at a pile of wood sitting beside the hearth. Some of those sticks were heavy.

Ira saw her glance and laughed. "I wouldn't get any ideas like that. You're a strong wench, but I'm stronger. And you know it."

Lotus gave him a sullen look, her black eyes slitted. Yes, she did know that. He'd proved it on many an occasion. She didn't mind her men a little rough, but Ira got mean sometimes. "You expect to stay here and help us dig for dat gold?" she demanded again. "You think nobody gonna tell de Missus?"

Ira got up, letting the chair bang against the floor. He advanced until he was only a foot away from Lotus, then reached out and grabbed her breast. He squeezed until he saw tears in her eyes, but she stared back at him, not flinching. He dropped his hand and gave her a cold, deadly look.

"I expect you'll make sure no one knows I'm here," he told her, his voice as cold as his expression. "Because if they find out, you'll be sorry."

Lotus stared back at him defiantly, but inside she was scared and shaking. More scared than she'd ever been in her life. She feared this man, but she feared being sold off the plantation more. If Ira were discovered in her cabin, that would happen; she had no doubt at all.

Hate rose like bile, almost choking her. He had her trapped now, but she'd find some way of getting rid of him. She and Zeke were the only ones going to share the gold. And maybe not Zeke once they escaped and got up North. She wouldn't need him then.

"Awright," she said sullenly. "You can stay. But you bettah be careful. If anybody see you, we both be in a heap o' trouble."

Ira put a heavy hand on each of her slim shoulders and pulled her to him. "I plan to be careful." He began unbuttoning her dress. "You're a mean bitch, but you know how to make a man feel good," he said as he stripped her dress off her shoulder.

Lotus felt heat rising in her at his touch. Maybe this wouldn't be so bad in some ways. Lately, Zeke had been so worried about what they were doing he wasn't much good at night. She gave Ira a slow smile and shrugged out of the dress, letting it fall to her bare feet, then slipped out of her rough cotton undergarment.

She stood naked before him, her head flung back proudly. She heard Ira's breathing change, become harsh. She was completely ready for him when he grabbed her roughly against him and pulled her down to the pallet on the floor.

* * *

"My dear, that was a superb meal. Your seafood is indeed as wonderful as is claimed." Jerome leaned back on the settee in the sitting room, smiling at Calista. The mid-December evening was cool, and a bright fire burned in the grate.

Calista smiled back. "Thank you, Mr. Kingsley. It's kind of you to say so." Lucinda sat beside Jerome, not touching him, but it was clear both of them longed for privacy. Jerome had arrived this morning to stay for the weekend. Calista had extended an invitation after her aunt's not so subtle hints.

"Don't you think it's time you called me Jerome, my dear? After all, I consider us to be good friends now. And maybe much more than that in time." He gave Lucinda a fond, warm look.

Calista felt happy for her aunt as she watched Lucinda blush rosily from her hairline to the neck of her gown. But she also felt a twinge of regret. Aunt Lucie would marry Jerome eventually. And that would be wonderful for them.

But after Lucinda left, she'd be alone on Meadowmarsh. How could she do without her only real friend?

You shouldn't be alone, a small voice inside told her. *You have a husband in Charleston. A handsome, virile husband.*

And he doesn't want me, and I don't want him, she returned.

Jerome cleared his throat and glanced quickly at Lucinda. She gave him a slight nod, and he turned back to Calista. "My dear, I have news that I feel I must tell you. Lucinda informs me it's my duty."

Calista sat up straighter in her Queen Anne chair, surprise and alarm going through her. Jerome sounded so solemn. Had something happened to Ryan? Her alarm turned to fear, which she quickly subdued. She nodded. "Of course, Mr. King—Jerome."

"It seems your husband's family has fallen upon unfortunate circumstances. His father has lost his plantation, everything he has, to bankruptcy."

She felt her tension ease. Ryan was fine, then. She tightened her lips. Why should she care? He didn't love her. "I'm sorry to hear that."

He seemed to hear the question in her voice. He turned to Lucinda again.

Lucinda looked across at her beloved niece. This was the right thing to do. She knew it was. For everyone. But especially for Ryan and Calista. "Ryan's family is penniless," she said quietly. "Ryan has taken them in, but he has a very small house. Everyone is miserable."

Calista at last understood why she'd been given this information. She was Ryan's wife. Obviously, Jerome and Lucinda expected her to offer hospitality to Ryan's impoverished family. Just a few moments ago, the thought of being alone on Meadowmarsh had dismayed her. Now, the thought of several strangers intruding on her life and privacy was even worse.

She swallowed and summoned a small smile. "Why don't I invite them to stay here for a while? We have plenty of room."

Lucinda's face relaxed. "Oh, would you do that, dear? That would help so much. Wouldn't it, Jerome?" she asked innocently, as if the thought had never occurred to either of them.

He nodded vigorously. "It would be a godsend."

This was something she knew she must do, hate it though she did. *Are you sure about that?* a tiny voice asked. *Ryan would have to bring them out, wouldn't he? You'd get to see him again.*

"But what if Ryan won't let them come? After all, he doesn't want anything to do with me or Meadowmarsh. He made that perfectly clear."

Jerome gave her a satisfied smile. "My dear, you can rest assured Ryan will agree to this plan," he said confidently. "I can almost guarantee you that."

Calista firmly pushed down the small thrill of anticipation that shot through her at his words. It didn't matter if Ryan came.

"Then, that's settled," she said. "I'll write a note inviting them to stay. You can take it back when you return to Charleston on Monday."

There was no reason to think Ryan's feelings or opinions about her had changed in the month since their marriage. Neither had her own, of course. He was a rogue, a would-be seducer. She wanted nothing to do with him.

Ryan scowled at the note in his hand. Calista's handwriting was neat and firm and easy to read. No mistaking what her words meant. His *wife* was graciously inviting his family to come to her island for an indefinite stay. Visions of his house back to normal—all the turmoil of three extra people living in a small house not meant for a family ended—swept over him.

Arva would stop complaining about the extra work and about how his sister Gabrielle tried to help and just got in the way. He wouldn't have Andrew popping in at his office six times a day, asking him if he had any new leads for some backing for his father. And most of all, he wouldn't have Emory's heavy, sullen presence when he returned home at night.

But to accept help from the woman who'd tricked him into this travesty of a marriage? Who'd ruined his life?

He crumpled the sheet of paper in his hand, then threw it on his desk.

"A generous offer, don't you think?" Jerome said from the doorway.

"Quite," Ryan answered, coldly. "But of course I can't accept it."

"Why in the world not, my boy?" Jerome asked, irritation in his strong voice. "Calista has plenty of room. It's the perfect answer to your problem. And don't try to tell me there's no problem. You haven't been fit to do a day's work here since they arrived." Since his marriage, but Jerome wouldn't say that.

Ryan's head came up. "If you'd rather I resigned so that you can find a more satisfactory partner, you have only to ask."

Sighing, Jerome sat down in one of Ryan's client chairs. "Don't be a fool. That's not what I mean, and you know it. You're a fine attorney—but lately your heart's not in this office."

Ryan returned his level look. He knew Jerome was right, and it wasn't fair to his partner to let his personal problems come into the office, interfere with his work. But just the same, he couldn't accept what amounted to charity from the wife he'd refused to live with.

He glanced up at a noise from the doorway. Andrew entered holding a sheet of paper, excitement on his face. He came into the room and handed the paper to Ryan.

"Miss Howard gave me this note. She suggests that Papa and I ask her father for backing to buy new land."

When had Leora seen Andrew? Had she come to the house again? He knew for a fact his brother hadn't been invited to the Howard home. No, that wasn't likely! He glanced at the note, written in Leora's rounded, schoolgirlish hand, then gave it back to Andrew.

"This is a ridiculous idea. The Howards have taken their business affairs to another law firm. We have no contact, either business or personal, with them."

"Oh, Leora explained that mix-up to me," Andrew said, his voice still eager and confident. "She says her parents have calmed down a lot now."

Ryan felt like shaking his younger brother. He threw a glance at Jerome. The older man shook his head, a small smile on his face. "I suppose you've already talked to Father and gotten him all stirred up."

"Naturally, I've told him," Andrew said, the eagerness fading from his face. "He's making plans to see Mr. Howard tomorrow. Leora is going to talk to him first, of course."

Ryan didn't at all like the casual way his brother kept dropping the girl's name into the conversation. "When have you seen Leora?"

"Why, uh, I've met her on the street when she was walking with her maidservant," Andrew stammered, not quite meeting Ryan's eyes.

And also when she wasn't walking with her maidservant, Ryan guessed. Visions of another humiliating scene like the one a few weeks ago filled his mind. Another forced marriage? Oh, no, not to a member of that odious family!

Ryan got up and pushed his chair back. "Forget all that. I just received an invitation from my wife for all of you to visit her plantation. I have accepted for you already."

"Mrs. Burke has a most splendid plantation house," Jerome put in. "Lots of room. Wonderful food. Oysters and clams and shrimp. One of her servant-girls cooks delectable dainties."

Ryan could see that Jerome's words were tempting

Andrew. No wonder. Now he shared a small room and bed with his father and complained that Emory snored loud enough to wake the dead. Arva's cooking couldn't be called inspired by anyone, either.

"I don't know if Papa will want to do this," Andrew said, doubtfully. "He's set on visiting the Howard household tomorrow."

Deciding to appeal to Andrew's reason, Ryan said, "Andrew, you know this plan has no chance of succeeding. You and Father would be lucky if all Farley Howard did was have you thrown out into the street. He'd be a lot more likely to accuse you of trying to seduce his daughter."

Andrew's blue eyes widened in alarm. Clearly, this had never occurred to him. He swallowed. "I believe that you're right, older brother. Gabrielle would be in ecstasy to get into a larger house, and frankly so would I."

"And Father?" Ryan asked bluntly. "Can you undo your foolish work and make him see reason?"

His confidence back, Andrew nodded. "I believe you can safely leave that to me."

Ryan let out his breath. Damn, but he hated this. Again, he was being pushed into a corner against his will. He hardened his heart against Calista. He didn't want to be obligated to her in any way. That's why he'd relinquished all his marital rights to Meadowmarsh. But he had to get his family out of Charleston before Andrew or his father did something completely asinine.

"Then that's settled. I will send word to—Mrs. Burke to expect us." A small tremor went through him as he said Mrs. Burke. It sounded so strange, but yet somehow so right. Don't be a bloody fool, he told himself savagely. He had to escort his family to the island, but he didn't have to stay. He didn't know what devious trick Calista planned now. But he would be no part of it. He'd take his family to Meadowmarsh and then come back to Charleston and pick up the pieces of his life again.

And forget her.

He ignored the taunting voice asking him how that would be possible with his family cozily ensconced in Calista's house.

Chapter Eight

Ryan, followed by his family, stepped off the wooden dock onto the grassy banks where Lucinda and Calista waited, welcoming smiles on their faces. Calista moved her hand and the sun flashed on the wedding ring on her third finger.

Calista, his *wife*.

Damn! he swore inwardly. He'd promised himself he wouldn't think about their relationship. He'd just bring his family here, stay as short a time as possible to get them settled, then leave.

But how could he do that when her radiant beauty made him draw in his breath? She still wore black, of course; but it only made her skin more lustrous, her eyes and hair more brilliant.

Calista tried to avoid meeting Ryan's deep blue gaze, tried to calm her racing pulse. She'd steeled herself for this moment, told herself she was prepared; but now that it was upon her, she realized all her preparations had been for naught.

He looked so wonderful in his midnight-blue frock coat, his garnet waistcoat and crisp white shirt contrasting with his golden-hued skin. He'd flung a dark-blue cloak carelessly over his arm, since the day was pleasant. Her gaze was drawn to his mouth as she remembered how that same mouth had ardently pressed against hers, those strong hands inflamed her senses.

She drew in her breath. Yes, and this man had also caused the most humiliating scene she'd ever endured. But he'd saved her home, the very ground on which they all stood.

Ryan stepped forward and made the introductions.

Calista smiled at Ryan's father, hoping the smile was warmer than it felt. "Welcome to Meadowmarsh, Mr. Burke. We are honored to have you visit us." At least her voice sounded properly cordial.

"Thank you for asking us to stay, *Mrs.* Burke," Emory replied, his voice stiff and cool, as he emphasized her married state. He wore a plain, black coat and carried a black cloak. He was not a man who cared what he wore, she decided.

He didn't welcome her to their family. He didn't ask her to call him father. He wasn't happy about the marriage, and he didn't want to be here, Calista further decided. Ryan must have put pressure on him to make him agree to this.

She hoped he wouldn't be difficult to entertain, because she had a lot of work to oversee at this time of year. "Please, you must call me Calista," she said firmly.

Andrew stepped forward, resplendent in a bright-blue frock coat with a robin's egg-blue brocade waistcoat under it. His white shirt was fluted and his cloak scarlet. Ryan's brother appeared to be something of a dandy. He bent over her hand with a flourish, admiration in his blue eyes, so much like Ryan's.

"You indeed have a wondrously beautiful island, Sister

Calista," he proclaimed. "But the surroundings cannot compare with your own surpassing beauty."

Sister? Andrew must not know the real situation between her and Ryan. All right, she could keep up the fiction, too. It would make the visit go more smoothly. She managed to turn her amused smile at his extravagant compliment into one of welcome. "I thank you, *Brother* Andrew, for both compliments."

Ryan gave Andrew an amazed look, as if he couldn't believe his ears. He turned his head, and his eyes met Calista's full on for the first time. A shock wave ran through her body. As at that first dinner party, she felt he could see into the depths of her, almost read her mind.

Widening her smile, she quickly turned to Gabrielle, who wore a demure rose-colored gown. The girl looked shy and uncertain of her welcome. "I've always wanted a sister. Welcome, Gabrielle."

"As have I," Gabrielle answered eagerly, her blue eyes warming as she smiled at Calista.

She liked the girl, Calista thought. They should get along fine.

Emory looked around him with a frown. "Never been on an island plantation before. I would think it might be a bit confining."

Neither would Andrew be a problem, she guessed, but his father was a different story. His first glimpses of Meadowmarsh hadn't charmed him in the slightest. She had an intuition that the plantation never would. Could she blame him? He'd just lost all he owned. He probably hated the world right now.

"Oh, no," she answered, her voice still pleasant. "We have plenty of room since we own the entire island. The plantation house is on high ground overlooking the sea, so we don't need a separate summer dwelling. It's quite a walk, so I've had the carriage brought around."

She gestured to where Gideon waited with the large, two-horse carriage on the oyster-shell road. The carriage seated four easily, five a little tightly. She planned to walk back to the house. Even to herself she wouldn't admit she wanted to delay being with Ryan as long as possible.

But to her surprise, Andrew insisted on walking back with her. "Of course, if you want." She glanced at Ryan, who stood before the carriage door, frowning at his brother.

Ryan was not pleased with Andrew's behavior. The young fool was bowled over by Calista's beauty and made no effort to hide his admiration. Damn it! He acted as if she weren't a married woman. What's that to you? his mind asked. You don't want her. You don't plan to ever live with her.

That didn't matter. She was still his wife. "That sounds like an excellent idea." He gave Calista and Andrew a tight smile. "I need the exercise, too."

A moment later, Calista found herself walking between the two handsome men who looked so much alike. She could feel Ryan's disapproval of his brother, even though he hadn't said a word.

She could also feel the heat coming from his muscled body, so close to hers, bringing back memories she wanted to forget. She moved to the right a few inches, nearer to Andrew.

This was an awkward situation, Calista thought, irritated with both Ryan and Andrew. She should have gotten into the carriage and let the men walk with each other. "So you like what you've seen of Meadowmarsh?" she asked Andrew, ignoring Ryan.

Andrew nodded, his black-lashed blue gaze lingering on her. "Yes, indeed. I hear things on the Sea Islands are done differently than on the mainland. Would it be possible to see a little more before we go to the house? Father and I will soon be buying more land and start planting again."

Beside her, Calista felt Ryan stiffen and give a snort of disapproval. Her irritation increased. Her *husband* was not only an unprincipled rogue, but also rude and disagreeable. She liked Andrew, she decided. He was friendly and open and pleasant. Which his older brother certainly wasn't.

She turned to Ryan. "Will your father be offended if I leave Aunt Lucie to entertain him and Gabrielle?" she asked, forcing her voice to be calm and friendly.

Ryan glared at her for a moment, then his face smoothed out, and he gave her the mocking smile she remembered so well. "I doubt if anything you could do would please my father—unless you can provide him with the financial backing which he and my brother so desire." He threw an ironic glance at Andrew.

Damn it! He hadn't meant to say that. It had just slipped out. He didn't hold Andrew responsible for the final failure of Ainsley Hall. His brother had a sound business head. His father he wasn't so sure about.

Calista felt her indignation rise even more as she turned to Andrew and saw his handsome face flush. Ryan was a cad! Why did he taunt his poor brother like this? Impulsively, she said, "Meadowmarsh has had several very good years of late. If your father is interested, I'd be pleased to make him a loan." Satisfaction filled her as she saw the eager light return to Andrew's face.

Shock filled Ryan at her unexpected words. He jerked his head around to stare at her. She stared back, her gaze challenging. She'd only said that to annoy him; she had no idea of the quagmire into which she'd sink if she started giving his father loans—as he'd done for years. "You can't do that," Ryan said, his voice and face hard. "I won't allow it."

"Oh?" she questioned sweetly. "And how can you prevent me, *husband?* Since you gave up all your legal rights to Meadowmarsh before our marriage."

Damn her—he wished he hadn't. But how could he have foreseen this problem? And his pride wouldn't have let him do otherwise. His frustration and anger grew. His wife enjoyed rubbing it in that she controlled her plantation.

Just as his mother had done. His face tightened. He gave Calista a small, stiff bow. "You are correct. There is no legal way I can prevent you from doing anything you wish with either your property or income, no matter how unwise."

Calista swallowed, her satisfaction fading. Ryan was very angry—more so than the situation called for. She felt as if she'd disturbed muddy waters with no knowledge of what lay beneath.

Turning back to Andrew, Calista saw the hurt in his face at his brother's words. She felt sorry for him, but wished she hadn't agreed on this plantation tour. She had no desire to spend the next hour or two in the company of her angry husband.

"On second thought, I believe we'd better wait until morning. The plantation is large; we'll have to be on horseback to see all of it."

"That's fine with me," Ryan said curtly. "I have no wish to see any of it. I grew up on a plantation and couldn't wait to get away."

That wasn't wholly true. He'd loved his plantation home as a young child—before he had grown old enough to see and feel the dislike between his parents.

Calista turned to Andrew again. She'd take him out alone tomorrow. What a wonderful relief that her *husband* had expressed no desire to live with her. How fortunate that she didn't have to try to please the surly, hateful man!

"Tell me all about Ainsley Hall," she said amiably, then paused. "Unless it pains you to talk of your lost home."

Andrew shook his head. "No, I'm over that." He squared his shoulders manfully. "One has to look toward the future. And now, maybe Father and I can start planning again for that future." He gave Calista a grateful, warm smile.

She smiled back, tucking her hand in the bend of Andrew's elbow.

Ryan scowled at them both. Another day should be long enough for him to remain here. He could plead pressing business at his law firm.

He threw another glance at Calista and Andrew, his scowl deepening. Not that it would matter to his *wife*. She probably wouldn't even notice if he left right now.

And that was the way he wanted it, of course. He turned his eyes straight ahead and marched up the oyster-shell road, doing his best to ignore Calista's sweet laughter.

Lotus lay on her pallet, sweat running down her body. Fear snaked its way into her consciousness. It wasn't supposed to be this bad. She'd taken the herbs before and been up and about in just a few hours.

A groan filled the small cabin; and she realized, through her haze of fear and pain, that it came from her. She closed her eyes and began to pant. "Oh, lordy. Somethin's bad wrong. I knows it is."

Dimly, as if it came from a great distance, she heard her door creak open, then shut again. Who was coming into her cabin? Zeke? Ira? They were supposed to be out digging for the gold. And none of the slaves would dare to enter without her permission.

She felt a presence and heard a long, trembly sigh. She opened her eyes a slit. Old Maum Fronie, the childminder, crouched beside her. Maum Fronie was also the plantation midwife.

Lotus scowled at the other woman. "Git out o' heah! I don't want you." Another pain took her and she doubled over.

"Chile, you needs help bad," the old woman said, her hand pressing down on Lotus's convulsing abdomen. "If I don't help you, you gonna die."

Die? She couldn't die! She was young and strong and had lots of plans for her life. Lotus tried to give Maum Fronie another fierce glare, but a pain caught her, worse than any of the others. She felt as if she were being torn apart. In spite of herself, she screamed, a long, almost-howl that frightened her more than the pain. She felt blood trickling down between her legs, soaking the pallet.

"Awright," she mumbled when the pain finally eased, leaving her limp and weak. "Den help me. But if you tells anyone what went on heah tonight, I kill you!"

Maum Fronie ignored her. She scooted her pine straw basket closer and removed something that glinted in the feeble light of the candle.

Lotus's eyes widened with fear. "No! Don' you use dat on me!"

Maum Fronie's wrinkled old face remained impassive as she pushed Lotus's legs apart and brought the forceps closer. "Dey's nothin' else I can do, and you knows it. You gonna bleed to death if I don't. You push when I tells you to, and let me do what I has to."

The next pain seized her in its iron grip. Lotus picked up her kerchief and pressed it into her mouth to hold back the scream trying to break free.

"Now, push as hard as you can!" Maum Fronie ordered.

Lotus pushed and pushed and felt the hard, cruel edge of the metal enter her. She bit on the kerchief, then blessed darkness drew her down and down in a spiraling whirlpool and she knew no more.

Calista lay wide awake in bed, staring at her ceiling, listening to the night sounds of the house. Had there always been this many creaks and groans? Why couldn't she sleep tonight? She was certainly tired enough. The day had been exhausting.

She'd gotten up when Zeke had blown the conch, not waiting for her morning ritual of tea in bed. She'd scarcely sat down all day, preparing for Ryan's family to arrive. She had wanted everything to be perfect. And it had been.

When she and Andrew and Ryan arrived at the house, after their half-hour walk, she could tell both men were favorably impressed with the beautiful house. Andrew asked her knowledgeable questions about architecture; and although Ryan said nothing, she saw the surprised, appreciative look in his eyes.

Delphinia opened the door before they got to it, immaculate in white apron and kerchief, bowing them inside. She supposed she should have a butler as most of the big plantations did; but her parents, and now she, had never felt the need.

The house shone with cleanliness and smelled of lemon oil. The sitting room smelled pleasantly of fragrant, white, tea-olive blooms; and a fire was ready to be lit in the immaculate grate.

Looking up from one of the settees, Lucinda gave them a welcoming smile. "There you are! We were just going to have tea." She rose and went to the pie-crust table where the tea service was arranged.

Gabrielle also smiled at the three newcomers and rose quickly from Calista's favorite Queen Anne chair. "I'll help you," she said eagerly, her deft fingers soon busy with cakes and napkins.

Ryan's father stood before one of the large, front windows, gazing down over the lawns that led to the bluffs overlooking the sea. He didn't turn at their entrance, didn't even seem aware of it.

When his daughter handed him a cup of tea and a plate with two cakes on it, he took it, then turned away from the window and moved heavily over to a chair and seated himself.

"Did you have a nice walk?" Lucinda asked brightly, pouring more tea, her eyes searching her niece's.

"Very nice," Calista lied. She seated herself on the settee her aunt had vacated and forced a smile. She glanced at Andrew, who was giving his father an eager look as if bursting to talk to him. She now regretted her promise to offer her in-laws financial backing. It wasn't like her to be that impulsive without thinking things through. She'd never have done it if she hadn't been angry with Ryan.

She didn't know what it would take for her father-in-law to make a fresh start or how much money she could safely lend. She'd have to consult with her lawyer, who wouldn't be pleased with the idea.

And, until her birthday next month, when she turned twenty-one, full control of the plantation and all its assets wouldn't be hers. But Ryan didn't have to know all that. She tightened her mouth. It wasn't any of his business.

Ryan sat beside Lucinda on a settee, making pleasant conversation. She'd have to give him credit for that. He genuinely liked her aunt and the feeling was mutual. He turned her way, and she quickly gave her attention to Gabrielle, who'd finished serving and now sat beside her.

"Did you enjoy Charleston?" she asked the younger woman. "It's a beautiful city."

Gabrielle made a face. "I *hate* Charleston! I miss my

home so much. I don't know what to do with myself now."

Calista reached over and squeezed her hand. "I know how you feel. I don't like towns, either. You're welcome to stay here as long as you like. And I'm sure Aunt Lucie would be glad of your help with the housekeeping routine."

Smiling, Gabrielle squeezed Calista's hand in return. "Thank you, Calista. I'll be happy to do anything I can. Ryan was most fortunate in marrying you."

Her last words came during a sudden lull in the conversation and seemed to echo in the room. Calista felt her skin reddening and, in spite of herself, glanced in Ryan's direction.

He gave his sister a startled look, which changed to a frown. Gabrielle gazed back at him, plainly puzzled at his disapproval. Calista saw she'd been right. Obviously, Ryan's family didn't know the reasons they were living apart.

"I believe we all need another cup of tea," Lucinda had said, rising and moving to the tea table.

The awkward moment had been smoothed over, Calista thought now, as she tried yet another position in bed. But the rest of the evening had had a distinct chill on it, due mostly to Ryan's father's morose silence. Even the sumptuous meal she'd planned hadn't eased the tension.

She'd been relieved to finally go to bed. If she could only sleep! The full moon cast its beams across her bed through an opening in her curtains. That didn't help. She turned over again, seeking a more comfortable position. She must be too tired to relax.

Why don't you admit it? she asked herself at last. It wasn't the moon and it wasn't exhaustion. She couldn't sleep because her husband slept in the next room. That thought made her change her position again, to no avail.

Finally, she flung back the covers. She needed a cup of warm milk. That had always worked when she had been a child. Why not now? She put on her wrapper and slippers and quietly opened her door. The wide hall was dark and still. No one else seemed to be having her problem.

She descended the staircase and made her way to the back of the house and outside. The brilliant moon lit up the night as if it were day. No, not quite. It cast strange, grotesque shadows, making a shiver go down her spine.

Calista unbolted the kitchen door and stepped inside. She knew her way around the big room, and besides enough light came through the windows from the moon to make out where things were. She soon located a pan of milk on a long table, set there so the cream would rise overnight.

She moved the thin skin of cream already formed to one side, dipped milk into a small pan, and put it on the still-glowing embers of the hearth fire.

A soft sound at the door made her jerk her head around. She drew in her breath and her heart gave a hard thump. Ryan stood there, silhouetted in the doorway. "What are you doing here?" she asked.

He leaned against the door frame, that familiar, mocking smile on his face. He wore a dark dressing gown tied with a sash. "I might ask you the same thing," he drawled.

Calista's nostrils flared. "It *does* happen to be my home," she said coolly. "I may go where I wish."

Ryan moved away from the doorway, closing the door behind him. He stopped a few feet from her. "Why are you so touchy, Calista? Even if we don't plan to live together, we could at least exchange a few civil words occasionally, don't you think?"

"You've said scarcely a civil word to me since you got here! And it wasn't *my* idea to live apart," she returned hotly, then was at once appalled. She'd never wanted him to know how badly his cold, cruel treatment of her that night had hurt.

Ryan was absolutely still for a moment, then he gave her another ironic smile. "You are so right, little wife. I was rude earlier, I'm sorry to say. And the other was, indeed, my decision. But made for very good reasons, don't you think? No man likes to find he's been tricked into marriage."

So he still believed that. Of course he did. He'd always believe it. Nothing she could say or do would change his views. She wouldn't even try. She gave him a cool stare. "I don't know why you followed me, but I don't want you here. Please leave."

Instead, Ryan moved closer until only a foot separated them. She could feel his heat, smell his masculine scent of soap and spice. Her knees began to tremble. She braced her legs to stop the weakness she couldn't bear for him to detect.

He reached out his hand to lazily touch her cheek. "What *do* you want, Calista?" he asked, his voice so soft it seemed she felt, rather than heard it.

Her knees trembled worse, and his hand on her face felt like fire. She stood as still as she could, afraid to move, which might reveal her weakness to his mockery. His hand slid down her cheek to her neck, caressingly, until it reached her breast. Slowly, gently, he cupped the round softness, his gaze not leaving hers.

Calista felt as she had that night under the cedar tree. Will-less, mindless, wanting nothing but his touch, his kiss. He moved his hand to more fully encompass her breast, and his thumb circled the nipple. With a last desperate effort she commanded her mind not to betray her to her ridiculous passions.

"I want you to leave me alone," she told him, but her voice trembled, betraying the lie.

Ryan's gaze held hers for an eternity before finally dropping to her mouth. Slowly, he lowered his face to hers. She felt the whisper of his breath teasing her lips, then his mouth was covering hers, devouring hers. Calista could no more keep herself from returning his kiss than she could stop breathing.

Then, his hand dropped away from her breast and he stepped back. He gave her a mocking bow. "As you wish, madam," he said formally. "Good night."

He walked outside, closing the door behind him without a backward look. Calista stood as if turned to stone, still feeling his kiss, his touch. The smell of something burning finally penetrated her daze. The pan of milk boiled over, splashing onto the coals.

She grabbed the handle with the hem of her dressing gown and set the pan on the table. The milk was scorched and ruined. She didn't want it anyway. She knew now she wouldn't sleep tonight, no matter how many pans of milk she drank.

Calista left the kitchen, stopping just outside the door. There was no sign of Ryan. He must have gone back inside the house.

A cloud moved across the moon, plunging the yard into sudden darkness, and a sound seemed to drift up from somewhere below. A disturbing sound—like the echo of a scream . . .

Her head cocked, she listened intently, but no repetition of the sound came; the night was as still as death. Only her imagination, she decided. Her nerves were on edge. Shivering, she picked up her skirts and hurried inside, relieved to get away from the night which now seemed full of creeping, hidden dangers.

* * *

Back in his comfortable room, Ryan lay in his bed, hands behind his head. Damn it! What had possessed him to follow Calista outside, into the kitchen? Why had he touched her again, kissed her again, when he'd sworn never to do so? She was a beautiful woman and she was his wife, but she'd also proven to be a cold, calculating vixen.

Cold? His mind asked him, mockingly. He scowled at the ceiling, his body tense with anger at himself. Only *anger?* His mind mocked him again.

He threw back the covers and strode to the window, sweeping the curtains aside. His room looked down on the back of the house; that's how he'd seen Calista leave a few minutes ago.

Now, he saw her again. Standing in the moonlight, her black hair gleaming in its rays, her soft, seductive body outlined by the nightclothes she wore. She seemed to be listening to something, her head tilted to one side.

He could have had her tonight if he'd kept on with his love play. No matter what she'd said, she was as eager for it as he. If he wanted to, if he handled her right, he could have her for his wife in all ways.

But he wouldn't do it! She'd tricked him into marriage, and he couldn't forgive that. In addition, she was committed to a way of life he wanted nothing to do with.

He'd stay away from her tomorrow. Not go with her and his besotted brother on their tour of her beautiful island plantation. And early the next morning, his duty fulfilled, he'd head back to Charleston and his law practice where he belonged.

Yes, his mind taunted him, back to your stuffy office, back to your boring clients and endless hours of paperwork. He turned it off and jerked the curtains closed again, just as Calista left his range of vision and came inside.

Chapter Nine

"This Sea Island cotton requires much more time and labor than the short staple variety we grow," Andrew said.

Calista looked with pride at her cotton field filled with workers. "Yes, but it also brings a higher price, which makes it worth while."

She was enjoying this tour. Andrew was interested in every detail of her plantation. She firmly pushed back the thought that she'd enjoy it more if Ryan were with them. No, she wouldn't. He'd be sarcastic and disagreeable and spoil everything. She was glad he'd stayed back at the house with the others.

"So this is the last picking of the season?" Andrew asked.

"Yes. There'll be some cotton left on the plants, but we must finish with the moting and the ginning now to get it to market."

"How do you transport it and to where?"

"We have a sailboat and flatboats to take it to Beaufort.

From there, it's sent on to Charleston. Our finest grade has a standing contract with a French mill."

He looked suitably impressed. "It seems a shame to leave any cotton in the fields. Wouldn't it be better to have another picking?"

Calista gave him a half-amused look. This wasn't the first suggestion Andrew had made concerning her management of Meadowmarsh. He was a young man of decided opinions. *Just like his brother.* Never mind Ryan; she wouldn't think about him.

She shook her head. "No. It's only a small amount, and soon we'll need to get the ground ready for next season's planting. It must be fertilized and a cover crop planted."

"You bother with all that every year?"

"Of course. Since we live on an island, our land is limited. We must take care of it. We can't use up our fields, then go on to new ones as mainland planters often do."

His face grew thoughtful as he pondered her words. Finally, he glanced up at her. "For a woman, you are remarkably well-informed, Calista," he told her, his blue eyes sparkling.

She gave him an indignant look, then had to smile herself. Andrew had no malice. He was also intelligent and strong willed. All good qualities in a young man.

His expression became serious. "I haven't spoken to my father about your generous offer. I thought perhaps you'd rather approach him yourself."

"I'm glad you haven't," she answered, relieved. "I'll have to consult with my lawyer in Beaufort before I can make a definite offer." She would also have to wait until her birthday next month, but he didn't need to know that.

Andrew couldn't quite hide his disappointment, but he nodded, then smiled again. "Yes, naturally you will."

Her relief grew. Good, he wasn't going to press the issue. "I think I've showed you everything on Meadowmarsh. And it's nearly dinner time. Shall we ride back to the house?"

"I hope we're going to have more of your wonderful seafood," he said eagerly.

"Of course we are. I'm so happy you and your family enjoy it as much as Aunt Lucie and I do." The mention of dinner and food reminded her that she wanted to send Junie down to the quarters with some broth for Lotus.

This morning, before she and Andrew had started their tour of the plantation, she'd stopped at Zeke's cabin to inquire if anyone had been sick during the night. He'd said no; but when she'd reached the cabin where the field workers' children were cared for, she'd found Maum Fronie alone.

When she'd asked about Lotus, the old woman said she was ailing, but quickly added Calista didn't have to see her or send for the doctor. Just a stomach upset, and she'd tended to Lotus herself. Something about her manner seemed evasive, but Calista didn't question her further. She trusted Fronie, and she didn't want to see Lotus unless it was absolutely necessary.

Ryan made his sixty-eighth circuit of the veranda. He'd paced restlessly for the last two hours, refusing to admit he wished he'd gone with Andrew and Calista on their plantation tour. No, he didn't want to see the damned plantation.

But the day was glorious, and it was a shame to stay indoors. He spent enough such days in his Charleston office dealing with the endless paperwork, trying to soothe irate clients or, even worse, explain some dry legalese to said clients.

He paused and sniffed the air appreciatively. It reminded him of his childhood home and, at the same time, the balmy sea breeze with its tang of salt held an exotic, unfamiliar, therefore exciting scent. It made him even more restless.

He started pacing again. It was a wasted day so far. He wanted to talk to his father before leaving for Charleston tomorrow; but Emory came down for breakfast, then went straight back to his room. And there he still was. When Ryan tapped on his door, he said he wasn't feeling well.

Hell, he didn't know what he'd say to his father anyway. He couldn't tell him to refuse any offers Calista might make. That demand, coming from him, would only get Emory's back up. And, as his wife had pointed out yesterday, he had no legal say over what she did with her plantation or its income.

He frowned, wishing he hadn't been so hasty in relinquishing all his marital rights to Meadowmarsh. But how could he have foreseen this situation? He'd known his father and Andrew were heavily in debt, as were most plantation owners. His father had asked him for money and he'd given them a substantial amount only a few weeks ago, leaving himself quite short.

Now, Ainsley Hall was gone forever. Ryan felt a sharp pain in his midriff at that thought. He could remember happy times there from his early childhood. Gone, too, was all the money he'd advanced Emory and Andrew over the years. He hadn't known they'd lost everything until his father had written him, asking if he and Andrew and Gabrielle could stay with him for a while until they "got on their feet again."

His father was fifty-five, an old man. Ryan knew he would find it almost impossible to obtain a loan. Andrew was young and bright, but he now possessed no assets. He'd have a hard time borrowing money, too.

He could probably find Andrew a place somewhere in Charleston, maybe with a law firm or as an assistant for one of the factors. But his brother would hate it. His whole life had been the plantation. Gabrielle, too, wasn't cut out for city life, and as for Emory—Ryan shook his head as he rounded the corner again.

The truth of the matter was, as far as the world was concerned, his father was finished. And, even more than his son and daughter, he'd be miserable living in town.

"Ryan, would you like something to drink?" Lucinda asked, coming out the front door. She, too, drew a deep breath. "Umm, the air's nice today. You'd never know it's winter, would you?"

Pausing opposite her, he summoned a smile. "It's a wonderful day. No, I think I'll wait until dinner, thank you, for a drink."

He could see why Jerome wanted to marry Lucinda. She was intelligent, witty, and still very attractive. And with a mind of her own. He hoped his partner's courtship would eventually be successful. This was one marriage he believed would have a chance of working out. One of the very few.

Lucinda walked over and sat down in one of the veranda chairs. She patted the seat beside her; and Ryan, who'd rather have continued pacing, seated himself. "I do hope your father isn't coming down with one of the fevers."

"I don't believe so," Ryan assured her. No, he didn't think his father was physically ill. It was a sickness of the spirit that ailed him. That, and the fact he was drinking too much.

"Good. Gabrielle is such a dear girl, and a big help. She's fitted right in. You'd think she'd lived here for years. I declare, I didn't know how many miles I walked in a day until your sister walked some of them for me this morning."

"She ran the house for my father since my mother died five years ago."

The sound of horses' hooves made him glance up. Andrew and Calista galloped up the oyster-shell drive. His brother looked handsome and fit. Calista, her green eyes sparkling, her fair skin rosy from the exercise, rode astride a black Arabian mare.

Some men might have found this shocking, but he didn't, he realized. Instead, he felt intrigued. His wife seemed completely natural and at ease. Also thoroughly enjoying herself.

A sting of what felt suspiciously like jealousy went through Ryan. His wife and his brother had just spent a wonderful morning together out in the fresh air and sunshine while he'd wasted the time counting off steps on this blasted porch.

The two riders reined their mounts in front of the house.
"You're just in time for dinner," Lucinda called.

Gideon came out of the house and took the horses' reins, then headed for the stables.

"Yes, we know," Andrew said. "That's why we're here." He threw a laughing, somehow intimate glance toward Calista as if they shared a secret. Her answering smile seemed to hold the same secret intimacy.

Ryan watched them walk toward the house, a frown between his brows. Calista's dark riding habit fit her to perfection; and her black hair, pulled back and fastened at the nape of her neck, gleamed in the sun. She was damned lovely, and he didn't want to leave his good-looking brother, who apparently had an eye for all attractive women, here on Meadowmarsh with her.

* * *

Calista glanced across the dinner table at Ryan. All morning, she'd managed not to think about that midnight scene last night in the kitchen. But now, with Ryan only a few feet away, it came flooding back. Red suffused her face as she felt once again his burning kiss, his warm hand curving around her breast, and heard his whispered words. If she'd been willing, she could have had Ryan in her bed last night.

Willing? something inside asked her. *Oh, you were willing all right. You were just too big a coward to take a chance on the aftermath.* Calista turned quickly to Emory on her right.

"Mr. Burke, I hope you're feeling better."

"Tolerably," he answered shortly, reaching for his wine glass and finishing half the contents before returning it to its place.

He'd smelled of liquor when he'd sat down at the table. What had Ryan gotten her into? She had no experience with people who drank too much. Her father had been a very moderate imbiber of spirits.

She glanced again at Ryan, who watched his father, a frown on his face. He, too, was worried about Emory's drinking, she suddenly knew. So that must mean the older man did too much of it.

Ryan hoped his father would control his liquor-intake and not create an ugly scene as he sometimes had at Ryan's house. Misgivings hit him. Maybe he shouldn't have brought Emory here. He'd been in such a hurry to get him out of Charleston, it hadn't occurred to him to worry about this problem.

He felt eyes on him and glanced up to find Calista looking at him. She quickly looked away, pink blooming on her smooth cheeks. Damn it! He didn't think he could sit through this dinner with Calista across the table from him. As if it were still last night, he could feel her rounded breast, her warm, soft lips beneath his own. He was a fool for not taking her to bed. Maybe that's what he needed to do to get her out of his system.

The thought took root in his mind and grew as the meal progressed. Try as he might to ignore her, he was aware of every word she said, every movement of her graceful hands, every smile that curved her lovely mouth. He couldn't seem to help gazing at her.

Calista became increasingly uncomfortable. Every time she looked up, Ryan was staring at her. The look in his eyes made her wonder if he, too, were reliving those moments last night.

Would this dinner never end? Finally, after dessert was served and the men retired to the library with brandy and cigars, she grabbed her cloak. "I'm going for a walk," she told Lucinda and Gabrielle. "Do either of you want to go with me?"

Lucinda shook her head. "I want to work on some embroidery this afternoon." She turned to Gabrielle. "Would you like me to show you that bouillon stitch?"

Gabrielle's blue eyes lit up. "Oh, would you? It looks so pretty on your collar."

Her aunt was giving her an opportunity to be alone, Calista realized, gratefully. The older woman knew she had to have these moments of solitude. It was hard for her to adjust after years of almost no visitors, either friends or strangers, at Meadowmarsh.

Strangers? Calista drew on her cloak and let herself out of the house. No, already Andrew and Gabrielle were beginning to seem like family. Yesterday, she'd answered in kind when the two had called her sister only to be polite. But today, she honestly felt she could get close to them.

She walked slowly down the sloping road toward the lagoon, her brow furrowed as she thought over this unexpected development. Did she want to get close to Ryan's family? Was it a good idea, considering that she and Ryan would never live together.

Never? *That's a long time,* her mind protested. *You and Ryan are both young. You're talking about years and years. The rest of your life.*

She ignored that and continued with her train of thought. Whether she wanted to or not, there wasn't much she could do since the Burkes were already here for an indefinite stay. She couldn't snub all of them, not that she would think of doing such a thing.

Finally, she shrugged, deciding not to worry about it. She had enough worries as it was. She'd been so busy since yesterday morning, she'd almost forgotten the conviction that something almost evil had invaded her island plantation. But now that she was alone again, it was back.

It was another unseasonably warm day for December. All the hands were ginning today. Zeke was in charge and she had full confidence in him, but later on she'd ride down to the ginning barns to see how things were going. The hands went through the wooden rollers by the dozen. She'd soon have to send Zeke over to Beaufort to get a new supply.

As usual, a flight of birds took to the skies in alarm as she approached the lagoon. She spread her unneeded cloak on the grassy bank and settled her skirts under her. Closing her eyes, she let the peace of her sanctuary steal over her and released her worries for a little while.

But her peace and solitude weren't complete. Again, she felt observed by unseen eyes. Her eyes flew open. Looking around carefully, she saw nothing. Then, she heard a rustling in the underbrush across the lagoon.

Ryan appeared on the opposite bank. He hesitated, then walked toward her. All her serenity fled as she watched him. What was he doing here?

From the window of the library, he'd seen Calista leave. Making excuses, he'd followed her; but he was sure Lucinda knew where he went. She'd given him a knowing, pleased smile as he'd left.

Now, seeing Calista's body tense, her eyes widen, he cursed himself for a fool. His sweet, docile wife was a lot more likely to push him into the lagoon than welcome him with open arms. But he felt his body hardening just at the sight of her.

Damn it! He seemed to have no control when he was in Calista's presence. Just this instant, unthinking, physical reaction. And that's why he was here, he reminded himself. He intended to consummate his marriage on these grassy banks. Maybe then, the burning urge to possess her would die.

"What are you doing here?" Calista demanded. She tried to put indignation into her voice, but realized that wasn't how she felt. Ryan had destroyed her tranquility, but he'd brought excitement in its place.

"I wanted to be with you."

His voice held no trace of sarcasm or annoyance. Then he smiled. A warm smile, like the ones he'd given her the night of the failed elopement. It transformed his face and made her catch her breath.

He eased himself down beside her, sitting so close his gray trousers brushed her skirt. She felt his enticing warmth. She had to get up, get away before he drew her down into the mindless spell that had held her that other night. And last night.

Instead, she found herself looking at his mouth, which had given her such intense pleasure. Quickly, she glanced out over the lagoon and moved away from him a few inches. "I wanted to be alone," she said, trying to sound firm and cool. She didn't think she was very successful.

Neither did Ryan. She wanted him to stay, he decided, satisfaction filling him. He let her new distance stand for the moment. "I know," he said, his voice still warm. He didn't say anything else, just sat there beside her looking out over the placid blue water.

Well, tell him to leave, her mind urged. *He gave you a perfect opportunity.* Instead, she heard herself say, "This is my favorite place." Her voice was softened, warm, not firm and controlled the way it should have been.

After another pause, Ryan answered. "I can see why. It's beautiful and peaceful." Should he move closer to her again? *No, take it slow and easy,* he warned himself.

Calista held herself tense, waiting for Ryan to make a move. But he seemed content to drink in the calm beauty surrounding him. Hadn't he admitted he'd come here to be with her? He certainly didn't act as if he wanted that.

She realized she felt miffed. *You idiot!* she told herself. If Ryan wanted them to be merely decent to each other, she should have been relieved. And that must have been what he had in mind. Hadn't he said in the kitchen just last night that they ought to be able to exchange a few civil words?

Of course they should. She pulled herself up, straightening her spine. "It is a lovely day. Very fine for December," she said, still not looking at him.

Maybe he was going *too* slow. Calista's voice had taken on a cool tinge. Ryan eased a few inches closer to her again. "It is indeed," Ryan agreed pleasantly, waiting to see if she'd retreat again. To his satisfaction, she remained where she was.

She ignored the surge of pleasure she felt when Ryan moved so close that, once again, their clothes were touching. Maybe she should try to find out more about his father's financial problems. But that would probably start another quarrel. She didn't want to do that. This was too pleasant.

An egret made a graceful landing at the edge of the lagoon. Calista hoped the old alligator wouldn't decide he wanted the bird for his dinner. That would certainly spoil the mood. But the water remained calm and placid. "We have many sea birds here in the winter," Calista said politely.

"Egrets are attractive birds." *Now what?* he asked himself. He was beginning to feel as if he were talking to Lucinda or Gabrielle. Should he ask about her plantation? No, he wouldn't pretend even a polite interest. How did one insinuate a seduction into this bland talk? *You should know,* his mind goaded. *You've engaged in enough of them.*

Calista realized she wanted Ryan to pull her into his arms and kiss her. As he had last night. No, she didn't! Yes, she did. Very much. She wanted him to do more than that. Alarmed, she struggled to her feet. "I must get back to the house."

The warmth of his hand penetrated the sleeve of her black gown, stopping her. "Wait, don't go." His voice was soft, as it had been last night in the kitchen, but without that sardonic note that had spoiled everything. Calista let him draw her back down beside him.

He slid his hand up to her shoulder, to her face, to gently cup her chin. "You are so very lovely." His blue, blue eyes gazed deeply into hers. *That's the way,* his mind encouraged him. *Flatter her. Make her think she's the most beautiful woman you've ever seen.*

Just like those other times, Calista felt her body tremble, that drugging weakness stealing over her. She should leave, now, while she still could . . .

Instead, she tilted her face up to Ryan's. Slowly, he

lowered his head until his mouth touched hers. Just a whisper of a touch, making her want more. She opened her mouth under his.

Ryan drew in his breath as Calista made it clear she invited his kiss. His lips pressed more firmly upon hers, and she returned the pressure. Her hand went to his neck, her fingers tangling in the hair at his nape.

Her warm response made him forget everything, just as it had that night under the tree. He only knew he wanted this woman with every fiber of his being. And he intended to have her.

He pulled her close against him, even through their clothes feeling the hard points of her nipples pressing against his chest. The touch inflamed him. His swollen manhood pushed against his trousers, begging for release. He lowered Calista to the ground, his mouth hot and hard against hers.

Calista felt the sweet-smelling grass beneath her, pillowing her head. She felt Ryan's fingers fumbling with the buttons on her gown. Smiling, she moved his hand aside and quickly finished what he'd started. She heard his sharp intake of breath, then he pushed her gown off her shoulders, along with her chemise.

The air felt cool on her heated, bare flesh as Ryan moved away from her. Her eyes still closed, she lifted her hands to pull him back. "No," she murmured. She heard his deep, satisfied laugh and slowly opened her eyes.

He looked upon her bare breasts as if feasting on the sight. Calista's mouth curved in a smile. "Do I please you?" she asked softly.

Their gazes locked for an instant, a deep, deep look. Ryan smoothed the tumbled curls away from her flushed face.

"Wife," he whispered, hoarsely, "you please me perfectly." He lowered his head, his tongue slowly circling the engorged nipples.

She trembled even more violently, waiting for his next touch. It wasn't long in coming. He moved to the other breast, repeating his movements; then his mouth fastened upon the nipple and he gently suckled. Deep inside, in the very core of her, she felt a contracting, a pulling. She wanted to take him inside her, hold him deep within her.

She arched her body to his, feeling his hard manhood throbbing against her softness. Ryan's mouth left her breasts and went to her lips again. His tongue slipped between her teeth, and she opened her mouth for him. He thrust into her mouth as his body pressed against hers.

A strangled sound came from him, and he reached down to the hem of her gown, pushing it upward, the heat of his hand burning its way up her leg until he reached the soft skin of her upper thighs.

She'd waited for this all her life, without knowing what it was she wanted. Now she'd know; Ryan would give it to her . . .

A sudden horrendous noise erupted into the quiet afternoon. Ryan jerked against her, his hand leaving her flesh. "What the hell?" he muttered furiously. He moved away from her, turning toward the lagoon, from where the sound had come.

"It's a goddamned gator. After the egret." He got to his feet, turning his back on Calista to scowl out over the water. The egret had escaped, leaving behind only a few feathers. The old bull alligator lumbered up on the bank, still making those god-awful noises.

Calista felt as if someone had dashed cold water in her face. She realized she lay in the grass in broad daylight, her dress and petticoats up to her waist, her breasts exposed.

She sat up and jerked her skirts down, then quickly

buttoned her bodice. Thank God it was only a gator. It could just as easily have been one of the slaves or someone from the house. She pressed her lips together in embarrassment.

He turned back to Calista to see her standing, smoothing down her skirts. She raised her head, and their eyes met. She quickly looked away, but not before Ryan saw the blush of shame on her face.

Dammit it all to hell! Five minutes ago, she'd been willing and warm and totally giving. She'd offered herself to him as naturally as a flower opens itself to the sun.

His wife was not cold. She burned with a passion to rival his own. As he looked at her bent head, he could no longer believe she'd feigned ardor that night under the cedar tree. Or last night in the kitchen.

That didn't mean she hadn't tried to trap him—then or now. But he hadn't been in any way reluctant—he'd burned with hunger for her those other times—just as he had today.

They were equally to blame.

"It's a good thing that gator interrupted," he said tightly. "Even if it did ruin both our plans."

Her head shot up, her green eyes startled. "What do you mean?"

"Don't try to act the trusting innocent with me again," he drawled. "It won't work this time."

Her eyes flashed with anger. "I don't know what you're talking about!"

"I think you do. Didn't you tell me only last night it wasn't your idea we were living apart?"

"What does that have to do with this?"

"Everything. We want each other. But you also want the appearance of a normal marriage. What better way to keep me here than with desire?"

"So you think I was trying to trap you again? Just as I trapped you into marriage?" Her voice was still angry, but now it trembled, too.

His mouth curved in a sardonic smile, even while something inside was touched by that evidence of her vulnerability. "Yes. But I had plans, today, too. I came here to seduce you. To have you just one time. To get you out of my system."

Disbelief and hurt widened her eyes. She backed away from him. "You are despicable!"

He faced her, still smiling. "Maybe so. But what do you call yourself? Wasn't marrying me enough? Did you also have to try to entice me to stay here with you on this island?"

Uncertainty clouded her eyes. "I—I didn't do that," she faltered. "That wasn't what . . ."

Ryan felt a moment of compunction. He wanted to stop his hard talk; he wanted to take her in his arms and tell her it didn't matter. But he wouldn't. *Couldn't!* If he did, he'd start down the road that would destroy his life. Confused anger swept over him, wiping away the other feelings.

"I don't believe you. But that doesn't matter. Neither of our motives were pure. And neither of us can have what we want. I want your lovely body, and you want the semblance of a happy marriage. I won't be trapped into a living hell such as my parents called a marriage," he bit out. "And the situations are too similar for anything to ever work out between us."

"What do you mean?" she asked again.

He sighed, suddenly sick to death of this whole mess. "Never mind. All that matters is for you to accept once and for all that I'm never going to live here. We're never going to have a real marriage. And since we seem to be so physically attracted we lose our heads when we're alone together, I'll make sure that won't happen again. I'll leave tomorrow."

He bowed formally, his face set in cold, hard lines. "Good day, madam. I'm deeply sorry for what just occurred between us."

And that was a goddamn lie, one of the biggest lies he'd ever spoken. His logical mind might be sorry, but his body still craved this woman. He passionately wished they were still lying together in the sweet grass.

Calista inclined her head. "I accept your apologies, Mr. Burke," she said coolly. She turned and walked away, her slim back very straight, her head held high.

He had to admire her spirit, Ryan thought, following, not trying to catch up with her swift steps. She didn't want to walk back to the house with him. Now that passion no longer held her in its throes, she didn't want to have any more to do with him than he did with her.

And that was another lie, at least on his part. He liked more than just her spirit. He liked everything about her. Her courage, her sweetness, her essential goodness.

Lots of successful marriages have been built on no more than physical desire, his mind told him. No! He didn't believe that. Because there were very few good marriages. Most husbands and wives barely tolerated each other—at best. At worst, they felt a mutual hatred—as his parents had.

He slammed the door on that illogical part of him that kept trying to keep him and Calista together. It was best to end it now. And stay away from her. And this time he would keep his vow.

Because if he didn't, *he* would be the one springing the trap on himself by succumbing to the hunger that still achingly spiraled through his body.

Chapter Ten

Calista walked across the floor of the ginning room in time to hear Andrew say to one of the gin operators, "You're feeding the cotton through the rollers wrong. Here, let me show you." He then demonstrated his idea of the proper way to do the job.

She bit her lip to keep from ordering Andrew out of the room. These last two weeks since Ryan's brother had arrived, the workers were producing a third less ginned cotton a day than before. It couldn't be just a coincidence.

Jacob, the machine's operator, had a half-sullen, half-amused expression on his face. Jacob had done this job ever since Calista could remember coming out with her parents to the barns, and he was good. One of the best and most skillful workers on Meadowmarsh.

But like the others, he preferred to be left alone to do his job with no harassment. Calista's parents had understood this fundamental principle and had done just that, trusting the driver to oversee his fellow workers. Zeke had been the driver now for ten years, and there had been very few problems.

Andrew looked up and saw her, and a pleased smile lit his handsome face. "Good morning, Calista. I was just showing Jacob a better method." He proudly indicated the machine which now wasn't in use at all. Jacob stood idly by, watching to see what his mistress would do.

Now that he came out with her on her rounds every day, Andrew had exchanged his flamboyant brocade waistcoats for simple shirts and trousers. But he still reminded her so strongly of Ryan that a pain shot through her midsection as she forced herself to return his smile.

"Good morning, Andrew." She couldn't reprimand him in front of Jacob and the others. "Would you come outside with me for a moment?"

"Of course, but I can't spare too much time. I need to get over to the sorting rooms next." His tone and manner suggested he was the plantation owner and she merely someone interrupting his important duties.

Andrew nodded to Jacob to recommence his work. Jacob glanced at Calista, who also calmly nodded, although inside she fumed at Andrew's attitude. Then Jacob leisurely began operating the foot pedal again.

She led the way outside and kept walking until they were far enough away no one in the barns could hear them. Stopping under a big magnolia tree, she drew her cloak around her. The weather had turned cold.

This was a delicate task. She didn't want to fight with Andrew because she liked the young man. In fact, she was growing very fond of him and his sister.

For the moment, they were ahead of schedule and he hadn't done any real harm. But this couldn't continue. She sighed inwardly. Andrew badly needed a plantation of his own. But he also needed a few lessons in learning to let people work unhindered unless it was necessary to direct or reprimand them.

She took a deep breath and let it out. "I appreciate all the work you're doing on Meadowmarsh."

Andrew gave her a wide smile, admiration shining from his blue eyes, so like Ryan's. "It's the least I can do to repay you for your kindness in allowing us to stay here. It was very generous of you to take us in."

Instant compunction smote her. She didn't want him to feel that he and his family existed on her charity. "I enjoy having you here. Anyone would have done the same."

Andrew shook his head in denial. "No, not anyone. You're a very good woman, Calista." His admiring glance deepened. He moved a step closer and took her hand. "My brother is a fool. If you were *my* wife, I would be with you all day. And night." His last words were filled with significance.

Dismay swept over her. She drew her hand out of his and moved back a step, looking at him in consternation. This wasn't going at all as she'd planned. She took another deep breath and held it a moment before releasing it.

She'd ignore his last few statements. "Andrew," she began once more, trying to infuse her words with authority and dignity. "You and your family are welcome to stay here on Meadowmarsh as long as you wish and have need to. But I—"

"And we appreciate that," Andrew's eager voice interrupted. "But we hope to have our own plantation again before too long." He paused, and looked at her again, this time with another kind of significance.

How did he keep turning the conversation away from what she had to tell him? This was the first mention since the day they'd arrived that Andrew had made of her offer to lend him and his father money. She hadn't talked to her attorney yet. But she must give Andrew some kind of answer before she got into the unpleasant subject of how he had to stop trying to run Meadowmarsh.

She decided to be totally frank. "I don't have complete control over Meadowmarsh until my twenty-first birthday. My lawyer in Beaufort has to approve any disbursals of money until then."

Andrew nodded. "I understand. I wouldn't want you to think I was pressing you. It's just that Father is drinking too much and I know if we had our own plantation again, he would stop. He isn't used to this idle life."

Guilt and worry hit Calista in the pit of her stomach. Also annoyance. There was no reason for her to feel guilty. She couldn't do anything about this situation now. And Andrew had no right to burden her with his worries about his father's increasing drinking.

But to be fair, she didn't think he was trying to upset her. He just needed someone with whom to share his own anxiety about his father. He shouldn't have this whole load on his shoulders.

She moved forward a step and laid her hand across his arm. "Please don't worry too much," she told him, warm concern in her voice. "My birthday is only two weeks away. I'm sure something can be worked out."

She didn't look forward to the interview with her lawyer. Mr. Hadley was sure to disapprove. But she intended to follow through on her offer anyway.

Andrew squeezed her hand. "Thank you, dear Calista. My brother is a double fool for treating you as he does. And my stomach is telling me it's almost dinner time. The sorting room will have to wait until later."

Thank God for that. Calista gave Andrew a relieved smile. For the first time, she realized his gallantry and flirting meant nothing serious. He liked her as a person and admired her as a woman. She had a feeling Andrew liked *all* women. And that was fine with her. She no longer had to worry about his admiration getting out of hand.

"You're right, Andrew." She slid her hand around the crook of his elbow. "I'm starving, too. Let's go back to the house."

They'd mounted their horses and were halfway back to the plantation house before Calista realized she hadn't said a word to him about his interfering, bossy ways. It could wait until after dinner. She wanted to enjoy the ride. The fresh, invigorating air blew her hair out of its chignon and made her feel more alive than she had since Ryan had left two weeks ago.

Since that episode on the lagoon banks. Even now, just thinking about it brought a rush of color to her face. Oh, how could she have so shamelessly offered herself to Ryan on his terms.

Which were no terms at all. He'd made it brutally clear he'd never be her real husband. He only wanted her body. Well, didn't she also want his? Her lips pressed together. No! Not anymore. She pushed down the thought that she wanted much more than that from him. She'd forget him and be happy with her life here as she had before.

Calista turned to Andrew with a brilliant smile. "Let's race the rest of the way."

Urging her mare into a canter, then a gallop, she firmly put thoughts of Ryan out of her mind and angrily blinked back the foolish tears threatening to overflow.

She was an idiot to waste her tears on such a man.

Ryan glanced around the large, crowded ballroom, wondering if his boredom showed on his face. He didn't much give a damn and regretted accepting the invitation to the Hamiltons' Christmas ball. He'd hoped the music and gaiety might lift his spirits, but that hadn't happened.

It only made him wonder what he was doing here with a crowd of people he cared nothing about, trying to pretend to be merry. Despite his efforts, his mind drifted back to Meadowmarsh. He'd offered to stay and keep the law office open during this week of Christmas festivities so that Jerome could spend the time with Lucinda.

Jerome had urged him to come, too, saying they could close the office down for all the work they'd do during this season. But he'd insisted. When Jerome had left yesterday, his goodbyes had been heavy with unspoken disapproval.

Why wouldn't Jerome leave him alone? Ryan slapped his palm against the stone column he leaned against, then, as a pain shot through his hand, wished he hadn't. His law partner seemed to have taken on the office of substitute father. And Ryan didn't like it! Jerome might as well give up and accept that Ryan never intended to go back to Meadowmarsh.

Except when he removed his family to some other residence. And he must do something about that soon. He couldn't expect Calista to have them as guests for much longer since their marriage was such a sham.

"Ryan Burke! I didn't expect to see you here."

The soft, feminine voice brought him out of his fog. He focused on the young woman standing in front of him. Leora Howard's pretty face was flushed, her blue dress very becoming.

He pushed back his disturbing thoughts and managed a smile. "How are you, Leora? I haven't seen you for a while." No, not since that day she'd come to his house. At least she hadn't tried that caper again.

"I'm fine." She gave him a demure smile. "I would have

thought you'd be on Meadowmarsh during the holiday season. Since all your family is there."

Damn it! If *she* started in on him about his behavior, he'd leave. But before he could tell her to mind her own business, she continued.

"How is everyone in your family? Are your father and Gabrielle well?"

"Very well, thank you," Ryan answered, relieved she hadn't mentioned Calista. He moved back, ready to make his escape. Since she apparently wasn't going to scold, she could have but one other thing in mind: Continuing her flirtation with him.

"And Andrew?" she asked innocently, but the color rose in her cheeks.

With a jolt, Ryan realized what all this had been leading up to and felt a mixture of relief and disquiet. Her interest had switched to his brother. He'd have to nip that in the bud. Leora was a sweet girl, but young and silly. She couldn't help it that her parents were such abominable people, but he didn't want his brother involved with the Howards.

"Andrew is well. He's keeping himself busy at the plantation."

"I'm happy to hear that. When you see him during the holidays, be sure to give him my best wishes," she said primly, but her cheeks turned even redder.

Ryan inclined his head. "I will." She didn't have to know he wouldn't be at Meadowmarsh now or any time. He searched his mind for something that would destroy any illusions Leora might have about Andrew. He couldn't hint that his brother was seriously interested in another woman, because he was isolated on the island plantation.

However, Leora had no idea who might be visiting there, did she? "I believe there will be visitors to Meadowmarsh during this Christmas week." Well, *Jerome* was a visitor; he hadn't said who the visitors were.

Her blush faded, and she looked at him intently. He shrugged and gave her a bland smile. "I would very much like the honor of your company for the next dance." She was an attractive female and danced well. Maybe that would get his mind off things he had no business thinking about.

Leora looked surprised, then flattered. "I believe I have the next dance free."

"Good." Ryan gave her one of his best smiles, then was annoyed with himself for thinking the effect he created mattered. He took her arm and led her to the dance floor. The orchestra was playing a lively waltz. As they glided over the floor, Ryan tried to enjoy the dance and the pretty girl in his arms.

But in his mind's eye, he saw quite another scene. A blue lagoon with grassy banks. And Calista lying in that grass, smiling up at him, sweet invitation on her lovely face.

The night was moonless and dark, good for their purposes. Lotus had moved the dim-burning lantern away from the hole they were digging so the two angry men wouldn't knock it over.

Grunts and curses came from Zeke and Ira as they grappled with each other near the excavation's edge. She didn't know who was winning, but the two were evenly matched.

She leaned against a palmetto, her hands crossed on her chest, amusement filling her. Zeke was angry and jealous that Ira not only shared Lotus's bed, but was also staying in her cabin. Zeke had started the fight, trying to force Ira to leave the island. Ira had insolently refused, and Zeke had plunged his fist into Ira's soft midsection. Ira had responded in kind.

Lotus had no illusions that Ira was fighting because he cared for her; but still, two strong men were trying to kill each other because of her. It was gratifying.

After watching for a few more minutes, she decided to break it up. They might hurt each other, and she needed both of them healthy and able-bodied until the treasure was found and dug up. Once that was accomplished, she wouldn't need Ira any more; but she still hadn't thought of any way to get rid of him.

She pushed herself away from the tree and walked toward them. Just as she reached the men, Zeke gave Ira an uppercut to the jaw that staggered him. He stood next to the hole and, his arms flailing wildly, he fell backwards into it.

"Why you do dat?" Lotus asked Zeke in a fierce whisper. "We needs him." Since the night she'd almost died, her strength hadn't come back. She let the two men do the digging now while she kept watch.

She looked down into the hole. Ira was just getting to his feet. The top of it only came to his waist, so he was soon out of it, back up on the bank.

"I'll fix you for that, Zeke," Ira growled, his face ugly with anger.

Lotus stepped between them. "Now you two stop dat fightin'. We ain't got time fo' such foolishness. We has a job to do."

For a moment, she thought Ira would fling her out of his way, but then he took a deep breath and picked up his discarded spade again. "Don't think I'll forget this," he told Zeke over his shoulder, his voice deadly cold.

Zeke didn't answer. He picked up his own spade, and Lotus got the lantern and re-positioned it. The sight of Ira down in that hole had given her an idea. When they found the gold, it would be in a big chest of some kind. And when they took the chest out of the ground, it would leave a large, empty space.

She recommenced her lookout as the two men again grunted over their spades. Her back turned to them, a slow, satisfied smile spread across her face.

The problem of what to do with Ira when she no longer needed him had been solved.

Calista sat before the library fire, sipping a glass of wine. Emory and Andrew sat across from her with glasses of brandy. Ordinarily, she loved the comfortably furnished, book-lined room. But not this evening.

Andrew gave her an eager, expectant glance. He knew why they were here. She wasn't sure about Emory. He'd come along docilely enough when she'd said she had something to discuss with them, but he'd had so much to drink today he seemed in a fog. Which wasn't unusual.

It was one of the main reasons for this talk. The other was Andrew. She'd tactfully tried to tell him she didn't need his help. Instead of getting her point, he'd thought she was worried about his doing too much work. She knew the blunt truth would hurt him deeply, which she didn't want. In desperation, she'd asked him to go with Zeke on his trips to St. Helena for the mail and to Beaufort to pick up supplies and sell produce and fish. That kept him out of trouble most of the time, but she wasn't sure how long he'd be satisfied.

Both he and Emory badly needed their own plantation again. She'd celebrated her twenty-first birthday yesterday by going to see her Beaufort lawyer. Predictably, he'd been horrified at what she wanted to do.

But she'd stood firm and made him admit Meadowmarsh had a large cash surplus. And, unlike most plantation owners, she owed nothing to her factor. Her father had always dealt in cash, not credit, and she and her mother had continued that policy. Mr. Hadley had further admitted she could do as she liked with the money, no matter how foolish he thought her plans.

As she'd left, he had handed her an envelope. "Before her death, your mother asked me to give you this today," he had said gruffly, his disapproval still plainly visible on his face.

She'd glanced at the envelope, tears coming to her eyes at the sight of her mother's familiar, strong handwriting. "For Calista," it said.

"Thank you," she'd told Mr. Hadley, putting it into her reticule. She'd wait until tonight to read it, alone in her bedroom.

Now she frowned as she looked at Andrew and Emory. How should she start? Just plunge in with her offer? No, she'd better lead up to it gradually.

She took another sip of wine, a long one, to fortify herself, then set her glass down on a small table next to her chair. "Mr. Burke, I know how much you want another plantation."

Emory finished his brandy, looked disappointed there was no more, and set his glass down heavily. He glanced at Calista. "Of course I want another plantation. Would you like to give me Meadowmarsh?" His voice held a derisive, malicious note.

Calista felt a chill of foreboding go down her spine as she realized her father-in-law didn't like her. And it had nothing to do with her marriage to his son. No, he was burning with envy because she owned a prosperous plantation and he'd lost everything. Maybe that was natural, but he wasn't a nice man. She didn't much like him, either.

She glanced at Andrew. He was frowning at his father

and looked as if he wanted to say something to the other man, but he didn't.

Calista summoned a smile and directed it toward Emory as if his last comment were meant to be a joke. "I'm afraid I can't do that, Mr. Burke. Where on earth would I live if I gave you my home?" she asked, her tone light.

His surly expression didn't change. He picked up his empty glass and drained the last drops clinging to the bottom. "Why don't you get to the point? If you're tired of us sponging on you, just say so."

Calista's eyes widened with shock that he would think she'd bring them in here to say such a thing. "No, of course I don't want you to leave!"

That wasn't entirely true. She *did* wish they were gone, but as much for their own welfare as for hers.

He leaned back in his Hepplewhite chair. "Then why *did* you want to talk to us?"

She'd have to be as blunt as he, she decided. He left her no choice. "To offer you a loan to buy more land."

Emory's heavy face lost its sullen look. He stared at her as if he hadn't heard her correctly. "What did you say?"

She glanced at Andrew again. He nodded, eagerly. "I'd like to make you a loan," she repeated.

Emory pushed back his chair so hard it took the Persian carpet along with it. He stood glaring at her, his hands shaking. "I never thought I'd live to see the day when a slip of a girl offered me money to get back on my feet."

Calista stared at him, stunned. She'd never dreamed he'd take her offer like this. He sounded as if she'd insulted him in the worst way possible. A surge of annoyance swept through her. What was the matter with this man?

But she got up, too, and crossed the few feet separating

them. She put her hand on Emory's beefy arm. "Mr. Burke, I'm sorry if I offended you. I had no intention of doing so," she placated—mostly for Andrew's sake, she realized.

He shook her hand off as if it were no more than an irritating fly. "It's bad enough to have to stay here, accepting your charity," he roared, his face turning almost purple with rage. "But I'll be damned and in hell before I accept money from you!"

"Papa!" Andrew hurried to his father, placing his own hand on the man's other arm. "Calista meant no harm. Don't talk to her in such a manner. She offered us a chance to have our own plantation again."

Emory shook off his son's hand as easily as he had Calista's. "Get out of my way." Heading for the door, he stumbled and almost fell, but righted himself and left the room, slamming the heavy door behind him.

Calista started to go after him, but Andrew took her arm. "Let him be," he said, his voice resigned. "When he gets like this, there's no reasoning with him."

She let him hold her back, relieved. She had a feeling that Andrew was used to these moods. "So what do we do now?"

"I don't know," he admitted ruefully. "I thought he'd be as eager to accept your offer as I was."

"It's because I'm a woman, isn't it?"

Andrew looked at her. "Yes, probably so."

"But why? Does he hate all women?"

"No," he said after a silence. "Just the ones who own property in their own right."

"Tell me what is wrong, Andrew," she urged.

A frown creased his brow. Finally, he nodded. "All right. You're part of our family now, so you should know. Our plantation belonged to my mother. Her father left it to her with the provision that she must retain legal control during her lifetime and leave it to her eldest child—not her husband. My grandfather hated my father."

Calista stared at him. *"Ryan* owned Ainsley Hall?" she asked in disbelief. "But how—"

He quickly shook his head. "Ryan refused to accept ownership when Mama died. Since he couldn't sign it over to Papa, he made me legal owner. My brother also advanced us many loans over the years." Andrew paused, giving her a rueful smile. "My parents had a very unhappy marriage. After Mama realized Papa married her for the plantation, she never let him forget she was the legal owner."

"So, your father never owned Ainsley Hall?"

Andrew sighed. "No. And it rankled with him that he had to defer, first to Mama, then to me, even though I tried to make him believe he was the true owner, if not the legal one."

Now she understood what Ryan had meant when he'd told her their marriage could never work out. No wonder he had such a jaundiced view not only of marriage, but also of plantation life. Especially plantations owned by the wife alone. And no wonder he'd been so angry with Andrew and with her for offering his father this loan. He'd lost a great deal of his own money when the plantation fell to bankruptcy. He didn't want her to experience the same thing. He must care for her a little then . . .

Cold washed down her spine. No, she was indulging in wishful thinking. Of course Ryan didn't want her to lose all her money. Then, as her legal husband, *he'd* be responsible for her. Just because she understood his bitterness didn't change anything. It didn't mean things would ever work out for her and Ryan.

She pushed thoughts of Ryan away and concentrated on the issue at hand. Maybe it was a risk, but she had to continue with this. She looked at Andrew. "He'll never accept a loan from me, will he?"

He held her look for a long time, his mouth pinched together. "No," he said shortly and turned away from her to stride to the big front window.

"Maybe there is a solution. I can lend *you* the money to buy the land. And you can keep up the fiction that it belongs to your father. You are of age, aren't you?"

He swung around, pain and disappointment in his face. "Yes, I'm of age. But I'm afraid your ingenious plan won't work. Not anymore. Papa is determined this time he'll be successful and he'll do it on his own."

She let out her breath in a long sigh, stopping herself from asking how Emory planned to accomplish all this. "Then, I guess that's the end of it." She gave him a quick look. "Except that the offer to lend *you* money still stands, Andrew. Money to buy a plantation for yourself and the family you'll have one day."

His face lit up briefly, then clouded over again. "I much appreciate your offer, but I can't accept. To do so would hurt my father too much," he said regretfully.

"But he's not being fair to you!"

Andrew looked at her, his face solemn. "I love my father. That's the way it has to be." He walked out of the room and upstairs.

Calista left the library, too. She was exhausted and longed for bed. Too much had happened today. First, the argument with her lawyer, then this one with Emory. But the worst thing was learning the reason for Ryan's bitterness. Depression settled over her. She entered her room and closed the door.

A two-branched candle holder was lit on her mahogany highboy, warming her room, making it welcoming. Junie had turned down her bed and laid out her nightdress. And put her mother's letter on the pillow.

She turned it over in her hand before finding a letter opener and slitting the paper. It contained a single folded sheet. She unfolded it, both longing and dreading to see what her mother had written. The first words brought tears to her eyes and a lump to her throat.

> My darling girl,
> When you read this you will be twenty-one.
> The deadline I gave you for marrying will be reached. Over these last few months I'm sure you've wondered many times why I made such a seemingly cruel demand of you.
> "But by now, being the brave, intelligent girl I know you to be, I'm confident you've found a suitable husband, one you can live with happily for many years.
> "Maybe you've even guessed my motives. Yes, I was afraid that, left to your own devices, and loving Meadowmarsh as you do, you'd never bother to marry. And so miss what is the most wonderful experience a woman can have.
> "I trained you in my footsteps—not only to be a good plantation mistress—but to be its *master* as well. You don't need anyone, Calista, and that is sad. A woman should have a man by her side who needs her as much as she needs him.
> "So, my dear, a final goodbye. By now, I pray you'll not only have a good husband, but you may also be with child. Be happy.
>
> Your loving mother

Big wet drops fell onto the ink, blurring some of the words. Carefully, Calista blotted them with her handkerchief. She folded the letter and put it back in its envelope and then in the top drawer of the highboy.

SWEET ENCHANTMENT

She donned her nightclothes, blew out the candles, and climbed into bed. But she knew sleep would be a long time coming.

"You planned well and cleverly, Mama," she said softly into the darkness of the room. "How could you foresee what a mess I've made of things? With child! Oh, that I were!"

She heard her last words with a small shock. Did she really wish that? Did she wish that Ryan had made love to her, planted his seed deep inside her? Yes, she did, she realized, angry with herself.

At least that way she'd have some small part of him to keep forever.

Chapter Eleven

"Aunt Lucie, what am I going to do? Mr. Burke can't stay in his room much longer without eating." Calista paced the sitting room floor. Emory hadn't left his room since the night he'd gotten so angry with her. Guilt struck her anew. "This is my fault! I shouldn't have offered him the loan."

"No, it isn't," Lucinda said. "You had no way of knowing he'd react so irrationally."

"But Ryan told me not to do it, and I ignored him." Just the mention of Ryan's name made a tremor go down her spine.

Lucinda sighed. They'd gone through this several times before. "You wouldn't have if you'd known something like this might happen. Ryan didn't tell you that. Neither did Andrew. Stop blaming yourself."

Calista sighed, too. "I'll try. But we have to do something about it!"

"True. And he's still drinking. I can hear him stumbling

around in his room at all hours. I've heard glass breaking, too."

"I know; so have I. And there's several bottles missing from the spirits cabinet. I should have locked it." Calista walked to the window and gazed down at the lawns leading to the sea bluffs.

She turned back around. "Andrew can't do a thing with him. Neither can Gabrielle. And you know what a soft spot he has for her."

Giving her niece a wary look, Lucinda decided to speak her mind. "You'll have to send for Ryan."

Calista stopped dead a few feet from the window. "Ryan?" Oh, she couldn't do that! Not after what had happened between them at the lagoon. Once more, he'd humiliated her in the most hurtful way possible and made it brutally clear he didn't intend to set foot on the island ever again.

Lucinda nodded firmly, knowing she wasn't suggesting this only to get Ryan and Calista back together, although that was an end greatly to be desired. Ryan was needed here. "He's the eldest son. You must send for him."

Could she bring herself to talk to her aunt about what had happened that day? No, she decided. It was still too painful. And if Ryan came back, how could she bear to face him again?

But Lucinda was right. Emory couldn't go on much longer keeping himself locked in his room, refusing food. Drinking heavily. It would kill him.

She could handle Ryan's visit. Of course, she'd have to tell him what caused his father to do this. He'd be furious with her, but she could handle that, too.

And she'd make sure there were no opportunities for him to find her alone. Her husband still wanted to seduce her. He'd admitted that. But never again would she give her physical weakness for him a chance to destroy her.

Destroy her? Wasn't she overstating the situation? No. Some knowledge deep inside told her that if she let Ryan possess her, make love to her, and then leave her, she'd never be the same again and she'd regret it for the rest of her life.

"Well, Andrew, is the situation with Father as desperate as my wife would have me believe?" Ryan asked, as Andrew met him at Meadowmarsh's dock. He was in a foul mood. When Calista's note had arrived yesterday, he had been handling a matter for one of their most important clients. But Jerome had assured him he could take care of Ryan's business affairs. That wasn't the only reason he didn't want to be here, but he'd been left with no choice.

A worried frown between his dark brows, Andrew nodded. "It is indeed. He hasn't left his room for five days. Nor taken any nourishment."

"That's impossible. Not even water?"

Andrew glanced away. "He's managed to keep a supply of spirits," he admitted. "He's been quiet since last night, so I believe he must have exhausted it."

"Goddamn it to hell! Do you mean an entire household of people can't cope with one old man?"

"No, we can't. He won't even speak to Gabrielle, and she's pleaded and cried outside his door."

Ryan swore again as they entered the waiting carriage and Gideon started to the plantation house. "I've never exactly been Father's favorite. What do you expect me to do? Short of breaking down the door, I can't think of any way to persuade him."

"Maybe it will come to that. Breaking down the door, I mean."

"And you couldn't accomplish that simple act without

dragging me out here?" Ryan asked savagely. "To this damnable island that I never wanted to set foot on again?"

Andrew gave him a hard look. "You must put aside your differences with your wife and deal with a problem that concerns us all. We'll have to move back to your house until other arrangements can be made. You can't expect Calista to keep on putting up with this kind of thing."

Ryan frowned and drummed his boot heel on the carriage floor. He knew his brother was right. Certainly his family had overstayed their welcome. He turned back to Andrew. "All right, if Father won't come out, I *will* break the cursed door down!"

Andrew's face cleared. He smiled at Ryan. "Good. I'll help you."

In a few more minutes, the carriage drew up before the house. In spite of himself, Ryan felt a surge of admiration for the well-designed structure. If he ever built a house, it would be one similar to this. He drew his thoughts up short.

No, he wouldn't. No matter how appealing the house, he wanted no reminder of how the woman who owned it had ruined his life. He got out and walked up the steps to the imposing front entrance, Andrew beside him. Junie opened the door, her smile wide. "Welcome home, Maussa Ryan. We all glad to see you."

"Thank you, Junie," Ryan answered, tight-lipped. What did she mean? Did they think he was here to stay? The spacious entryway was clean and neat, with that pleasant lemony smell he'd noticed before. Somehow, the feel of this house was welcoming, as if he were, in truth, coming home.

Damn it! He hadn't gotten beyond the entrance and already the spell of this place was beginning to draw him in again. He turned to Andrew, his frown fierce. "Let's get this over with."

Andrew gaped at him. "But you haven't even greeted anyone yet."

"That can wait. I want to—"

"How good to see you, Ryan." Lucinda came out of the sitting room, holding out both hands, her smile too genuinely delighted to be false.

Ryan forced an answering smile as he bowed over her hands, his mood softening. "You're looking well, Miss Shelby." He liked this woman. In spite of how he felt about marriage in general, he hoped she and Jerome made a match of it.

"I am well. I'm sorry you had to return for a reason such as this." Her smile faded, a concerned look replacing it. "Your father has been quiet all day. Too quiet."

"Ryan!" Gabrielle appeared beside Lucinda, then ran forward to hug him.

A rush of affection swept over Ryan as he returned her embrace. His sister was a sweet girl. He'd have to try to make things come out right for her. "How are you, Gabby?" he asked, using the old nickname he'd given her years ago.

She smiled up at him, then moved back. "I'm fine. I love it here, but Papa . . ." She threw a worried glance toward the stairway.

Ryan let out his breath. "Let's go see what we can do about this." And where was Calista, his wife? Why wasn't she here to add her welcome to the others? He tried to repress the thoughts, telling himself he hadn't *wanted* her to greet him, but they persisted.

Lucinda led the way up the gracefully curving staircase. "Calista is down at the ginning barns, but she should be back before too long."

He nodded as they walked down the hall to Emory's room. Junie had joined their group, he noticed, her dark eyes wide with excitement.

No sound came from behind the door. As Lucinda had said, it was too quiet. He raised his fist and brought it down against the wooden panels.

"Father," he called, his voice loud, his tone authoritative. "It's Ryan. Let me in." Still no sound came from the room. He turned the doorknob, but as he'd expected the door was locked.

"Oh, I'm so afraid something has happened to him!" Gabrielle said, her voice trembling.

For the first time since he'd received Calista's note, Ryan seriously began considering the same possibility. He rapped again, harder and longer. "Father, let us in!" he demanded loudly.

Receiving no answer again, he turned to Lucinda. "We may have to break down the door."

"I'm afraid you will, since the only key is inside the room. No one locks doors here on Meadowmarsh. But don't you want me to get one or two of the field hands to do it?"

Ryan shook his head. He turned to his brother. "Are you ready?"

Andrew nodded, stepping up beside Ryan. Both of them moved back, then slammed their shoulders against the door. The wood shuddered, but held. Another determined effort and the door splintered near the knob. Ryan reached inside and turned the key, then swung the door open.

Emory lay face down on the Persian carpet by his bed, unmoving. The room was a shambles, the bed covers pulled nearly off onto the floor. A whiskey bottle had been smashed against the wall, dark stains marring the wallpaper. Broken glass was scattered around the floor. Several wine bottles lay upended.

"Papa!" Gabrielle cried. She ran across the room and knelt before him, wringing her hands.

The others followed. Ryan, too, knelt beside his father. He turned the older man over onto his back, relieved to see his chest rising and falling at regular intervals. Now and then he let out a sighing snore. Ryan stood up. "He's just drunk," he said coldly.

He turned to Lucinda. "Miss Shelby, I'm sorry you had to endure all this. I'll arrange for your door to be repaired, and I'll take my family off your hands as soon as possible."

He heard a gasp behind him. "Ryan, you're going to take us away from Meadowmarsh?"

Ryan turned to Gabrielle, softening as he saw the anxiety in her face. "Gabby, you can surely see I must."

Out in the hall, Calista felt her heart lurch at the sound of Ryan's voice, then dismay filled her at his words.

She knew he had to do this, but she'd miss them. At least Andrew and Gabrielle. And if his family were no longer here, there would be no reason for Ryan to ever return.

That was fine with her. She stepped into the room, her eyes going to Emory. He looked terrible. Her stomach tightened. No matter what Lucinda said, she still felt at least partly to blame for his condition.

She dreaded having to tell Ryan. "Good afternoon," she said to his back, her voice cool and controlled even though she felt far from composed.

Stiffening at the sound of her voice, Ryan slowly turned to face her. He was struck again at her beauty. Her face was rosy and windblown, a small smudge on one cheek.

And more than her beauty drew him. It was all the different things he saw in her—the way she cared for people, yes, even her damned efficiency at running this plantation. He inclined his head. "Good afternoon, Calista."

Calista swallowed a huge lump in her throat as she looked at him. She tried to summon the anger she'd felt when he'd left two weeks ago, but it seemed to have disappeared. All she could think about were those moments in his arms at the lagoon.

"I'll have Junie bring Gideon and someone else up to lift him into bed," she said.

Ryan quickly shook his head. "Andrew and I can do it."

Junie hurried to get the bed back in order, and the two sons lifted the heavy man and placed him between the sheets. Emory roused only enough to utter a hollow groan.

Neither she nor Lucinda had ever dealt with a situation like this before. The blacks were rarely allowed spirits and then only in small quantities on special holidays. Calista turned to Ryan. "What should we do for him?"

He shrugged. "Nothing. Let him sleep it off. He'll be all right." He gave Calista a cynical smile to hide that, even in the midst of this unpleasant incident, her nearness made him feel more alive than since that day at the lagoon.

She frowned uncertainly. "But he looks so sick! Surely we should do something." She knew part of her concern was because she still felt responsible, but Emory did look awful. And being close to Ryan was having its usual effect. Her breath came faster, and her knees felt weak and trembly.

"Ryan is right," Andrew said. He paused, then continued, his words slow as if they were painful for him to say. "This isn't the first time he's done this. But he's never locked the door before." He gave Calista an apologetic glance.

She stared at him, surprise and relief sweeping through her. So this wasn't an isolated event, caused by her actions? Her guilt faded, replaced by annoyance. She sensed Andrew's embarrassment; but just the same, he should have told her this before.

"Let's leave the poor man alone," Lucinda said firmly. She led the way downstairs.

Ryan forced his gaze to meet Calista's. Something in the green depths of her eyes looked hurt and vulnerable. He felt a stirring in the vicinity of his heart. Damn it! He didn't want to feel anything for her.

"I'm sorry this happened—and it won't again. As soon as my father recovers, which shouldn't be more than a day or so, I'll take my family back to Charleston."

He'd concentrate on why he'd come here, and not look at her again. Andrew's words upstairs had disturbed him. Apparently his father had gone on binges like this before they'd lost the plantation. If he'd known that, he'd never have brought his family here. He owed Calista an apology for inflicting this mess on her.

They'd reached the bottom of the stairs. Delphinia emerged from the dining room, her eyes big. Junie had already spread the news, Calista thought. "Dinnah is ready," Delphinia announced.

The tension around the table was so thick it was almost palpable. Gabrielle was near tears, and Calista's heart ached for her. She'd come to love the girl like a sister during these few weeks.

A muscle jumped in Ryan's taut jaw. He avoided glancing her way, which was fine with her, she assured herself. He kept giving Andrew searching glances, and Andrew looked like a small boy who'd said or done something that would get him into trouble. She thought she knew what it was, too. Those remarks Andrew had made about his father's drinking.

But it was none of her concern, she told herself firmly. And she'd changed her mind—she wouldn't tell Ryan what had precipitated this latest episode after all. In the light of Andrew's revelations, it really didn't matter.

Ryan would take his family away, and she'd probably never see any of them again. A hollow, empty feeling hit her stomach. He kept his glance away from her, Calista noticed, just as she avoided his eyes.

The meal over, she hurried from the house, heading for the ginning rooms. She hadn't planned to go back this afternoon, but she wouldn't be around Ryan any more than absolutely necessary.

The rest of the cotton was almost ready to ship to Beaufort. And then it would be time to prepare the ground for next year's crop.

Lotus was over her illness, but didn't have her previous zest. She was quieter and moved more slowly. She helped tend the children satisfactorily, even though Calista was sure she didn't enjoy it. She didn't cause any trouble, though.

But something was still wrong on Meadowmarsh. Calista could sense it in the very air. Every now and then she'd catch a slave giving her a furtive look, as if he or she knew something Calista didn't.

Calista reined Sable in and dismounted near the packing room. A hand took the mare to turn her into the nearby field. Zeke was just coming out of the packing room. Impulsively, Calista called to him. "I'd like to talk to you."

She frowned at the way his eyes darted to hers, then quickly away, in an almost stealthy manner, as he followed her to a distance away from the packing room. Zeke had changed the last few months. Ever since Lotus had become his woman. Most plantation owners would have insisted they marry, but she didn't want Zeke to marry Lotus. She hoped if she ignored the situation their liaison would end naturally.

"Ever since I went to Charleston, something's wrong on Meadowmarsh," she said without preamble, her voice firm. "I don't know what it is, but I think you do."

Something leaped in Zeke's dark eyes. For a moment, he looked as if he would tell her what she needed to know. But then whatever it was disappeared. He gave Calista an innocent, puzzled look. "The cotton is 'bout ready to go, and I ain't had no trouble with the hands. I don't know what you mean, Miz Calista."

Impatience rose in her, which she repressed. It would do no good to get angry with Zeke, she well knew. He'd only withdraw further. Whatever the problem, he wasn't ready to confide in her yet. She gave him another straight look. "When you want to talk about it, come to me. You hear?"

He nodded. "Yes'm, I hears." He watched Calista move off and enter the packing room, her back very straight, disapproval in every line of her slender figure. Lordy, if only he could tell her everything!

He was tired of spending half the night digging for pirate gold. Tired of sharing Lotus with Ira Atwood. Most of all, he hated the way he let Lotus get anything she wanted out of him. He wished he'd never let her talk him into this scheme. And with all his heart and soul he wished he'd never laid eyes on her.

"All right, tell me what's going on with Father," Ryan demanded of Andrew as they sat on the veranda after dinner. "I gather this isn't the first time he's done this, from what you said upstairs. What caused him to go on this binge?"

Andrew looked uncomfortable. "No, it isn't the first

time. The last few months he—drank too much several times."

"And this time? What prompted it?"

"Isn't losing our plantation enough cause?"

Andrew's voice was evasive. He was hiding something. "I think something else happened," Ryan said flatly. "I intend to find out what it was."

"All right," Andrew said. "But I want you to know that none of this was Calista's fault."

Ryan's pulse quickened at the mention of Calista's name. "Why should it be her fault? Did she ask Father to leave?"

"No, of course not. She merely offered him the loan she mentioned that day we arrived here. And he became enraged and refused. Then, he stomped upstairs and locked the door and wouldn't come out."

Surprised anger swept over Ryan. Had he actually thought Calista would heed him when he'd insisted she not offer his father a loan? Lose a chance to show him *she* controlled her plantation and its income? Of course she wouldn't.

His mother never had. He supposed that's why he'd kept on lending his father money after his mother's death. Emory had never had a chance to show what he could do. Ryan had wanted to give it to him. If he'd thought that would help the relationship between him and his father, he'd been very wrong.

And if Calista hadn't started all that the day he brought his family here, this mess wouldn't have happened. His anger grew. And he'd planned to find her and apologize for his father's behavior! "I see," he said shortly. He'd still find her, but his message would be different.

"It wasn't Calista's fault," Andrew repeated. "Papa just went berserk."

His anger growing by the second, Ryan only half heard

him. Ever since he'd first set eyes on Calista, he'd had nothing but trouble. If she'd minded her own business, his father wouldn't be stretched out on the bed upstairs like a common drunk.

He would take his family and be gone from here as soon as possible. But before he left, he'd tell his wife a few things she badly needed to know about tending to her own affairs.

"I nevuh in my life seen such a mess!" Junie picked up another piece of broken glass and threw it into the refuse basket she carried, disgust on her face.

Righting a picture that had been knocked askew, Delphinia nodded. "Maussa Ryan's papa is a bad man."

Junie picked up the last glass shard, then tilted her head, considering the other woman's words. "No, he just a weak man," she finally said. "He one o' dem men who cain't handle de spirits."

"He a sorry man," Delphinia repeated, stubbornly. In her eyes, anyone who gave Miz Calista grief was no good. "I'm glad all dat passel of folks gonna be out of heah befo' long. Dey ain't nothin' but trouble."

"Miz Calista not be glad. She like all of Maussa Ryan's fambly 'cept dis one." Junie looked around the room again, to be sure it was set to rights, then gave Delphinia a sly grin. "Spec'lly she like Maussa Ryan."

Her hand on the doorknob, Delphinia turned and gave Junie a cold look. "He ain't good 'nuff to wipe her feet on."

Following her to the hall, Junie quietly closed the door behind her. "He all right," she told Delphinia as they walked toward the stairs. "He just mad at Miz Calista. Someday, dey git over all dat."

Delphinia flounced to the stairs, still unconvinced, then

paused, her hand on the top rail. "Has you heard the stories goin' round de quarters?" she asked, her voice pitched low.

Junie looked uncomfortable. She shrugged, not meeting the other woman's glance. "Don't reckon so."

"You is lyin,'" Delphinia said flatly, giving her a hard look. "Gideon tell me dat overseeuh back on Meadowmarsh and him and Zeke and dat no-good Lotus diggin' for pirate gold."

Junie nodded, reluctantly. "Dat's what I heared, too. But maybe ain't nothin' to it."

"Gideon, he don't say stuff 'less it true."

"Is you and Gideon fixin' to jump de broom?" Junie grinned at her.

Delphinia grinned back. "Maybe," she admitted, then returned to her former worry. "We needs to tell Miz Calista 'bout all dis."

They'd reached the bottom of the stairs. Junie drew in her breath and quickly shook her head. "I ain't gonna git mixed up in nothin' like dat. Lotus is a mean one. I feared of her."

"I feared of her, too, but Miz Calista need to know."

"*You* can tell her," Junie said, her voice firm and sure.

"Maybe I will," Delphinia answered.

The two girls moved apart as Lucinda came out of the dining room.

"We just finish reddin' up Mistuh Emory's room," Junie said hastily, holding out the basket containing the trash they'd collected as evidence.

Lucinda smiled and nodded. "That's fine. How does he look? Is he still sleeping?"

Junie and Delphinia glanced at each other. Neither had paid much attention to the man in the bed. But they supposed he was still breathing.

"Yes'm," Delphinia said. "He sleepin' like a babe when we left him."

Lucinda glanced up the stairs, a worried frown on her face. "I think I'd better go look in on him." She followed her words with action, climbing the stairs gracefully.

"Miz Lucinda awful spry for bein' so old," Delphinia whispered.

"Dat 'cause she sweet on Mistuh Kingsley," Junie whispered back, poking Delphinia in the side.

Delphinia smothered a giggle. "Cain't you talk 'bout nothin' else? Come on, lets go out to de cook house and help with suppah."

Lucinda quietly opened the battered door to Emory's bedroom and walked across to the bed. He still lay on his back, as they'd left him several hours ago. But now his face was a deeper red, his breathing heavier, with a rasping quality. After every few breaths, she heard a tiny pause.

Alarmed, she reached for his wrist. His pulse was rapid and shallow. Could it be pneumonia? The disease was common among the slaves. She and Calista had helped nurse many a hand. She'd better tell Ryan they needed to get a doctor.

Lucinda hoped it was only pneumonia, not perepneumonia. Pressing her lips together, she hurried downstairs. She found only Andrew and Gabrielle on the veranda. Andrew looked harried and worried. The girl's face was flushed, and traces of recently shed tears marked her cheeks. Lucinda guessed she'd been pleading with her brother to let her stay on Meadowmarsh and he'd refused.

If only she could intercede on the girl's behalf; she was a joy to have around. And she'd been a big help.

Lucinda now left a large portion of the daily routine to her. Soon, Gabrielle would be capable of managing alone, and she wouldn't have to worry if she and Jerome married.

Lucinda felt a flush coming to her own face and dismissed these thoughts. None of that was important now. "Where is Ryan?" Lucinda asked. "I must talk with him."

Andrew's handsome face looked even more harried. "He took a horse from the stables and went to find Calista." His gaze sharpened on Lucinda's face. "What's wrong?"

"Your father's ill. Not just the drink—it looks like pneumonia."

He quickly rose. "Are you sure?"

"No—we must get a doctor. But Calista and I have nursed a lot of the slaves through pneumonia. I recognize the symptoms."

Andrew was halfway through the door, Gabrielle beside him. He turned to the girl. "Will you send someone for Ryan?"

"Of course," she answered, her young face fearful, and hurried down the hall toward the back of the house.

"Is our doctor all right or do you have one you would prefer? Ours lives on St. Helena and can get here faster."

His hand on the stair rail, Andrew turned and gave her a distracted look. "That's fine, Miss Shelby." He hurried on up the stairs.

Lucinda went to find Gideon to fetch the doctor. She hoped he was available and not out at some other plantation.

Andrew took the last two stairs in one and almost ran down the hall. He flung open his father's door and hurried to the bed. His heart sank as he looked at the older man. He had no experience of pneumonia, but it was obvious something serious was wrong.

Placing his hand on the other man's forehead, he was shocked at how hot it felt. What should he do until the doctor came? Emory must have a high fever, so he supposed the main thing was to keep him from getting chilled.

"Mistuh Andrew, Miss Lucinda send me up heah," Junie's voice came from behind him. "Can I do anythin'?"

He nodded. "He needs more bedcovers."

"Yes'suh," Junie said. She went to a carved wooden chest at the foot of the bed and took out a quilt.

Andrew took the covering from her and spread it over Emory up to his chin. Then he found a chair and brought it to the bedside. He felt guilty about all of this, but he didn't know what to do except sit here with his father. He wouldn't leave until the doctor came.

Chapter Twelve

Ryan rode the bay gelding down the oyster-shell lane, strung up so tight he had to forcibly restrain himself from urging the mount into a gallop. But that wasn't why he was out here, he reminded himself, settling for a smooth canter.

No, he was going to find Calista and tell her what he thought of her interfering, meddling ways. Deep inside, he knew that wasn't the only reason he wanted to find her, but he ignored this insight.

When he'd almost reached the barns where the cotton was processed for market, he saw her riding toward him on her black Arab mare. As usual, she rode astride with a cloak thrown over her shoulders. Her head was down, tendrils of black hair escaping from her chignon. She looked as if her mind was a million miles away.

Then, she heard his mount's hooves and her head jerked up, her face tightening. She nodded, coolly, as Ryan came alongside, but didn't stop or even slow down.

"Wait! I want to talk to you," Ryan called after her.

For a moment he thought she'd keep on going, but then she reined her mare and waited for him to turn and catch up.

Tension hit Calista as she noted his tightened mouth and jaw. Now what? Had Andrew told him about the loan offer?

"Where can we go?" he asked curtly when his mount was even with hers. "Not back to the house. I want some privacy."

A shiver slid down her spine as she remembered the last time they'd been alone together. She'd have no repeat of that disastrous scene. But she probably had no worries along that line. He looked as if he couldn't stand the sight of her.

Just the same, she wouldn't be any more alone with him than they were right now. "We can talk as we ride back to the house."

He frowned, finally nodding. "All right."

Calista started Sable off again at a walk, Ryan beside her. He was silent so long she finally looked across at him. "I thought you had something to say to me."

Blast it, he didn't want to talk as they jounced along on horseback! But since she refused any other arrangement, then he must.

"I would appreciate it," he clipped out, "if you'd tend to your plantation affairs and not meddle in those of my family."

Andrew *had* told him, and he blamed her—even though she felt sure Andrew hadn't laid the responsibility for his father's actions on her. All right, she'd accept some of it. Maybe she should have told Ryan what she'd planned to do. "I'm sorry—"

"That won't help now," he interrupted, his voice hard and cold. "If you'd taken my advice and not offered Father a loan, none of this would have happened."

Calista halted her mare. "I tried to help your father. How was I to know he'd react as he did? Who could have predicted that?"

He stopped his mount alongside hers. "I warned you against this the day I brought my family here," he reminded her, his voice superior and lordly.

The last remnants of her remorse fled. "Warned me? I don't recall you doing anything but losing your temper. You gave me no good reasons why I shouldn't. Your only objection, as I recall, was that *you* didn't approve of it."

"A wife is supposed to obey her husband!" Ryan roared, goaded beyond thought of what he was saying.

Calista raised her brows in mock surprise. She'd much rather deal with anger than that superior attitude. "Why, Mr. Burke, are you suggesting we honor our vows? Living in separate homes makes it a bit difficult for me to obey you, does it not?"

Even as she taunted him, pain filled her. In spite of everything, some part of her still wished they could have had a real marriage.

Her words were like a slap across his face. Ryan stared at her for an endless moment. Why had he made that asinine remark? He'd left himself wide open for her derisive rejoinder. He inclined his head.

"I haven't the slightest wish to oversee your daily life, have no fear. It's only in the matter of my family that I command you to mind your own business!" He picked up his reins again and urged his mount into a canter.

A film of unwanted tears dimmed Calista's vision as she watched him disappear around a bend in the lane. Oh, he was so cruel! She *hated* him! She wished he'd leave this instant and she'd never have to lay eyes on him again. Even as she thought this, she knew it wasn't true.

Rounding the bend, Ryan saw Gideon galloping toward

him. "Maussa Ryan," he said, reining up beside him. "Your papa is took bad!"

"What are you talking about?" Ryan demanded, stopping his own horse. "My father was sound asleep when I left."

"Oh, he still asleep. But it not from de drink now. Miz Lucinda think he got pneumonie."

"How does she know? Did a doctor examine him?" Ryan found the man's words hard to believe. His father hadn't seemed sick.

Gideon shook his head. "Dat's where I goin' now. To fetch de doctuh. I got to hurry." He urged his mount on down the lane.

Ryan watched him go, frowning. Lucinda was not one to get alarmed over nothing. He kicked his booted feet against the horse's sides, and the animal responded with a burst of speed. At the house, he gave his mount to another house servant and hurried inside. No one seemed to be in the spacious downstairs.

"Dey's all up in Mistuh Emory's room," Junie told him, popping her head around the edge of the sitting room door, her eyes wide with excitement.

He took the stairs two at a time. The splintered door was wide open and, as Junie had said, Andrew, Gabrielle, and Lucinda were in the room. Lucinda wrung out a cloth from a basin of water, then applied it to Emory's forehead. She looked up and saw him, and a relieved smile came onto her face. "Oh, there you are, Ryan. Gideon must have found you."

"Yes, he did." Andrew and Gabrielle appeared numb with worry, Ryan saw as he approached the bed. And no wonder. His father looked very ill, his eyes sunk in his head, his breathing rasping and shallow. He glanced at Lucinda. "How could he get this sick so fast?"

"It happens like that sometimes," she said. "He must

have taken a chill from lying asleep on the floor for so long."

Guilt smote Ryan for his earlier callous attitude. Calista had been worried about his father, and he'd brushed off her concern. But hell, how was he to know Emory was ill? He'd always been as healthy as an ox, seldom suffering from any ailment.

He heard a noise behind him and from the corner of his eye saw Calista enter the room just as Emory coughed raspily, then groaned as if in pain. She walked over to stand beside Ryan. "It does look like pneumonia," she said quietly to Lucinda. "I hope Gideon can locate Dr. Norman."

Ryan heard genuine concern in her soft voice, and his guilt and irritation at himself grew. After the things he'd just told her, she'd be completely justified in telling him to take his family away from her island this minute. But he knew she wouldn't. No matter what he'd said, Calista would make sure his father got the best care possible.

He looked at Emory again, wishing he'd tried to get along better with his father instead of taking the easy way out and seldom seeing him. Lending him money instead. He found a chair and pulled it up beside Emory's bed. All he could do now was help with his care—and hope he pulled through.

Ira Atwood leaned against a palmetto, a bottle in his hand. He lifted it to his mouth and took a long swallow, giving Zeke, who'd just lifted a spadeful of dirt out of the crater they were working on tonight, a baleful look. "We're never goin' to find no pirate gold. Who had this stupid idea in the first place?"

He turned his head to glare at Lotus, standing beside Zeke, also holding a spade. "It was *you,* wasn' it? Had to be you. Zeke's not got enough brains to figure anythin' like this out."

Zeke tensed, his hands tightening on the now-empty spade. "I'm gonna knock that man down," he snarled. "I cain't listen to him no more."

Lotus grabbed his arm. The former overseer was drunk, and when he was drunk, he got even meaner than usual. "No, you ain't," she hissed.

Ira lifted the bottle to his mouth again, then flung it aside and wiped his mouth. He leered at Lotus. "You're only good for one thin', and that's not enough to keep me on this godforsaken island any longer."

Giving him a sidelong glance, Lotus tried to gauge how drunk he was. Not enough to pass out, unfortunately. Just enough to fight or do something crazy and stupid.

She laid her spade aside and wiped her hands on her woolen skirt. She walked across to Ira, swinging her hips, forcing a seductive smile to her mouth. "Let's go back to de cabin. We done digged enough for tonight." She moved closer, rubbing her breasts against his chest.

Behind her, she heard Zeke's angry indrawn breath, but she didn't care how he felt. She had to calm Ira down, and Zeke should have sense enough to know it.

Ira pulled her roughly against him and gave her an even rougher kiss. Then, he pushed her away so hard Lotus stumbled and fell at his feet.

He looked down at her with contempt. "I told you, I'm not diggin' at all no more. I'm leavin' this damn island."

Relief swelled inside her. Now that she had her strength back, she and Zeke didn't need Ira. It would be wonderful to have him gone! She flung back her head and looked up at him. "If dat's how you feel, I reckon you bettuh' go."

"You darkies'd be glad to get rid of me, wouldn't you?

You think I'll leave without seein' you two get what's comin' to you?" He laughed nastily.

Her body tensing, Lotus asked, "What you talkin' 'bout?"

"I'm gonna have a talk with Missus Burke before I go. I'm sure she'll be innerested in what I have to say."

Alarm filled Lotus. Behind her, she heard Zeke approaching. She managed a scornful laugh. "You cain't do dat. Miz Calista have you locked up in de jailhouse for bein' here all dis time and helpin' us do all dis diggin'."

Ira laughed again. "No, she won't. She'll just throw me off her island. But she'll sell you two for trying to steal her gold, and most plantations aren't like Meadowmarsh. You'd have a harder life."

Cold swept through Lotus. She knew he spoke the truth. And even if he left without telling anyone their secret, she'd never feel safe as long as he was alive. She had to get rid of him the way she'd planned. She glanced over her shoulder at Zeke. He stood behind her, his spade in his hand. Could they overpower Ira?

Ira sneered at the black man. "Come on," he told him. "You know you'll be strung from the nearest tree if you hurt a white man."

Only a muscle worked in Zeke's jaw, revealing his tension. He wouldn't do anything, she knew. Fear gripped Lotus. Ira had them trapped. She looked up at him, her mouth agape.

Ira reached down and jerked her upright again. His beady eyes raked over her. "We're goin' back to the cabin." With one last triumphant glance at the still-rigid Zeke, he staggered down the lane, holding Lotus clutched to his side.

A red film of anger clouding his vision, Zeke watched them go. His hand gripped the spade handle so tightly a sharp pain shot up his forearm. Ira and Lotus disappeared from view, and Zeke let out his breath in a whoosh. How he hated Ira! He trudged back to the gaping hole. Might as well cover it up again.

A rock from his first spadeful of dirt tumbled into the hole, and Zeke heard a sharp, metallic sound. Puzzled, he looked down. A corner of corroded metal stuck out from the far side. Zeke froze, then, his heart pounding, jumped into the hole and scrabbled at the sandy dirt covering the object.

Ten minutes later, gasping from exertion, he looked at what he'd uncovered. The curved-top chest was old and rusty, and he'd have to get a bar to break the lock. But not tonight. His mouth turned down in a grimace. Lotus and Ira would be on her pallet together by now. Ira was drunk besides. Maybe by tomorrow the overseer would have forgotten his threats and just leave. And they'd have the treasure to themselves.

If not, Zeke would have to tell him. He scrambled out of the hole and shoveled the dirt back in, then smoothed it out. He pulled fallen palmetto fronds over the disturbed earth, then stood back.

It looked all right, he decided. No one could tell. As always, they'd dug under a large tree. This time a huge old magnolia, the biggest one he'd ever seen. It shouldn't be hard to find again. But just in case, Zeke took out his knife and carefully marked an X low down on the trunk where no one would notice.

He headed for home, but his excitement had gone. Even if it were pirate gold in the chest, he had a bad feeling that they'd never get away with it. For a moment, he was tempted to forget it, to not tell either Lotus or Ira.

But Ira could leave any time he wanted. He and Lotus couldn't—without the gold. And he wanted to go up north and live as a free man, didn't he?

SWEET ENCHANTMENT

* * *

"I'll be glad to keep watch with you tonight, Ryan," Gabrielle said softly. She smiled at her brother, her blue eyes dark-ringed with anxiety.

He shook his head. "Before Father is out of danger, we'll all have plenty of midnight hours to put in."

"I'm sure you're right," Gabrielle said, not arguing with him. She kissed his cheek. "Good night. I'm glad you're back. I've missed you."

Ryan hugged her warmly. "I've missed you, too, Gabby. As soon as Father is well enough to travel, I'll take you all back to my house."

And then, the former hell would start over again, he added silently. Gabby was no trouble to anyone, but she wasn't happy in Charleston, any more than Emory or Andrew was. They'd only be content on a plantation again. But that wasn't likely to happen—and he couldn't help them further.

His sister bit her lip and turned away, but not before Ryan saw the sadness in her eyes. Damn it! He knew she didn't want to leave here, but they must once his father recovered enough to be moved.

He couldn't expect Calista to endure this situation any longer than necessary. Not after that tongue-lashing he'd given her this afternoon. The reality of his father's illness had cooled his temper. He'd no reason to believe Calista had offered his father a loan for any other purpose than to help him and Andrew. Shame went over him. He'd behaved like an ass. And the next time he saw her, he'd apologize. So far there had been no opportunity.

"Would you like some company?" Lucinda entered the room, her smile tired and anxious. She looked over at the bed where Emory still slept, but restlessly now. His breathing was harsh, and he coughed frequently.

"I'd be delighted with your company," Ryan said gallantly, "but you look exhausted. You've been here all afternoon and evening."

Lucinda walked to the bed and placed her flattened palm against Emory's forehead, then shook her head. "His fever is still very high." She sat down beside Ryan. "The leeches and the bloodletting didn't seem to help."

"No." Ryan moved restlessly in his chair. He hated feeling helpless like this, not able to make his father any better.

Lucinda sighed. "I feel somewhat responsible for this, Ryan. We should have gone ahead and forced entry into the room rather than wait until you arrived."

"Don't," he ordered. "You did what anyone would have done under the circumstances." He managed a reassuring smile.

She smiled back. Oh, she was glad he was here! She'd felt so much better the minute he'd walked in the house today. She marveled at her thoughts. For years, Meadowmarsh had been a plantation of women. Calista's mother, Calista, and herself. And she'd never felt any need for a man to make things complete.

Maybe it was because she'd come to love Jerome. She felt her face warm at the thought, but there was no use in denying it. She *did* love him, and she would marry him—but not right away. She couldn't leave Calista now. Not while she was so unhappy. And she had to get Meadowmarsh in perfect shape so that her successor would have no trouble taking over the management.

If only Gabrielle were staying. The girl was a natural-born plantation mistress. Of course, she would be staying for a while now that her father was so ill. All of them would.

She smiled at Ryan again. "These illnesses must run their course."

"What's this perepneumonia that Dr. Norman mentioned?" Ryan asked, again moving restlessly in his chair.

Lucinda gave him a quick glance, surprised he wasn't familiar with the disease. But then, he'd left his family plantation some time ago. Maybe it wasn't as common in Charleston. Should she worry him further by explaining?

A sound made her turn. Calista stood framed in the doorway. "Come in, dear," Lucinda said, relieved at her niece's fortuitous arrival. She rose. "I was just leaving. You can keep Ryan company for a while."

She gave Calista a bland smile, ignoring the younger woman's frown. Ryan and Calista belonged together, and she intended to take advantage of anything she could to help matters along. "If you need me, just call," she told Calista pleasantly, then slipped out of the room.

Ryan looked at Calista, then quickly away. Yes, he owed her an apology. Not only for his hasty, ill-tempered words, but for ignoring her when she thought Emory was ill earlier today. No matter how the words stuck in his throat, he'd give it to her.

And here was his opportunity. Lucinda had gotten out of here as fast as she could, all too obviously giving them a chance to be alone together. Wouldn't she and Jerome ever give up?

Calista hesitated, then walked across the room and seated herself beside Ryan. His profile looked hard and cold. He wasn't happy with her presence. She'd stay long enough to inquire about his father, then leave. She certainly had no intention of forcing her company on him.

She cleared her throat. "Has there been any improvement since Dr. Norman left?" Her voice sounded stiff and cool, but she couldn't help that. She still smarted from Ryan's words this afternoon.

He shook his head, not turning toward her. "I don't

think so. His fever is still high. And the doctor said the crisis may not come for another day and night."

"Yes, that's often true," Calista agreed, "and if it's perepneumonia, the pain will be worse and—" She broke off as Ryan turned swiftly toward her.

"What in hell is this perepneumonia?" he asked, frowning, his voice taut with strain.

Calista realized Lucinda hadn't told him of this probability. "It's pneumonia and pleurisy combined," she said, then paused. He looked exhausted. There was no reason to tell him the fatality rate was much higher with this disease.

But she hadn't reckoned with Ryan's sharp intuition. "And it's a more serious disease, isn't it?"

"Oh, I don't know about that," she hedged. "Maybe—"

"Tell me the truth," he demanded roughly. "Do you think you have to shield me as you would Gabrielle?"

Yes, he had a right to know this, she decided. "It is. Quite a bit more. Most of our slaves that contract it die, but white people are more resistant. Often, they pull through."

Shock widened his blue eyes. His face paled. For the first time, she saw him with all his defenses down. Then, with a visible effort, he pulled himself together. A small, wry smile turned up one corner of his mouth.

"Now, that wasn't so hard, was it?" he asked, his voice soft, but with a clear, ironic note in it. "You and Lucinda have lived in a household of women so long that you're entirely too careful of everyone's sensibilities."

A small shock traveled down her nerve endings. That was perceptive of him. He was right, but she hadn't realized it until he'd pointed it out. "That's probably true," she said, her voice trembling with fatigue.

Ryan, expecting an argument, blinked at her agreement. Her green eyes looked so tired and haunted he wanted to reach over and pull her into his arms and comfort her. He fought the urge. Why should *she* be worried? It wasn't *her* father on the bed.

No, her father was long gone, and her mother, too. There was no one except Lucinda who cared about her. *Are you sure about that?* the taunting voice in his mind questioned.

"You look exhausted. Why don't you go on to bed?" In spite of everything he'd told himself since he'd arrived here, the mention of bed presented a vision to his mind. Calista's black hair spread across a white pillow, her brilliant eyes, her parted, full lips beckoning to him.

Calista nodded and rose. "I have had a very tiring day. I met Andrew downstairs, and he said he would take over here at midnight. But, of course, if you need me . . ."

Ryan also stood and, without conscious thought, his hand reached out to touch her sleeve. Another vision came to him, a real one this time. Calista on the lagoon bank, as eager as he. . . . He pushed that aside. "Wait a minute, please. I want to apologize to you."

She stood very still, his warmth coming through the fabric of her gown, into her flesh. "What did you just say?" Was he really going to tell her he was sorry for those harsh, unfair words he'd spoken earlier today?

Ryan gave her another wry smile. "I know what you must be thinking. I don't often apologize for something I've said or done." He knew he should remove his hand, step back, but he didn't want to.

The warmth of his hand seemed to flow up her arm, into her shoulder. Calista realized she wanted him to take her into his arms as he had that night at the Howards'. For comfort. It would feel so wonderful to rest her tired head against his broad chest, listen to the sound of his heart beating beneath her cheek . . .

"I'm sorry for ignoring your concerns about my father

earlier today," Ryan continued, his voice softened. "If I'd listened, if we'd gotten the doctor then, maybe he wouldn't be so sick now."

Calista stared at him, his words like a dash of cold water. What a fool she was. Of course he wouldn't apologize for saying those hurtful things this afternoon. He'd meant them then, and he still did.

She drew herself up. "I accept your apology."

Ryan removed his hand from her arm and stepped back, puzzled by her sudden coolness, but glad of it. For a moment he'd felt so close to her it had frightened him. He didn't want to feel that way about her. He didn't want to feel that way about any woman. "That wasn't all. I wanted to—"

"You couldn't be expected to know," she interrupted, her voice cold. "You don't have the experience of illness that Lucinda and I do here on the plantation. We're faced with it almost constantly."

Ryan's contrite mood vanished. She wouldn't listen to him, and she seemed to think he sat around all day doing nothing of importance.

"Ah, yes," he said smoothly. "How could I have forgotten that? Your years of experience as a plantation mistress make you an expert on just about everything, I'm sure."

Calista gave him an even cooler stare. Would she never learn that Ryan intended to keep that shield over his emotions forever? Why had she thought for a moment he was lowering that guard, about to let her into his heart? His life?

She stepped back, tilting her chin up. "Good night, Mr. Burke. If I am needed, call me."

She turned and left the room, her head high, and Ryan stared after her. Damn it to hell! Couldn't he do a simple thing like apologize without it turning into whatever this had turned into?

A sudden deep cough came from the bed. Ryan pressed his lips together and walked to the bedside and touched his father's forehead. It burned his hand. His father's breathing was rough and harsh; he still coughed deeply and often. He'd stay in here and watch over his father, and he wouldn't think of Calista again.

He also wouldn't be taking his family back to Charleston in the next few days as he'd planned. The doctor had made it plain his father couldn't be moved for weeks. And he wouldn't leave these two women to cope with his father's illness.

No matter how much he hated it, he was stuck on Meadowarsh.

Chapter Thirteen

"I still can't believe Estelle and Farley would send Leora here—after the way they practically threw us out of their house!" Calista sat beside Lucinda in the carriage on the way to their dock to meet the girl in question.

Lucinda smiled. "I can. Estelle has a convenient memory about such things. Now that she needs your help, all that unpleasantness has completely left her mind."

"I also can't imagine Leora involved with a married man," Calista continued. "Why, the girl isn't any older than Gabrielle; and although she likes to flirt, I always thought she had good sense."

"At least you won't have to worry about her still having a yen for Ryan," Lucinda ventured, giving her niece a sideways look.

A week had passed since Ryan's return to Meadowmarsh. His father, indeed, had perepneumonia and, although he'd survived the crisis, was far from recovered. Dr. Norman had said he couldn't be removed to Charleston for at least another month.

Ryan was still here, too. Apparently he was determined no one on Meadowmarsh would have to deal with any more emergencies. He'd brought work with him, and Jerome was coming in a few days with more legal briefs. Lucinda felt her heart beat faster with anticipation. She hadn't seen Jerome for weeks. She missed him more than she'd have thought possible.

Calista pressed her lips together. "It makes no difference to me if she has or not, although I wouldn't like the girl to make a fool of herself." She wasn't going to think about Ryan. She hadn't been alone with him since that night in his father's room. And she didn't want to be, of course.

Young people could be so obstinate, Lucinda thought, holding back a frustrated sigh. Why did these two continue to act as if they couldn't stand the sight of each other when it was obvious they wanted nothing so much as to be together? Then, she smiled wryly. Who was she to criticize young people for being obstinate? Jerome often accused her of the same failing.

The carriage pulled up and stopped, and the two women got out. In a few minutes, Zeke poled the flatboat up to the dock. He'd taken it down the creeks to meet the steamboat from Charleston. Leora, dressed in the height of fashion in a frothy white-and-pink gown, perched on a large trunk. Her maid Summer sat on another smaller one.

"I take it she means to stay awhile," Lucinda whispered to Calista.

"Yes, I guess so." Calista looked with dismay at the evidence of a prolonged sojourn. In spite of what she'd just told her aunt, she dreaded this visit. Her last encounter with Leora had been far from pleasant.

"Aunt Lucie, do you think she still hates me because

she believes I stole Ryan from her? I wonder if she'll be sullen and disagreeable since she's been banished to Meadowmarsh?"

Watching the girl disembark with Summer's help, a bright smile on her face, anticipation in every feature, Lucinda said, "No, dear, I don't think you have to worry about that. She certainly doesn't appear to be suffering from a broken heart."

The two women stepped forward to welcome Leora. Her aunt was right, Calista thought. Leora seemed delighted to be here. And that acknowledgment did nothing to allay Calista's worries.

Her cousin could well be pleased because she looked forward to seeing Ryan again. Wrenched from her Charleston romance, would she try to renew her flirtation with Ryan? If she'd gotten involved with one married man, what was to stop her from doing it again?

She didn't care, of course, Calista tried to convince herself, but she wouldn't let the girl make a laughingstock of her.

Is that all that worries you? Her mind nudged her. You're not at all concerned that maybe your husband, since he obviously cares nothing for you, might welcome attention from someone as young and pretty as Leora?

The girl rushed forward, her arms held out, Summer following. "Calista! Aunt Lucinda! Oh, it's so good to see you." She hugged both women effusively, then stepped back and glanced toward the waiting carriage. A disappointed expression showed on her face for a moment before she erased it.

Calista froze. She'd been right. That look was occasioned because Ryan hadn't come along to welcome her. "It's good to see you, too, Leora."

Leora looked around, pulling her fur-trimmed cloak

closer. "It's cooler here than in Charleston," she commented. "I'd forgotten it was so beautiful! I can see why you stay here all the time, Calista."

She was laying it on just a trifle thick. Lucinda gave Calista a quick look. Her favorite niece's face was even more tense than a few moments before. More than she'd mentioned worried her, and Lucinda was certain she knew the cause.

If this little chit continued the outrageous flirtation she'd tried to carry on with Ryan in Charleston, she would personally pack her up and send her back to Estelle and Farley, Lucinda thought grimly.

"We like it," she answered. "Shall we go on up to the house?" Zeke had already loaded the trunks onto the carriage, and now he helped Summer up beside Gideon. Lucinda saw the appreciative look the driver gave the attractive girl. That wouldn't sit well with Delphinia.

The three women seated themselves, and Leora looked eagerly around during the drive up the curving lane to the house. Leora hadn't been to Meadowmarsh for years, Calista thought. Maybe she was genuinely glad to be here. It was possible that glance into the carriage meant nothing.

"I understand your husband's family is still here, Cousin?" Leora inquired pleasantly.

"Yes, they plan to stay for another month, until Mr Burke is well enough to be moved," Calista answered, surprised at the way the girl had worded her question. She supposed Leora had enough manners to not inquire directly about Ryan. *Not jealous, are you?* her mind prodded. She tried to ignore it.

Leora's pretty face became even more animated. "Oh, good. Then I shall have a chance for a nice visit with them. I only just met them for a short time in Charleston."

Calista's surprise grew. "I didn't know you'd met them at all."

Her cousin's dark eyes widened for a moment, as if she realized she'd said more than she intended. Then, she smiled prettily again. "Oh, yes, at Ryan's house."

And why had she been at Ryan's house? After her parents' breaking off all social and business relations with Ryan? Calista barely managed to hold back a scowl. "Gabrielle is about your age," she said stiffly. "You should get along well."

Leora blinked, then nodded. "Yes, Gabrielle is indeed a nice girl," she agreed.

The carriage pulled up before the plantation house, and the three women alighted. "Oh, it's such a *beautiful* house!" Leora said. "It's been so long since I was here, I'd forgotten that."

Delphinia opened the door, throwing a smiling glance toward Gideon, which changed into a surprised frown when she saw Summer getting down from her seat beside him. The women entered the spacious hallway. "Is dinner ready?" Calista asked Delphinia.

"Yes'm, Miz Calista, you is just in time." She darted a quick, unfriendly glance at Summer, who stood behind Leora.

"Good. This is my cousin's maid. Will you take her out to the kitchen for her meal?" Calista asked, relieved her voice sounded so calm and unruffled. Her stomach was tied in knots, dreading the moment Leora and Ryan met again.

Delphinia nodded, her eyes cold as she looked at the slim, attractive black girl who now stepped forward.

Her concerns were justified, Calista told herself grimly, when everyone was seated around the long table. Leora had dimpled and smiled at Ryan just as she had at her parents' house in Charleston; and now, seated at his right, she still simpered and blushed.

Calista felt like shaking her. Didn't she realize what a spectacle she was making of herself? Especially when she'd been sent here because of similar behavior? Or worse. Calista refused to dwell on that thought.

It didn't help matters that Ryan, who'd donned a garnet waistcoat and deep-blue frock coat for the meal, was so handsome she could feel her heart speeding up its beat. No wonder Leora flirted with him. And Leora was young and beautiful in her pink-and-white dress, her hair in perfect blond ringlets.

She, on the other hand, looked every bit the part of a no-nonsense plantation mistress in her plain, black dress, her hair pulled back in its chignon. Calista glumly turned her attention to the excellent meal.

"It's wonderful to see you again, Ryan." Leora glanced up at him from under her long, dark lashes. "I still remember our dance at the Hamiltons' Christmas ball." Her voice was pitched just loud enough so that it could be heard by everyone at the table.

Damnation! What did the girl think she was doing? Her attentions to him were so blatantly feigned, she should realize everyone at the dinner table could see through them. His glance collided with Calista's at the other end of the table, and a small shock went through him.

Maybe not. If looks could kill, he'd be very dead. Could it be possible his beautiful wife was jealous of her cousin? That thought didn't fill him with amusement as it once would have. Instead, he felt irritation and, deny it as he would, satisfaction.

He smiled at Leora. "It was a pleasure I, too, remember," he said gallantly, his own voice a shade louder than necessary.

He glanced at Calista again to find her attention firmly fixed on her dinner plate. Becoming aware of another stare, he realized Andrew regarded him with a far-from-friendly look. His brother had taken special pains with his clothes, Ryan noticed, wearing his best powder-blue waistcoat.

Double damnation! He'd thought his conversation with Andrew in Charleston had cooled any ardor his brother might have for Leora. That had obviously been a hasty conclusion on his part. His brother had been here on this island for weeks, seeing no young women except Calista. And, Ryan had to admit, Andrew's manner toward her was merely warm and friendly. Even if he hadn't been attracted to Leora before, he certainly would be now.

"I'd love to see the plantation," Leora said, smiling sweetly. "Would it be possible for you to show me around this afternoon, *Cousin* Ryan?"

Ryan's eyes narrowed at her last words. No doubt she'd emphasized "cousin" to nullify any need for Lucinda or Summer to act as chaperon on her proposed expedition.

He had no intention of granting her request for more than one reason, the most important being he didn't want to spend the afternoon touring his wife's precious plantation. He planned to get the hell off the island as soon as possible. But his father convalesced very slowly.

He gave Leora a regretful smile. "I'm sorry, but I have legal work I must do. Perhaps Calista could spare the time."

There, he thought, that should fix Miss Leora's plans, whatever they were. He glanced at Calista just in time to see her startled expression.

"I would be delighted to show Cousin Leora the plantation," Andrew quickly put in before Calista had a chance to reply to Ryan's suggestion. "Calista is so busy overseeing the preparation of the cotton for market." He gave everyone a bland smile.

"Thank you, Andrew." Calista tried not to let everyone see the relief she felt at his unexpected offer. She was also grateful to Ryan for sidestepping Leora's request—for whatever reason he'd done it. "I *am* very busy just now."

Actually, as it happened, she wasn't for the moment. Just yesterday, the last of the cotton had been baled and stored in the cotton house. Zeke and some of the other field hands would take it to Beaufort in a few days. But she was tired.

"That's kind of you, *Cousin* Andrew." Leora gave Andrew a pleasant smile. "I do hope I'm not taking you from more important duties."

"No, there's nothing for me to do here. Calista has a very smooth-running operation." His voice held a hint of chagrin.

Leora managed to suppress any disappointment in the foiling of her plans, Calista noted. The girl was a good actress. And Andrew chafed at his inactivity. He still went with Zeke to Beaufort occasionally, and sitting with his father took up a lot of his time, too. But she knew he was bored and restless.

Ryan tried to catch Andrew's eye, but his brother wouldn't so much as glance in his direction. He'd waylay that young man later on this evening for a talk. And his *dear* wife obviously had no idea Leora had maneuvered this outcome so that she could be alone with Andrew. He'd underestimated the girl's cleverness, he admitted.

When she had been interested in him, she'd been single-minded in her pursuit. Since she'd switched her affections to Andrew, he'd had no reason to think she'd be any less dedicated to her cause. He glanced at Calista to find her eyes on him, speculatively.

Maybe he should have a talk with his wife about this situation, let her know which way the wind blew. The more he thought about it, the more convinced he became that's what he should do. He was sure Calista would be

Wish You Were Here?

You can be, every month, with Zebra Historical Romance Novels.

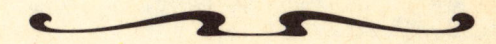

AND TO GET YOU STARTED, ALLOW US TO SEND YOU

Historical Romances Free

A $19.96 VALUE!
With absolutely no obligation to buy anything.

YOU ARE CORDIALLY INVITED TO GET SWEPT AWAY INTO NEW WORLDS OF PASSION AND ADVENTURE.

AND IT WON'T COST YOU A PENNY!

Receive 4 Zebra Historical Romances, Absolutely *Free*!

(A $19.96 value)

Now you can have your pick of handsome, noble adventurers with romance in their hearts and you on their minds. Zebra publishes Historical Romances That Burn With The Fire Of History by the world's finest romance authors.

This very special FREE offer entitles you to 4 Zebra novels at absolutely no cost, with no obligation to buy anything, ever. It's an offer designed to excite your most vivid dreams and desires...and save you almost $20!

And that's not all you get...

Your Home Subscription Saves You Money Every Month.

After you've enjoyed your initial FREE package of 4 books, you'll begin receive monthly shipments of new Zebra titles. These novels are delivered direct to your home as soon as they are published...sometimes even before the bookstores get them! Each monthly shipment of 4 books will be yours to examine for 10 days. Then if you decide to keep the books, you'll pay the preferred subscriber's price of just $4.00 per title. That's $16 for all 4 books...a savings of almost $4 off the publisher's price.

We Also Add To Your Savings With FREE Home Delivery!
There Is No Minimum Purchase. And Your Continued Satisfaction Is Guarantee

We're so sure that you'll appreciate the money-saving convenience of home delivery that we guarantee your complete satisfaction. You may return any shipment...for any reason...within 10 days and pay nothing that month. And if you want us to stop sending books, just say the word. There is no minimum number of books you must buy.

It's a no-lose proposition, so send for your 4 FREE books today!

YOU'RE GOING TO LOVE GETTING

4 FREE BOOKS

These books worth almost $20, are yours without cost or obligation when you fill out and mail this certificate.
(If the certificate is missing below, write to: Zebra Home Subscription Service, Inc., 120 Brighton Road, P.O. Box 5214, Clifton, New Jersey 07015-5214

Complete and mail this card to receive 4 Free books!

Yes! Please send me 4 Zebra Historical Romances without cost or obligation. I understand that each month thereafter I will be able to preview 4 new Zebra Historical Romances FREE for 10 days. Then, if I should decide to keep them, I will pay the money-saving preferred publisher's price of just $4.00 each...a total of $16. That's almost $4 less than the publisher's price, and there is no additional charge for shipping and handling. I may return any shipment within 10 days and owe nothing, and I may cancel this subscription at any time. The 4 FREE books will be mine to keep in any case.

Name _____

Address _____ Apt. _____

City _____ State _____ Zip _____

Telephone ( ) _____

Signature _____ LF0895
(If under 18, parent or guardian must sign.)

Terms, offer and prices subject to change without notice. Subscription subject to acceptance by Zebra Books. Zebra Books reserves the right to reject any order or cancel any subscription.

TREAT YOURSELF TO 4 FREE BOOKS.

A $19.96 value.
FREE!

No obligation to buy anything, ever.

ZEBRA HOME SUBSCRIPTION SERVICE, INC.

120 BRIGHTON ROAD
P.O. BOX 5214
CLIFTON, NEW JERSEY 07015-5214

AFFIX STAMP HERE

as horrified as he at the prospect of a romance developing between Andrew and Leora.

His eyes lingered on Calista's face. Even though she always wore black mourning gowns, she didn't look dowdy and drab. Far from it. The black set off her fair skin, and the lack of jewelry or other adornment only drew attention to her classically lovely features, her lissome figure.

Her face grew rosy under his scrutiny, as if she could feel his thoughts. Ryan summoned an ironic smile and aimed it at her. Her face changed, hardened, and she gave him a cool stare.

Her damn beauty didn't mean anything to him. That time between them at the lagoon constantly stayed in his mind only because he was stuck here on Meadowmarsh, Ryan told himself savagely, even as his hardening body gave the lie to that assertion.

As soon as he took his family and left here, everything would be all right. He'd go back to his normal routine at the law offices, find a woman to make him forget all that had happened here. He'd be happy again.

He pushed down the thoughts clamoring at the edges of his consciousness telling him it was far too late for that. It had been too late from the first moment he'd seen Calista.

Delphinia stood with Junie inside the kitchen door, watching Summer daintily eat her dinner. "Who she think she is?" Delphinia muttered. "She talk an' act like she belong in de Big House with de white folks."

Junie giggled, giving Delphinia a sideways glance. "You just mad 'cause you see de way Gideon look at her."

"Hush your mouth," Delphinia told her friend, scowling. "I ain't worried 'bout dat little old city gal. Why, she don't know how to do nothin'. All she ever done is wait on Miss Leora."

Junie giggled again. "What difference you think dat make to a man? Gideon ain't lookin' for a maid."

"He ain't lookin' at dis gal for anythin'," Delphinia insisted, her scowl deeper. "Why you sayin' all these things?"

Realizing she'd gone too far, Junie backtracked. "I was just funnin' with you," she said quickly. "I didn't mean nothin'. I knows Gideon's your man."

Watching as Gideon came into the big room with a tray of dirty dishes and gave Summer a furtive sideways glance, Delphinia felt her former rock-sureness of that fact falter.

She hadn't felt any urgency before to set a wedding date, but now she did. Turning to Junie, she forced a smile. "You right. Reckon it 'bout time Gideon and me jumped de broom. I'm goin' to talk to Miss Calista real soon."

Andrew cleared his throat and turned to Leora. Both of them stood by their tied horses under a huge magnolia tree. He'd just finished showing her most of the plantation. He didn't want to discuss this with her, but he'd grown too fond of Calista to risk seeing her hurt. That was why he'd objected to Leora's blatant flirting with Ryan at the dinner table. The only reason, he assured himself.

She turned toward him at the same time, and their glances met. He seemed drawn into the dark pools of her eyes. She gave him a dazzling smile, and he suddenly felt dizzy. "I've enjoyed this, Andrew," she said softly. "More so, because I was with you. I was just trying to make you jealous at the dinner table, you know."

Surprise washed over Andrew, mixed with what felt

suspiciously like relief. So that business with Ryan had only been an act? He continued to stare at her, watching the play of the afternoon sunlight on her fair skin, the sweep of her long lashes.

He drew himself together. No, no, he wasn't going to succumb to her flirting ways again. She'd tried that on him in Charleston, and he'd barely avoided catastrophe. If Ryan hadn't brought him to his senses, hadn't made him realize just how deeply involved he was getting, there was no telling what might have happened.

Andrew hastily pushed those thoughts aside and gave her a friendly return smile. "It was a pleasure to escort you, Cousin Leora," he said formally.

She tilted her head of blond curls, and her smile became impish. "Now that we're by ourselves, you don't have to keep on calling me cousin."

His heart leaped at her words and manner in spite of everything he'd told himself. He moved back a step and tried to frown at her.

"I believe that I should," he said, but his voice lacked conviction even to himself.

"Why?" She moved a step forward so that they were as near as before. "My parents are a long way off, and no one will tell them about this."

Her words alarmed at the same time they excited him. He didn't retreat further. "About *what?* That I've taken you on an unchaperoned tour of Meadowmarsh?"

She laughed, a merry sound that floated on the air, then pouted prettily. "Oh, Andrew. Surely, you haven't forgotten all those things you said to me in Charleston."

No, and neither had he forgotten how he'd felt, and that was the trouble. He still felt that way, he discovered, more so with every passing moment. Looking down into her tipped-up face, he wanted desperately to pull her into his arms and kiss her.

Summoning every ounce of will power he possessed, he backed up and cleared his throat again. "That was a mistake. I never should have said anything to you."

Her pout turned into a hurt expression. "Then, you didn't mean any of those sweet words? You were just playing me for a fool?" Tears formed on the ends of her lashes, sparkling like jewels.

"No!" He couldn't stand seeing her hurt. He stepped forward, putting his hands on her shoulders. She felt so good. Just as he remembered. "I meant every one of them," he said huskily, watching her rosebud mouth.

She blinked away her tears, a tremulous smile starting to form. "I don't understand, then. Because I meant everything I said, too. And now, I'm here at Meadowmarsh. And I'll be here for *weeks.*"

Andrew shuddered. He drew Leora into his arms and kissed her. When they finally pulled apart, she looked at him with stars in her eyes.

He abruptly removed his hands from her shoulders and stepped back. Damn! Now he'd done it. "I'm sorry," he said stiffly. "I shouldn't have done that. It won't happen again."

Leora's smile was radiant. "I'm not sorry. And I hope it will happen often."

Andrew's eyes widened. He'd forgotten how plain spoken she could be. "Leora, your parents would never approve of me," he told her, his voice heavy with regret.

Her smile faded, and she grew as serious as he. "I know, Andrew. That's why I managed to get myself sent here for a long visit."

He shook his head with finality. "No, we can't sneak around behind everyone's back. I won't be a party to any such behavior. We'd best be getting back to the house."

He turned to his mount, not wanting Leora to see his face. He'd have to make sure they weren't alone together, because he didn't feel nearly as positive as his words had sounded.

Calista stood on the gallery outside her room, a cloak thrown over her nightdress, glad of the brisk breeze. It banished the mosquitoes even if it were chilly. She wished she could sleep! In spite of her physical exhaustion, she hadn't been able to sleep well since Ryan had returned to Meadowmarsh.

She'd tried many times to convince herself her inner turmoil was caused by all the problems Ryan's coming into her life had created. But tonight she was too tired to continue that fiction. She couldn't sleep because she knew her husband, a man to whom she was strongly attracted, occupied the bedchamber next to hers.

Why couldn't she suppress these wild, useless longings that assailed her many times a day? And night. A small sound made her turn her head. Ryan walked out onto the gallery from his room, like her, a cloak thrown over his nightclothes.

Her heart thumped as she looked at him in the shadowy light. The sliver of moon emphasized the cleft in his chin, darkened his eyes until they looked almost black.

"I see you couldn't sleep either," he said, leaning on the rail beside her. He tried to ignore the knowledge that coming out here was a mistake. "I've been wanting to talk to you all day."

She wouldn't move away, Calista told herself. She would stand her ground, no matter how she felt. "What about?" she asked warily. "I was just going back inside."

"This won't take long." No, he'd make sure of that. "I only want to make you aware of a situation you apparently know nothing about."

Something superior in his tone put her back up. She

welcomed the feeling. It took her mind off other emotions she didn't want to think about. She raised her brows. "Oh? And what might that be?"

"Leora isn't interested in me. She only flirted with me at dinner to make Andrew jealous."

Calista stared at him, truly surprised now. "Andrew? But I thought she hardly knew your family."

Light from the candles in Calista's bedroom came through the undrawn curtains, making shifting shadows across her face. A warm, sweet scent drifted from her across to him. In spite of the cool night, he felt moisture bead his brow, his upper lip.

"That's what I thought, too, until Andrew let it slip he and Leora had been seeing each other. One of the reasons I agreed to bring my family out to Meadowmarsh was to get those two away from each other."

He looked so tired, Calista noted, dark circles under his eyes. He'd also had a lot to contend with, she admitted, reluctantly, her heart softening a little. "Yes, I suppose that wouldn't sit well with Aunt Estelle and Uncle Farley."

Ryan raked a long-fingered hand through his black hair. If he stayed out here much longer, he'd pick her up and carry her to his bed. He *had* to do something to get them fighting with each other again.

"It didn't sit well with me! The last thing I want is *another* forced marriage!"

Calista stiffened, her newly softened feelings toward him evaporating. "I suppose you think Leora is trying to trick him into marriage, as you feel I did you?"

"You saw how she acted at the dinner table." He tried to be pleased his strategy had worked. "She can pretend anything to get what she wants."

"And I'm sure that's meant as another slur. I didn't try

to trick you into marrying me, but I know you'll never believe that."

He looked at her for a long minute, wishing he'd never started this, wishing he'd waited until tomorrow to talk to her in some public place. But fighting was better than the alternative. He'd never risk making love to her again. It was far too dangerous. Once she was in his arms, he cared about nothing else—not even that she wanted him to surrender to her, to the spell of this island. To put himself under her control. "You got what you wanted, didn't you?"

"No!" she said without stopping to think what she was revealing. "Do you think I'd choose to have a husband who won't live with me?"

His mouth curved in one of his old, ironic grins. One brow lifted. "That's right—you wanted Timid Timothy, whom you could keep under your thumb."

He was wrong there, too. As soon as Ryan had taken her in his arms, she'd realized Baxter had prevented her from making a terrible mistake. But she'd never let this maddening man know that. She raised her chin. "At least Timothy wanted to live at Meadowmarsh."

"Not like me, eh? You're right. I'm not interested in your damned plantation. I never will be."

He raked his hands savagely through his hair again. His strategy was working too well. His anger, never very far from the surface these days, was genuine now. "Never mind all that. All I want from you is your promise to help me keep Andrew and Leora apart."

Some perverse imp took hold of her. She agreed with Ryan in principle—a match between Leora and Andrew would be fraught with problems. But she still stung when she remembered his high-handed manner, his scathing words, that day on horseback.

"Oh? I seem to recall you told me to stop meddling with your family. To keep hands off."

He glared at her to hide his admiration of her spirit. "This isn't the same thing and you know it."

She gave him a cool smile and started to go around him. "I don't see that it's any different. Meddling is meddling. If Andrew and Leora love each other, then I have no intention of interfering."

He caught at her arm as she passed him, stopping her. "Wait a minute. You're only saying that to annoy me."

His hand burned her flesh, even through the cloak. Would she always have this physical reaction to him, no matter how she felt about him otherwise? "Let me go," she said tightly, trying to pull away.

Ryan silently cursed himself as his body reacted instantly to the touch. He'd have to goad her again, make her angry. "Not until you stop acting like a spoiled child and promise to help me in this."

They were so close to each other, she could feel his warm breath on her neck. That peculiar weakness when she was with him assailed her again. "I'll *never* promise that. Now let me go!" She jerked her arm again.

Ryan's grip subtly changed as their gazes locked and held. It was still firm enough to keep her fast, but an awareness had come into it. He grasped her as a woman now, a woman he desired.

"Calista?" he asked, softly, his gaze holding hers with an intensity that made her feel as if her bones were melting. She could escape if she really wanted to. Ryan would never hold her against her will. All she had to do was glare at him, say something cold and hurtful.

Instead, she felt herself sway toward him, knowing what a fool she was. His hand moved up her arm to her shoulders; and the other one found her waist, pulling her close against his hard length.

Her unfastened cloak spread apart, just as his own had done. The heat of their bodies burned through the thin cloth of their nightclothes. She felt his aroused body press against her softness, and a long shudder went through her.

She lifted her face to his and he lowered his mouth to hers. She wouldn't open her mouth to him this time, she vowed, desperately, even as his hot, probing tongue slid across her lips, urging her to do just that.

Closing her eyes, she relaxed her mouth and his tongue slid triumphantly into the opening. A white-hot tremor shot through her, and she slipped her arms around his neck, urging him even closer.

She inhaled his clean masculine scent of soap and smoke. Smoke? That was strange, not a cigar kind of smell, but smoke like a fire burning . . .

The smoke smell became stronger. Calista stiffened in his arms and pulled away. She looked over the gallery railing, down toward the plantation outbuildings.

"What is it?" Ryan asked as he also moved to the rail.

Her heart stopped for a moment. The night was dark, and she could make out only the outline of the structures, but she saw a thick trail of smoke spiraling upward.

Ryan was so close she felt his body tense against her side. "What's burning?"

Calista willed herself into movement, running for the door to her room, jerking at her cloak, looking for her day clothes.

"The cotton house!" she flung over her shoulder. "And all the baled cotton is inside. Half the year's crop!"

Chapter Fourteen

"Throw that water over here!" Zeke directed the first field hand in the long line, all holding pails of water from the creek. A few lanterns lent a dim light to the scene. Reuben cast the contents of his pail against the side of the cotton house, extinguishing what appeared to be the last smoldering embers.

Zeke had the next three hands also add their water to be absolutely sure the fire was out. He wiped his sooty forehead, heaving a relieved sigh. That was a close call. If he hadn't been wakeful and smelled the first smoke, the cotton house would be gone. And half a year's crop with it.

Sweat ran down his back at that thought and his mouth tightened as he saw Lotus far back in the now disintegrating line. She didn't look worried or anxious like the others. No, he would swear that was a disappointed look on her beautiful face.

He didn't think the fire was an accident. And he didn't think any of the field hands had started it, either. He didn't know why Lotus would do this, except that her hatred for all the people up at the Big House grew stronger every day.

He couldn't prove it, though. His mouth tightened more. But he was going to scare her into not doing anything like this again. And how would he do that? Lotus didn't scare easily. If he threatened her, she'd only remind him of how firmly enmeshed in this treasure-seeking scheme they all were. He was in every bit as deep as she and Ira.

Today, when he'd caught a glimpse of Miz Leora and Mister Andrew standing under that big magnolia, his heart had stopped. But they were too wrapped up in each other to notice any sign of disturbed ground around the tree.

He had to tell Lotus and Ira about the old chest. He knew why he was putting it off. If it *were* the treasure, once it was divided between them, he and Lotus would take their share and leave Meadowmarsh forever. He still wasn't sure he wanted to do that.

He glanced up at the sound of horses' hooves and saw Calista and Ryan galloping toward him. They reined in outside the cotton house and dismounted.

Calista looked swiftly at the damaged wall and the scorched cotton bales on the ground outside the building.

"Good work, Zeke!" she told him, smiling her gratitude. "How much damage inside?" Already heading toward the door, she took a few deep breaths to calm her racing heart. She'd never dressed so fast or made the trip down here as swiftly in her life.

"It not too bad, Mistress." He followed her, Ryan behind him.

Scanning the blackened wall, the cotton bales pulled away from it, she let out her breath in a sigh of relief. Her legs shook in delayed reaction. "Only the two bales outside were damaged, then?"

"Yes'm. That's all. And they ain't ruint. Just the outside is burned some."

Ryan had moved up beside her, surveying the interior of the big room. Now that her fear for the loss of the cotton was gone, she became aware of his nearness.

Her skin reddened, and she moved away a few inches. Again, she'd given in to her desire for him. Even after he'd told her once more that he didn't trust her, that he still believed she'd tricked him into marriage. Why was she such a fool?

"How did this happen?" Ryan asked Zeke. He noticed Calista's withdrawal, and his mouth tightened. He didn't blame her. He'd handled everything all wrong—again.

Damnation! Hadn't he told himself a dozen times not to allow himself to be alone with her? Of course, he'd needed to talk to her about Andrew and Leora, but had that only been a pretext? Deep inside, he admitted he'd wanted more than that. And if it hadn't been for the fire, there would have been more than just one interrupted kiss . . .

There was no changing things now—he'd try to forget it. And make sure not to be alone with her ever again. The promise sounded hollow to him. He'd made and broken that vow too many times.

Zeke shrugged his heavy shoulders. "I don't know. I just smelled smoke and come runnin'." His face was blank and innocent.

Something in the other man's attitude didn't ring true to Ryan. He glanced at Calista to find her giving Zeke a searching look, as if she also weren't happy with his answer.

"How could a fire start tonight?" Ryan asked sharply. "There was no storm, no lightning strike."

Zeke nodded again, his black glance sliding away from

Ryan's. "Yes'suh, I knows that." He scratched the back of his head, as if deep in thought. "I cain't figure it out, no way."

Ryan's irritation rose. Zeke should be commended for his quick action in putting out the fire, but he knew more about this than he told. Again, Ryan glanced at Calista to see how she'd handle this.

He saw the tightening of her mouth as she looked at Zeke for a long moment. Then, she pushed her hair back from her forehead, her gesture bone-weary.

"I'm happy it was no worse, and you're to thank for that." She gave him another grateful smile. "See to getting the damaged bales back in the cotton house. And you'd better post a watch tonight, just to make sure the fire is completely out."

Zeke nodded, obviously relieved not to be further questioned. "Yes'm, Mistress, I shore do that."

Ryan frowned. Calista's tired gesture touched him, while at the same time he disapproved of her letting Zeke go with no further attempt to find out the fire's origin.

And though she hadn't stated it, he felt sure she meant the watch to prevent another attempt to burn the cotton house rather than to make sure this fire was extinguished.

He glanced at Zeke to find the driver's gaze on him.

"Put a trustworthy man on guard. Or stay yourself."

Again, Zeke nodded. "Yes'suh, Maussa Ryan," he agreed quickly.

Calista turned and walked outside the cotton house without looking at either of the men. Ryan followed her. Most of the field hands had gone back to their cabins. Only a few still stood in small groups, talking quietly.

A tall, striking, very dark woman stood off to herself. The silver bracelets on her ankles struck gleams from the lantern light. She raised her head and saw him staring at her, and a slow, unmistakably seductive smile spread over her face.

Shock traveled down his nerve ends. He knew what went on at a lot of plantations, maybe even at Ainsley Hall, but he didn't expect to find this at Meadowmarsh. He turned away from the woman, but not before he'd caught her satisfied smirk.

Calista pulled scorched cotton away from the outside of a round, hard-packed bale, the frown back on her tired face.

He joined her, still strangely shaken by the small incident with the black woman. "The scorch doesn't go very deep. You won't lose too much from this bale."

"Yes," she answered, not looking at him. She moved to the other bale, tugging at the outer layer of cotton.

Her voice was definitely cool, and that was fine with him. Best they keep their distance from each other. He gave a sideways glance to the spot where the Negro woman had stood. She'd vanished as if never there. A small, uneasy feeling slid down his spine. "Who is the tall woman with silver anklets?"

She shot him a quick, startled glance. For a moment he thought he saw fear in her eyes. Then, whatever it was passed. Her mouth turned down. "You must mean Lotus. She helps mind the field hands' children."

Ryan's eyebrows raised in surprise. "I can't picture her caring for children."

Lucinda had said almost the same thing, Calista thought. Weeks ago. "She seems to be doing her job well enough. At least Maum Fronie has no complaints."

"Maum Fronie?"

"The plantation midwife. She also has charge of the children."

The feeling she'd had ever since she'd returned from

Charleston was still with her. The nagging foreboding that something was very wrong here on Meadowmarsh. Tonight's fire had intensified it.

Zeke came outside the cotton house and walked over to a group of field workers. Several of them hurried to the building and carried the cotton bales inside. Zeke came over to Calista and Ryan.

"I'll stay here the rest of the night," he told Ryan. "I think that be best."

Ryan nodded. "Good. So do I."

The rest of the field hands melted away into the darkness, and Zeke settled down outside the building.

Ryan turned to Calista, forcing a smile. "Well, I guess that's settled. We can go back to the house."

She gave him another, even cooler look. "Oh, do I have your permission for that, *Maussa* Ryan?"

Abruptly, Ryan understood the reason for her coolness. It had nothing to do with the incident on the gallery. His mouth twisted. He'd usurped her authority. That was much more important to her than an interrupted kiss. For the last few minutes he'd acted as if he were, truly, the master of Meadowmarsh. He'd questioned Zeke, given him orders, and Zeke had instantly obeyed. And it had seemed normal and right.

His face tightened, and he returned his wife's look with an aloof smile. "Since you seemed to be almost asleep on your feet, I just went ahead and told Zeke what I thought was needed."

She turned away and walked over to Zeke, who was sitting, shivering, on the cold ground. "Go home and get a blanket and your coat. We'll watch until you come back."

Zeke hurried off toward his cabin, leaving Calista and Ryan alone by the cotton house. She came back to where Ryan still stood.

"I didn't contradict your order, no matter what motivated it, for the sake of plantation discipline. But I depend on Zeke to oversee every aspect of the plantation work. If he stays up all night guarding the cotton house, he won't be able to do that tomorrow."

Ryan inclined his dark head in a small, mocking bow. "A point well taken, *Mistress*. So why don't you have Zeke select someone else to stand watch?"

"Why don't you mind your own business?" she said hotly. "Stop meddling in my life, as you've told me so often not to interfere in yours!"

She glared at him, wondering why she'd flared up like that. Was she deliberately trying to make him angry with her again? To ward off other feelings she didn't want to have to deal with? To keep from remembering he'd kissed her on the gallery not long ago? The chilly breeze increased, and she drew her cloak around her, shivering.

He guessed he deserved that. All the mockery gone from his voice he said, "You're cold. Go back to the house. I'll stay here and wait for Zeke."

"All right, I will." She turned away and headed for her mare, tethered to a tree. Her fingers fumbled as she untied Sable and mounted.

Swaying tiredly in the saddle, she rode off up the oyster-shell lane. Just ahead, to her left, beside a big oak tree, a metallic-looking gleam appeared. Calista turned for a better look, but saw nothing. Only her imagination, she told herself, and the fitful moonlight. But she felt a shiver down her spine. In a few moments, she heard another horse's hooves behind and relief shot through her. Ryan. She slowed to a walk.

"Why didn't you question Zeke further about the fire?" he asked as he came alongside. Why was he doing this? He didn't give a damn if all of Meadowmarsh burned!

Calista's hands tightened on the reins, her relief at his presence fading. "I don't want to talk about it."

"Zeke knew more than he told," Ryan insisted, wondering what demon drove him on. "We both know that."

The interminable, worrisome day and night caught up with her. She had to be alone! She couldn't deal with any more problems, think of any more solutions. She kicked her startled mare hard, and Sable took off.

Ryan watched her flying figure in astonishment. She was riding as if the very devil were after her. Chagrin hit him. Maybe she did feel that way about him. He couldn't blame her. He shouldn't have kept on at her, not tonight, when she was so obviously exhausted.

He wouldn't try to catch up. He'd let her go. Best to leave things where they stood. She was right. He had no business meddling in her plantation affairs. And he had no desire to do so. He'd never do it again.

He heard the diminishing sound of her horse's hooves ahead of him, and then he heard something else. A horse's startled whinny rent the dark night, followed by a sharp cry. *Calista's voice.* His gut tightened. He kicked his horse into a gallop.

Rounding the same bend where he'd met Gideon a few weeks ago with news of his father's illness, he reined his mount in quickly and swung himself off. In the dimness, he made out Sable still galloping ahead, but Calista lay prone across the lane, unmoving, her black hair, loosened from its knot, spread around her. Something must have startled the mare, and she'd fallen.

He knelt beside her, fear making his hands shake. Should he turn her over or might that injure her more? "What happened?" he asked urgently. "Are you all right?"

A small moan came from her, making him weak with relief. She was at least partly conscious. She moved, trying to turn over, and Ryan helped her, sucking in his breath when he saw her face. Her eyes were closed, and she had a large, bleeding lump on her forehead.

"Calista," he said, his voice shaking. "Can you hear me?"

She moaned again, but gave no indication she heard him. Fear snaked through him again at her deathly pallor. He sat back on his heels, thinking. He didn't know if anyone at the house was aware of the fire. He and Calista had been in too big a rush to wake the others.

Probably they weren't, or they would have been here by now. He couldn't count on help. He had to get her back to the house. And he dared not jostle her on the horse. He tied his mount's reins so the horse wouldn't entangle itself, then gave him a hard slap on the rump.

"Go home!" he commanded. The startled animal bounded up the lane. Ryan wrapped Calista's cloak around her as best he could, then slid a hand under her neck, the other beneath her knees, and gently lifted her into his arms.

It wasn't far to the house from here, thank God. He adjusted his precious burden and set off up the lane, carefully easing his feet down with each step so he wouldn't jar her.

He murmured a frantic, hasty prayer—the first time he'd prayed in a long, long time. And he was too worried about his wife to even marvel at that fact.

The gray light of dawn came feebly through the windows of Calista's room. Her face was still as white as the lace-edged pillow on which she lay, the ugly lump on her forehead standing out starkly. But at least she'd regained consciousness. A wave of relief swept over Ryan as he stood at her bedside. Now, she seemed to be in a half-dazed state, alternately waking and sleeping. At the moment, her eyes were closed, her fringe of black lashes smudging her pale cheeks.

Everyone except Ryan and Lucinda had been sent from the room while the doctor examined Calista. Thankfully, no bones were broken. But Dr. Norman had frowned as he carefully moved and flexed her swollen and bruised ankle, then moved away to let Lucinda arrange the bedclothes again.

Now, Andrew, Gabrielle, and Leora were back in the room, anxiously hovering near the door.

Dr. Norman turned first to Lucinda, then Ryan, including them both in what he had to say. "The lump on her head isn't serious. Her ankle isn't broken, but it's a bad sprain. She must stay off her feet for at least two weeks. A month would be better."

Calista's eyes fluttered open at his words, alarm in their emerald depths. She struggled to sit up, but Dr. Norman restrained her.

Ryan saw perspiration break out on her forehead, and she winced. He winced inwardly himself at her obvious pain, and guilt hit him again. If he hadn't kept on badgering her, she wouldn't have taken off on her horse, she wouldn't have fallen . . .

"I *can't* do that!" she told the middle-aged doctor. "The rest of the cotton has to be sent to Beaufort during the next couple of weeks. And the listing needs to be started. I have to—"

"You have to stay off this ankle," the doctor interrupted, his voice firm, "or you'll damage it further. Then it will take months, not weeks, to heal."

He turned to Ryan. "I trust you to see that your wife follows my orders."

A wry smile tilted Ryan's lips as he remembered his furious demand that Calista obey him the day his father took ill. And her instant rejoinder, mocking him with her reminder of the unusual circumstances of their marriage. But Dr. Norman obviously didn't know this.

He heard someone's footsteps, and Andrew moved up beside him. "Calista," he said earnestly. "I would be more than happy to act as overseer in your place."

Her eyes took on an anxious look, and her face seemed to pale even more. She managed a tremulous smile at her brother-in-law. "Thank you, Andrew," she murmured, "that's most kind of you, but I wouldn't expect—"

"It is nothing," Andrew interrupted. "I insist."

Calista's eyes had fluttered closed. She looked hurt and exhausted, Ryan saw, his guilt and anxiety deepening. Before he could suggest they leave her alone, Dr. Norman did it for him.

"Mrs. Burke needs quiet and rest," he said. He gazed directly at Ryan as he closed his medical bag and picked it up. "See that she gets it."

Ryan nodded stiffly, feeling like the worst kind of imposter. "Of course."

"We'd better leave," Gabrielle whispered to Andrew. He nodded, frowning, and followed her out, Leora on Gabrielle's other side.

"I'll look in on her tomorrow," Dr. Norman told Ryan, "when I see your father."

Ryan nodded again, and the doctor left the room. Ryan glanced at Lucinda. "I'll go, too."

Calista's eyes flew open again. "Wait, I—I need to talk to you," she whispered, the distressed look back in her eyes. She turned to Lucinda. "Aunt Lucie, would you mind . . ."

The other woman patted her hand. "Of course, dear. I'll leave you with your husband." She smiled at Ryan and left, closing the door behind her.

Ryan frowned after her. He admired and liked Lucinda, but did the woman think that addressing him as Calista's husband in such a manner would change their farce of a marriage into the real thing?

He turned back to Calista. Her eyes were still open, fixed intently on him.

"I need your help, Ryan." She flinched at having to say those words. She'd thought never to have to beg him for aid.

But the cotton must be taken to market. It was already contracted for, and the buyers were expecting it. Zeke could manage without her supervision. But after tonight's unexplained fire, the uneasiness, the feeling of things not being right, she'd felt since returning from Charleston had increased a hundred-fold. She braced herself for his answer.

As she'd expected, an ironic smile formed on Ryan's mouth. "I can't believe my ears," he drawled. "You're requesting *my* help when my brother has already volunteered?"

He was going to make this difficult. She flushed, grimacing as a movement of her injured ankle made a sharp pain shoot up her leg.

Ryan caught both actions, and his conscience smote him. It was mostly his fault she was hurt, he reminded himself. And whatever help she needed from him would be minor.

She hadn't liked it when he'd merely given Zeke an unthinking order tonight. She'd much rather accept Andrew's aid, even though he was still puzzled at her seeming alarm when his brother had stepped forward.

"I'm sorry," he said, simply and sincerely. "Go on."

Her flush deepened. She gave him a direct look. "I appreciate Andrew's offer." She paused, not quite knowing how to say this. Ryan knew nothing of her troubles with Andrew because of his too-eager, too-take-over attitude and methods. She'd have to be blunt.

"Andrew tries to run things too rigidly. He won't leave

the workers alone to do their jobs. He tells them every move and then checks to see that they're doing it exactly as he ordered."

Ryan stared at her, an uneasy feeling crawling up his spine. "What do you want me to do about it?" he asked, just as bluntly.

"I'd like for you to go along with Andrew, see that he leaves Zeke alone. Zeke knows exactly what needs to be done. He's done this for years."

Ryan barely stopped the refusal trying to explode from his mouth. Damnation! He wanted nothing to do with her plantation. She knew that. He wasn't going to do this; he'd get someone else; he'd . . .

His chaotic thoughts stopped as he saw the imploring look in her beautiful eyes. Double damnation! She was in a bad situation and had no one else to turn to but him.

Even though he'd been unaware of Andrew's interference here, he well knew his brother's headstrong ways. He didn't for a minute think Calista exaggerated the trouble Andrew could cause at this crucial time.

His mouth pressed together, and he frowned fiercely. Seconds ticked by while they looked at each other. Finally, he expelled an impatient breath. "I will do as you wish."

Calista's lips parted in a relieved smile. "Oh, thank you, Ryan!"

She knew he was only doing this under duress, that he hated the idea, but she didn't care. All that mattered to her now was getting the crop to market, starting to prepare the fields for next year's crop—and making sure nothing else happened.

Her heart quailed at that thought. Surely the fire was just an accident! It *had* to be. A hazy memory swam into her mind. A glimmer beside a tree along the lane last night, then a few minutes later something . . . white? A fluttering piece of cloth? Tossed at Sable's head? The mare had reared. She'd fallen . . . just as she fell she'd heard a soft, triumphant laugh . . .

Chilled, Calista forced those blurry images back. No, that couldn't be. She'd hurt her head; she'd imagined all that. Sable had only stumbled, and she'd slid off. No one here on Meadowmarsh would try to harm her. But just the same, she'd rest easier knowing the reins of the plantation rested in Ryan's capable hands.

His face didn't lighten at her words of gratitude. "You know I left this life years ago. I have no experience at overseeing plantation operations. Andrew is much more knowledgeable than I."

She nodded, daring a small smile. "I'm aware of that. Actually, Zeke could probably manage alone, but after last night's fire . . ."

So, she, too, wasn't satisfied the fire had been an accident. Ryan expelled another irritated breath.

"All right, I'll do it. And now I'll leave you to rest." He turned and left the room.

She watched him go, his back very straight in his ruffled white shirt, his black hair catching a gleam of candlelight. He hated the task she'd maneuvered him into. But Calista knew he'd do it to the best of his ability.

Her husband was honest and trustworthy. He also had a kind heart—even though he tried to hide that fact. He'd never leave anyone who was hurt and in pain to suffer. She'd found that out when he'd carried her to the house last night, up the dark, winding road.

Without warning, her heart turned over and tenderness spread through her. She marveled at this strange feeling and what it meant, refusing for a long moment to admit the answer to her consciousness.

But finally she must. She could deny it no longer. In spite of all that had happened between them, in spite of every evidence that Ryan cared nothing for her, she'd fallen in love with her husband. When it had happened, she didn't know, but the fact remained.

She loved Ryan Burke. And he wanted nothing as much as to be free of her and her plantation as soon as possible.

Chapter Fifteen

"That bale needs to be tied down tighter," Andrew told Zeke, his voice officious as he looked over every inch of the loaded flatboat. A strong gust of wind buffeted the boat, making it rock.

"Yes'suh, Mistuh Andrew," Zeke said.

Even though Zeke had stood watch over the cotton house all night, only getting a few hours sleep this morning, he looked alert, Ryan noted. And there'd been no more attempts at a fire.

Zeke turned away to do Andrew's bidding, but not before Ryan saw the flash of annoyance cross his face. After having watched Zeke direct the field hands as they had loaded the boat, Ryan realized how good the driver was at his job. He commanded respect and obedience without once raising his voice. Andrew should be able to see that, too. But he didn't.

Zeke was irritated with Andrew, although the driver hid his feelings well. Ryan didn't blame him. Since he and Andrew had begun working together this morning, he'd been tempted to wring his brother's neck at least a dozen times.

If Andrew had managed the hands on his own plantation this way, it must have hurt productivity and caused many problems.

And Ryan couldn't reprimand him in front of the field hands, although it got harder not to do so every minute. Talking to Andrew privately would doubtless do no good either. His brother possessed a great deal of pride and was still young enough to get offended easily. Too, as far as plantation matters went, Andrew was the one with the experience. He'd probably tell Ryan to mind his own business.

His wife had gotten him involved in a situation with no solution, short of ordering Andrew back to the house. Or walking off himself, which sorely tempted him. He watched his brother make another circuit of the flat, checking everything for the dozenth time.

Ryan swore inwardly. He couldn't take two weeks of this. But he couldn't quit, either. He'd promised Calista, and he was a man of his word.

"The flat looks well-packed." Ryan stepped up beside his brother, trying to keep the impatience out of his voice. "Shall we let Zeke get underway? After all, he must make the tide to reach Beaufort today. And a storm may be brewing."

Frowning, Andrew turned to Ryan. "I'm well aware of that, Brother. But you admit to knowing nothing about plantation procedures. It's up to me to see that everything is done properly."

Ryan's slim store of patience evaporated. "If you ran Ainsley Hall like this, no wonder you—"

"Andrew! Ryan!" A lilting, feminine voice called, breaking in on Ryan's rejoinder.

Both men turned toward the source of the voice. Leora walked her horse toward them.

"I wanted to watch the cotton being loaded," she pouted, prettily. "But I guess I'm too late."

Ryan gave her a wry smile in return. Couldn't the girl think of a better excuse to seek Andrew's company than that? But he was glad she'd interrupted.

No doubt he and Andrew would by now be into a rousing argument, right here at the docks, with half-a-dozen workers as interested spectators. And that would have played hell with the already-shaky solidarity between them.

"Yes," Andrew answered stiffly. He gestured toward the loaded boat, Zeke and three other hands atop it. "It's all ready to go."

Ryan let out a sigh of relief. Leora's arrival had done another bit of good. The boat should make Beaufort today after all.

"Perhaps tomorrow I can watch. Would you help me dismount?" Leora asked Andrew prettily.

He frowned, hesitating. "Of course," he said finally, walking over to her.

Surprised at his brother's reluctance, Ryan motioned to Zeke to get underway. With a relieved smile, Zeke picked up his pole, the field hands their oars, and the boat moved away from the dock, out into the creek.

What had happened between Andrew and Leora on yesterday's plantation tour? Leora was still obviously infatuated with Andrew, but his brother's attitude was now wary. He touched Leora as little as possible while helping her down from her mount.

But then their glances met and lingered, and that told all. Andrew might be trying to avoid Leora, but not because he wanted to.

"It's almost dinner time," Ryan said. "We'll wait until afterwards to move the cattle to another cotton field."

Leora's dark eyes brightened. "Oh, could I go with you?" she asked, glancing from Ryan to Andrew.

Andrew shook his head, avoiding her eyes. "No, I don't think that would be a good idea."

The glimmering of a plan came to Ryan. Leora was a city girl, through and through, used to parties and entertainment. If she saw first-hand how a plantation was run, discovered that the owners spent most of their time supervising the work, it should do a lot to discourage her interest in Andrew.

"I don't see why not." Ryan gave Leora an affable smile. "We'll all go after dinner." Out of the corner of his eye, he saw Andrew's glower, but ignored it.

The cattle were placed in movable pens on the cotton fields, where they spent a few days in each one, trampling down the old plants and softening and fertilizing the soil. It was a messy, smelly operation.

Leora should quickly get enough. It would be a good start toward disillusioning her about the glamour of plantation life. Her interest in Andrew might die a swift death.

Ryan's mouth twisted. He could expect no help from Calista. She'd made that clear last night. And, to be honest, he couldn't blame her. He *had* been pretty overbearing when he'd told her not to meddle in his family affairs earlier.

Andrew rode ahead on the way back to the house, leaving Leora to ride beside Ryan. The girl kept up a lively conversation, mostly for Andrew's benefit, Ryan thought, torn between amusement and irritation. He had enough complications in his life without this added one.

The wind was coming up strong and cold, the sky darkening, he noticed, frowning. Would Zeke be able to get to Beaufort before the storm struck? If not, how much damage could it do to the load of cotton?

Ryan stopped in the sitting room doorway, surprise widening his eyes. Calista sat in her favorite Queen Anne chair, her injured ankle propped on a low footstool, her hair arranged to cover the lump on her forehead. He hadn't expected her to be downstairs this soon. She looked across the room and smiled at him. The smile lit her face. Her beauty made him catch his breath.

"Good afternoon, Ryan." Her voice came out much softer and warmer than she'd intended. She tried to ignore the way her heart sped up when Ryan walked through the door. Dressed in a plain white shirt and dark trousers, he looked just as handsome as he did in formal dress. Feeling heat in her cheeks, she hoped Ryan didn't notice.

She hadn't slept much last night. And she couldn't blame all of her restlessness on pain from her injuries. Trying to come to terms with her newfound love for her husband had caused most of her disquiet.

Pleasure joined Ryan's surprise. He couldn't deny he was glad to see her, glad she'd join them for dinner. He smiled back as he greeted her and the other two women, his irritation with the way the day had gone so far easing.

"I'm relieved there was no more trouble with the fire," Calista said, trying to make her voice sound as it normally did when she spoke to him.

But she was aware of Ryan's every movement. Her whole self seemed sensitized to him. It was a strange feeling, pain and pleasure mixed. "Did Zeke and the hands get off to Beaufort with another load of cotton?"

Her voice had lost its warmth and softness, Ryan noticed, only affability remaining. His pleasure evaporated, and his irritation returned.

Would he never learn her first and only concern was the plantation? Since at present he did her a favor, naturally she'd try to be agreeable.

"Yes, they did," Andrew said from behind him, coming into the room. "Never fear, I made sure the cotton was loaded and secured properly."

His voice sounded so pompous Ryan wanted to shake him. He settled for a frown, which Andrew didn't seem to notice as he seated himself on a settee beside Lucinda.

"That's wonderful." Calista fussed with a pillow to hide her own annoyance at Andrew's tone. She knew Ryan had suffered a trying time with him today. But it would only make things more difficult now if she insisted Andrew stay at the house and let Ryan take charge.

In addition, even if Andrew were overly bossy, he *did* know what needed to be done. She wasn't sure Ryan did since he'd been away from plantation life so long. She sighed inwardly. This seemed to be the best arrangement, even if far from satisfactory.

"And what are your plans for the afternoon?" She smiled at Andrew, then at Ryan, to make the question apply to both of them.

"We'll turn the cattle onto a new cotton field and set the hands to hoeing under the old plants in the one they've been in," Ryan answered before Andrew could.

Could that be a spark of interest she heard in his rich, deep voice? "That's fine." She nodded her approval.

The room was darkening, Ryan noticed, frowning. "We should have done this before coming up to dinner. The storm is moving in faster than I'd anticipated."

Calista threw a quick, surprised glance toward the front windows. "Why, yes, it does darken to storm, I fear. I hope Zeke makes it to Beaufort with the cotton. Of course, often these storms are localized."

Inwardly, she fumed, annoyed with herself. She'd been

so caught up in her lovesick fancies, she hadn't even noticed the coming storm!

"I'll see to the moving of the cattle now," Andrew said, rising. He waved his hand at Ryan before he could get up. "No, go ahead and have your dinner. *I* can tend to this."

"Oh, do let me come with you!" Leora jumped up from her chair, an eager expression on her pretty face.

Andrew stared at her in astonishment. "That would be entirely unsuitable, *Cousin* Leora," he told her stiffly, then turned and left the room.

The girl bit her lip as she stared after him, her eager look replaced with disappointment. Finally, she sat back down.

Ryan glared after him. The young pipsqueak! He'd grabbed at the chance to show Ryan up. Shocked, Ryan realized he felt as if his brother were his rival. That he had to compete with him. For what? Calista's approval?

Damnation! And his wife expected him to put up with this for two weeks? He couldn't do it, he fumed. He'd plead pressing work at his law office and have Zeke take him to meet the steamboat tomorrow.

Coward, his mind taunted him. *You're going to run back to Charleston and hide in your nice, quiet office? And leave your injured wife, who needs your help, to cope with all this? Not only the plantation, but your sick father upstairs?*

"Dinnah is served," Delphinia announced from the doorway.

No, just as he'd known last night, his conscience would make him stay here as long as necessary. Ryan rose, realizing Calista needed to be helped to the table. He went to her. Before he thought, he swept her up into his arms and walked toward the dining room.

Automatically, her hands went around his neck. She

stared up at him, hoping he couldn't feel the pounding of her heart. His strong hands beneath her knees, under her arms, felt so good she never wanted him to let her down.

"I could have had Junie and Delphinia assist me," she told him primly.

He gazed down into her brilliant green eyes. "You forget I carried you to the house yesterday when your mare threw you. That was a much longer journey than this."

She looked into the depths of his deep-blue eyes. Yes, she remembered that trip. She'd gone into and out of consciousness, very aware of his warm, strong arms holding her. She'd felt secure and safe.

She gave him an impish smile to hide her true feelings. "So it was. I'm surprised you are not down in the back today."

"You're not heavy," he told her, his voice softening. For a moment he forgot where they were, that Gabrielle and Lucinda and Leora stood behind them. He and Calista seemed alone in their own private world. The scent of mingled flowers and citrus that always seemed to cling to her drifted up to his nostrils.

He realized he'd stopped walking and stood halfway across the sitting room holding her. And they were looking into each other's eyes as if they'd never get enough of each other.

"Don't worry. My back is strong," he assured her, starting to walk again.

His tone was once more smooth and slightly ironic. A disappointed pang went through her. What had she expected? That Ryan's feelings for her and Meadowmarsh would change just because she'd foolishly fallen in love with him?

In the dining room, he eased her onto her chair, careful

not to bump her swollen ankle. "There you are." He gave her a smile that matched his voice and moved to the other end of the table.

Why should he change? Calista asked herself dully, sipping her wine. He'd told her from the start that his life in Charleston suited him perfectly. One morning of riding around Meadowmarsh wouldn't alter that. Most important, he still believed she'd tricked him into this marriage. He'd made that clear last night on the gallery.

The dinner was, as always, excellent. He was getting used to these wonderful meals. He'd have nothing to compare with this back at his small house in Charleston, with Arva cooking.

That didn't matter. He only wanted to get away from this island, to be his own man. To live his own life again. Somehow, his assurances rang hollow in his mind's ear.

Did he actually feel like this, now? Or was he just repeating by rote all the things he had since the first time he'd stepped onto Meadowmarsh's shores? Impatiently, he shrugged that errant thought off and turned his attention to his meal.

The room steadily darkened, so much so that Junie lit the candelabra over the table halfway through dinner. The storm hit with fury as they finished dessert. Lightning streaked across the sky, and thunder shook the house.

Frowning, Calista glanced at the dark windows streaming with wind-driven rain. "I do hope Andrew isn't caught out in this."

A flash of irrational jealousy hit Ryan, bringing a frown to his own face. Andrew was a grown man. He should be able to take care of himself by now.

Had she developed something more than friendly affection toward his brother during these weeks Andrew had been here? A vivid memory of that day they'd raced up to the house on horseback entered his mind. How lovely and vital Calista had looked—her hair coming loose, her cheeks flushed. And she'd given Andrew a secret smile . . .

His hand pressed his fork so hard the embossing on the handle dug into his fingers. He loosened his grip and smoothed out his frown. What was wrong with him? Those kinds of thoughts belonged to a callow boy during his first infatuation.

"Yes," Lucinda put in. "It's gotten much colder in the last hour. He could come down with fever if he got drenched."

Ryan pushed back his chair. "I'll check on Father; and if Andrew isn't back after that, I'll go see if everything is all right."

Calista gave him a relieved smile. "Oh, would you, Ryan?"

She didn't seem concerned if *he* got soaked, Ryan observed. Presumably, he was made of tougher stuff than Andrew. He bowed stiffly and left the dining room.

His father was awake, propped up in bed with a tray across his lap. He glanced up as Ryan entered the room, but no spark of interest lit his slack, pale face.

He hadn't eaten much, Ryan noticed. He didn't think his father ever did lately. He'd lost a lot of weight since his illness. "How are you, Father?" Ryan tried to make his voice cheerful.

Grimacing, Emory pushed the tray away. "How do you think I am, stuck in this bed day after day?"

"You're looking better." Ryan forced a smile. He knew his father had suffered a debilitating illness, but surely by now he should be starting to recover.

The other man scowled at him. "Don't bother lying to me. Both of us know I don't look a damn bit better. And I feel worse. I don't think that doctor knows what he's doing. He's bled me every day, and it hasn't helped a bit."

"Do you want me to send for another doctor? Perhaps the one you used at Ainsley Hall?"

His father's scowl deepened. "No, I don't. You know we can't afford any such thing. If it weren't for the charity of your *wife,* I wouldn't even have this bed to rot in."

Ryan fought down an angry reply. As usual, his father was managing to get Ryan's temper up with his sour disposition, but he wouldn't answer in kind. Not with Emory still so ill.

"You know I'd pay for another doctor, just as I am Dr. Norman," Ryan said stiffly. "And Calista is happy to have you here." He doubted that last statement, but since his father couldn't be moved yet, there was no help for the situation.

"Happy?" Emory's laugh was more bitter than his words had been. "Oh, yes, I'm sure she's overjoyed to have a sick old man on her ha—"

A deep, racking cough that shook his whole body interrupted the speech, making his tray tilt precariously. Ryan grabbed it before it fell, his brow knit with worry. He put the tray on a chest, then picked up a glass of water and held it to the older man's mouth.

"You'd better not talk anymore," Ryan said, replacing the glass. "I'll leave you to get some rest."

"Rest? That's all I've done, and it isn't helping a damn bit. I can rest when I'm dead. I want to get out of this bed! I want Andrew and me settled on our own plantation again!"

Irritation with his blindly stubborn parent overcame Ryan's concern for the other man's health. When would his father face up to reality? "That isn't likely to happen soon. You'll have to come back to my house in Charleston."

His father's pale face turned bright red, and he glared at Ryan. "Like hell I will!" he bellowed. "I've had enough of that miserable excuse for a dwelling!"

His outburst caused another fit of coughing, worse than the first. Alarmed, Ryan supported his father's head, offering him water again.

Damn! Why had he said that? Even if true, it was no time to remind his father of the unpleasant facts of his future life.

In a few moments the spasm passed and he shivered with cold. Ryan eased him back down on his pillow, pulling the quilt up to his chin. He unfolded another quilt at the foot of the bed and spread that over him, too.

"Can I get you anything else?"

Emory glared at him again. "Just get yourself out of my sight," he whispered hoarsely. "Send Andrew up."

"Yes, Father," Ryan said, his voice strained. He wouldn't upset his father more by telling him Andrew might be out in this storm somewhere. In any case his brother would be back soon. And he could calm Emory down when no one else could.

The other man's eyelids fluttered closed. He looked old and sick and exhausted. Ryan's conscience smote him. Why couldn't he be around his father for more than five minutes without their getting into an argument? He was sick; it was up to Ryan to tolerate his outbursts.

And he would, Ryan promised himself as he quietly left the room and went downstairs. From now on he'd hold his tongue if it killed him.

Lucinda came out of the sitting room just as he reached it, but he saw no one else in the room. Good. He didn't want to see Calista now. He didn't want to remember how soft and warm she'd felt in his arms when he'd carried her into the dining room. How odd and shaken he'd felt when their eyes had met in that long, long look.

Lucinda smiled at him. "How is your father?"

Ryan frowned. "Not very well. Shouldn't he be showing signs of improvement by now?"

"It takes longer to recover from perepneumonia. And he had a severe case," she told him.

"I know, but he's still coughing so much and eating very little."

"I'm sure he'll start perking up soon. And then he'll be all right before you know it." Lucinda wished she felt as certain as she sounded. She also didn't like the way Emory looked. Dr. Norman wasn't saying much, either— never a good sign. But no use worrying Ryan further.

Ryan let out a sigh of frustration, then found a smile for Lucinda. "Did Andrew return?"

"He came in while you were with your father, soaked to the skin and freezing, poor boy. He went upstairs to change. And Junie took him up a hot rum toddy along with his dinner."

"Good," Ryan answered, relieved. The storm had died down into a steady, hard rain. The field hands could do nothing else outside today. He hoped Zeke had outrun the storm or that, as Calista had said, it was localized and had missed them.

Lucinda seemed to read his mind. "Zeke will come to the house when he returns from Beaufort. I just hope the storm didn't hit the flatboat and capsize it."

Ryan had been concerned about damage to the cotton, but he hadn't thought of a complete loss, not only of property, but possibly lives. His frown deepened. "Is that likely? The boat looked very sturdy."

She put her hand on his arm, smiling reassuringly. "It is. Don't fret. I'm sure nothing happened to it."

She glanced up the stairs, then back at him, her smile fading. "Calista went to her room with a headache. I suppose she isn't over the head injury yet. It worries me."

It worried him, too, Ryan admitted. He fought a strong desire to check on her. No, he wouldn't. She was probably asleep. "Dr. Norman said all she needed was plenty of rest."

Lucinda nodded regretfully. "I'm sure you're right. After all, the accident only happened last night. She shouldn't have come downstairs so soon."

Ryan couldn't quite hide the smile pulling his mouth upward. Lucinda was at it again. She'd use any excuse to try to get him and Calista in the same room together.

Alone. That thought reverberated in his mind, conjuring images he didn't want to dwell on. "I'm going out on the veranda to watch the storm."

She looked startled. "Oh, my, don't do that. It's cold, and the wind is still blowing hard. We don't want you to take a chance of coming down with fever, too."

As well as Andrew, she meant. And then there would be no one to oversee the running of the plantation while his wife was incapacitated. Of course, there was no reason to think Andrew would get sick.

"The storm's changed direction," he pointed out. "The wind's blowing against the back of the house now."

She frowned, still not convinced. "Don't stay out there too long."

"I won't." He turned and headed purposefully for the front entrance. He'd stay as long as it took to cool off. He passed Junie in the hall, and she stared at him in amazement as he pulled open the massive door.

It *was* cold outside. The temperature had dropped a good deal in the last hour. He walked to the railing and took deep breaths of the damp, bracing air, enjoying the feel of the raindrops that splattered onto his arms and chest.

Even after the long dinner, even after the upsetting scene with his father, his body still throbbed with heat just from the memory of those moments when he'd held Calista in his arms.

He couldn't forget how she'd felt, so soft and warm and sweet, or that look they'd exchanged. That long, long look. He brought his hands down on the cold, wet railing in frustration.

Every day, every hour, he stayed here on this island, he was becoming more ensnared in her spell—no matter how much he tried to convince himself a real marriage between them would be impossible. He didn't trust her motives, feared the control she might come to have over him. When he was with her, none of that seemed to matter. It would be damned hard to leave here in a few weeks.

And he was no longer certain he wanted to go.

Chapter Sixteen

The short, cold winter day was almost over, dusk beginning to fall. Zeke watched as the women and children knelt on the ground, shelling the weekly ration of corn. Some used mortars made of big logs, hollow at one end. Others merely rubbed one cob against another.

His glance found Lotus, who used one of the makeshift mortars, and lingered. He hadn't talked to her about the fire yet, but he intended to this evening. He wasn't looking forward to it.

As if sensing his gaze, she looked up, her long, almond-shaped black eyes gleaming in the near twilight. She gave him a sly grin.

It made a cold chill race down his spine. For an instant he wondered, crazily, if she'd had something to do with Miz Calista's fall from her horse. No, of course not, he told himself. How could she?

Her grin fading, her eyes narrowing, Lotus returned her attention to her work.

At last the shelling was finished and the corn kernels

poured onto a big blanket spread on the ground. Zeke made quick work of dividing it, and the women placed their portions into woven pine straw and palmetto baskets.

As the women and children straggled off, Zeke caught Lotus's arm. "Wait a minute. I want to talk to you."

She gave him an unfriendly, sloe-eyed glance and shook his hand off. "What about? I ain't got time."

But Zeke wasn't to be put off. He grabbed her arm again. "Never mind that. Come on."

Lotus decided to let him lead her to his cabin. Lately, she'd spent more time with Ira than Zeke. Not long ago, that fact would have made him crazy with jealousy. She had to figure out how to get him that way again. She could feel her power over him fading.

Once inside, Zeke closed the door securely. Lotus sidled over and ran her hand down his body, lingering when she got below his belt.

He pushed her hand away, reluctantly. But it wasn't as hard to do as it would have been a few weeks before.

"What ailin' you?" Lotus asked petulantly.

Zeke decided to come straight to the point. No way to lead up to it. "You set that fire in the cotton house, didn't you?" he demanded.

Lotus tossed her head, an insolent smile curving her mouth as she remembered that night. Then the smile faded, her face hardening. That white woman was blessed with luck. The fall from the horse should have killed her! Why hadn't it?

She'd thought she'd never again have to look at the mistress's hated face, so much like that other face she loathed. Then the satisfied smile returned. It didn't matter. There'd be another time, another chance . . .

"Why you think I do somethin' like dat?" Should she tell him what she'd done to the mistress? Would that frighten him enough to bind him to her again?

He advanced on her. "That's what I want to know. *Why?*"

Her smile turned into a smirk. "Why you care if I burn dat old cotton? It ain't nothin' out of our pockets if it all burn."

"You a fool, you know that?" he asked her, his hands clenching at his sides. "If the cotton go, Mistress won't have no money for next year's crop. She have to sell some of the slaves, even. You might be one of them," he threatened.

She tossed her head again. No, she'd wait awhile to tell him. Tonight it would give her no advantage. "Still ain't nothin' to us. We have de gold and be out o' here befo' next year."

Zeke felt a hard knot form in his stomach. "Maybe we ain't gonna find no treasure."

"Don't you say dat!" Lotus said fiercely, her black eyes flashing. She advanced again, stopping when she was almost touching him. "You been actin' awful funny lately. Like you don't care if we find de gold."

He felt the heat from her body and began to sweat, gathering all his resources to resist her earthy pull. She was coming too close to the truth, and he couldn't weaken now. Somehow, he had to regain the upper hand with her.

"Course I care," he said, trying to put conviction into his voice. "But we just about digged up the whole island and we ain't found nothin' yet."

He'd halfway planned to tell her tonight about the chest he'd found; but now that the time was here, he couldn't bring himself to do it.

Lotus's beautiful face grew stubborn. "I ain't givin' up. Dat gold is here somewhere, and we bound to find it soon." She moved closer to him.

He backed up a few inches, even though he wanted to pull her down onto his pallet and bury himself deep within her body. But that was the way she kept her hold on him. He had to resist her.

"Then we better git to diggin'," he said.

Her face became sullen. "You know we cain't tonight. Dere's de big singin' and dancin'." As if in response to her words, the sound of banjos and drums started from the large open area in front of the row of cabins.

Zeke remembered Calista had given permission for this extra evening of celebration. Today the last load of baled cotton had been taken to Beaufort. Relief filled him at the reprieve. He turned away and opened the cabin door. "Let's get on over there," he said.

He hurried out, leaving the door open for her to follow. Frustrated, he realized he hadn't accomplished a thing. Even though certain now that Lotus had set the fire, he could do nothing about it because he had no proof. And his threat that she might be sold hadn't bothered her at all.

She was so caught up in the treasure hunting, so sure they'd eventually find pirate gold, nothing else mattered to her. Except her growing resentment and hatred of Miz Calista. He felt a cold chill at this thought.

Soon he'd have to tell Lotus and Ira about the chest he'd uncovered. *Or did he?* No one else knew about it. Maybe it didn't even hold any gold.

Ira was about ready to give up. Soon he'd leave the island. After that, Zeke could refuse to search anymore with Lotus. His ability to refuse her a few moments ago had strengthened him and, for the first time since their relationship had begun, he felt like his own man again.

If he never told, whatever the chest held could remain there, safely buried forever. And he could stay at Meadowmarsh.

* * *

SWEET ENCHANTMENT

Leora came out of her room just in time to see Delphinia, carrying a tray, pause before Andrew's door. She hurried down the hall.

"What do you have there?"

Delphinia smiled at her. She liked Miss Leora. She was friendly and never acted hateful or uppity with her or Junie. "Some of de chicken soup we had fo' dinnuh. Mistuh Andrew need nourishment. He mighty weak since de fever."

"Yes, he is," Leora agreed. She reached for the tray. "Here, I'll take it in. You must have a lot to do."

The other woman tried to keep her astonishment from showing. Miss Leora knew it wasn't proper for a young lady to go into a gentleman's bedchamber alone, even if he was as sick as a dog. She shrugged mentally. It wasn't any of her concern what the white folks did. "Yes'm," she said, giving the tray up.

The tray was heavier than Leora had expected. It held a silver-domed bowl as well as a china cup and small teapot and some spicy plum preserve tarts.

She tiptoed into the room and placed the tray on the chest next to Andrew's bed. His eyes were closed, and he was pale. But he looked better than yesterday, she thought. He'd had a raging fever that had lasted several days after his drenching in the storm. She'd been numb with worry.

But that was almost two weeks ago. She smiled down at him tenderly. Oh, how she loved him! What could she do to make him realize he loved her, too? She knew he kept her at a distance only because he had no money and her parents would never give their consent for them to marry.

Well, they didn't *have* to give their consent. There were other ways of getting married. Her smile widened. Marie, her best friend, had eloped with her sweetheart, just as

Calista had tried to elope with Timothy. It had been over a week before Marie's parents had found them. So they had had to let the marriage stand. After all, as Summer had said, Marie might have already been with child.

As for the money—she had some of her own. Papa had been most generous on her last birthday, only a month ago, and she hadn't spent any of it.

Andrew's eyelids fluttered open. His heart skipped a beat as he saw Leora standing by his bed wearing a pale blue gown that defined her figure, a sweet smile on her pretty face. Why was she here, alone with him in his room? With the door closed, too.

"You'd better leave," he said, trying to put authority into his voice.

"I just brought you some soup," Leora said, her eyes wide and innocent. "Here, I'll help you sit up to eat it." She lifted his head and positioned the pillow behind it. Her fingers itched to smooth the hair back from his face, but she guessed she'd better not do that. Not yet, anyway.

Andrew pushed himself up a little farther, still feeling the touch of her warm hands on his neck. He wouldn't think of that, he told himself resolutely as Leora arranged the tray across his lap.

"There!" she said, smiling. "All set." Touching his neck had felt so good. She wanted him to kiss her again, as he had the first day she'd arrived here. Growing a little breathless at that thought, she lifted the domed lid off the soup bowl and a savory aroma floated up.

Andrew breathed deeply, and, to his embarrassment, his stomach rumbled loudly. For the first time since he'd gotten the fever, he was ravenous. "That smells delicious."

"Oh, it is," she assured him. "We had it for dinner. And Junie made a wonderful dessert." She poured him a cup of the tea, added honey, and stirred it.

Mesmerized, Andrew watched the movements of her slender, deft fingers. She had such pretty hands, so soft and white. What would her hands feel like touching him in intimate places? "You shouldn't have brought this up," he told her, gathering his senses.

"Oh, Delphinia brought it up; I only brought it *inside,*" she said, deliberately misunderstanding his meaning. "She and Junie are always so busy. I thought I'd help a little."

She moved back and found a chair by the bedside. Demurely folding her hands in her lap, Leora watched as Andrew picked up his soup spoon and began to eat.

Andrew decided not to argue anymore. His stomach quivering from hunger and something else he shouldn't think about, he made quick work of the soup and then attacked the dessert. Sipping the hot tea, he smiled contentedly. "That was wonderful. Thank you."

Leora got up. "I'll take the tray out of your way." She put it back on the chest, then turned to him. "You look much better today, Cousin Andrew." Her voice was as demure as her posture had been a few minutes ago. But her eyes twinkled.

"Here, let me fluff your pillow." One of her slender hands slid behind his neck again, lifting his head, lingering longer than necessary as she pulled the pillow away.

She put it on the edge of the bed and pushed and pounded vigorously. Andrew hastily lifted his head so she wouldn't have to touch him.

Leora replaced the pillow, patting it into shape. "Now, isn't that better?" she asked him brightly. She stood right against his bed, so close he could smell her faint scent of violets. Her hands lay on the top of the quilt.

"Yes, thank you, *Cousin* Leora." Stressing their only-by-marriage relationship didn't help a bit, Andrew realized, feeling his body hardening. His hand closed over one of hers. She didn't move away, just gave him another of those warm, melting smiles, then turned her hand over under his, her fingers tracing circles in his palm.

He drew in his breath. Her boldness shocked and inflamed him. She leaned over the bed, her movements making her breasts move enticingly. Andrew swallowed. He reached for her and pulled her close, his mouth eagerly finding her willing lips.

The kiss was as sweet as the first one. Sweeter. It made him want more. It made him want to pull her down under him on the bed. He pushed her away with his last remaining will power. "You must leave! What if someone came in and found us?"

Leora slowly moved away from him, her smile satisfied. "And what if they did? It wouldn't be the end of the world!" She picked up the tray and, giving him one last smile, moved across the room.

At the door she turned and looked back. "Do you need anything else, *Cousin* Andrew?" Her black eyes twinkled merrily. A smile tugged at the corners of her mouth.

Andrew quickly shook his head. "No, that will be quite sufficient," he answered, trying to make his voice brisk and unconcerned. He wondered uneasily what they'd started, and where it would lead. One thing he knew for sure now. Leora wasn't giving up on him.

And he knew something else, too. He couldn't forget Leora, no matter what her parents thought of the Burke family.

"Thank you, Delphinia. The tea was most enjoyable." Calista smiled at the servant. After nearly two weeks of physical inactivity, she was beginning to fret.

Her eyes strayed to the door. It was late afternoon— time for Ryan to come, to report on his day. Tension hit her stomach at that thought. Their time together was exquisite torment.

Delphinia still lingered, and Calista glanced at her again. The young woman looked fidgety and anxious. "Did you want to talk to me about something?"

"Yes'm, I did," Delphinia admitted. She paused, then blurted out, "Gideon and me wants to git married." There, it was finally out. Delphinia relaxed. Once she and Gideon were safely married, she could quit worrying about that maid of Miz Leora's.

A wide smile lit Calista's face. "Why, that's wonderful! I suppose you want to have the ceremony soon?"

"Yes'm," Delphinia said again, trying not to let too much eagerness show.

"It's too cold now to have it outdoors in the orchard, so how about the dining room? We'll plan a nice feast. Let's say two weeks from now?"

Tomorrow would have suited Delphinia better, but she knew she couldn't say so. "Dat be fine," she agreed, giving Calista a broad grin.

Would this be a good time to tell the mistress about what Lotus and Ira and Zeke were doing at night? She considered a moment, then decided against it. Of course, she could tell Maussa Ryan . . .

No, she wouldn't do that, either. This was something Miz Calista needed to know first. Even if Maussa Ryan was taking hold lately just as if he planned to stay here for good. And that would be the best thing that ever happened. He'd turned out to be a good man, after all.

"Then I'll start planning for it." Calista was certain that something else was bothering Delphinia, but the girl wasn't ready to tell her about it yet. Could it have anything to do with the unrest she felt here on her island? For an instant, a picture flashed through her mind. A white cloth fluttering . . . Sable rearing. Quickly, she forced it away.

She'd only imagined that, because of her head injury. Sable had stumbled, and she'd slid off. No matter what was wrong here, why would anyone want to hurt her?

She'd be back at her usual duties in a day or so, she told herself. That's what she needed. This forced inactivity gave rise to foolish fancies.

"Thank you, Miz Calista." Delphinia scooped up the tea tray and walked across the room. Almost at the door, she stopped abruptly.

Ryan stood framed in the open doorway. "Good afternoon, Maussa Ryan," Delphinia said, giving him a beaming smile. Lawsy, he was just what Miz Calista needed, whether she knew it or not.

"Afternoon, Delphinia." Ryan smiled back, feeling the now-familiar tension grip him. These late afternoon sessions grew harder and harder to get through. *No, be honest,* he told himself. *They are torture.* Yes, but a sweet torture.

His wife, sitting on top of the quilt, hastily arranged her skirts and pulled another quilt up over her legs. He was sure she, too, felt it.

"You're looking well," he said, smiling at her as he walked across the room. She looked more than merely "well." She looked flushed and rosy, as if she'd just awakened from a nap. She looked sublimely kissable. He seated himself in a chair by her bed.

She sighed, making a face. "I'm feeling very well. And my ankle is fine, too. Now, all I have to do is convince Dr. Norman."

And it couldn't be soon enough for her. She didn't know how she could take many more of these sessions alone with Ryan. She pushed away the knowledge she could stop them now. All she had to do was make sure she was up from the rest Dr. Norman insisted she take every afternoon and downstairs by the time Ryan arrived.

Ryan had obviously just come in from the fields. His hair was mussed, and the cool wind had whipped color into his face. He'd taken off his cloak, which left him in a plain white shirt and dark trousers. As always, in his presence, her heart beat faster.

"It's been almost two weeks," Ryan agreed. Two weeks ago, no one could have made him believe he'd assume overseeing this plantation when Andrew fell ill. But he'd had no choice. And doing the job alone was considerably easier than trying to work with his overly fussy brother.

In spite of his deliberately distracting thoughts, he felt his trousers becoming uncomfortably tight. He hoped Calista didn't notice.

"I trust the last load of cotton got off all right." She carefully kept her eyes focused a few inches to the left of Ryan's face.

"Yes, Zeke made the early tide and got back just a little while ago." She wasn't looking directly at him. Didn't she want their glances to meet?

"Good." Calista gave Ryan a wide, relieved smile. "Even if there have been no more fires, or any other trouble, I'm glad it's over, the crop safely marketed for the year."

"Yes." From below, in the quarters, the strains of banjoes and fiddles drifted faintly up. "I can hear the celebration beginning."

Her radiant smile did nothing for the state of his trousers. He hastily tried her trick, looking to the side of her face.

True, there had been no more fires or overt trouble, but now that he worked on the plantation every day, he sensed something not quite right in the atmosphere. Lotus's face swam briefly into his mind. He didn't trust the woman, and it seemed that at least once a day he encountered her. And every time, she gave him that seductive look. He didn't like it—he didn't like *her*. But this was no time to talk to Calista about it.

"And most of it was fine grade," he said instead. "This Sea Island cotton is impressive."

"My parents improved the strains by experimenting with new seeds, and I plan to do the same."

Her mind was only half on the plantation, she realized, shocked, trying to shake off her reactions to Ryan. She cast about for a new subject.

"Did the hands get the Irish potatoes planted?"

"Yes. And after that, we started running out the land." Ryan listened to himself in amazement as the heretofore unknown Sea Island terms came out of his mouth as if he'd been born and raised here on Meadowmarsh.

"Oh, good," she murmured, still trying not to look directly at Ryan. He was just too distracting. "Are you getting used to our ways of doing things by now?"

He smiled wryly. "Driving stakes to mark off each field worker's 'task' still seems odd, but the system appears to work very well."

"Yes, it does. The hands get their allotted job done as fast as possible so they'll have the rest of the day free to do what they want. Most of the women tend a garden patch and raise chickens and hogs. The men spend a lot of time fishing."

Their glances met, and Calista quickly looked away. She knew she rattled on to keep Ryan unaware of how he affected her.

"It's a far cry from the way most plantations are run on the mainland."

Ryan finally understood her tension was as great as his own. That realization did nothing to ease his torment.

"It's also a more efficient way, because the workers

are content and happy. We encourage them to be as independent as possible."

She loved the way Ryan's black hair curled on the back of his neck . . .

He gave her another wry smile. "Considering they're not free people, that seems a contradiction in terms."

She probably didn't realize her shining dark hair had come loose from its knot and was curling around her rosy face . . .

"Not really. They're free in many ways. They can sell their produce and stock in Beaufort, or to me, at market price. Or trade for molasses and extra beef. We buy all our eggs from the Negroes."

Her fingers ached to comb through his hair, feel the crisp curls wind around her fingers . . .

"The way of life here is so different from that on the plantation where I grew up, there's really no comparison."

Her gown had the first two buttons undone, for comfort during her rest, he supposed. He was sure she'd forgotten that. A vivid mental picture of how she'd looked that day at the lagoon flashed through his mind. His trousers tightened even more.

"That's why I love it so much here," she said softly. "Why I could never live anywhere else in the world."

A muscle flexed in Ryan's strong jaw. His black mustache gleamed, and the cleft in his chin seemed more pronounced. He'd looked like that when he'd bent over her at the lagoon that day . . .

"I can understand that," Ryan agreed. Her soft words touched him somewhere deep inside, made the tender feelings he'd had from the first for this woman surface again.

Somehow, Ryan was on his feet; somehow, he was standing next to her. She let her glance meet his again, and this time she didn't look away. Nor did he. Calista made a small, involuntary movement, toward the center of her bed. She wasn't aware she'd made that innocently welcoming move.

But Ryan was. He sat down on the edge of the bed, his glance still locked with hers. He could feel his heart pounding so hard he wondered if she could see it moving his shirt.

"Calista," he breathed. He ached to pull her into his arms, to crush her against his chest until their heartbeats mingled, until they couldn't tell where one left off and the other began. He'd been a fool to think he could resist her. He no longer wanted to try.

She reached out to him first, her hand moving to the back of his neck. Just as she'd imagined, his hair curled crisply around her fingers. She moved her hand to the front of his neck, up to his firm chin, her fingers tracing the outline of the cleft.

"Calista," he said again, hoarsely. He pushed her gently back on her pillow, much as he'd pushed her down on the soft grass of the lagoon that day. But no longer did that oft-remembered scene send bittersweet thrills through him.

No, today all the feelings rushing through him were purely sweet—and hot. She looked up at him from those emerald eyes, her full lips parted, as if she, too, remembered that day. And again welcomed his touch, his caress . . .

At last, each yearning mouth found the one it sought. Ryan groaned as the honey of her kiss flooded through him. He heard an answering sigh from her as her lips opened wider, anticipating the thrust of his tongue . . .

Dimly, he was aware of a noise outside the room, but it wasn't important. Nothing mattered but this moment he'd wanted for so long.

SWEET ENCHANTMENT

"Oh! Excuse me, I'm sorry."

Lucinda's surprised but pleased voice abruptly penetrated the sensual spell holding them in thrall. For a moment, Ryan's mouth stayed on Calista's, then he pushed himself away from her and stood.

The other woman had vanished. They were alone again. But in this household anyone could, and probably would, come barging in next.

Ryan looked down at Calista. She still lay where he'd left her, her lovely face flushed, her delectable mouth still half-open.

It was all he could do not to cross the room and close the door and lock it. But, as everyone knew, no one locked doors at Meadowmarsh. First he'd have to hunt up a key. The absurdity of that thought brought an ironic smile to his mouth.

"If it isn't a damned alligator, it's one of your family," he said before he thought, then could have kicked himself. Was he trying to get her angry? To defuse whatever was between them?

Her eyes met his again and she smiled, much as she had that day at the lagoon when she'd bared her breasts for him. An innocent, yet totally unembarrassed smile. His heart contracted painfully.

"Tonight, no one would disturb us," she told him softly.

A rush of feelings swept through him, desire mixed with tenderness and something else that he didn't give a name to wrapping the two together.

"Yes." He picked up her hand from the quilt top and brought it to his mouth. As he kissed the sensitive palm, he felt her tremble, echoing his own shudder. He put her hand back down.

"Tonight, no one will disturb us."

Chapter Seventeen

Was that the knob turning? Calista's eyes flew to her bedchamber door. No. A mixture of relief and disappointment went through her when she saw she'd been mistaken.

One lone candle flickered in the two-branched candelabra on the chest near her bed, giving a soft, muted light to the room. The wine-red curtains on the veranda doors securely closed the room into an intimate cocoon.

Not long out of a scented bath, Calista adjusted her bedgown for the dozenth time. Her hair cascaded down her back, not confined tonight to its usual thick braid. It felt strange and heavy against her neck.

She didn't know how she'd gotten through supper. Every time her glance crossed Ryan's, a ripple of mingled tension and anticipation racked her. Trying to make small talk in the sitting room, with Ryan only a few feet away, would have been impossible.

She'd excused herself early, pleading fatigue, which brought concerned inquiries from Leora and Gabrielle.

And a look from Lucinda that seemed to be more interested and speculative than worried.

Now, she was in her bed, waiting for her husband to come to her so they might at last enjoy their long-delayed wedding night. A blush suffused her face and neck at that thought.

Her eyes went to the small clock on the chest. It was getting late. After that interrupted kiss this afternoon, she'd been sure Ryan wanted this as much as she did. But as the hours had passed, her certainty had waned. What if he didn't come? Maybe he'd believed her when she'd said she was very tired . . .

A small noise at the door made her head jerk quickly toward it, then she drew in her breath. The knob *was* turning this time, slowly but unmistakably. It had to be Ryan. Lucinda or anyone else would have knocked.

She was propped up in the bed, the candle lit. Was that too brazen? Should she have been demurely settled down in a dark room, pretending to be asleep?

The door moved inward on silent hinges. Ryan stood framed in the opening for a moment before he just as quietly closed the door behind him.

He wore the same dressing gown as that night he'd come to the kitchen. She wondered if he wore anything beneath it. She swallowed at that thought. His black hair was rumpled as if he'd just run his hands through it. His glance encompassed the drawn curtains, the single candle.

Too late now for maidenly modesty, Calista decided. And besides, he already knew she was as eager for this as he. She cleared her throat. "Would you please lock the door?" She'd found a long-unused key in the top chest-drawer this evening.

Ryan looked startled, then a slow smile transformed his face. Strange, Calista thought, her heart skipping a beat, how few genuine smiles of pleasure he'd given her since they'd met. He inclined his head in a small bow, but not the mocking kind she was used to receiving from him.

"I will be delighted," he told her, his voice soft, yet vibrant. He turned to accomplish the small act.

The sound of the key turning in the lock seemed to echo through the room. Calista flinched. What if everyone else heard that sound and realized what it meant? She bit her lip, sliding down in the bed, moving back into the shelter of the pillow. Had she made the wrong decision? Was it too late to change her mind?

Ryan turned back around, the smile gone now, a look that took her breath away replacing it. Calista stopped her attempt to disappear beneath the bedclothes. Yes, it was far too late for that.

God, she was so beautiful, Ryan thought, as he approached the bed. The dim, flickering candlelight half-illumined, half-shadowed her face. Her luminous eyes stared into his. Her full red lips were parted, and the memory of that interrupted kiss this afternoon returned full force. Her bedgown, with its high neck and long sleeves, made her look like a little girl. Until his roaming gaze reached her swelling breasts.

His body hardened with a swiftness that startled him. His manhood became a throbbing ache, lusting for fulfillment. He took a few deep breaths, trying to slow his physical reactions. He didn't want this first time to be rushed.

At supper he'd seen her withdrawn gaze, her obvious reluctance to talk with him. *He'd* had no second thoughts. He'd allowed no thoughts at all to temper his desire. Soon after supper, she'd excused herself. He'd been in agony, wondering if she'd changed her mind, regretted her tacit invitation to her bed later that evening.

But one glance at her when he had opened the door

had relieved his mind of that fear. And she'd even found a key for the door. His lips curved upward in a smile as he looked at her, remembering again how she'd opened her dress for him at the lagoon. Once his bride made up her mind to something, shyness left her.

However, right now she seemed to be having a belated attack of doubt. He needed to reassure her, and pushing her down in the bed and giving in to the urge throbbing below his belly wouldn't accomplish that. Besides, he wanted to kiss her again, devour her with kisses . . .

He sat down on the edge of the bed, much as he had this afternoon, and reached for one of her small hands. "You are so beautiful," he murmured. For a long moment, they only looked into each other's eyes.

But soon that wasn't enough. Not nearly enough. He moved fully onto the bed, stretching out beside her, but not quite touching her yet. He would let her get used to his nearness first.

Calista felt the heat of Ryan's body; and knowing he was so close, yet still not touching her, made an ache begin in her most private part. She wanted him closer. Oh, yes, much closer. But, remembering her brazen behavior that day at the lagoon, she resisted her impulse to take the initiative and move closer to him.

No, that wasn't how properly brought up young women behaved. She'd wait. Accordingly, she lay breathlessly still, waiting for Ryan's next move.

Was she afraid of him? Ryan wondered, checking his strong urge to gather her into his arms. Did she regret her agreement to this? No, that couldn't be, his raging body insisted. *She wants you; go ahead. What are you waiting for?*

Ryan took a deep breath and let it out, then another. As much as he wanted her, he had to make certain this was what she also truly wanted. "Calista," he said, his voice low and vibrant, "if you aren't sure about this, just tell me. I'll leave."

Shock ran through her at his words. The very thought of his leaving widened her eyes with horror. "No!" she said before she could stop herself. "Of course I want you. Please don't go!"

The moment the last words were out of her mouth, she bit her lip in chagrin. She'd done it again. Oh, she was shameless, shameless. What did he think of her? She dared a glance at him.

He didn't look shocked at all. A tender smile curved his mouth, making the cleft in his chin deepen. The ache in her lower regions increased. "Then, come here, and let me love you," he whispered, holding out his arms to her.

Her heart almost stopped. *Let me love you,* he'd said. Could that mean he felt about her as she did him? She slid into his arms. She wasn't going to worry anymore about what was or wasn't proper to do with her husband on her at-last-arrived wedding night.

As her pliant body fitted itself against his own, Ryan's manhood leaped and hardened even more. His teeth clenched as he struggled to keep from pulling her under him, making her his. Instead, he lowered his head and found her waiting mouth with his own.

Calista opened her mouth to him, knowing what was coming and eager for it. His velvet tongue slid inside, finding the sensitive caverns never before explored. Tentatively, she let her own tongue do some venturing of its own.

Rewarded by Ryan's small gasp, she became bolder, drawing her tongue back to outline his lips lightly.

Oh, God, he couldn't take much more of this without exploding! And they'd just begun to make love! What a lover she was going to be! What he could, would teach her! A niggling thought crept into his mind. That sounded as if he planned to have her in his bed for more than just a few nights here.

He pushed it aside. Tonight, he refused to worry about anything except pleasing the exquisite woman beside him—and, in so doing, pleasing himself. His trembling fingers unbuttoned her gown. He pulled it off her shoulders, down past those rosy-tipped, ivory mounds he remembered so well.

Ryan's mouth found her breast, his tongue teasing first, circling the nipple; then he began to suckle. That same drawing sensation, from deep within her, made Calista gasp in amazed surprise and delight. She pressed down on the back of his head, pushing him closer to her, at the same time straining upward to meet the lower part of his body with her own.

All Ryan's good intentions evaporated. He couldn't go slow; he couldn't wait. Quickly, he pulled Calista's gown from her willing body. The flickering candlelight revealed her slender waist, her rounded hips, the shadowy dark triangle between her legs.

Calista felt her breath coming in shallow gasps as Ryan raised himself to dispose of his dressing gown. As it slid off his shoulders, she saw that he wore nothing beneath. Her gaze roamed over his muscled torso, which tapered to a flat stomach and slim hips. Then her gaze moved farther downward. His fully aroused manhood sprang out, and her eyes widened in startled shock.

Oh, my. She'd imagined this moment often since that time at the lagoon, but she'd never dreamed that a man looked like this. So *big* . . . how in the world could . . .

Ryan threw the dressing gown to the floor and moved over her, the length of his hard body pressing against the soft length of her own. God, she felt so good! Exactly as he'd imagined she would during those sleepless nights he'd spent since that time at the lagoon.

Go slow, he desperately told his eager body. *Don't scare her. This is her first time with a man.* He pressed closer against her, and her legs moved apart for him.

Calista swallowed. Why had she done that? She didn't want him to . . . no, she didn't. She was scared. He was too big . . . It would hurt her . . .

Ryan's mouth found hers again and covered it. She forgot everything but the wonder and magic of the kiss. Then she became aware she'd moved her legs even farther apart. And the throbbing ache inside her had intensified until it made her squirm. Her body urgently told her that what she needed to get rid of the ache was to let Ryan thrust his huge member inside her. She squirmed again, fighting against that idea. No, she couldn't.

Her writhing movements inflamed Ryan further. He groaned, knowing he could wait no longer. He reached downward and guided himself to the small, tight opening between her legs, just nudging her.

Calista gasped and tried to move away. "No, stop. It will hurt. It will . . ." she whispered, her trembling increasing.

Hearing the real fear in her voice, Ryan desperately held himself in check. "No, sweetheart," he whispered in her ear. "It's all right. I'll be gentle. It will only hurt for a moment."

Only hurt for a moment? Then it was all right for it to hurt? It wouldn't do something terrible to her. Absorbing his words, she relaxed enough to realize that the tip of Ryan's manhood, just barely inside her, felt good. Not merely good, it felt wondrous. The need began growing in her again, telling her it would feel even more wondrous if he were all the way inside her.

She wasn't sure of that, but still she inched her thighs apart a tiny bit more and heard Ryan's gasp. He moved deeper inside her. Her eyes widened at the sensations that created. She pulled Ryan's dark head down to her again and hungrily sought his mouth.

He groaned against her lips, and his body moved back from hers a little, then pushed into her again. But this time he didn't stop; he kept on pushing, until he was halted by something.

Ryan raised his head and looked at her. "All right, sweetheart, after this there will be nothing but pleasure."

Before she knew what he meant, he thrust hard against her. She felt a sharp pain, and the barrier gave way; and then he was inside her, fully, completely. Her mind had thought that was impossible; but oh, it had been wrong. Her body was right and Ryan was right, too. It had only hurt for a second. And now he filled her as she'd never known she needed to be filled until this moment.

He rested against her, then he lifted his head and looked at her. His blue eyes blazed with passion but they held concern, too. "Are you all right?" His rich voice was rough with desire, yet solicitous for her feelings.

Love swelled within her. She gave him a radiant smile. "Oh, yes, I'm fine." She almost laughed at the absurd understatement of those words. She reached to the back of his neck and pulled him to her again. "I'm *wonderful!*"

His arms tightened around her and hers around him until she hardly knew where one body left off and the other began. "Yes, you are wonderful, my darling," he whispered hoarsely in her ear.

Gently at first, he began to move within her; and instinctively, she answered his movements with age-old ones of her own. The tempo increased, and she felt something new building again within her core. Something more urgent and demanding than she'd ever felt before.

Clinging to Ryan as their movements became ever more frenzied, the need grew within her until she truly felt as if she were going to explode. Waves of intense pleasure flowed over her, bathing her in ecstasy. She heard herself moan; she heard herself cry out Ryan's name; then just at the moment of her most intense bliss, she felt him release his seed deep inside her in spasms of his own pleasure.

Ryan collapsed against her, his breathing ragged and harsh. His full weight was heavy, but she welcomed it. He felt so right there. She could stay this way forever. But too soon, he lifted his head and kissed her lingeringly, then moved off her to lie on his side and pull her close against him.

Wonder filled him. He was dazed with fulfillment and completion. He felt alive in every cell of his body—exhausted, yet revitalized. A wave of tenderness and something else—an unfamiliar, yet somehow right feeling—went through him, and he pulled Calista even closer.

Was this woman a witch? Had she truly bewitched him so that he could never let her go? If so, he decided, drowsily, it was a good bewitchment. He would never try again to disentangle himself from her silken web. Deeply content, he drifted off to sleep.

Calista lay awake, looking at his closed eyelids, the sooty sweep of his black lashes against his face. She tenderly stroked a fallen lock of hair back from his forehead, love swelling within her, deeper and stronger than she could ever have imagined.

Oh, yes, she loved him! And it was right to do so. She felt its rightness in every part of her. She would love him until the moment she died.

But even as she thought this, even as he still, in sleep, clung to her, a tiny thread of doubt crept into her mind. Ryan had loved her with his body, as he'd promised he would. He had loved her to a depth she'd never dreamed possible.

She could never again doubt that he desired her as much as she desired him. And he'd been concerned for her, too, not wanting to hurt her, wishing her to be pleasured as much as he was. Surely that meant, had to mean, he cared for her.

The last thought echoed in her mind uneasily. She'd had those same thoughts, felt the same way, the first time Ryan had taken her into his arms those months ago.

And she'd been wrong, so very wrong. Coldness swept over her. Just like the first time, like the day at the lagoon, tonight he'd spoken no words of love to her, none at all. Not even in the most intense moments of his desire.

Oh, but tonight was different from those other times. She turned the wide gold band on her left hand. She was truly married now. They'd become as close as two people could. Almost become one person . . . that had to mean something to him . . .

How was it different? the logical part of her brain asked. Just because their marriage had at last been physically consummated didn't have to mean anything to a man. Most men would have taken their marital rights long before this, no matter how they felt about their wives.

Just because this had happened between them tonight didn't mean Ryan intended to stay with her, to make this a real marriage. He'd said nothing about that, either. It was quite possible, probable even, that he intended to do what he'd planned from the beginning.

Stay here on Meadowmarsh until his father recovered, then go back to Charleston and take his family with him. And never return to Meadowmarsh—and her—again.

Chapter Eighteen

The sound of Zeke blowing the conch woke Calista. She was alone. A sense of loss swept over her, renewing and intensifying her misgivings of the night before. She didn't know when Ryan had left.

Sometime during the night, he'd awakened her with kisses and they'd made love again, slowly and lingeringly. If she'd thought the first time the most sublime experience of her life, Ryan had soon changed her mind.

But now her doubts were back. Had he left because he didn't want Delphinia to find him in her bed? Why? Out of concern for her, or for himself?

Was last night the only time she'd know his love? No, she corrected herself, his *lovemaking*. A world of difference lay between the two. And maybe she'd never know which it was.

She forced the dark thoughts from her mind and stretched widely. The sun shone; it was a beautiful day, and she refused to worry, she told herself with determination.

She'd assume Ryan left out of consideration for her. And she fully intended to spend the day with him.

Flinging off the covers, she slid out of bed, relieved when her ankle gave not the slightest twinge when she placed her weight on it. She hastily washed and dressed, twisted her hair back into its chignon, and hurried out of the room, meeting Delphinia with her tea tray on the stairs.

"What you doin' out of bed so early, Mistress?" Delphinia asked, her face astonished.

Embarrassment swept over Calista. Did she look different this morning? Did what had happened between her and Ryan show on her face? She smiled, hoping it looked natural and ordinary. "I'm going downstairs for breakfast, and then out to the fields."

"But de doctor ain't said you could do dat!"

"I feel fine." Thankfully, Delphinia was too concerned with her health to notice anything else. Calista lifted her teacup from the tray and took a long, appreciative drink, then put it back. "Please bring the tray to the dining room, Delphinia, and tell Gideon to have Sable saddled."

"Yes'm," the other woman muttered, her voice disapproving, as she followed along behind Calista.

In spite of her determination, a knot formed in Calista's stomach as she approached the dining room. She both wanted desperately to see Ryan and dreaded to do so. At the doorway, she paused.

Ryan sat at the far end of the table, but not alone. Leora, dressed in her riding habit, sat on his right, smiling up at him. Ryan smiled back at her.

A flash of jealousy went through Calista, which she at once pushed down. She was being ridiculous, just because she was unsure of Ryan's feelings for her.

Ryan glanced up and saw her standing in the doorway. The smile left his face, replaced by surprise. He stared at her for a long moment. Then, he smiled again—at her. The smile made her heart turn over with renewed love.

"Good morning, Calista," he said, striving to make his voice merely friendly and pleasant. "I didn't expect to see you down here so early."

Her beautiful face was rosy, her eyes shone. Just as he'd known, possessing her hadn't sated his desire in the slightest. Only increased it. He wanted to take her in his arms and kiss her passionately. Then, sweep her up and carry her back upstairs and make love to her all day. But of course he couldn't do that.

She felt her face warm. Was that a reference to the fact they'd had very little sleep last night? She smiled back, just as pleasantly. "I've had enough of lazing around the house."

Leora turned her head and gave her cousin a bright smile. "You must be feeling a lot better."

Embarrassment hit her again at her cousin's innocent words. "Yes, I am." Calista came into the dining room, seating herself at the other end of the table.

Delphinia placed her teacup on the table, and the small dish of oysters, her movements heavy with disapproval.

"Thank you, Delphinia," Calista said.

"Yes'm. But you needs to wait till de doctuh sees you before you go out in de fields."

"I'm *fine*," she told the other woman again, her voice firm. She helped herself to a biscuit, then glanced down the table at Ryan.

He was looking at her, but his face didn't reveal his thoughts. Did he remember last night with delight or wish it had never happened?

"Are you going out in the fields today?" Leora asked, eagerly. "So am I. Ryan has been showing me how you do things here."

"Oh. I didn't know that." Leora talked as if Calista

were a guest here, like herself. As if Ryan were truly the master of Meadowmarsh. Well, didn't she want him to be? Her irritation mixed with bewilderment. Yes, of course she did, but she didn't want him to take over . . .

It also sounded as if Leora had gone out on rounds with Ryan before. More than once. Another flash of jealousy joined her mixed-up emotions. Maybe she'd been right to think the smile Ryan and Leora had exchanged as she entered the dining room was too friendly. Was her cousin a hopeless flirt? With Andrew temporarily unavailable, had her earlier interest in Calista's husband revived?

"Meadowmarsh is such a wonderful place," Leora went on, her voice still eager.

Ryan swore inwardly as he saw the changing emotions flicker across Calista's face. He should have told her he'd taken Leora out with him several times, but he hadn't wanted her to know his ulterior purpose in doing so because he was certain she'd disapprove.

He'd planned to discourage Leora's interest in Andrew by making the girl realize plantation life involved endless work, not the round of parties and dinners she was accustomed to in Charleston.

But Leora hadn't reacted as he'd expected. She asked intelligent questions and seemed genuinely interested in all aspects of cotton-growing and plantation life. Since Andrew was bound to marry someone soon, Ryan had come to the reluctant conclusion she'd make his brother an excellent wife—if her parents condoned. Which of course was highly unlikely.

He cleared his throat and looked at Calista at the other end of the big table. Why did she have to sit so far away? He wanted her next to him. He wanted to kiss the throbbing vein in her white neck . . .

"I *never* want to go back to Charleston," Leora chattered

on, apparently oblivious to the undercurrents passing between Calista and Ryan. "I'd love to live on a plantation."

"Good morning, all!" Andrew's voice said from the doorway.

"Andrew!" Leora squeaked. "Should you be downstairs?"

"Yes," he said firmly, "I should." He entered the room and walked to the table, seating himself across from Leora.

She looked startled, rather than delighted, to see him, Calista noted, fighting another attack of jealousy.

Delphinia came back in the room, bearing a plate of fresh biscuits and one of delicately fried fish. She poured Andrew a cup of tea, then left again.

"I can't stay in bed forever," Andrew said briskly. He helped himself to a piece of fish, then looked at his brother. "I'm sorry this all had to fall on you, Ryan. But I'm quite recovered now. I plan to go out with you today."

Alarm hit Ryan at his brother's words. He couldn't stand having Andrew with them, fussing over everything, making all the work twice as difficult. He shot a glance at Calista. She looked the way he felt.

"Oh, no, Andrew," Calista said hastily, "it's too soon after your fever. It's a chilly day, too. And there's no need. I plan to go out myself."

"You still look pale," Leora added. "I don't think you should go outside yet."

Andrew frowned at everyone. "Will all of you stop acting as if I'm an invalid?"

"What's this about an invalid?" Lucinda asked cheerfully, coming into the room, Gabrielle behind her. "Calista! Andrew! It's good to see you both at the breakfast table again!"

Calista felt the older woman's shrewd glance looking her over thoroughly, and her face reddened again. Maybe no one else had noticed, but she was sure her aunt could tell she wasn't the same woman she'd been yesterday.

"It's good to be on my feet again," Calista agreed. She pushed back her chair and rose, glancing at Ryan, who'd also risen. "Today, we need to finish running out the land," she told him briskly. In a way she was relieved Leora was going with them. She both desired and dreaded being alone with Ryan again.

"Yes, that's what I had planned," Ryan answered stiffly. He felt annoyed that she hadn't consulted with him before announcing her plans for the day. Well, what had he expected? That one night of lovemaking would change her possessive feelings about Meadowmarsh?

The plantation had always been her strongest passion. And it was still. No matter that they'd lain in each other's arms all last night.

Calista turned to leave the room, surprised Lucinda hadn't objected to her taking over her duties again without consulting with Dr. Norman, then realized why the other woman was applying herself to her breakfast. Lucinda wouldn't object to anything that kept Ryan and Calista together.

She became aware that Leora hadn't risen. "I've changed my mind. I believe I'll stay here at the house today," the girl said primly as Calista's inquiring gaze rested on her.

Andrew's head shot up, and he gave Leora a surprised look. The girl didn't meet his gaze, looking down at her plate instead.

Now that Andrew was up and about, Leora obviously didn't want him to know she'd been going out to the fields with Ryan, Calista decided.

By now Ryan had reached her side. He waited, courteously, for her to leave the room ahead of him. He was so close she could smell his mingled scent of soap and spicy cologne. Her knees felt shaky as memories of last night swept over her again.

She gave him a quick look from under her lashes. If he, too, had the same kind of thoughts, it didn't show. His face looked bland, almost remote. No hint in it of the passion that had taken her to heights she'd never dreamed of just last night.

Calista drew herself up, tilting her chin. She gave him a cool smile even as she burned inside. "Shall we go?"

Ryan crooked his arm and bowed slightly. "At your service, Mrs. Burke," he told her.

His voice had that ironic tone again. She didn't want to touch him, but she also didn't want the watching people at the table to notice any hesitancy on her part. So she placed her hand in the bend of his elbow. She felt his body heat through the fabric of his white shirt, and a shiver went through her.

"Cold?" he asked, his voice concerned. "Perhaps you shouldn't go today."

Fool, she told him silently. *Can't you see how I feel? Don't you care?* "I'm fine," she repeated for the third or fourth time this morning.

At the door, Junie fastened her cloak securely around her neck. Gideon placed Ryan's on his shoulders, then opened the door. A chilly breeze swept across the veranda, and she shivered again.

One of the grooms held their mounts. In spite of the tumult raging inside her, Calista smiled as she saw Sable, brushed and sleek. It would be good to be on horseback again. Maybe a brisk ride would make her forget that the husband who'd roused her passions to fever-pitch last night probably didn't love her.

And that he might be leaving her within a short while, never to return.

* * *

"Mistress!" Zeke smiled widely at Calista as she and Ryan drew their mounts up before one of the cotton fields. "It good to see you out here again."

Calista smiled back. "That's how I feel, too," she assured him. She felt breathless and windblown, exhilarated and happy. The brisk ride had blown the cobwebs out of her brain, just as she'd hoped.

"Maussa Ryan, I put some of the hands to listin' this field, like you tell me yesterday."

Ryan nodded. Two weeks ago he wouldn't have had the slightest idea that "listing" meant hoeing the marsh grass under the soil. "That's fine, Zeke. We should be able to get the rest of the tasks laid out today."

"Yes'suh, we ought to." Zeke turned to Calista. "Maussa Ryan just take to this plantation work like he was born to it."

Calista smiled again, even though, for some reason, she felt annoyed. "Well, he *was* born on a plantation, Zeke."

"Yes'm, I knows that, but he ain't lived on one for a long time now."

"No, I haven't," Ryan interjected, irritated that Zeke and Calista were talking about him as if he weren't there. "And I'm sure that's been obvious, Zeke, in spite of your flattery."

"No'suh," Zeke said earnestly. "It ain't. Are you ready to go to the other field?"

"Yes, we are," Calista said crisply, before Ryan could answer. Now she knew why she felt annoyed. Zeke was acting as if Ryan had been at Meadowmarsh for years instead of only a few weeks. Why, he hadn't even glanced at her when he'd asked Ryan that last question!

Zeke's head swung back around to Calista, a surprised look in his eyes. "Yes'm," he said quickly, nodding at her, but she knew what that look meant. If the master were finally taking over the plantation, as he should have from the beginning, why, then, of course, Zeke would answer to him.

Her annoyance grew. So all these years, when first her mother alone, later joined by Calista, then finally Calista alone, had competently run Meadowmarsh, hadn't meant a thing to the driver. As far as he was concerned, a man was still needed.

Abruptly, the final words of her mother's last letter came into her mind. *"You've not only been Meadowmarsh's mistress, you've been its master, too. You don't need anyone. . . . a woman should have a man who needs her as she needs him. . . ."*

She swallowed, glancing over at Ryan. His profile was presented to her, and a muscle moved in his firm jaw. *He* was also annoyed, she realized, and for the same reasons—in reverse. And she was wrong, she knew, to feel as she did, to have made it clear just now how she felt. Ryan had every right to be annoyed.

She'd begged him to take over while her injuries healed; and, even though he obviously didn't want to, he'd agreed. She should feel nothing but gratitude. And the more interested Ryan grew in Meadowmarsh, the more likely he was to stay here . . .

The very last words of her mother's letter came into her mind then. *"By now I pray you'll not only have a good husband, but you'll also be with child."*

A tremor ran through her. It was possible her mother's last wish had already been granted. She darted another glance at Ryan. This time he was looking at her, frowning. But there was something in his deep, blue eyes that belied the frown. Something that told her he also remembered last night. His eyes moved to her mouth, then lower, to the neckline of her cloak.

She felt her breathing quicken. Hadn't she told herself she was going to forget her doubts about Ryan's intentions and just enjoy the day with him? She smiled, making it as warm and tender as she could. "Are you ready to go?"

Ryan's frown smoothed out as he looked at Calista's lovely, smiling face. Naturally, she couldn't help resenting Zeke's new-found loyalty to Ryan and his over enthusiastic praise. He no longer felt annoyed. He wanted to lift her from her mount and carry her off to the lagoon and make love to her.

He sighed inwardly. But since that wasn't possible at the moment, he'd have to get as much pleasure as he could out of just having her near, of being able to feast his eyes on her whenever he wanted, and of remembering last night.

And anticipating the night to come.

His answering smile was as warm as her own. "I am, indeed, wife."

Calista's spirits lifted, and her smile widened as they looked into each other's eyes with a hidden wealth of meaning. *Wife*. Often since their marriage, he'd used the term ironically, hurtfully. But that wasn't how he'd said it just now. No, his voice had been soft and it had lingered over the word as if he found it appealing.

Maybe she'd been right when she'd told herself last night that Ryan had to care for her, that his actions, if not his words, made that clear.

Maybe, after all, there was a future for them.
Together.

* * *

SWEET ENCHANTMENT

That evening, a balmy sea breeze blew, belying the late January date, and kept the mosquitoes at bay. The long veranda, stretching across the front of the house, was full of people enjoying the evening.

And all were couples, Calista thought contentedly, smiling at Ryan, who sat close beside her. "You'd think it was spring instead of winter."

He smiled back. "It is unseasonably warm," he agreed.

"Yes, but that's not what I meant." She gestured at Lucinda and Jerome, who sat together in the middle, and at Andrew and Leora, at the far end. "You'd think it was the mating season."

Ryan laughed, a pleasant, rich sound in the gathering twilight. "I see what you mean." He reached for her hand, drawing it to his side and covering it with his own. A sense of *déjà vu* swept over him as he remembered the first time he'd taken her hand in his.

What a lot had happened since then. He no longer felt that his wife had tricked him into marriage. He hadn't felt that way since the day at the lagoon, but he hadn't admitted it. Even to himself—let alone Calista—until last night.

And he sure as hell knew she wasn't cold and calculating. He squeezed her hand and was rewarded with an answering squeeze. "How long do we have to stay out here?" he asked her in a low tone, his voice suggestive.

She gave him an impish smile, feeling her face grow warm. "Jerome *did* come all the way from Charleston to see you," she mock-rebuked him.

"Like hell he did. He came to see Lucinda, and well you know it." He placed his arm across her shoulders and pulled her closer to him, cursing the arms of the rockers that prevented any closer contact.

Calista laughed, throwing a glance toward the couple

in question. As near as she could make out in the gathering dusk, Jerome also held her aunt's hand, and Lucinda was gazing up at him as if she'd indeed missed him very much.

She must talk to Ryan about another matter, and she didn't want to. This was too pleasant. But she might as well get it over with. "Ryan, you don't have to come out to the fields with me anymore. That sheaf of papers Jerome brought will keep you busy for weeks."

His hand tightened on her shoulder. "Don't you want me to go out with you?" he asked.

His voice sounded odd, she thought. She couldn't decide what his question meant. Whether he wanted to, or not.

"Of course I do," she hurried to assure him. And she did, really she did, even if it felt strange to share the management of Meadowmarsh with someone else. She'd get used to it. "But I know you must have a lot to catch up on."

Ryan laughed again, and she wasn't sure what the laugh meant either. "Nothing Jerome brought is important. He's keeping up with everything just fine. A young man who's studying law comes in to help part-time. Jerome's singing his praises, hinting he might make him a junior partner. If I never went back to the firm, it wouldn't hurt Jerome's practice a bit."

"Oh," Calista said after a moment. She started to ask him what about his *own* practice, then changed her mind. What was he telling her? That he didn't care if he never went back to Charleston? No, she was afraid to hope he meant that. She pushed down the fleeting thought that the idea scared her, too.

Ryan heard the uncertainty in her voice. Damn! Why had he said that? He didn't know how he felt about the possibility of staying here on Meadowmarsh for good. He was considering it, that was true, but he wasn't committed to the idea yet. *Go slow,* he advised himself. *Don't rush into anything.*

"Would you like that, Calista?" he heard himself asking, and swore at himself again. What had happened to him in the space of less than twenty-four hours?

She drew in her breath at his words. *Would she like that?* "Ryan," she began. "Of—"

A chair scraped on the veranda's wooden floor. Jerome got jerkily to his feet. Even in the dim light, Calista could see the barely controlled anger on his face. He turned and went inside without a backward glance at Lucinda.

"Oh, what happened between them?" Calista whispered to Ryan.

He felt a mixture of disappointment and relief that she hadn't finished her sentence. Had she planned to say of course she wanted him to stay? Or of course they needed to wait a while to decide?

And damn again! Most men wouldn't even be asking their legal wives if they wanted them to live with them. Most men he knew would bluntly tell the wives the way it was going to be.

But he knew he wouldn't force himself on her—not now, not ever, not in any way. He'd seen too much of that kind of thing between his parents. They'd ended up hating each other over a piece of property. His face tightened. His father had married his mother only to get the plantation he coveted. Then he'd discovered he'd never have it, and his mother had found out Ainsley Hall was all his father wanted or cared about. *All right, enough of that,* he told himself. He'd brooded over those things for too many years.

Another chair scraped on the veranda floor, and Andrew

rose to his feet. He marched back toward the front door, his face grim and set. He came on past the door and stopped before Ryan.

"Ryan, Calista," he began, hurt and anger in every word. "Leora says you don't need me to help with the plantation duties. That, in fact, you were both relieved when I took ill and couldn't interfere. She tells me I am far too bossy and opinionated."

He paused, as if waiting for their instant contradiction. Calista sat with her mouth open in surprise. She finally cleared her throat, but didn't say anything. Instead, she glanced at Ryan.

Ryan had a sudden vision of repeats of this kind of conversation going on for years, even after Andrew had his own plantation again—with nothing resolved and his brother never realizing he needed to change. The only way to get through to Andrew was to be absolutely blunt, he knew from experience.

He took a deep breath and let it out, resigned. He hated to do this, but as the older brother he guessed it was up to him to settle this issue once and for all.

"Hell, yes, that's true, Andrew," he said, but with a grin to take the sting off. "You're a worse fussbudget than any old lady I ever saw. I'm sorry you took ill, but I was damned glad not to have to work with you!"

His words rang out in the evening air. He saw Leora coming toward them, looking uneasy. Lucinda had risen, too, and looked quite upset, whether at his words or her quarrel with Jerome, he wasn't sure.

Andrew's face paled visibly. The anger left his features, replaced with hurt and surprise. He stood there for a moment, then, without a word, wheeled and hurried inside the house.

Ryan stared after him, frowning. Oh, hell. He supposed

he'd been too blunt. But it was too late now to do anything about it.

Leora had reached Calista and Ryan. She glanced after Andrew, then back at the other two.

"Thank you, Cousin Ryan, for backing me up. Andrew is a bit of a prig, isn't he? I couldn't live with him the way he is." She paused and gave them a smile.

"And since I plan to live with him for many years, he must do some changing." The smile left her face, and she sighed and shook her head. "But right now, I guess I'll have to go and soothe his ruffled feelings."

She, too, turned and left the veranda and Lucinda followed her, leaving Calista and Ryan alone.

Ryan decided Leora had a much better chance of mollifying Andrew than he did. He'd leave her to the job.

Calista gazed after Leora, then turned back to him. "It looks as if your efforts to discourage Leora and Andrew were for naught." She gave him a sly smile.

He nodded, mischief and something else alight in his blue eyes. "I decided that awhile back." He bowed. "Madam, I believe we should go inside, too. It's getting late and since we have to be up early, we need to retire."

Calista's face flamed at the emphasis he put on the last words, but she rose. "I agree with you, Mr. Burke," she said primly. "Let's go upstairs to bed."

Her face reddened even more at her last words. She'd been too bold again, but surely Ryan's words meant that he planned to share her bed again tonight.

The front door opened once more, and Gabrielle stood framed in the opening, her young face alarmed.

"Ryan, Papa has taken a turn for the worse—he can't seem to stop coughing. Will you send for the doctor at once?"

Chapter Nineteen

Calista's gaze strayed to the closed door of her room, willing the knob to turn.

It was very late. The whole household had been in an uproar for hours after Emory's sudden attack. Dr. Norman had come immediately, but his usual ministrations had had little effect. Finally, he had given Emory a large dose of laudanum and the racking paroxysms of coughing had eased enough that the man could drift into an exhausted sleep.

"I don't like to give him that much laudanum," Dr. Norman had said, frowning. "He's too weak. But he's also too weak to stand the coughing fits."

"Why isn't he getting better?" Ryan had demanded. His black hair had been rumpled and worry lines had creased his brow. "It's been over a month now since he had the pneumonia."

"Perepneumonia," Dr. Norman had corrected. "It's a much more serious disease than ordinary pneumonia."

"All right," Ryan had conceded, "but he should still be improving."

"These things often take longer than we think they should," the doctor had answered, soothingly, his smile as evasive as his words. Calista liked Dr. Norman, but getting him to commit himself to blunt answers was difficult. He preferred a hearty, optimistic attitude toward all illness.

Clearly not reassured, Ryan had stared, frowning, at his father, who slept restlessly in spite of the sedative. "I don't like it," he had muttered, turning to Dr. Norman, his words and manner challenging.

The doctor had picked up his medical bag and given Ryan another smile. "None of us do, my boy," he had said. "But there's nothing we can do about it."

Once he'd gone, and with Emory finally asleep, everyone except Andrew, who had insisted on keeping watch alone the rest of the night, had left the room. "I don't seem to be of much use around here in any other capacity," he had said.

Obviously, he was still hurt and angry because of Ryan's stinging words earlier. Leora had looked as if she wanted to offer to stay with him, but after another glance at his glowering countenance, she didn't. Jerome and Lucinda hadn't spoken a word to each other, either. Whatever had happened between them on the veranda must have been serious.

Ryan had been so worried about his father, he'd hardly seemed aware of Calista's presence. After Andrew's taunting words, he'd tightened his mouth and gone to his bedchamber, closing the door firmly behind him.

Now, an hour later, Calista waited for him and wondered if she were a fool for doing so. Ryan had probably gone straight to his own bed after the exhausting evening.

Or maybe he thought *she* was too tired to be interested in lovemaking.

They needed to talk, too, she admitted reluctantly. Ryan's question before Gabrielle had interrupted kept running through her mind. *Did* Ryan plan to stay on Meadowmarsh permanently? He must at least be considering it. Otherwise, why ask her if she'd like that? And why was she reluctant to discuss it?

Of course, she wanted him to stay! True, she had a bit of a problem adjusting to the idea of a man—even the one she dearly loved—usurping some of her authority. But it could be worked out.

Not tonight, though. Tonight, all she wanted was Ryan's arms around her, his mouth and body hot against her own. For a moment, she toyed with the idea of walking down to his room and letting herself in. Sliding into bed with him, waking him with kisses . . .

No, of course she couldn't do anything like that! She'd already been far too brazen with him. She took a deep breath and let it out. If he didn't want to share her bed, that was fine with her. She blew out the candle, then settled herself for sleep.

After half an hour of restless tossing, she conceded that that objective wouldn't be easy to attain. After another hour, exhaustion finally claimed her.

. . . Something was tickling the back of her neck. Had a mosquito found its way inside? Drowsily, Calista reached her hand back to brush off the offender and encountered firm, warm flesh. Her hand moved slowly upward and found a mouth, then a silky mustache. The mouth slowly drew one of her fingers inside and began to suck on it.

A tremor shook her half-asleep body. The mouth stilled on her hand. "Oh, don't stop!" she mumbled, rolling over.

Her face came up against a firm, hard chest, which also shook. "My sweet, demure bride, I have no intention of stopping," Ryan's warm, amused voice said in her ear.

At last he'd come, but he was laughing at her! Oh, why did she keep saying these things? Mortified, Calista moved away. But not far, because his other hand and arm were around her neck, pulling her close to him again.

"I can't keep on with what I was doing if you don't stay put," he whispered.

"That's all right; I don't want you to," she said hastily to hide her embarrassment. She lied. She wanted him to keep on . . . and on . . .

"I don't believe you," Ryan murmured. "Let's see if you really mean that." His tongue traced the outline of her ear, then moved further inside.

Calista shuddered and felt a stirring in the deepest part of her womanhood, just like last night. Abandoning her futile attempts at maidenly modesty, she pressed against him, gratified to feel his body swiftly hardening to her touch.

She lifted her face to his. A moonbeam threw a line of silver light across the bed, showing her Ryan's face as he lowered his head. His amusement was gone. He looked intent, aroused, and eager. His mouth found her own and claimed it, and she let out a small sigh of joy.

Tonight, she would entertain no doubts. She'd give herself over to his wonderful lovemaking and not think of anything, only feel. And love.

Ryan drew her closer, cradling her soft body against his hard contours. Why had he fought with himself before coming to her? Why—when he'd wanted this more than anything he'd ever desired? He couldn't withstand her bewitching appeal. He wouldn't try to again. He would make love to her; he would let her love him.

And tomorrow could take care of itself.

SWEET ENCHANTMENT

* * *

Lotus eased open Zeke's cabin door and quickly slid inside. She closed it behind her, then leaned against it, shaking rain from her clothes and hair. She hadn't been here much lately. She'd thought to tease Zeke, make him hungry for her, but her strategy hadn't worked. He didn't seem to care.

Zeke jerked his head up from the pan of cow peas he stirred over the hearth. "What you doin' here?" he asked, his voice not at all welcoming.

Lotus came further inside, smiling seductively. "Ain't you glad to see me?" she asked, a knot of worry forming in her stomach. She had to get Zeke back the way he'd been—so eager for her he'd do anything. Ira sharing her cabin didn't help matters. It was hard to get away from him at night.

Today, she'd managed to sneak some liquor from the Big House, and now he snored away in a drunken stupor, leaving her free to come to Zeke.

Zeke just shrugged his broad shoulders and turned back to his cooking. He scooped two big, steaming yams from the hearth, blowing ashes away from them, then laid them on the table.

A few months ago, she'd have pressed herself against him and Zeke would have forgotten about eating supper until much later. Now, she wasn't at all sure that would work. "Dat smell good," she said instead, kneeling beside the hearth. "I ain't had no supper."

"Why not?" Zeke didn't want to look at her because he feared the hold she still might have on him. He hadn't tested it lately, and he wasn't in the mood to now. He was hungry. There'd be no digging for gold tonight because of the rain, for which he was grateful.

Lotus frowned. She couldn't entice him if he wouldn't

even glance at her. She got up and sat down in one of the two chairs, then picked up a yam and cautiously peeled the skin back from its steaming surface.

She took a small bite, then laid the yam back down. She rose again, found wooden bowls on a shelf, and held one out to Zeke. "Dat stuff 'bout ready to eat?"

Zeke saw her movement out of the corner of his eye and reached for the bowl. His fingers closed over hers, and for a moment the old weakness and desire came over him. But he fought it, pulling the bowl away from her slim fingers.

He ladled the cow peas into the bowl and handed it back to her, then took the other bowl she held out, still not looking directly at her. He sat down across from her and began eating.

"Ira 'bout ready to give up and leave Meadowmarsh," Lotus said in a minute. "He say he only help dig for two more weeks, and if we don't find de gold by then, he leavin'."

Zeke's head shot up, and he looked at her with undisguised eagerness. "Did he say that?" he demanded.

Not long ago, that look would have meant he couldn't wait to pull her down with him on the pallet, Lotus thought sourly. She'd soon have him that way again. "Yes, he did. He told me dat just tonight." She smiled. "He not gonna say nothin' to de mistress."

A worried frown replaced Zeke's excitement. He'd forgotten that threat of Ira's. "You believe he mean that?"

She nodded. "He know he git hisself in a heap of trouble, too, if he tell. Even if he white, he still been tryin' to steal gold dat belong to Meadowmarsh."

Zeke felt a great weight lift off his shoulders. If Ira left, he'd have plenty of time to decide what to do about the old chest he'd found.

He'd refuse to go out digging with Lotus anymore. He

could stay here at Meadowmarsh, if he wanted to. He was happy here. He enjoyed his life. "That's good," he said in heartfelt relief. "That's real good."

"Yes, that means you and me can keep all de gold," Lotus agreed. She was tiring of the hunt herself, but she wouldn't give up. Not after all the effort they'd already put into it.

Zeke looked at her fully for the first time since she'd entered his cabin. The flickering candle highlighted the planes of her beautiful dark face, and even the loose-fitting wool dress couldn't conceal her lush body. He let his eyes roam freely over her, testing himself, relieved when his body didn't harden. All he wanted was for her to leave.

But maybe she was right and it would be better to be free and up north. And with half the gold instead of only a third. If that was gold in the chest. He'd never know unless he opened it.

It was his decision, and he didn't have to make it now. "I'm tired of all the diggin', too. We already dug up most of the island, and we ain't found nothin' yet." He hesitated, then went on. "I think we wastin' our time. They's no gold here."

Lotus stared at him, her yam halfway to her mouth. There'd been a strange note in his voice just now. Like he knew something he didn't want her to know about the treasure.

What could it be? He'd never gone out digging alone, so he couldn't have found anything by himself. No, they'd always done this together, none of the three trusting any of the others.

A half-forgotten memory entered her mind. That night, weeks ago, when Ira had again been drunk and threatening. When she'd enticed him back to her cabin to keep him from carrying out his threats . . .

She'd left Zeke alone to refill the hole they'd been excavating. What if, after she and Ira had left, he'd found something in it? She kept on staring at Zeke, thinking about this new idea.

"What you lookin' at me like that for?" Zeke demanded roughly. "You look like you never seen me before."

Lotus put her yam down on the table and wiped her hands on the sides of her dress. Yes, she thought, excitement building in her. That could be why Zeke was acting so funny lately. Why he never wanted to search for the treasure. Of course he didn't, if he'd already found it. And what if he planned to get the gold one night all by himself? Her eyes narrowed. That's what *he* thought!

But she didn't want him to suspect she was onto him. She smoothed out her face and smiled. "You lookin' good tonight," she purred. "I tired of dat old Ira in my cabin. I be so glad when he goes."

Zeke nodded, ignoring her blatant invitation. "Me, too. But I meant what I said. There ain't no gold here on Meadowmarsh. We fools to keep on diggin'."

He should have gotten a bar and opened the chest the night he'd found it. Sighing inwardly, he knew he had to dig it up again. He had to find out what was in it. If it was gold, then he'd wait until Ira left to decide what he wanted to do.

Again, there was the slightest bit of hesitation in his voice, convincing Lotus she was right. Her mind worked quickly as she made her plans. She'd try once more to seduce Zeke tonight. And if that didn't work, no matter. Ira would soon leave Meadowmarsh, and she'd pretend to lose interest in the quest.

They'd dug in so many places, she had no idea where they'd been that night. But that didn't matter, either.

Because from now on, she'd keep watch on Zeke and

follow him if he left his cabin at night. When he dug up the gold, she'd be right there to claim her share.

Her lips curved in a smile that made a shiver go down Zeke's spine. But before they left here, she had something else planned for Miz high and mighty Calista.

Lucinda read the letter, and her face paled until it was as white as the paper she held. She stared straight ahead, and the sheet dropped from her nerveless fingers onto the sitting room floor.

Calista sprang to her feet and went to her aunt, kneeling beside her. "What is it, Aunt Lucie? What's happened?"

Pressing her bloodless lips together, Lucinda gazed up at Calista. "Jerome is very sick with a fever. His housekeeper says he's not expected to live." She got up quickly. "I must go to him!"

"Of course you must," Calista agreed.

"Oh, why did we have that senseless quarrel when he was here?" Lucinda asked, her voice filled with pain.

"What did you quarrel about?" Calista ventured, wondering if her aunt would tell her.

Lucinda sighed. "Jerome asked me point blank if I was ever going to agree to marry him and, if so, to set the date. When I wouldn't do that, he accused me of being afraid of marriage and said he was tired of waiting."

She turned to her niece, tears filling her eyes. "Oh, what a fool I've been! He was right—I was afraid. I've wasted all this time when we could have been together. And now maybe we never will be!"

Calista put her arm around her aunt's shoulder. "Of course you will. Jerome is strong—he'll pull through this."

"But he's no longer young, the point he kept trying to

make," Lucinda said, her voice quivering. "Neither one of us is."

A sound at the door made Calista turn. Ryan stood in the doorway, frowning. He'd obviously heard at least some of the conversation. He hurried across the room and gave Calista a strained smile, then turned to Lucinda. "I'll go with you. You need an escort, and Jerome will need my help at the office."

Calista stared at him, cold washing over her. Oh, he couldn't leave, not again. Not now, when they were so happy. The last few days had been the most joyous of her life.

He turned back to Calista, giving her a searching look. "Father isn't in any immediate danger. Will you be all right here with Andrew and Gabrielle?"

She took a deep breath and let it out. "Of course I will. You must go." She forced a reassuring smile she didn't feel.

He gave her a relieved one in return, as if he'd expected her to raise objections. "We'd better hurry if we want to make the tide today."

"Yes." Calista tried not to think about the fact she and Ryan would be separated for what could be a long time. She helped Lucinda get a few things together, telling her she'd pack her trunk to send later.

Within half an hour, they were all three at the dock. It was high tide and Zeke should be able to get to Beaufort in time to make the steamboat to Charleston.

"If Jerome pulls through this, we'll marry the instant he can say his vows!" Lucinda said fervently.

Calista forced a warm smile. "Good for you. Don't let anything stop you." Ryan stood beside her, holding her hand. Oh, how she'd miss him! Would he miss her?

"I won't." Lucinda looked at Calista and Ryan and frowned. "I'm sorry you have to go," she told Ryan.

He squeezed Calista's hand tighter. "So am I, but it can't be helped. We'd better go before the tide turns." He pulled Calista into his arms and covered her mouth with his own, despite the fact Lucinda and Zeke were watching.

Calista tried to put all her love for him into the kiss so he'd remember it, remember her, while he was gone. She tried to imprint the feel of his hard, strong body into her mind, her heart. Oh, but she wouldn't forget him!

"Goodbye," he whispered against her mouth. "I'll be back as soon as possible." He seemed to hesitate for a moment, as if considering whether to say something else.

Calista held her breath, wondering, hoping, that he would say he loved her. But he didn't. She felt his small sighing breath, then he released her.

"Goodbye." She forced a warm smile for both him and Lucinda. She had to let him go, and she couldn't show her worries and fears.

The two women exchanged embraces, and Calista watched as Zeke poled the flatboat out into the creek. She waved; Ryan and Lucinda waved, and then the boat disappeared from view. Calista blinked away the tears so that Gideon wouldn't see and got into the carriage.

Would he come back? Or would this time away from the island make him decide once and for all he didn't want this kind of life?

Didn't want *her*.

"Where can Summer and Andrew and Leora be?" Calista and Gabrielle stood on a street corner in Beaufort, where they'd come for some supplies and to do some shopping. Ryan had been gone a week. The longest week Calista could ever remember, one reason for this expedition.

She missed him more than she'd ever have believed possible. She could hardly sleep in the wide, lonely bed. She put in long hours in the fields to see if that would help. But nothing did.

A note had come from Lucinda. Jerome was better, but still not out of danger. Ryan had sent an even briefer one, telling her he didn't know how long he'd have to stay. He'd signed it merely "Ryan".

The note hadn't made her feel any better. Maybe worse. If Ryan truly cared for her, surely he'd have written more than that. Would at least have said he missed her. Ended it with some term of affection. Maybe he *didn't* miss her. Maybe he was glad to be back in Charleston, back in his old, familiar life.

Maybe their time together had only been an interlude for him, a way to amuse himself while he had had to stay on the island. She tried to force these thoughts from her head and keep even busier. With Ryan gone, her uneasiness, her sense of something amiss on Meadowmarsh, had returned. So had the dream-like, frightening visions of the night she'd fallen from Sable.

Emory's health hadn't improved. Neither had his disposition. But Gabrielle was a joy. She'd taken over the household reins from Lucinda as capably as if she were twice her age.

Another reason for the Beaufort trip. The girl needed to get away for a few hours. But now it was time to return to Meadowmarsh, and the other three members of their party weren't here on this street corner as they'd arranged.

Someone hurried toward them—Summer, Calista saw with relief. Andrew and Leora couldn't be far behind.

Summer reached them, out of breath, with a folded piece of paper in her hand. "Miss Leora said to give you this."

SWEET ENCHANTMENT

Frowning, Calista took the note. A few moments later, she looked up at Gabrielle, astonishment in every feature. "Andrew and Leora have eloped!"

"Eloped?" Gabrielle squealed, her eyes widening in equal amazement.

Calista sighed. "So that's why they were so eager to come with us today." She turned to Summer. "Did you know anything about this?"

Summer shook her head, her dark eyes frightened. "No ma'am. When we got down to the docks, Miss Leora said to hurry and take this note to you. I told her it wasn't seemly for her to be there alone with Mr. Andrew, but you know how stubborn Miss Leora can be."

Calista nodded. "Yes, I certainly do. Has the steamboat left yet?"

"Yes, ma'am. I heard the whistle right after I left them. Miss Leora's mama and papa are going to be mighty upset about this," Summer said, her voice worried. "They'll blame me for leaving her alone with Mr. Andrew."

Calista patted her shoulder. "No, they won't. I'll explain to them what happened." Oh, and wouldn't *that* be fun? The Howards would not only blame Summer, they'd heap blame on Calista, too, she had absolutely no doubt. They'd do everything in their power to keep the young couple from carrying out their plan.

Just as they had to prevent her from marrying Timothy—and then Ryan. Calista pressed her lips together, frowning.

Gabrielle looked from Calista to Summer. "Andrew will take good care of Leora," she said, a challenging note in her usually soft voice. "They love each other."

Calista had no doubt of that. It was clear in every glance and smile they exchanged. Didn't they deserve their chance at happiness? Obviously Leora must have some money, since they'd taken the steamboat. Calista's frown cleared.

"Let's go back to Meadowmarsh. I don't believe there's any great hurry to contact the Howards." She turned to Summer. "I'll take full responsibility for this. Gabrielle is right. Andrew is a sensible young man. He'll take good care of your mistress."

Summer looked from one to the other of them, then a smile broke out on her face. She nodded. "Yes, ma'am, I know he will." She shook her head, then laughed.

"I declare, I should have known that girl was planning something when she kept asking me so many questions about that friend of hers who eloped a few months ago. Miss Maria's maid and me are friends—she told me all about it. By the time her parents caught up with them, well, it was too late, if you know what I mean."

Calista nodded. She knew what Summer meant. If Leora and Andrew married at once, which she was sure the young couple planned, the Howards would probably not try to have the marriage annulled. Because Leora could possibly already be with child.

She felt her face, her whole body, warming at that thought. As she, too, might be. Every night since Ryan had left, she prayed, not only for his return to the island, but also for that possibility.

And she wouldn't tell the Howards what had happened until it was too late to stop the marriage.

Calista stood under an orange tree in the grove, watching as Delphinia, dressed in the white gown Calista had had made for her, looked up at Gideon with a radiant face. He looked down at her with love in his eyes.

The day had turned out warm and pleasant, and Delphinia had wanted the ceremony in the orchard. Now, it was over and the feasting had begun. Planks covered with white cloths lay across sawhorses. A huge pot of savory beef-and-rice stew sat on the makeshift table along with a cake already half-devoured. Molasses had been added to big pitchers of water for a sweet drink.

Ryan came up beside her, slipping his arm around her waist. "Well, Mistress, do you feel as if you've given away one of your children?" he asked teasingly. God, she was lovely. He'd missed her so much while he'd been away. He never wanted to leave again. But getting away from her, from the spell of this island, had made him face the fact that they had to settle some things. That's why his note to her had been so noncommittal.

She gave him a happy, radiant smile, still not quite believing her prayer had been answered: He was actually here on the island. He'd returned yesterday with no warning. They'd spent a glorious night together with no room in it for anything but love.

But Calista knew they had to talk about their future. Her smile turned inward, became secretive. It was too soon to know, but maybe another prayer had been answered as well. "At least I got to organize *one* wedding."

He laughed, intoxicated with her, with the balmy day. "Lucinda warned you before she left. She said she'd marry Jerome the minute he was well enough to repeat his vows."

Calista's smile widened. "Having the ceremony by Jerome's bedside wasn't very romantic, but I'm so happy for them, even though I miss Aunt Lucie."

She glanced up at Ryan. "I don't know what I'd have done without Gabrielle. She's taken over the housekeeping duties as if she's done it all her life."

Ryan's answering smile was filled with pride for his sister. "She's a good girl. She likes nothing better than being in charge of the house."

"I feel guilty, though, for taking advantage of her good qualities. At her age she should be going to parties, having beaux flock around her."

"Were you doing that at her age?"

Calista darted a look at him, then slowly shook her head. "No. I never cared for that kind of thing. But—"

Ryan placed a finger across her mouth. "Stop your fretting. Neither does Gabrielle. She never has. She's perfectly content." He had to get his wife away from this crowd. To be alone with her.

His hand slid down to her throat, tracing a line of fire where he touched her. Calista drew in her breath, her heart speeding its beat. It still amazed her that his touch did this to her, every time. How long would the enchantment last?

Ryan drew her further away from the people crowding around the improvised table, back into the shadows of the trees. Once there, he pulled her into his arms and kissed her passionately. "Mrs. Burke," he said thickly, "I've wanted to do that all day."

Calista nestled against him, feeling the pounding of his heart against her cheek. "So have I." She pulled away from him regretfully. "But we should be getting back."

A dart of irritation stabbed him. He shook his head. "Always the conscientious plantation mistress."

A serious note, almost of disapproval, in his voice made Calista look quickly at him. "Yes. I was brought up that way. I don't know any other way to be."

Maybe this was a good time to talk with her. Before he told her what he'd done. He leaned over and gently traced the outline of her mouth with his hand. "And you don't *want* to be any other way, either, do you?" he asked lazily.

But she saw a glint in his deep, blue eyes. She shook

her head slowly. "No, I can't imagine not having the responsibilities of plantation life."

He felt tension hit his nerve ends. "There is such a thing as sharing responsibilities."

What did he mean? Was he trying to tell her he wanted to share the duties of Meadowmarsh with her? Permanently? Her heart leaped with gladness at that thought. But alongside the joy was a tiny, niggling doubt. Did she want to give up some of her authority? Most of it, perhaps? Could she do it?

Voices drifted up from the road leading down to the docks. Sharp-toned, *familiar* voices. They both turned in that direction.

Farley and Estelle Howard trudged up the lane, followed by Baxter. All three looked hot and tired and extremely unhappy.

Goddamn it to hell! Ryan swore inwardly. Why did they have to show up now? Just when he and his wife were finally talking about their future together.

Calista drew in her breath. Along with dismay at her relatives' arrival, she felt a sense of relief that this discussion had to be postponed. She placed her hand on Ryan's arm. "I've been expecting this since I sent word yesterday. But at least Andrew and Leora have had enough time to get married—and *be* married."

"Yes," Ryan agreed, trying not to let his anger show.

Together they went to meet the group.

Chapter Twenty

"Maybe I should have told them sooner," Calista said to Ryan as they hurried across the orchard.

Her voice sounded so uncertain Ryan forgot his irritation at the interruption. She needed his help now. Their talk could come later. He squeezed her hand in reassurance. "No, you shouldn't have," he answered firmly. "You did the right thing."

"You certainly have changed your mind. You wanted to prevent this before," she reminded him. "And you wanted my help in doing that."

"I was wrong," he admitted. "On both counts. I'll have to try to find Andrew some kind of position in Charleston, though. Since he doesn't have a penny. And I know they can't expect to get anything out of the Howards." He gave Calista an apologetic smile. "I don't mean to offend you; I know they're your relatives."

She squeezed his hand back, wondering if she should mention she'd offered Andrew a loan. Even though he'd refused then, he might reconsider now. No, she decided. This wasn't the time.

"You're not offending me. I'd like to forget that fact most of the time. You know I haven't seen them since they kicked Lucinda and me out of their house..."

Her voice trailed off, and she darted a look at Ryan. Despite the glorious nights of shared lovemaking, they'd never discussed the evening that had caused them to be married. With a small shock, she realized she didn't even know if Ryan still believed she'd tricked him into marriage.

"Neither have I," he said grimly. "And I can't say I've had any desire to, either."

No, surely, he no longer believed that. Or if he did, he'd forgiven her for it. Otherwise, he'd never have come to her that first night; he wouldn't keep on coming back...

The Howards had reached the wide lawns in front of the plantation house. At close range, they appeared even more out of sorts, Calista saw, her heart sinking.

Estelle looked at Calista with sorrowful anger. A tear formed at the corner of one eye, then rolled slowly down her full cheek. "To think my dear niece, who's meant as much to me as my own daughter, would allow such a thing to happen at her home!" Her voice trembled dramatically.

Stepping up beside his wife, Farley's expression was also one of mournful indignation. "We entrusted our daughter to your safekeeping, thinking you would watch over her, just as we were always there for you."

Baxter moved next to his father. He, too, looked angry, but Calista saw that his glance lingered, traveling insolently down her body.

She shivered and edged closer to Ryan. The Howards were such overpowering people, they could make you believe you'd done wrong, even if you knew better. And in truth, she'd had second thoughts—and third—since Andrew and Leora had eloped ten days ago.

Leora *was* young; and until recently, she'd appeared fickle. She'd gone from a strong infatuation with Ryan straight to Andrew with hardly any time in between. What if her affections for Andrew were equally transient?

The marriage could be a complete disaster. In which case, Leora's parents had every right to be furious with her for not notifying them in time to stop the pair.

But she couldn't undo what had happened, and they couldn't stand out here arguing. She forced as pleasant an expression as she could manage onto her face. "Won't you all come inside for some refreshments? I know you must be tired from your walk. We can discuss this in comfort."

Baxter scowled. "There's nothing to discuss, and we don't intend to stay. We only came to find out if—"

A quelling glance from his mother stopped him in mid-sentence. "We hoped you might be honorable enough to give us any information you have about Leora and, and. . . ."

Her voice quavered again, and Farley patted her shoulder. "There, there, my dear," he said ponderously, then turned to Ryan. "Do you know where your scoundrel of a brother has taken my daughter?"

Ryan's jaw clenched. "My brother is no scoundrel, Mr. Howard."

"That's debatable." Baxter's lip curled as he looked at Ryan. "You're evading my father's question."

The slimy toad hadn't forgotten how Ryan had humiliated him that night, Ryan realized, his anger growing as he returned Baxter's cold stare. "My wife and I have no idea where Andrew and Leora went. But I'm quite sure they are married."

Estelle let out a piercing half-sob, half-shriek. "Oh!

My baby!" She swayed toward Farley, and he grasped her shoulders.

"We *must* go inside," Calista said firmly. "Aunt Estelle, you need to lie down and rest for a while." As much as she disliked the idea, she knew she had to offer them the hospitality of her home—at least overnight.

She glanced at Ryan to find his gaze still locked with Baxter's. Intense dislike masked both their faces. Oh, no, things were already bad enough. She didn't want Ryan and her detested cousin getting into a fight on her front lawn!

To her relief, Estelle nodded weakly. "Yes, I am exhausted. I fear I am going to have an attack of palpitations. Farley, dear, take me inside."

Lotus stayed well behind Zeke as he made his way through the grove of trees, carrying a lantern, a spade, and an iron bar. She was sure he planned to dig up the treasure he'd found—and open the chest. Otherwise, why would he have the bar?

The celebration of Delphinia and Gideon's marriage had lasted well into the night. Now all the field hands slept in their cabins. She didn't have to worry about anyone following them. Not even Ira.

She'd given him a long tumble on the pallet, and then he'd drunk himself into a sodden sleep with liquor she'd sneaked from the Big House.

Her anticipation grew when Zeke stopped at a big magnolia and bent down as if to see something on the bottom of the trunk. He straightened, then began digging under the tree, the smoky lantern giving a fitful light. Quietly, she moved closer until she stood behind him.

If he turned suddenly, he'd see her; but he seemed too intent on his task to be suspicious. And she didn't much

SWEET ENCHANTMENT

care anyway. Half this treasure belonged to her. More than half. After all, it had been her idea.

The digging went slowly because Zeke was alone. After a while, when the hole was big enough, he jumped down into it. Lotus's palms grew damp with impatience, her legs tired. She sank to a crouching posture, peering out from behind a palmetto clump.

Zeke lowered the spade again, and she heard the dull ring of metal striking metal. She drew in her breath and rose to her feet, edging nearer.

Excitement slammed through her. Zeke stood over a rusted, old chest. While she watched, he tried to fit the bar into the corroded lock, but it slipped loose and banged against his leg. He muttered a curse and tried several more times with the same results. Uttering another curse, he climbed out of the hole.

Lotus shrank back into the shadows of the palmetto, holding herself rigidly still. Zeke stood on the edge of the excavation, looking all around, tilting his head in a listening pose. Finally, apparently satisfied, he climbed back into the hole again.

A loud clang came from the pit as Lotus edged forward once more. Zeke raised the bar and hit the lock again, hard. This time the ancient metal broke into two pieces and fell onto the earth.

Zeke stood just looking at the chest for so long Lotus thought he'd changed his mind about opening it. Then, moving slowly, he fit the flat edge of the bar under the lid and pried upward.

With a shrieking of long unused hinges, the lid gave and Zeke pushed it further upward. Hardly breathing, Lotus inched forward. Zeke stood as he had before, staring into the chest's interior.

As she got close enough to see what was inside, she let out a deep, disappointed breath. This chest didn't hold any treasure! It was piled with what looked like rotted cloth. It was just an old chest full of someone's old clothes!

Sick with disappointment, she jumped down into the hole, an ugly scowl twisting her features. "Why you spend all dis time hidin' dis old chest?"

Zeke jerked around to stare at her in shock and alarm. "What you doin' here?"

"What you think I doin' here?" she mocked him, hands on slim hips. "I knowed you was hidin' somethin'. Why didn't you tell me?" she demanded.

Zeke cursed his carelessness in letting her follow him. "I was goin' to after Ira left," he muttered. "Where is Ira? He comin' along behind you?"

"No. He out for de night. Why you care? Dey ain't no gold here."

Relieved, he turned to stare at the chest again. It was too late to hide anything now. And he'd gone this far, he might as well be sure there wasn't anything valuable inside.

He stuck the end of the bar into the moldy, rotted cloth and pulled some of it away. A heap of coins showed through the rips in the cloth, most of them black with tarnish, but some with a dull gleam.

Lotus peered into the chest, her interest revived. "What's that stuff? It don't look like gold to me."

"I don't know," Zeke admitted. Like Lotus, he'd envisioned the treasure, if they ever found it, as piles of shiny gold pieces gleaming so brightly they would hurt their eyes. Gingerly, he reached into the chest and picked up a couple of the coins. One was large, roughly circular in shape, so badly tarnished he could barely make out the carvings on it. The other was smaller, but glinted dully, like brass.

"Well, well, and what have we here?" a voice said

from so close by both of them jerked in surprise and turned in unison.

Ira stood a few feet away, smirking at them. Then he, too, jumped into the hole. He peered into the chest, and both of them heard his sharp intake of breath.

"My god. Look at this!" He reached in the chest and scooped up a handful of coins, letting them slide through his fingers.

Lotus sniffed disdainfully. "Hah! Dis ain't nothin' but some old coins. It ain't pirate gold." All the work they'd done, all she'd put up with from both Ira and Zeke, for this!

"Oh, yes, it is!" Ira laughed and scooped up another handful, his eyes lit with unholy excitement.

He sneered at Lotus. "Did you think they'd look like new coins? No tellin' how long it's been buried here."

Her face still skeptical; she scooped up a handful of the coins again and looked at them, closely this time. "You mean we all rich?"

Ira's laugh was ugly. "Not quite, you stupid bitch." He grabbed her arm roughly, making her flinch and drop the coins back in the chest. "Did you two think you could get away with this? Tryin' to get me drunk so you could keep all of it for yourselves?"

He shoved her, and she staggered and fell to her knees. Ira kicked her, hard, in the ribs. She gasped with pain and fell backward.

"You stop that!" Zeke moved forward. He was finished with Lotus, but he'd never been a man to beat on a woman, or watch anyone else do it.

Ira turned to him, his face deadly serious now. "Don't try to tell me what to do, Nigra. I can still let your mistress know what you two have been up to."

Zeke frowned uncertainly. "No, you won't. You as deep in this as us."

Ira reached down and picked up the spade. "That's what you think." He lifted the spade threateningly. "Go on. Get out of here. You tried to cheat me out of my fair share; now you won't get any of it. And neither will the bitch."

Behind him, Lotus got quietly to her feet, holding the iron bar. Just as silently, she lifted it and brought it down with all her strength on the back of his skull.

Ira dropped the spade and collapsed face-forward into the chest. The force of his fall made the lid drop onto the back of his neck. He lay there, grotesquely caught by the treasure he'd so wanted.

As if carved from stone, Zeke stared at the erstwhile overseer. Lotus, still clutching the bar, crept to his side.

Zeke turned to her, his eyes wild, fear racing through his body. "You done killed him! You know what they gonna do to you for killin' a white man?"

Lotus's beautiful face was unmoved. She stared at Ira, then back at Zeke. "They ain't gonna do nothin' to me. Cause no one ain't gonna ever find him."

"What you talkin' about?" Zeke demanded roughly.

She gave him an impatient glance. "I mean we git this chest out of here and Ira gonna take its place. Come on. We ain't got all night."

She dropped the bar and lifted the chest lid. The rough metal had sliced into Ira's neck, but that wasn't what had killed him. One side of his skull was smashed in.

Lotus gave a satisfied smile. It was all working out just as she'd planned weeks ago. She glanced up at Zeke again, who was still standing there, unmoving.

"Come on," she said again. "There ain't nothin' else we can do, and you knows it. If you don't help me, I tell the mistress you killed Ira."

Zeke came out of his fearful stupor, dull despair filling him. Now that it was too late, he saw what a fool he'd been to get involved with Lotus, to let her talk him into this scheme.

He was caught in her web again, and this time he'd never be able to get free.

After she settled the Howards' into rooms for the night, Calista had Junie bring them all supper trays. "I hope that will keep them in their bedchambers until tomorrow," she told Ryan as they ate their own late supper with Gabrielle in the dining room.

She toyed with the beef and potatoes on her plate, not at all hungry after the wedding celebration and the stress of the Howards' descent on them.

Ryan glanced at her, unsmiling. "That would be too much to hope for. As soon as Estelle gets her second wind, she'll come sailing down, ready to tear into both of us again."

In spite of his best efforts, he couldn't lose his irritation with this whole situation. He wanted to talk to Calista, but she was too preoccupied with her relatives tonight. And he'd like nothing better than to flatten Baxter. He still simmered over the toad's lustful looks at his wife.

Calista frowned at Ryan's ironic tones. He sounded as he had when she'd first met him, and it made an uneasy frisson go down her spine.

"I'm sorry you had to get involved with this," she told him. "It really shouldn't concern you. It was my idea not to let them know about Andrew and Leora, and they *are* my family."

Ryan's mouth turned up, but the smile held no pleasure. "That sounds like an echo of something I said to you not long ago." Damn it! What was he trying to do? Start an argument?

She gave him a quick, surprised look. "I didn't mean it that way." She heard the edge of irritation in her voice.

"Never mind," he told her, his voice still rough. He needed to get away by himself for a while before he made things any worse. He applied himself to his meal. Afterwards, he went out onto the veranda, not asking her to come with him.

Frowning, Calista watched him go. Something was bothering him, but he didn't want to discuss it with her. Uneasiness, mixed with hurt, flooded over her.

Gabrielle went up to read to her father, who was still confined to his room most of the time. Emory couldn't seem to regain his strength, and he still had a racking cough.

Calista stayed in the sitting room for an hour, bracing herself for the Howards's expected descent. But as time passed and she heard no footsteps on the stairs, her nerves eased.

Apparently, they were all exhausted and had gone to bed. The other footsteps she strained to hear were also not forthcoming. Ryan hadn't left the veranda; and though she longed to join him, she wouldn't. If he'd wanted her to, he'd have asked her.

She pressed her lips together and went upstairs herself. Leaving a candle burning, she tried to sleep. An hour later, when Ryan finally came in, she was still wide awake.

He undressed quietly, then slid in beside her. She waited tensely for him to move close to her, to encircle her with his strong arms, but he didn't. He snuffed the candle, then turned his back to her.

Now, another hour later, she knew sleep would elude her unless she helped it along. A cup of warm milk might do that.

Ryan didn't budge as she eased open the bedroom door and closed it behind her. The hall was silent and dark, but she knew the way so well she required no light. A half-moon rode the cloudy night skies, and a cold wind had come up. She closed the back door and, shivering, pulled her wrapper tighter around her.

Stopping for a moment on the wooden walkway, she looked down the slope toward the quarters. A small light bobbed along. Someone was up and about, which surprised her. The hands had celebrated the wedding well into the evening. They should all be abed by now. She dismissed her concern. If anyone were ill, Zeke would ride up to tell her.

The kitchen was warm, the embers of the evening fire still smoldering in the hearth. The moonlight came fitfully through the windows, casting strange shadows. But it gave enough light for her needs.

Calista skimmed back the cream on top of the bowl and ladled milk into her cup, remembering the other time she'd done this, months ago. Ryan had followed her. She'd realized that night she'd never be free of wanting him.

She heard the sound of the door opening, then closing. She set the cup on the table, her heart leaping with relief and joy as she quickly turned. Ryan had come to find her. Just as he had that other time.

Clouds moved across the moon, plunging the room into a deeper dimness. He walked toward her, only a dim outline in the room, and she went to meet him, a smile of welcome on her face. "I was just making myself a cup of warm milk. Do you want one, too?"

A laugh came over to her, again making her heart leap in her chest. But not from joy this time.

"Not particularly," Baxter's oily voice said. He stepped forward until only a foot of space separated them. "But you can give me what I do want."

Before she realized his intent and could move away,

one hand slid around her neck and shoulder, the other around her waist. Pulling her tightly against his robe-clad body, he pinned her arms to her sides. He lowered his head and covered her mouth with his own.

Revulsion made her gag as she tried futilely to get away from him. He was stronger than she'd expected, and having her arms pinned made it impossible to push against him. She tried to jerk her entire body away, but he only laughed again, his arms and hands clamping more tightly around her.

"Go ahead, struggle, little cousin," he said against her mouth. "That only makes the conquest that much sweeter."

A chill of alarm shot through her. Conquest? What did he mean by that? Surely not what it sounded like.

Should she scream? Have everyone in the house out here? Including Ryan? Her mind quailed at that prospect. Baxter would deny everything, and she'd feel like an idiot. No, she'd try to make him see how foolishly he was behaving.

His mouth slackened on hers, and she gasped for breath. "Let me go, Baxter," she said, forcing her voice to stay calm. "I'm married, now. Have you forgotten that?"

He laughed unpleasantly. "Everyone knows what kind of a marriage you and that crooked attorney have. You've got to be ready for a real man."

"You're an ass, Baxter!" Calista said furiously, forgetting her vow to remain calm. "You've always been an ass!" She jerked her head away, trying again to release herself.

His hand left her shoulder to wrench her head back around. His black eyes burned into hers with a combination of lust and anger. "An ass, am I? We'll see about that!"

He fumbled with the ribbon at the top of her wrapper,

and his grip loosened. She jerked one arm free and gave him a stinging slap.

The moon came out from the clouds, making the room brighter again. His head jerked back, the imprint of her fingers plain on his cheek, fury in every line of his face. His grip tightened. "You little bitch! I'll make you sorry you did that!"

He reached for her wrapper again, tearing at the neckline. Calista heard the fabric rip and shock washed through her, mixed with the beginnings of real fear.

Oh, no, he couldn't be planning to try to force her! Not here in her own kitchen, with her husband sleeping in the house behind them. He couldn't be that stupid.

Abruptly, her mind went back to that other time, when she had been fourteen, and her heart began hammering in her chest. Baxter had found her on the veranda one evening, alone. She'd escaped with a torn bodice, leaving a soundly slapped and surprised Baxter behind.

But that was years ago. Baxter was much stronger now. No smarter, but even more determined. She began to struggle in earnest, managing to get a foot back far enough to kick him in the leg.

He moved away from her a little, his hands still tightly clasping her upper arms, his black eyes gleaming in the dim light. "That's right," he gloated. "Go ahead. Fight me. It won't make any difference in the end."

She'd have to scream, Calista realized, fear pounding through her veins. She opened her mouth, but before a sound could escape, Baxter pressed his hand roughly across her lips. Even in the dim light, she could see his leer. She saw something else, too. The kitchen door opened, and another figure stepped into the room.

"Oh, no, you don't. I've wanted you for years, and nothing's going to stop me from having you now."

"That's where you're wrong, you bastard!" Ryan's grim

voice erupted in the room. His hand clamped down on the other man's shoulder. Taken by surprise, Baxter released Calista. She staggered and nearly fell, catching herself on a table's edge.

Ryan spun Baxter around to face him, then his hard fist connected solidly with the other man's jaw. Baxter staggered, then righted himself, and Ryan hit him again, even harder. Baxter went down heavily, and Ryan stood over him.

"What do you mean attacking me? I haven't done anything," Baxter blustered, struggling to his feet. "Your sweet little wife asked me to meet her out here."

Ryan hit him for the third time, and again Baxter went down. "You'd better stay there, you slimy son-of-a-bitch," Ryan warned, each word clipped and deadly cold.

The other man lay still. A ray of moonlight came through a window, showing Baxter staring up at Ryan, fear on his face. He wet his lips. "This is an outrage," he said, his voice wobbly.

Ryan gave him a contemptuous look. "You're damned right it is. And if you ever look at my wife again, if you ever again set one foot in my home, I'll kill you."

He moved across the few feet separating him from Calista and pulled her to him. "Are you all right? Did he hurt you?"

"No. I'm fine." A thrill coursed through her. *His home.* Ryan had never spoken of Meadowmarsh as that before. It had to mean he'd decided to stay here with her. And she wanted that with all her heart, with no reservations, she knew at last.

How could she ever have doubted it? Love for him filled her with a white-hot flame. Nothing, not even her island plantation, meant more than that.

Ryan held her close. Thank God, he hadn't been able to sleep. If he'd arrived a few minutes later ... He wouldn't think about that. "Does the kitchen door have a lock?"

Surprised, she nodded. "An outside bolt to keep animals out."

She saw the gleam of Ryan's white teeth as he smiled at her. "That should be strong enough to keep in this human beast for the rest of the night." He took her hand and led her to the door.

"Wait!" Baxter called after them, panic in his voice as he got to his feet. "You surely can't mean to leave me here."

Ryan swung open the door, and Calista went out. "You can build up the fire if you get cold." He closed the door and slid the bolt home.

The half-moon illuminated Ryan's face as he looked down at her, his jaw hardening as his gaze lit upon her torn wrapper. "Are you sure you're all right? I should have killed him."

Calista nodded, smiling at him. "I'm fine," she said again. Oh, she was more than fine; she was alight with happiness. She felt as if she could float back to the house and up the stairs to their bedchamber.

"Won't Junie be surprised when she opens the kitchen door in the morning?" She put her hand in the bend of his elbow. Even though a chill wind still blew, colder even than before, she felt warm, delightfully warm.

"I imagine so." Ryan squeezed her hand with his arm as they walked across the wooden walkway to the house. They must talk tonight, now, he decided, before passion once more caught them in its spell.

"Are you feeling better?" she asked him as they entered the back hall.

"What do you mean?"

"You didn't seem to want to be around me earlier tonight."

He halted then, looking deeply into her eyes. "I'm sorry. I just wasn't fit company. The Howards made me so angry, it was all I could do to keep from personally rowing them to Charleston—tonight!"

"Oh. So that's all it was?" She guessed she had a lot to learn about husbands' moods.

This was the perfect opportunity for their talk. "No. I wanted to discuss something else," he said slowly.

A small tremor of unease dissipated some of her happiness. Had she been wrong, after all? Jumped to a hasty conclusion? "All right," she answered, just as slowly.

He let go of her hand and moved back a step, and her unease increased. "I told Jerome not to take on any more new cases for me. And while I was in Charleston I cleared up those still pending."

Her eyes widened as she gazed at him, her happiness returning. But she must have it in words to be certain. "Does that mean you plan to stay here—permanently?" she asked, her voice a breathless whisper.

He hesitated, then nodded. "Yes. If you're ready to accept me as an equal partner." He looked at her searchingly, then he drew in his breath at the blinding love that transformed her face.

"I'm fully ready," she said, her voice ringing with confidence. "Meadowmarsh isn't the most important part of my life."

"And what is?" He forced himself not to move forward and crush her against him. This had to be settled, once and for all.

"You are, my husband." Her voice was a soft whisper, but the words were clear and distinct. She moved forward a step until they were almost touching again. "I want you to stay."

"Then stay I will, my dear wife." Ryan drew her close

to his hard chest. "That's what I want, too." He tilted her chin up and lowered his head, his mouth closing over hers in a deep, hungry kiss.

Calista kissed him back, pressing herself against him, excitement beginning to build in her as she felt the evidence of his swiftly growing arousal.

"Come on," he growled into her ear. "Why are we standing here in the back hall when we have a comfortable bed waiting for us upstairs?"

Before she knew what he had in mind, he'd swept her up in his arms and was carrying her down the hall and up the wide staircase.

"Put me down," she whispered, but not very strongly. She thrilled to the feel of his arms and trembled with anticipation for the night ahead of them. "I must be heavy."

"My dear wife, how many times do I have to refute that statement?" He stopped on a stair and nuzzled her neck until she gasped with delight. "You are just right for me, in every way."

He went on up the stairs and through the open door into the bedchamber. He strode to the bed and deposited Calista gently upon it. He'd lit a candle before he'd come looking for her, and now in its flickering light, she thrilled to the passion in his face, in his deep blue eyes.

"How did you know where to find me?" she thought to ask him belatedly.

"I wasn't asleep when you left, and I remembered that other time you went to the kitchen in the middle of the night to make warm milk." He placed a warm finger across her mouth. "I don't want to talk about that. I have other more interesting things in mind."

"You do? Maybe you can tell me all about them," she said demurely. She sat up in bed and removed her wrapper.

Ryan's eyes darkened as he watched her pull her bedgown off one shoulder, half-exposing one full breast. He turned and hurried to the bedroom door, closed it, and she heard the click of the key in the lock.

Then he was back at the bed, untying his robe, pulling it off impatiently. "I have a better idea," he told her huskily as he slid into the bed beside her. "I will *show* you."

Her heart began pounding; her body started that pleasure-pain aching deep inside. She lifted her hands to Ryan and pulled him down upon her. "That sounds like a perfect idea," she murmured as his lips found hers and he finished removing the gown.

After that, there was a very long silence in the room, broken only by the soft sounds of lovemaking. The candle melted into a shapeless mass of wax, then went out, but neither of them paid it any mind.

Chapter Twenty-One

When Calista and Ryan came down for breakfast the next morning, Delphinia gave them a wide-eyed look.

"Dat Mistuh Baxter, he in de kitchen when I goes out to start de fire," she announced, looking from one to the other. "In his nightclothes."

"Go on, Delphinia," Calista said, feeling Ryan tense beside her at the mention of the other man's name. Love and tenderness filled her. She and Ryan had spent a wonderful night together. For the first time, no doubts or shadows had marred their lovemaking.

"He asked Junie to git his clothes from his bedchamber." She rolled her eyes. "He got a bruise on his jaw and de biggest black eye I ever seed!"

"Where is he now?" Ryan asked, his voice tight. He wouldn't put it past the bastard to be sitting at the dining room table awaiting breakfast!

"After he dress, he ask Gideon to git him a horse and he ride down toward de dock. Guess he in an all-fired hurry to leave Meadowmarsh."

Calista glanced at Ryan, and their eyes met. She was sure he saw the same gratified look in her eyes that she saw in his. Baxter had apparently taken Ryan at his word about never setting foot on Meadowmarsh again. She felt sure there'd be no more trouble from her detested cousin.

She turned back to Delphinia. "It sounds as if he were. But his parents are still here. They'll have breakfast with us."

"Yes'm. Will dey be leavin' today?"

"I'm almost certain they will."

A noise on the stairs made her glance that way. Estelle, her head high, sailed down the stairs, Farley beside her.

She'd quite recovered her aplomb, Calista saw. Wonderful what a good night's sleep could do.

"Dear Baxter isn't in his room," Estelle said, her voice frosty, as she reached Calista and Ryan. "I wonder where he could be?"

"I understand, madam, that he's on his way back to Charleston," Ryan said coolly as they all walked to the dining room. He hoped Calista wouldn't mind, but he intended to get this out in the open and finished.

Estelle stopped halfway through the doorway. She gave Ryan an amazed stare. "Why on earth would he have left so early, and without us?"

Calista glanced at him. Would he tell Estelle the whole story? Which, of course, both she and Farley would refuse to believe?

"Probably because I told him if he ever set foot on the island again, I would kill him," Ryan said pleasantly, bowing to let Estelle go ahead of him.

His glance met Calista's, and he saw the gleam of satisfaction in her eyes at his words. God, what a night they'd spent together! And in the cold light of morning, he had no regrets for the decision he'd made.

"Now see here, young man," Farley blustered, his face

darkening. "Isn't it bad enough you and your wife aided and abetted my daughter in marrying your penniless scamp of a brother? What do you mean by such discourtesy to my son?"

Junie, setting a plate of fish on the table, looked avidly at the group in the doorway. Gideon, behind them in the hall, also seemed very interested in the unfolding drama.

Calista realized she didn't care. All she wanted was to get these two unpleasant people out of her life for good.

"Last night I had to knock Baxter down to rescue my wife from his advances," Ryan said, every word distinct and icy. He challenged Farley with an equally cold look.

"Oh!" Estelle clutched at her ample bosom. "I don't believe I'm actually hearing such terrible lies—and from my own family, too. Farley, we must leave at once! I can't spend another minute in this house."

"Yes, my dear," Farley said, his face now an alarming shade of purple. He turned to Ryan. "Will you have the carriage brought around or do we have to walk as we did yesterday?"

Calista let out her breath in a sigh. "Of course, we'll bring the carriage. But don't you want breakfast before you leave?"

"Breakfast?" Estelle's voice rose an octave. "How can you suggest that after the dreadful lies your husband just told about dear Baxter?"

"Ryan told the exact truth, Aunt Estelle," Calista said firmly, holding the other woman's gaze.

Estelle's glance slid away from her niece's. "Oh! Farley, take me out of here now. Before I have a swooning spell."

His arm about his wife, Farley escorted her back into the entrance hall. Gideon hastily opened the front door, and they walked outside.

Calista heaved a heartfelt sigh of relief. "Junie, bring their traveling bags down."

"I think this will be the last time we'll be blessed with the Howards' presence on Meadowmarsh," Ryan said five minutes later, watching Estelle, head high, get into the carriage, followed by Farley. A glum Summer got up beside Gideon. He lifted the reins, and the carriage moved off down the lane.

He turned to Calista. "Will that bother you? After all, they and Lucinda are all the family you have left."

She smiled and squeezed his hand, a warm vibration going up her arm at the touch. "No, it won't bother me in the slightest, and you're wrong. Your family is mine, now."

Ryan's face softened as he returned her smile. He'd made the right decision. He wanted to stay here, with her. "Thank you for saying that. I've imposed them on you far too long."

"No, you haven't. I don't know how I could get along without Gabrielle now that Lucinda's gone. She's the sister I always wanted." Calista paused a moment, then went on. "I wish there were some way to make your father feel better."

Ryan released her hand and moved away from the window. "So do I, but I fear there's nothing."

"I believe he's some stronger," Calista said, not looking at Ryan. She didn't believe anything of the kind, but maybe Emory's health would improve eventually.

"Perhaps. Now, shall we go in to breakfast? I suppose you have a full day ahead?"

She tucked her hand in the crook of his elbow and smiled up at him. "*We* have a full day," she corrected him, satisfaction filling her. It wasn't going to be hard to share Meadowmarsh with Ryan. Why had she worried about it?

He smiled down at her, loving the curve of her mouth, the tilt of her eyes. Everything about her. A strong urge to pick her up in his arms and carry her back up the stairs, as he'd done last night, swept over him. He wanted to spend all day making love to her. Sighing, he subdued the desire.

But the night lay ahead—the long winter night. And many more to come. "Let's get on with it, wife."

A week later, Calista sat across from Andrew in the library. It had been a satisfying, busy week. She and Ryan had worked together every day and loved each other every night. She was happier than she'd ever have dreamed possible. Her mother had been right—she did need a man in her life. She'd needed Ryan. And now he was completely hers.

Leora and Andrew had come yesterday. "It's obvious married life agrees with you two," she told Andrew, smiling. "Leora's absolutely blooming."

Andrew had asked Calista if he could talk privately to her, and she'd brought him in here a few moments ago. He smiled back at her, but he looked nervous, she thought.

"Yes, we're very happy," he agreed. He cleared his throat. "That's what I wanted to talk to you about, Calista. If you recall, on that other unfortunate occasion, you offered to make me a loan with which to buy land."

Oh, so *that* was what this was all about! "Of course. Have you changed your mind about accepting my offer?"

"Yes, I have," he said, glancing at her half-apologetically. "Now that I'm a married man, I have responsibilities. Leora's money is paying for our rented house and our food." His mouth firmed. "I can't let that continue. Ryan has offered to try to find me work in a law office, but I know nothing of such affairs. All I know is plantation life."

"Yes, and you understand that very well," Calista said encouragingly.

Andrew grimaced. "Now that I've been shown the error of my ways, maybe I'll do better as a plantation master. In any case, I don't know what else I can do."

Calista leaned over and patted his hand. Amazing what a little humility had done for Andrew. Once he'd admitted the need for change, he'd done so. Leora had been right to force the issue that night on the veranda. "I will be delighted to lend you the money," she assured him.

He gave her a relieved smile. "Thank you. I appreciate your kind offer." He paused, then went on. "There is one other thing I'd like to ask of you."

"Of course. What is it?"

"I'd rather you said nothing to Ryan about this just at present. If you remember, he was against this before. I have no reason to think he's changed his mind."

Calista frowned and bit her lip, wishing she hadn't agreed so readily before she knew what Andrew would ask. She had every reason to believe Ryan had changed in many ways, but about this particular issue, she wasn't sure.

He was, as Andrew had just said, planning to try to find his brother a position in Jerome's law offices. He hadn't even mentioned the possibility of Andrew's buying land for a plantation.

Even if Ryan had decided to stay at Meadowmarsh, was his prejudice against plantation life in general still active? She didn't know; and if she got him involved with this, he might very well insist she not loan Andrew the money. And thereby deprive his brother of the only life for which he was suited. On the other hand, she didn't like the idea of keeping this from Ryan.

Andrew, seeing her hesitation, went on, eagerly. "It would only be for a little while. As soon as Ryan sees how well I can manage a plantation now, I'm sure he'll approve."

Finally, she nodded, but reluctantly. Everything Andrew said made sense. "All right, I won't tell him—for a while, anyway."

Andrew beamed. He rose, put his hands on Calista's shoulders, and kissed her cheek in a brotherly fashion. "Thank you again for your kindness. Now, I suppose I'd better go see what my bride is up to." Husbandly pride permeated his voice.

"I believe Gabrielle is filling her in on all the finer points of being a good plantation mistress." Calista gave him an affectionate smile as she, too, rose. "And Leora seems to be taking to it as if she were born on a plantation."

Ryan was coming down the stairs as they closed the library door behind them. He looked harried and exhausted, Calista thought, as he always did after sitting with his father.

Smiling, she quickly walked over and took his arm. "Tired?" she asked him. "Let's join the others in the sitting room for a glass of wine."

"That sounds good," Ryan agreed, smiling back at her. He turned to his brother. "Father didn't like the way I read tonight, Andrew. He's asking for you."

Andrew looked longingly toward the sitting room which held his new bride, then nodded. "Of course. Just let me speak to Leora for a moment." He hurried into the room, leaving Ryan and Calista to follow more slowly.

Already, she regretted her promise to Andrew. She should have told him she had to think about what he asked before giving her consent.

She and Ryan were husband and wife now, truly, and she wanted no secrets between them.

Andrew drew her aside the next day, a worried frown between his eyes. "I did something I'm afraid I shouldn't have. I suggested to Father that as soon as Leora and I get settled, he could come to live with us."

"And he didn't like that idea?" Calista asked, surprised. She would have supposed Emory would much rather live with Andrew than here. Her heart ached for Ryan when the three of them were together and his father's favoritism was so obvious.

"Oh, it's not that he'd mind living with us." Andrew paused. He looked at Calista, chagrin on his face. "You know I said earlier I couldn't accept a loan from you because it would hurt Father too much?"

"Yes," she answered, tensing, afraid she knew now what the problem was.

Andrew sighed, raking his hands through his dark hair. "He guessed you were the one lending me the money and made me admit it. It enraged him. Now, I fear it has sent him into a deeper depression, making him realize he'll never be able to have a plantation of his own."

Calista didn't know how to answer him, because that sad fact was all too true. "Things can change," she tried to reassure Andrew. "He may get better soon and then maybe—"

"What are you two talking about huddled here in the corner?" Leora asked, coming out of the sitting room. She put her arm possessively in Andrew's and smiled up him, adoration in her dark eyes.

Some of Calista's worry eased as she watched Andrew gaze back at his new wife, just as much love on his own face. At least she didn't have to be concerned anymore about these two. It was clear they were happy. Leora had lost, or at least subdued, her flirtatious ways and showed every sign of trying her best to be a good wife.

She'd done the right thing, after all, in not notifying the Howards about the elopement. But she wished she hadn't promised Andrew not to tell Ryan about the loan.

Now, within the next day or so, she must go to Beaufort to talk to her lawyer. Alone. Would Ryan wonder why she didn't ask him to come along? Or would he insist on coming?

The next day she and Ryan stood at the dock, waving, as Zeke took Andrew and Leora away on the flatboat. Guilt filled her. This was never going to work. She'd have to write Andrew and take back her promise. That decided, she relaxed. In fact, she'd tell Ryan tonight, ask him to go along with her to Beaufort. If he objected to her decision, she'd argue with him. They were partners now, true, but that didn't mean they had to agree on everything.

Ryan slipped his arm around her. "Well, Mrs. Burke, do you suppose things have finally settled down and we can be alone together for a while without any more crises developing?" he asked, only half-joking.

She smiled at him, loving the feel of his strong arm holding her close. She'd never tire of that. But the trouble was, his every touch made her want more, made desire flame up inside her. And there were other things to be done besides lovemaking.

"If I don't get Zeke started on the garden, we'll have a crisis when we want fresh vegetables a couple months from now," she said lightly. "Do you want to come along?"

"I wouldn't miss it for the world," he assured her. "Maybe I'll plant a few seeds of my own."

Later, as she stood by the garden area with Ryan, watching him carefully sowing muskmelon seeds in the potato patch, she smiled and pressed her hand against her flat stomach. Maybe another seed Ryan had planted had taken root and would bring forth fruit.

She wasn't sure yet, so she would say nothing to him

for a while. But her monthly course was two weeks late now, and she was always as regular as clockwork. How long she could keep from sharing this happy suspicion with him was debatable, though. Would he, too, be as excited and pleased as she?

He finished sowing the seeds and turned back to her, smiling, his expression happy and carefree. "Is it about dinner time?"

She laughed. "Not for an hour yet. But since we're finished here, I thought we might go by the lagoon before we ride up to the house for the meal."

His smile became mischievous. "That is an excellent idea. It's been awhile since we visited the lagoon," he said suggestively.

Calista smiled, too, as she remembered that day their lovemaking had been interrupted by the old bull alligator. "Yes, it has."

The day was balmy for the second week of March. As warm as May. They tethered their horses and walked across to the lagoon. A blue heron rose majestically at their approach and flew away.

Calista stood on the grassy bank, looking around. She had not been here since the time with Ryan. That episode, which had ended so bitterly, had spoiled her favorite place. But now that they were so happy, her pleasure in it had returned.

"At least I don't see that damned alligator anywhere. Or any egrets. Do you think we might try sitting on the bank for a while?"

His warm breath tickled her ear; his words made her shiver in anticipation. "That sounds pleasant," she agreed.

In a moment, they were situated close to the spot where they'd been before. But now Ryan sat very near, his body heat warming her even through the layers of clothing separating them.

"This is a lovely place. I can see why you like to come here."

"Yes." A small laugh escaped as she remembered that other occasion, when they'd sat here making inane conversation.

"What's so amusing?" he demanded, turning her face up to his.

"I was just thinking about the first time we were here, and we kept talking about the weather and the beauty of the lagoon and such things."

He stared down at her, his gaze hot and full of desire. "That's not what I had in mind this time," he said softly.

Her heart began beating faster. "And what did you have in mind, Mr. Burke?" she asked him demurely.

"This," he growled, swooping to cover her mouth with his own hot, questing lips.

She returned his kiss eagerly; and when his seeking tongue sought hers, she offered it freely with no touch of embarrassment. She heard his indrawn breath; then, as he'd done that other time, he pushed her gently backward onto the soft, sweet-smelling grass.

By now his hands had learned to be adept at her buttons, and soon he had her bodice open and her chemise pulled from her shoulders, exposing her breasts to his view.

"And do I please you?" she asked him impishly, just as she had that other time. But oh, things were so different now! She was sure he cared for her, even though he'd not yet spoken his love in words.

"You please me perfectly, Mrs. Burke." His smile told her he, too, remembered her words on that earlier occasion and his own response. His smoldering gaze seemed to scorch her exposed flesh. His thumb made small circles around one rose-tipped nipple, then the other. That drawing, throbbing sensation began inside her, and she pulled his beloved dark head down against her, holding him tight.

In a moment, he raised his head, and she reluctantly released her hold. He slid her skirts up to her waist and drew her drawers down. Gently, he pushed her legs apart and his searching tongue made those same maddening circles on her upper thighs, moving ever closer to the center of her womanhood.

"Oh, stop," she begged him, on fire with longing. "Come to me, now!"

"Patience, my bride," he whispered, smiling, his blue eyes soft with love. He lowered his head again, and his tongue once more began the slow teasing of her flesh. Calista held her breath as he left her thighs and at last found that most private part of her.

Sensations such as she'd never known existed swirled through her as his velvet tongue found the tiny nub it sought. Her lower body arched upward, and she heard his low, satisfied laugh.

"Enough!" she cried, holding out her arms to him as the now-familiar tension began swirling inside her. "Come to me," she begged him again.

"Not yet," he murmured. "Not quite yet." His mouth and tongue relentlessly continued their loving torment.

The wonderful, sweet ache began to concentrate in her lower body; and she arched against him again and again, her breathing coming faster, her heart pounding, until she could no longer hold back. She closed her eyes, letting the intensely pleasurable feelings wash over her.

In a moment, she felt Ryan's mouth on her closed eyelids, soft as down. "Did you enjoy that?" he asked her softly.

She opened her eyes, smiling at him drowsily. "Of course. But—"

"But what?" His mouth moved downward to hers. His

tongue outlined her lips, and she felt her body beginning to respond again.

"But I want you inside me," she told him, no longer worrying about her brazen words. She didn't care if properly brought up young ladies weren't supposed to talk and behave this way. Ryan had never complained, never acted in the least shocked.

He didn't now, either. "Then, that's what you shall get, my sweet wife," he said thickly as he lowered his body to hers. His mouth covered hers, his tongue thrust inside in an imitation of that other movement she so desired. To her amazement, the pleasuring just past had only whetted her appetite for more.

She arched her body against his, his hard, throbbing manhood pressing against her, inflaming her. "Oh, don't make me wait any longer!" she begged.

"I don't intend to." He parted her legs and thrust within her. She eagerly met his movements with her own, and the heated spiral of pleasure built within their bodies until finally, in the same joyous moment, their release came.

Ryan collapsed against her soft body, his heart hammering in his chest. She'd always given him enjoyment, from the first moment he'd taken her in his arms. But never had their lovemaking been this intense, this completely satisfying.

He wanted to stay here forever, never leave her embrace. But he knew he must. It was possible someone would come to the lagoon, even though unlikely. And even his uninhibited bride would be mortified if anyone found them.

Sighing with regret, he lifted his head and gave Calista one last, tender kiss. Then he pulled her skirts down and helped her fasten her bodice. "I can't believe your alligator friend hasn't surfaced," he said lightly as he adjusted his own clothing and helped her up.

"I told him he'd better not this time," she answered just as lightly.

They walked hand in hand to their tethered mounts, and Ryan helped her up on Sable, his hand lingering on her as his mouth had lingered oh, so recently. They walked their horses side by side, slowly, both reluctant to let the enchantment of the last hour end.

Calista heard the sound of galloping hooves first, coming toward them, and pulled to the right, motioning for Ryan to move in front of her. Who could that be in such a hurry? Zeke should still be in the garden, and—

Gideon came into view, pulling his mount up when he saw them.

A premonition hit Ryan as he looked at the man's face and remembered the other time he'd met him on this same road. The news Gideon brought then was bad, and somehow Ryan felt sure this time would be no different.

"Maussa Ryan," Gideon said, then paused, his eyes rolling wildly. "Oh, Maussa Ryan!"

The premonition hardened to a sick certainty. "What is it, Gideon," Ryan prodded, his voice tense. "What's the matter?"

"Your papa has done shot hisself," the other man answered, his words tumbling over themselves as he hurried to get them said. "He's dead!"

Chapter Twenty-Two

Calista gasped and clapped a hand to her mouth. She looked at Ryan. He stared at Gideon as if he couldn't take in the meaning of what the other man had said. Finally, the words penetrated. His face paled and tightened.

"What happened?" he asked, his voice as tight as his facial muscles.

"I don't know. Miss Gabrielle, she just come screamin' down the stairs, sayin' Mr. Emory was hurt bad. Me and Delphinia went runnin'." Gideon paused and then went on. "When we get upstairs, we see him on de floor with a gun by his hand."

Ryan swayed in the saddle, and Calista moved closer to him. "That's enough, Gideon," she said. "Go on back to the house; we'll follow."

"No," Ryan said. "Get out of my way!" He kicked his mount, and the animal responded with a burst of speed. Calista urged Sable on, too, trying to keep up with Ryan, Gideon bringing up the rear.

When they reached the house, Calista slid down from

the saddle and gave her reins to Gideon. Ryan was dismounted, already at the front door, not even glancing back at her. She hurried after him.

Her eyes wide and shocked, Junie let them in. Delphinia hovered just inside the door, the same expression on her face.

Gabrielle sat on the bottom step of the wide staircase, bent over, rocking back and forth, tears streaming down her face. When she saw Ryan, she jumped up and threw herself into his arms, her sobs increasing.

"Oh, Ryan, Papa's dead!" she cried, the anguish in her young voice making Calista's heart turn over with pity.

Ryan hugged his sister close, then put her away from him, his face still like stone. He hurried up the stairs, leaving the two women without a backward glance.

Calista hesitated, torn between following him and staying and comforting Gabrielle, who'd slumped back down on the bottom step again, her head in her hands. Finally, Calista sat down beside her and put her arm around the girl's shoulder.

"Why don't we take you upstairs?" Calista asked her softly. She caught Delphinia's attention and motioned for her to come over. "You need to lie down for a while."

"All right," Gabrielle said dully, letting Calista help her up. Calista and Delphinia supported the girl up the stairs and to her room. While Delphinia turned back the covers on her bed, Calista removed her slippers, then helped her between the sheets.

Five minutes later, Calista walked down the hall to Emory's room, steeling herself for what she must face. She'd persuaded Gabrielle to take a dose of laudanum and left Delphinia to sit with her.

The door was open. Emory lay on the floor beside his bed, sprawled much as he'd been that other time. But now a pool of blood spread out from his head and a pistol lay close by his right hand. Calista felt her stomach turn over. She took several deep breaths, trying to subdue the nausea.

Ryan knelt beside his father, his hands on his pulse. He must have been there all the time she'd dealt with Gabrielle. Her heart went out to him. Oh, how could she help him through this?

Finally, he lay Emory's hand back down. Before she realized what he planned, he lifted his father and placed him on the bed. Tears came to her eyes as she watched him close his father's eyelids and place Emory's hands across his chest. Then, he looked at him for an endless moment, his profile as hard as granite.

Her breath caught in her throat. She moved toward him, holding out her hands in a comforting gesture. "Ryan," she begged, "come out of here."

He turned and brushed by her, his blue eyes staring sightlessly, and left the room. Calista followed him, not knowing what to do to help. He walked down the stairs like a sleepwalker, she behind him.

He opened the front door and left the house, leaving the door standing wide open. Calista hurried to it, looking out to see him running toward Gideon and a groom, who were leading the horses to the stables.

Ryan's long strides soon caught him up to them. He swung himself up on Buck's back. He turned the horse and kicked him into a gallop, and the curving lane swallowed him up.

Oh, God! Please take care of him, she prayed. *Don't let Buck stumble. Don't let anything happen to him. I couldn't bear it!*

She came back inside and closed the door, then leaned against it. Fear for Ryan's safety mingled with shock, pity, and dismay. In a moment, she realized Junie was looking at her, fear on her face, her hands pulling the white apron she wore into a knotted ball.

Calista checked her wild impulse to go upstairs and throw herself on her own bed. Instead, she straightened, forcing a calm expression for Junie.

"Take the dinner food back to the kitchen," she directed the girl, relieved her voice sounded steady, giving no indication of her inner turmoil. "No one will be eating until later. But bring a pot of tea into the sitting room."

"Yes'um, Miz Calista," Junie said with alacrity, most of the fear leaving her face as her hands smoothed her wrinkled apron. She turned and hurried toward the dining room.

Calista forced her steps into the sitting room. She walked to the big front windows and stood there looking out, her mind a roiling mass of emotions. Why did this have to happen? Why hadn't any of them foreseen this possibility and tried to prevent it?

Ryan's reaction to his father's death had shocked her so badly she still felt stunned. She would have expected Andrew to show such intense feeling, but not Ryan. Ryan had told her he and his father had never gotten along, not even though in the last few weeks Ryan had made a tremendous effort to placate his parent in every way possible.

Hearing a noise, she turned to see Junie. The girl brought the tea tray in and put it on the pie-crust table. "Thank you, Junie," Calista said, again relieved her voice was steady. "Now, will you send someone down to fetch Maum Fronie?"

"Yes'm, Mistress." She left the room quickly.

Calista poured herself a cup of tea, added sugar, and drank half of it before lowering her cup. The hot brew felt comforting as it reached her stomach, settling the rolling somewhat. She finished the tea and poured herself another cup, carrying it back to the window.

There was no sign of Ryan. The knot in her stomach was back again. Should she go after him? Or send Gideon? No, she decided in a moment. He needed to be alone for a little while. She could understand that, even though she wished with all her being he'd wanted her with him.

She didn't know how long she stood there, but then her heart leapt as she saw a horse and rider come back up the lane. Ryan! He rode slowly now, his face lowered. But he was all right! He drew up before the house and reined the horse in.

Gideon appeared and took the horse's reins as Ryan dismounted. Calista hurried to the door, opening it before Ryan could, holding out her hands to him, streaks of tears on her face.

Ryan's hand came up to brush across her face. "I didn't mean to act like such a fool."

His voice was still tight with grief and some other emotion. His wild ride didn't seem to have helped.

She put her arms around his neck, relief making her muscles weak. His arms encircled her, holding her close. She still didn't know what to say or do to comfort him.

"I'm so sorry, Ryan," she said finally, quietly.

He touched her cheek gently, his face softening at her simple, heartfelt words. Even though his father had never treated her with friendliness, she'd always reciprocated with courtesy and kindness.

"I know you are." His face tightened again, with guilt, a muscle working in his jaw. "I shouldn't have left him alone!" he burst out. "I knew he was more deeply depressed the last day or so, but I didn't try to find out why or do anything about it. This is my fault!"

An icy knot formed in Calista's stomach as she listened to him and remembered what Andrew had told her yesterday. She knew why his father's depression had worsened. Oh, how she wished she'd never kept the loan to Andrew secret from Ryan!

"No, it's not your fault," she protested, knowing he needed to hear her say this. "It's not anyone's fault."

Did she believe that? Or was she at least partly to blame for the tragedy? If she hadn't given Andrew the loan, would Emory still be alive? A wave of nausea hit her at that thought. "He hated being sick," she continued. "I guess he finally realized he'd never be well again. Dr. Norman more or less told us that."

Ryan looked down at her, frowning, as if trying to decide whether or not to accept her words. "I know all that. But his health didn't get any worse in the last few days." His jaw muscle jerked again. "I should have locked his pistol up. But who would ever have thought he'd do something like this?"

"No one." Somehow she managed to keep her voice firm, but her guilt and remorse increased with every word Ryan said. "You have to stop blaming yourself." Why hadn't she told Andrew she couldn't make him the loan without discussing it with Ryan?

"Do you think he did this because with Andrew married he knew he wouldn't see much of him from now on?" His gaze burned into hers. "He and Andrew were always very close."

The cold knot in her stomach grew larger, twisted. Calista stared up at him, afraid her guilt showed on her face.

Ryan finally noticed her silence. His frown deepened. "What's wrong?" he asked. "Do you know something about this that I don't?" His hands went to her shoulders.

She swallowed, knowing she could keep this a secret no longer. "Yes. I do." She paused a moment, then went on in a rush, "I promised to lend Andrew money to buy land, and Emory found out. It upset him greatly."

Ryan's hands dropped from her shoulders. A new pain knifed through him, as if she'd struck him a physical blow. "You did this without saying anything to me about it?"

She took a deep breath and let it out. "Yes. I'd promised it to him earlier, and he'd refused. Now, since he's married, he changed his mind."

"Why didn't you discuss this with me?" he demanded. The pain of her betrayal merged with his other pain and guilt until it was almost unbearable. "I know I signed all my rights to Meadowmarsh over to you when we married and I have no legal claim to your plantation. But I thought things had changed between us. Didn't you promise me from now on we'd be full partners? Share everything? I see I was a fool to believe that."

Why had she confessed this now? He didn't understand; he'd never understand! "No! That's not the reason I didn't tell you. I—"

"What other reason could there be," he interrupted harshly, backing away from her, "except that you didn't want me interfering in your business affairs? You don't want me as a partner in your life any more than my mother wanted my father!" He knew he was saying things he didn't mean and that he'd regret later, but he couldn't stop himself.

"No!" she said again, desperately. "You're taking this all wrong! Andrew didn't want me to tell you, so I—"

The mention of his brother's name hit him like a dash of icy water. Irrational jealousy surged through him adding to the other painful emotions holding him in their grip.

"So you thought what my brother wanted was more important than sharing this with me? Even after my father reacted so violently to this same thing before? Didn't you realize Andrew couldn't keep from telling him? My brother has many good qualities, but holding his tongue isn't one of them."

"Please, listen to me, Ryan." She moved toward him, holding out her arms in a gesture of supplication. "You're twisting everything I say."

He wanted to believe her, wanted to take her in his arms and tell her everything was all right; but he couldn't. The old, bitter hurts of their past that he'd thought forgotten swarmed up in him. He moved away from her again.

"I don't think so. I think you're the one who's twisted what a real marriage is supposed to be like into what you want it to be. How could I forget that your first choice of a husband was Timid Timothy. When you lost him, you grabbed at me for only one reason—to save your precious Meadowmarsh!"

Hopeless despair flooded over her as she stared at him in disbelief, remembering the sweet hours of lovemaking they'd shared. The long, pleasant days out in the fields that she'd thought were drawing them closer together. He was right—nothing had changed between them. *Nothing!*

He still believed she'd tricked him into marriage and that all she cared about was her plantation home. Hopelessness filled her, making her feel dead inside. She turned away, not able to look at his accusing face any longer.

They had no real marriage after all. Nothing they'd shared had meant anything to him. As it had to her. She turned back around, her lips compressed, her own facial muscles tight. "You'll believe what you want. Nothing I say will make any difference."

"All you've done so far is try to make excuses for what you did—and what you didn't do that you should have."

Ryan listened to himself in disbelief. Some jealous, angry demon seemed to have control of his mind, his tongue. "I'm leaving this damnable island, Calista, just as I wanted to weeks ago."

Rage flared within her at his harsh, unforgiving words. "That's right—run away! That's what you've always done when there were things we needed to work out between us. But if you leave this time, Ryan, don't come back. I can manage. I don't need you!"

They stared at each other for another endless moment, then Ryan's mouth quirked upward in that hateful, ironic smile she'd grown to detest.

"You've never needed me, madam. Have no fears about my return. That will never happen."

He bowed to her, formally, coldly, then left the room, his head held high. Some sane part of him urged him to stop, go back, tell her he didn't mean those things, and beg her to forgive him for saying them. But the raging demon was still in control. He kept on going, not looking back.

Calista had never known that a heart could, literally, break. But that was what hers was doing at this moment.

The fact that she probably carried his baby inside her wouldn't matter to him, either. No, if she told him, he'd only think she was using that as a last desperate trick to keep him with her. So she wouldn't tell him.

He was leaving her again, just as he'd done that first time, and the second. But this time she knew he'd never, ever be back. And she didn't see how she could live without him.

Chapter Twenty-Three

Ryan picked up the stack of papers and tapped the bottom on his desk to straighten the edges. Then he laid it down again, staring blindly at the stack. He couldn't seem to concentrate on any of the affairs of the law office since he'd returned to Charleston two weeks ago. If he'd thought he was bored with this work before his sojourn at Meadowmarsh, that feeling was increased a hundredfold now.

He wasn't interested in resolving legal wrangles for his clients or setting up trusts and guardianships. It all seemed dry and lifeless.

Unbidden, Meadowmarsh's green fields, the blue lagoon, the beautiful house, sprang into his mind. And Calista's lovely face, looking hurt and bewildered and angry as it had the last time he'd seen her—at his father's funeral.

They'd taken his father's body back to Charleston to be buried next to his wife. Ryan had been shocked and saddened at the few people who attended. His father hadn't had many friends, he realized.

The guilt and blame he'd felt for his father's death had ebbed somewhat after several talks with Andrew, who also felt his own share of guilt. But both had finally agreed no one could have prevented the suicide. His father had no longer been able to cope with his life. So he'd ended it.

As Calista had tried to tell him. Instead of listening, driven by inner demons, he'd lashed out at her, tried to get rid of his own guilt by blaming her. He knew now he hadn't believed any of the accusations he'd hurled at her. He'd simply been almost crazy with regret that now it was too late for his father and him.

He'd finally come to terms with that fact. It had been too late for that for years. His father had preferred Andrew ever since the younger son was born. And nothing Ryan had done, such as the many loans, would alter that. Or nothing he could have done in the future if Emory's suicide hadn't cut his life short.

Mindlessly, he picked up the papers and tapped them on the desk again. Seeing Andrew and Leora so happy together sent a knife of pain through him. He could hardly bear to be with them.

"Ryan, my boy, don't you think it's time to call it a day?" Jerome's hearty voice questioned from behind him. "You've been shuffling those same papers for the last half-hour."

Ryan compressed his lips and set the stack to one side. "There's nothing here that requires my urgent attention," he said, his voice defensive.

Jerome sighed and sat down in front of Ryan's desk in a client chair. "I'm not hinting that you aren't pulling your weight around here. You're doing your usual good job, but your heart isn't in it anymore."

"What difference does that make?" Ryan asked angrily,

staring at Jerome. "Most people don't love the work they do for a living."

"That may be true, but not all of them hate their work, either." He put up his hand as if to ward off Ryan's angry retort. "I didn't come in here to argue with you again. I came to invite you to supper. Lucinda told me not to come home unless you were with me."

"Then it looks as if you are going to have to spend the night in the office."

He couldn't stand an evening with Lucinda and Jerome. Not only did their turtle-dove contentment pierce his heart even worse than being with his brother and Leora, but both of them were still determined to find some way to get Ryan and Calista back together.

Jerome rose to his feet. "I won't argue with you about this, either," he said. "You're the most bone-stubborn man I've ever seen when you want to be. I'm going home, but if you change your mind, just come on over."

Staring at his partner's back as he turned and left the room, Ryan knew he wouldn't do that. He'd go home to his empty house and eat one of Arva's uninspired meals.

Then he'd have a couple of brandies to try to dull the pain that was his constant companion. He'd never known a person's heart could hurt as his did, unrelentingly, day after day.

And night after night he lay and stared at the dark ceiling, trying to keep from remembering those other nights when Calista had lain in his arms. Sometimes he thought about swallowing his pride and going to her to beg her forgiveness, but he knew he couldn't do that.

She'd told him if he left not to come back. Not ever again. She'd told him she didn't need him. That hurt most of all.

Because he needed her as a man needs to draw breath into his lungs in order to live.

* * *

Holding onto the curving rail, Calista drew herself wearily up the long staircase. She'd stayed out in the fields later than she should have to try to make herself so tired she could sleep instead of lying awake and thinking about Ryan and how much she missed having him in the big bed next to her. And the nausea that was with her most of the time now had been especially bad today.

She knew now she carried Ryan's child. But she'd told no one, not even Lucinda or Gabrielle, for fear one of them would let Ryan know. Before too much longer, her condition would be obvious to everyone, but she'd worry about that when the time came.

The turbulent emotions she'd felt the day Ryan's father had died had settled down into a dull ache. She no longer blamed herself for Emory's death. She couldn't have denied Andrew the loan, and Emory was bound to have found out where his son obtained it sooner or later. No, the man's suicide had been his own doing. No one could have prevented it.

But she still felt guilt for not discussing the matter with Ryan and keeping her actions a secret from her husband. True, she'd regretted her decision and planned to tell him that very night. But that didn't alter the fact she'd been wrong.

Ryan had every right to feel she'd reneged on her promise to make him a full partner in Meadowmarsh, in her life, even though she'd thought she'd had good reasons for her actions. But it was too late now for second thoughts, and Ryan would never forgive her.

He'd meant all those hurtful, bitter words he'd said the day his father had died. He'd proved that. She'd had no word from him since the funeral. Gabrielle had come back to Meadowmarsh and she was a comfort. But no one could ever take the place of Ryan. And she needed him now more than she'd ever have believed she could need anyone.

She'd rest for a while before eating supper. It was almost dusk, and the candles in the sconce at the top of the stairs weren't lit. Frowning, Calista paused on the top step, looking down the dim hallway. It wasn't like Delphinia or Junie to be this careless.

Without warning, fear swept over her, like the unease she'd felt on Meadowmarsh since her return from Charleston, but intensified a dozen times. A sense of something evil seemed to fill the space around her. She was just being foolish and fanciful, she tried to tell herself, because she was so tired and unhappy. Nothing was wrong.

She made out something else just at the head of the stairs. Something that looked like a coil of thick rope. What could rope be doing in the upstairs hall? Puzzled, she put her foot on the top step and leaned over for a better look.

An ugly, wedge-shaped head lifted out of the mass, and a forked, flickering tongue shot out toward her. Unreasoning terror filled her as she recognized the object for what it was. A water moccasin. The snake began uncoiling and moved toward her, its head extended, and her terror became complete.

She turned to flee down the steps, but her feet caught in her skirts and she tripped. Then, she felt hard, strong hands on her shoulders, pushing. She heard a low, triumphant laugh, and she tumbled down the wide, long staircase. When she finally reached the bottom, she lay still and unmoving.

Delphinia ran out of the dining room at the sound. "Oh, my lord God, help us!" she screamed. "It the mistress— and she dead!"

At the top of the stairs, deep in the shadows, Lotus felt

a surge of exultant satisfaction as she heard Delphinia's words.

Finally, she'd done it. Never, ever again would she have to look at that white face, that silky black hair, those gloating green eyes.

That hated, detested woman who'd sent her away from the master who'd favored her . . .

She scooped up the snake with a pointed stick and thrust it into the bag she held.

Gabrielle, who'd been in the sitting room, came running, too. She knelt by Calista, who lay on her back, her eyes closed, and laid her ear against the other woman's chest. After a few moments, she lifted her head.

"She's not dead," she told Delphinia and Junie and Gideon, who were gathered around, fear and worry on their faces. A large bruise was already forming on one of Calista's pale cheeks, another on her forehead. Several scraped places on her neck and arms were bleeding.

"Let's take her up to her room," Gabrielle said, forcing her voice to sound calm and unworried. She had no idea how badly injured Calista was, but revealing her fear would only make the situation worse.

Her show of control had the effect she wanted, keeping the other three calm and steady as they slowly and carefully carried Calista up the stairs.

The candles burned at the head of the stairs now, and the polished hall floor was bare. A door further down the hall closed quietly just as the three people bearing Calista in their arms reached the top.

Gabrielle hurried to Calista's room and turned the covers on her bed back, and the others laid her gently between the sheets. Gabrielle pulled up the sheet and quilt to Calista's neck, then turned to Gideon. "Go fetch Dr. Norman. Tell him it's an emergency."

She turned to Junie. "Bring me a basin of warm water and a clean cloth and some of the salve we use for cuts."

Junie and Gideon hurried out of the room. Gabrielle unbuttoned the top two buttons on Calista's dress, loosening it from around her neck. Delphinia hovered on her other side, her face anxious.

"Miz Calista gonna be all right, ain't she?"

Gabrielle nodded. "Yes, I'm sure she will," she said, pretending a certainty she was far from feeling.

Her sister-in-law had looked terrible lately. Pale and exhausted—and Gabrielle well knew why, too. She missed Ryan. Gabrielle had managed to persuade Ryan to let her return to Meadowmarsh a few days after their father's funeral. He hadn't wanted her to, but she'd been as determined as he for once. She *wouldn't* let Calista stay there alone! Finally, weary of her pleading, he'd agreed.

Calista had been surprised but pleased at her return, Gabrielle was certain. She was furious with Ryan for leaving Calista again. She'd like to shake some sense into him.

"There's somethin' you ought to know," Delphinia said, her voice hesitant.

Gabrielle lifted her head. "What is it?"

The other woman swallowed visibly, obviously nervous about imparting this information. "The mistress, she in de fambly way. She don't want no one to know, but I thought you need to."

Shock washed over Gabrielle as she stared at the other woman. "Are you sure?" she demanded.

Delphinia nodded. "Yes'm. I seen a lot of women dis way. She cain't keep her food down in the mornin' and she gettin' bigger on her top." She indicated Calista's breasts.

Calista moaned and moved restlessly, and Gabrielle

jerked her attention back to her. Calista's eyes fluttered open for a second, then a look of horror swept over her face and she thrashed her head from side to side.

"Where is it?" she muttered, her eyes wild with fear. "Is it in the bed?"

Gabrielle frowned, her worry increasing. What was Calista talking about? Was she hurt worse than Gabrielle had thought? Whatever was wrong, the other woman clearly feared something. Tenderly, Gabrielle smoothed Calista's tumbled hair back from her forehead.

"It's all right," she soothed. "Nothing's in the bed, or anywhere else."

Calista's eyes opened again, and this time they looked awake and focused as she looked at Delphinia. "There was a snake, a moccasin, at the head of the stairs," she said. "And the light was out. And someone pushed me. And laughed."

The other woman's eyes widened with fright. She shook her head. "I lit de candles myself, Mistress," she said. "And wasn't no snake up dere when I did it." She darted a fearful glance at Gabrielle.

Shock and anger washed over Gabrielle, joining with her fear. Calista's story was true, she felt sure. But who would do such a horrible thing? And why?

Calista moaned again, and Gabrielle saw her hands move beneath the covers to clutch at her abdomen. "Hurts," she muttered.

No longer able to hide her fear, Gabrielle looked at Delphinia. The older woman nodded. "I better go get Maum Fronie," she said. "I feared she be losin' de baby."

"All right, you do that," Gabrielle agreed, trying to hold her voice steady.

Delphinia hurried out of the room just as Junie entered. "Here's de water and salve." She placed the items on the chest next to Calista's bed.

"Good," Gabrielle said, hearing the tremble in her voice in spite of her efforts. Uncertainty and fear swept over her. Oh, she didn't know what to do! How she wished Lucinda were here with her.

She dipped the cloth in the warm water and wrung it out, then gently wiped Calista's forehead. Her anger at Ryan increased. He shouldn't have left Calista here alone in the first place.

To leave her when she was carrying his child was unforgivable! But maybe he didn't know about it. Calista moaned once more, her hands still clutching at her abdomen, and Gabrielle's fear increased. What if Delphinia were right and her dear sister were losing the baby?

Not knowing what else to do, Gabrielle dipped the cloth into the water again, wrung it out, then placed it on Calista's forehead, covering her eyes, which seemed to soothe her.

Pressing her lips together in fear, frustration, and anger, she made up her mind. As soon as Dr. Norman arrived, she would send a message to Ryan telling him his wife was losing his baby.

And that he was desperately needed here and to come at once.

Chapter Twenty-Four

Ryan leaped out of the flatboat, securing it to the dock before Zeke had a chance to do so, then hurried to the waiting carriage.

Zeke watched him go, his brow furrowed. Two days had passed since Miz Calista had fallen down the stairs. He'd heard about the snake and now knew Lotus had done this terrible thing to the mistress.

Since Ira's death and the discovery of the gold, he'd managed to put Lotus off whenever she brought up leaving. The chest was in his cabin, and he lived in daily fear of someone's discovering it. A hundred times a day he wished he'd left the chest where it was. Ira would still be alive, and gone. And he could stay at Meadowmarsh.

Lotus had grown increasingly sullen; and from the sly glances he caught her throwing his way, he'd known uneasily that she'd been planning something else. But he hadn't even considered anything like this! Until she'd admitted it to him yesterday—at the same time admitting, no, bragging, that she'd also caused Miz Calista's earlier fall from her horse.

He'd known then Lotus was capable of anything. A fact he should have realized when she'd killed Ira with no apparent qualms, then or later. She'd tried to kill Miz Calista to force Zeke to leave with her. And she'd won. Too late, he knew he didn't want to go. This was his home. He'd been born here and lived here all his life.

But he had to get Lotus away from Meadowmarsh. She would do something else, even worse, if he didn't. And the next time she might succeed in her evil plans.

Everything was ready for their departure. The next dark night, when clouds hid the moon, they'd load the gold on the flatboat and leave Meadowmarsh forever.

"Good day, Mistuh Ryan," Junie said, opening the door, her smile restrained.

"Good day, Junie." This time there was no *Welcome home, Maussa Ryan,* he thought, pausing in the entry as the now-familiar smell of lemon oil and cleanliness filled his nostrils.

He couldn't blame her for that. His behavior had been abominable, he had to admit.

"Do you want some dinnuh? It be out in de kitchen, but I can bring you somethin'."

She sounded as if she didn't care if he starved. He couldn't blame her for that, either. "No. I don't want anything." He looked down the long hallway toward where the graceful staircase rose, trying to push down the anger that mingled with his guilt.

No matter how bitter their quarrel, Calista should have told him he was going to be a father.

Or maybe he wouldn't. Sorrow and regret joined the anger again as he strode down the hall and up the stairs.

Apparently, Calista was in great danger of losing the infant.

He paused again outside the open door of the room where they'd spent those wonderful nights of lovemaking. Which had resulted in this. He swore at himself inwardly. Why hadn't he thought of such a possibility when he'd left here?

Gabrielle sat by Calista's bed, intent on her needlework. She glanced up; but her smile, too, was reserved, not the delighted one he was accustomed to receiving from his only sister.

Damn it! He wasn't to blame for this situation. If he'd known Calista was pregnant, he'd never have left for good. No matter how angry they'd been with each other, what hurtful words they'd exchanged. He'd have returned with her as soon as his father's funeral was over.

At last Ryan forced himself to look toward the bed. Calista lay on her back, her glorious hair making an ebony fan on the pillow, her face as white as the bedgown she wore. Her eyes were closed, her sweep of dark lashes a smudge on her pale cheeks, one of which had an ugly bruise.

Compunction smote him, overriding all his other mixed emotions. He should have been with her from the start. She shouldn't have had to have gone through this alone. He walked to the bed and stood looking at her, remembering all that had happened between them, the good and the bad.

Her eyelids fluttered open, sleepily, then closed again. The next instant they flew open and her brilliant emerald eyes, filled with surprise, stared into his own.

"Hello, Calista," he said, forcing a smile.

"What are you doing here?" she whispered. Her glance went to Gabrielle, accusingly. "Did you send for him?"

Ryan's tender feelings fled, again replaced with anger.

"Yes, she did," he answered before his sister could reply. "Didn't you think I should know about this?"

Distress flickered over Calista's face. She wet her lips with her tongue as if she didn't know what to say.

Gabrielle rose quickly and took Ryan's arm and half-pulled him out of the room, closing the door behind them.

"I didn't send for you to make my dear sister even more miserable," she told him, her pretty face tight with anger. "Dr. Norman says she must have absolute peace and quiet. No one is to disturb her in any way or she will lose the baby for certain. If you can't control yourself, you had best go back to Charleston."

He stared at his normally docile, quiet sister in surprise. He felt as if he'd been attacked by a kitten. But he also felt a growing respect for Gabrielle and irritation with himself. He reached out and took her hand.

"I'm sorry, Gabby. I promise you I won't do that again."

"You'd better not," she said ominously. She glared at him for a moment longer, then her expression softened.

"How is she?" Ryan asked.

"Dr. Norman says that with each passing day, she has a better chance of keeping her child."

"What caused this? Has she been ill?"

Gabrielle bit her lip, glancing at him as if not sure how to answer his questions. "If I tell you the whole story, will you promise not to get angry again?"

Ryan nodded impatiently. "Yes, of course. Why the mystery?"

"Someone put a snake, a poisonous moccasin, at the head of the stairs. Calista fell down the steps trying to get away from it." She paused, then went on. "And whoever did it also pushed her."

Shock darkened his eyes until they appeared almost black. He grasped his sister's shoulders. "Do you mean

SWEET ENCHANTMENT

someone tried to kill her?" he demanded, his voice tight and hard.

"Let go; you're hurting me," Gabrielle complained. When he complied, she moved back a step. "Yes. Or at least hurt her."

"Who in hell did that? I'll kill the bastard!"

"You promised you'd stay calm," Gabrielle reminded him. "We have no idea who could have done it."

That wasn't entirely true. She suspected Delphinia and Gideon knew something more. But getting it out of them was a different story.

Fury darkened Ryan's face. "Dammit, I swear before God I will find out!" He drew a deep breath and let it out, visibly trying to regain his composure.

"The important thing now is to keep everything calm and peaceful for your wife."

"Of course," Ryan admitted, but inside he smoldered.

"You'd better give yourself time to calm down and Calista time to get used to your being back before you see her again."

Ryan scowled at her words, but knew she was right. If he caused his wife to lose the baby, he'd never forgive himself.

And he had plenty to do to occupy the next few hours. He'd find out who had done this to her, and the son-of-a-bitch would be lucky to escape with his skin intact.

"I don't care what you say, we needs to tell Maussa Ryan that Lotus is de one did it!" Delphinia, sitting on a kitchen stool, glared at her new husband.

She and Gideon seldom quarreled. In fact, since their wedding, and Summer's departure, Delphinia had been perfectly content and happy. Until this awful thing had happened. Then, all her old concerns about Lotus had resurfaced.

Gideon, not one to be browbeaten, glared back. "And what if she didn't? Dat woman git us for tellin'. Dere's somethin' wrong with her."

"I know. Dat's why we needs to git her off Meadowmarsh. Even if she didn't do dis, she do plenty other bad things."

Busy putting food away, Junie listened and wondered which one of them she agreed with. And which one would win this battle of wills. She thought probably Delphinia would.

And that might be good and it might not. She, too, heartily wished Lotus gone. Far away from the island. But if Lotus found out she was suspected, then she'd make sure the person who told Maussa Ryan would be very sorry for doing so.

Junie shuddered. She wasn't going to be the one to tell.

Turning up the collar of his cloak against the blustery March winds, Ryan strode to the boathouse by the dock. He'd ridden and walked around most of Meadowmarsh this afternoon talking to the hands.

No one would admit to knowing anything; but from the furtive glances they gave each other and the evasive answers to his questions, he was sure they at least suspected the identity of the culprit.

The sailboat was turned upside down, and Zeke was coating the bottom with coal tar. A flatboat was just coming back in with two field hands aboard.

By the time Ryan reached Zeke, the flatboat was secured, the hands holding up several large fish, their faces beaming with pride as Zeke looked over their catch.

"Afternoon, Maussa Ryan," Zeke greeted him, giving him a quick smile, then glancing away. "Look like it was a good day for drum fishin'."

Ryan nodded, studying the driver's face. There was something closed in Zeke's expression, too. And in his movements. And he hadn't even been questioned yet. Ryan watched as Zeke dispatched the two hands to the house with the fish; then the driver turned back to his work.

He looked up again in a minute. "Was there somethin' you wanted to talk to me about?"

Zeke had asked that question too innocently. "Yes," Ryan said, his voice hard. "I intend to find out who put the snake in the house." He paused, then went on, his gaze holding Zeke's. "And who pushed the mistress down the stairs. Do you know anything about it?"

The other man shook his head quickly. *Too* quickly, Ryan thought, his suspicions growing. He didn't for an instant think Zeke had done the deed, but he felt more sure all the time that the driver knew who had.

"No'suh, I don't know nothin' about it."

He kept his gaze steady, but Ryan could tell he was uneasy. Whom was he protecting and why? Would he cover up for any of the people here, just as a matter of principle? Or was there something else behind his silence? "You know your mistress could have been killed, don't you? That she is still in great danger of losing her child?"

"Yes'suh, I know that," Zeke assured him earnestly. "I sure am sorry. All of us are."

The driver's voice had hesitated a moment before that "all," Ryan noticed. As if perhaps one person wasn't sorry. Ryan's mouth tightened. Would it do any good to threaten the man?

No, he decided, reluctantly. Calista had complete faith in Zeke. Not only that, Ryan didn't have the authority to enforce any disciplinary action. He hadn't come back to Meadowmarsh to take over the reins of the plantation because Calista was temporarily unable to see to things.

He'd come because he'd been summoned by Gabrielle. Calista hadn't wanted him here, hadn't even wanted him to know about the baby. A cold knot formed in his stomach. He'd put off facing this realization for hours, covering it over with anger.

Now he could avoid it no longer. The day he'd left, Calista hadn't just said those final words to him in anger as he'd dared to hope. She'd meant them. She'd told him not to come back; and it was plain she still felt that way, because she certainly hadn't been glad to see him this morning.

"I think you know more than you're telling. And I intend to get to the bottom of this," he told the driver, his voice still hard, and walked to his mount. He might as well go back to the house. Maybe his newly-fierce sister would allow him to see his wife for a few minutes.

He took a deep breath of the air as he rode up the lane. It smelled like spring, and everyone was making ready for the new season. Most of the hands were hauling cartloads of marsh mud to spread on the cotton fields in preparation for planting in a few weeks.

On an impulse, he stopped by the garden. The melon seeds he'd planted in the potato patch were up, the tender new green of the fragile seedlings reminding him painfully of that day, that perfect hour he'd shared with Calista at the lagoon.

And of the mess he'd made of things later. He'd left her once too often; and now, he feared, it was too late to try to make amends. Especially, if she lost the baby. If that sad event happened, he'd have no second chance with her.

Because, as she'd told him that day he'd left, she didn't need him. She was perfectly capable of managing her life, running her plantation alone. And that wasn't the worst of it. He made himself face the final truth he'd so far avoided.

Maybe she no longer even wanted him.

"And how are things with Jerome and Lucinda?" Calista asked Ryan politely. It was early that evening, and Gabrielle had tiptoed in a few minutes ago to ask if she felt like talking to Ryan.

She'd agreed; but now, as he sat by her bedside, she wasn't sure that it had been a wise decision. His unexpected arrival this morning had badly shocked her. He looked tired and thinner, as if he hadn't been sleeping or eating well.

Could it be possible he'd missed her as much as she'd missed him? That he hadn't come back, as she'd been certain, only because of the baby?

"They're fine. Married life seems to agree with them," Ryan answered, his voice as carefully devoid of real feeling as hers.

Calista sat propped up in bed and looked a little less wan than this morning. He burned to take her in his arms and tell her how much he loved her, how much he'd missed her. But he didn't know how she felt about him and he didn't dare risk upsetting her to find out.

"I'm so happy for them. And Leora and Andrew?"

She didn't know if she were glad or sorry Ryan was here on Meadowmarsh again. She'd gone through so much these last few days she felt numb, half-dead inside. The cramping pains she still felt at intervals kept her nerves tightly wound because she knew what they meant.

Her body was trying to expel the baby growing inside her. She tried not to think about that because when she did it terrified her. She desperately wanted this baby!

"They, too, are well," he answered. "Andrew has found some excellent property not far from Charleston which he's negotiating to buy."

The sound of her soft voice had made tremors go up and down his spine. He would give anything to be able to take her pain and bear it himself. Should he tell her how much he regretted those hasty, angry words he'd said the day his father had died?

Surely, he could tell her how he felt without disturbing or hurting her. He got to his feet and walked the two steps to the bed. He smiled down at her and reached for her hand, which lay on top of the quilt. Her small hand was so cold it shocked him, and another dark bruise marred its whiteness, making him freshly aware of the precarious state of her health.

"We have to talk," he said, forcing his voice to stay calm and not reveal the intensity of his feelings.

Her hand moved slightly inside his grasp. She gave him a long, searching look, as if considering his words. Then her face contorted and her hand slid out from under his, both hands clutching her abdomen.

Terror filled Ryan as he watched her pain. What should he do? He hurried to the door and opened it. Delphinia was walking down the hall. "Get Gabrielle!" he called, then hurried back inside.

Without thinking, he lay down beside Calista and gently put his arms around her, hoping to comfort her. She was still in the throes of the cramps, her muscles drawn up, her face contorted. Tenderness swept over him. He wanted to hold her forever, to take away all her hurt and pain.

"Ryan! What are you doing?" Gabrielle came into the

SWEET ENCHANTMENT

room at a run. "Get out of the bed," she ordered, her voice horrified.

Ryan reluctantly slid his arm out from behind Calista's neck and then got off the bed. He backed away to give his sister room. Gabrielle dipped a cloth in a basin of water on the chest and placed it on Calista's forehead.

"Remember what Maum Fronie told you," Gabrielle said, her voice low and soothing, completely ignoring Ryan. "Try to relax all you can. Don't push or strain."

In a few more seconds, the spasm eased. Calista went limp, lying back on her pillow, sweat beading her forehead, her eyes closed.

Gabrielle shot him a worried look. "You'd better leave," she whispered. "Let her rest."

Ryan nodded, cursing his blundering self as he left the room. He'd tried to make things right between them, but all he'd succeeded in doing was upsetting her again and making things worse.

He made a fist and slammed it into his palm as hard as he could as he stood outside in the hall. He'd always believed that honor and strength and courage were all you needed to get by in the world.

Now, he'd just found out that sometimes none of those attributes meant anything. The woman he loved more than life itself was in pain and danger, and there was nothing he could do to help.

Except stay away from her.

Delphinia raised her hand and hesitated a moment, then knocked on Ryan's door. Oh, lordy, he wasn't goin' to like this, but she had to tell him, even if it were the middle of the night. Miz Calista was still in the bed. She couldn't deal with this. Maussa Ryan was the only one left.

The door opened and Ryan stood there in his nightshirt, frowning. A week had passed since he had returned to Meadowmarsh. Calista was better, the danger of a miscarriage thought to be over; but after what had happened the day he'd arrived, he hadn't dared try to talk to her yet. He hadn't discovered who'd attacked her either, a fact which galled him.

His face tightened. "What is it? Is my wife worse?" He started to go around her, heading for Calista's room.

Delphinia barred his way. "No, Maussa Ryan, nothin's wrong with Miz Calista." She paused a moment, then blurted out, "Zeke and Lotus are gonna run away—and dey takin' a chest of gold!"

"What in hell are you talking about?" Ryan demanded. "Have you lost your senses?"

She shook her head emphatically. "No, suh, I ain't got nothin' wrong with me. Gideon seen dem. You got to stop dem." She decided she might as well tell him all of it. "Lotus put the snake at de top of the stairs, too." She wasn't absolutely sure of this, but who else would have done such a thing?

Ryan's disbelief faded as he stared at her, his face tightening more, with anger now. "Wait right there," he commanded, "while I dress."

Ten minutes later, Ryan galloped toward the boat dock, Gideon alongside him. The night was pitch-dark, the sliver of moon hidden behind dense clouds. Perfect for such as this, he thought. Only the whiteness of the oyster-shell lane kept their mounts on track.

The two men slowed as they approached the landing, then stopped their horses and dismounted. Ryan could see nothing; but he heard faint sounds, grunts, and straining noises, as of people lifting some heavy object.

The chest of pirate gold, he supposed, if Delphinia and Gideon told the truth. The story was fantastic, but he had no reason to doubt them. Everyone had heard the tales, and some treasure had actually been found on these islands.

They tethered their mounts, then eased forward into the blackness. A faint glimmer of light came to them now. The two men crept on, finally coming out into the clearing at the landing. A dimmed lantern sat on the dock. Two figures struggled with a large, rectangular object, trying to get it onto one of the small flatboats.

"What do we do now?" Gideon whispered in Ryan's ear.

"We stop them." Ryan's anger overrode caution as he hurried forward, no longer trying to be quiet. This woman, this Lotus, who'd almost killed Calista, wouldn't escape. She'd stay here and be punished for her crime.

He burst into the clearing at a run, his boots crunching on the oyster shells underfoot. "Stop!" he shouted, indignant anger making his voice boom in the quiet night.

The figures froze, then two heads jerked around and stared at him. Even in the dimness, he could see the stupefied looks on their faces.

It was Lotus and Zeke all right. Ryan's anger increased. He'd liked and trusted the driver completely.

More fool he.

Chapter Twenty-Five

Zeke stared at Ryan. His worst nightmare had come true. Somehow he'd known he and Lotus wouldn't get away with this. His hands slid out from under the chest, and it landed with a thump on the edge of the flatboat. The boat tilted alarmingly, then righted itself.

Lotus glared at him and tried to push the chest further toward the middle. "What you doin', fool? You want dis gold to go to de bottom?"

"You the fool," he answered. "Cain't you see we're caught?"

Ryan reached the dock and leaped up on it. Gideon followed, staying beside the dock. Lotus backed away, hatred and defiance on her face.

"Zeke, I trusted you. How could you do such a thing?"

Shame washed over Zeke. He felt as low as a worm for his part in this. If only he hadn't gotten mixed up with Lotus in the first place. He hung his head, not seeing Lotus as she glided silently behind Ryan and lifted a heavy wooden oar.

"Look out, Maussa Ryan!" Gideon shouted. Ryan

turned, moving aside a split-second too late. The oar crashed down on his head. He staggered and fell to his knees.

Lotus, a triumphant smile on her face, lifted the oar again.

Before she could bring it down a second time, Zeke jumped at her, wrenching the oar from her hands and flinging it into the creek. "You crazy fool!" he spat at her. He pushed her away from Ryan and knelt before the other man.

Gideon leaped on the dock and started toward Lotus. The woman backed away from him, her hands extended like claws, malevolent fury contorting her features.

"You stay away from me," she hissed, "or I kill you."

Fear on his face, Gideon stopped. Lotus turned and, in one swift movement, grabbed the long pole from the dock and jumped into the boat. She pushed it out into the currents of the creek, the iron chest wobbling on the edge.

Gideon stared after her, then seemed to come to himself. He shook his head and hurried over to where Zeke still knelt beside Ryan. "Is Maussa Ryan hurt bad?"

"I don't know," Zeke said, cold sweeping through him as he saw the bloody gash on Ryan's forehead. Lotus had hit Maussa Ryan hard—maybe as hard as she'd hit Ira.

And Ira had died.

Forcing himself to stop thinking of that, he looked up at Gideon. "We got to get him back to the house. I'll stay here while you ride back and fetch the carriage. I'm feared to try to take him on the horse."

Nodding mutely, Gideon hurried off the dock and up the lane. In a few moments Zeke heard the sound of horse's hooves galloping away. He sat down on the dock and gently eased Ryan's head into his lap, hoping to see some signs of returning consciousness.

But there were none. Again, hopelessness and fear took

hold of Zeke. He'd done wrong, and now he would have to pay for it. As the sounds of the hoofbeats died away, the dark night grew very still.

Into the silence and darkness came another noise from somewhere down the creek. The sound of wood crashing into wood and splintering and a huge splash, then a woman's high-pitched scream. The hair on the back of Zeke's neck stood up. That was Lotus's voice, and he knew what had happened.

The chest, too near the edge, had made the boat hard to steer. Lotus had crashed into a tree along the bank, and the chest had tipped off. And so had Lotus. The gold lay on the bottom of the creek, and it could stay there forever as far as Zeke was concerned.

Lotus couldn't swim a lick, and neither could he. There was no way he could rescue her. Zeke felt only a great relief. He'd have to pay for his part in this mess, even if Maussa Ryan lived. But no one would ever have to know about Ira.

And maybe, if he were very lucky, Miz Calista wouldn't sell him off Meadowmarsh. He could stay here in his home.

In a comfortable chair, pillows stacked around her, Calista sat by Ryan's bedside. Gabrielle and Dr. Norman had fussed, reminding her that even if the danger of losing the baby was past, she was still supposed to stay in bed for a few more days. But she hadn't listened.

How could she possibly lie in bed, in another room, when her husband was perhaps badly injured? When no one knew if he'd ever regain consciousness?

Her heart stopped beating at that thought, and she put it hastily away from her. He *would* be all right. He couldn't die. She wouldn't let him.

Closing her eyes, she said a prayer for his recovery. When Zeke and Gideon had brought him up to the house late last night, the commotion had awakened her.

Calista forgave Zeke for his part in the affair because he'd prevented Lotus from hitting Ryan again, probably saving his life, and stayed with him. Of course, he must be punished, but she didn't intend to sell him.

In her heart she knew Lotus was responsible for the snake and pushing her down the stairs, as well as her fall from Sable. She could feel nothing but relief that the woman was gone, along with her malignant influence, lifting the pall that had hung over Meadowmarsh these last months.

When she'd seen Ryan stretched out on his bed, his face ashen, that horrible bleeding gash on his forehead, she had nearly fainted.

But she didn't. Instead, she sat by his bed the rest of the night, through the time when Dr. Norman came, examined him, stitched and bandaged his wound, and then left, giving no promises and not many encouraging words.

Now, it was almost noon of the next day and Ryan hadn't moved. Not even so much as an eyelash flickered on his still face. Fear and despair swept over her, but she firmly pushed them back. She would not give up!

She closed her eyes again for another prayer. "You can't let him die now, Lord," she said, not realizing she spoke aloud. "The baby is safe, and I love him too much. I need him too much. I can't give him up."

Ryan returned to himself just in time to hear her say these words. He moved his head, and an enormous pain split his skull. He scarcely noticed. *She needed him. His wife had just admitted she loved and needed him.*

"I don't think I am going to depart this world—not this time," he said, his voice weak and raspy.

Calista's eyes popped open. She jumped up from her chair and was at the bed in one step. Ryan gave her a shaky smile.

"Oh, Ryan," she breathed, a radiant smile breaking out on her face. "You're going to be all right!"

"I think so. However, this headache may kill me if the injury doesn't." He felt his forehead gingerly and encountered a bandage.

She shuddered, her smile fading. "Don't even joke about that."

The smile left his face, too. He gave her a serious look.

"Can you forgive me for those things I said? I didn't mean them. I blamed myself for Father's death, but I lashed out at you instead. I can understand why you didn't discuss the loan to Andrew with me. I'd acted like a jackass about it before."

She nodded cautiously. What was he saying? That he wanted to stay here with her? That he hadn't come back only because he felt duty-bound? "I forgave you long ago, Ryan. And you were right; I should have discussed it with you. I also said some things I didn't mean that day."

"Such as not to come back? That you didn't need me—even as a father to our child? Why didn't you tell me?" His eyes gazed deeply into hers.

She forced herself not to look away. "Because I feared you wouldn't believe me. That you'd think it only another trick to hold you here."

His blue gaze held steady. "Maybe I would have. I was a little crazy."

She took a deep breath. They had to get everything out in the open and resolved or their marriage had no chance of survival. "Do you still believe our marriage is like your parents'? That I want to control everything—including you?"

He reached for her hand and squeezed it. "No." His voice rang with conviction. "I was a fool to ever think that. And I love *you*, not your plantation. I want to be with you, always. I want that with all my heart."

Joy leaped in her breast, shone in her eyes. "I love you more than I can say, and I want that, too," she whispered. "That's all I've ever wanted."

"I'm stubborn and opinionated," he warned. "Used to getting my own way."

Calista smiled. "So am I. We'll probably do a lot of arguing. But we'll do a lot of loving, too."

She bent to kiss him, and he tugged her down beside him. As she nestled close to his warm body, contentment flooded over her. In a moment, she felt his hand on her abdomen, his fingers splayed.

"A part of both of us is growing inside you," he said, his voice alive with wonder. "What shall we name our son? Do you have any favorites?"

Calista placed her hand on top of his. She raised up on an elbow and gave him an impish smile.

"I think we'd better wait for the birthing to decide on names. You might end up with a daughter!"

He looked startled, as if that possibility had never occurred to him. Finally, he nodded. "You are correct, Mrs. Burke. And that will be entirely to my liking. However, if that's the case, we shall soon have to try again for a son."

She leaned over him and, just before their lips met, she whispered. "And that idea is entirely to *my* liking, Mr. Burke."

Dear Reader,

I hope you enjoyed SWEET ENCHANTMENT.

My next book will be COURTING EDEN. When an ex-Confederate officer falls in love with the pregnant, Yankee widow of a man he sent out to die in the last battle of the Civil War, the problems between them seem insoluble.

But somehow love finds a way!

Look for it in July 1996.

I enjoy hearing from my readers. You can write to me at P.O. Box 63021, Pensacola, FL. If you'll include a self-addressed, stamped envelope, I'll send you a bookmark.

Elizabeth Graham

Please turn the page for
an exciting sneak preview of
Elizabeth Graham's next historical romance
COURTING EDEN
coming in July 1996
from Zebra Books

Chapter One

North Carolina—May, 1865

"Dammit!" A sharp pain joined the constant ache in Jesse Bainbridge's wounded leg. He should have waited a few more days before starting home, as the kindly North Carolina farm woman who'd nursed him had urged. Jolting up these mountain trails on horseback wasn't helping any, either.

You don't have to do this, the sensible, critical part of his brain told him. *You could have gone straight home.*

But his conscience would give him no rest until he found Corporal Clayborne's cabin and delivered to his widow the man's personal effects. Why did he feel compelled to do this? He'd seen dozens, hundreds, of men die during the war. Why was this one death different?

He knew why. Guilt twisted his gut again. As company commander, Jesse should have sent Clayborne back home when he'd shown up in North Carolina in February, coughing his head off, too sick to fight; but he hadn't.

Joe Johnston had needed every man he could get, even though by that time Jesse, as well as most of the troops left in the ragged, hungry Army of Tennessee, had known the South was finished.

With no warning, a wave of dizziness swept over him, and he slumped in the saddle. Alarmed, he fought for control, but realized it was no use. He reined Ranger in, sliding from the saddle onto the trail only a moment before blackness engulfed him.

"Mister, are you ailin'?"

The young, anxious voice penetrated the gray fog. He felt a light touch on his butternut coat. Jesse opened his eyes. He lay on his side on the trail; and a slim, barefoot girl in a faded calico dress, her flaxen hair in two thick braids, crouched beside him. Her bright, blue eyes were as anxious as her voice had been. Her fingers loosened his shirt collar.

Jesse shook his head. "I'm all right." He'd managed to land on his good leg, barely missing a large, jagged-edged rock; but the injured one felt as if someone had started a fire under it. He tried to pull himself upright, and another wave of dizziness hit. When it passed, he carefully eased to his back, then raised to a sitting position, bracing himself with his hands.

He hadn't missed the rock after all. A gaping tear in his worn gray trousers showed blood oozing from his wound. Damnation!

He heard the girl draw in her breath in a shocked gasp. "Yore hurt! I knowed somethin' was wrong."

Jesse turned toward her, trying for a reassuring smile. "I'm all right," he said again. "I just need to rest for a few minutes."

"No, you ain't," the girl said, her voice very positive for one so young. "Yore leg is hurt bad. Did you git shot by a Yankee?"

The girl's forthrightness and total lack of fear surprised

him. But tucked up on this North Carolina ridge, her homestead probably hadn't been touched by marauders from either side. She hadn't learned to fear as had so many in Georgia after Sherman burned much of Atlanta and began his rapacious march to Savannah.

Jesse's face tightened as he thought of his mother. His ruined plantation. Annabelle, his fiancée, who'd tried to keep things together.

He nodded. "Yes, and I only reopened the wound. I'll put a new bandage on, and it'll be fine." The leg was far from fine, but he'd make camp for the night here and find Mrs. Clayborne's cabin tomorrow. Then he'd head on home to Annabelle.

The girl got to her feet. "You need doctorin'. I'll take you to the cabin. Reckon you can stay on the horse if I help you back on?"

Jesse struggled to his feet, fighting off a new wave of blackness. Reluctantly, he admitted the girl was right. He needed help and he didn't know if he could stay on Ranger. "I think I'd better walk. How far is the cabin?"

"A right smart piece. Maybe I ort to git Darcy and Pap." She frowned in thought, then her face brightened. "But Miz Hannah's ain't far. We'll go there. Kin you lean on me?" She presented a slender shoulder.

"If you can find me a walking stick, that would work better," he told her.

"Course I kin." She vanished, reappearing a few moments later with a sturdy tree limb. From a pocket, she produced a knife, expertly whittled off a protruding knob, and gave it to him. "Is this 'un all right?"

"It's fine," Jesse assured her, gratefully bracing himself with the stick. He glanced at Ranger, grazing a few feet away.

The girl followed his gaze. "Don't you worry none

'bout yore horse. I'll tether him and come back and git him later." She followed her words with swift action, securing Ranger to a tree in the shade.

Jesse felt warm blood trickling down his leg, accompanying the thrum of pain. He'd be a fool to argue further. A smart soldier knew when to quit. He'd learned that, if nothing more, from four years of war. "Lead the way."

"There's a path, but it's a ways. And you ain't in no shape to walk more'n you have to."

"You're right there," Jesse admitted. Sweat ran down his face, even though the May afternoon wasn't hot. He paused to remove his worn jacket and roll up his shirt sleeves. He guessed it was time they exchanged names.

"I'm—Jesse Bainbridge," he told her, barely stopping himself from adding "Major."

The Yankees had stripped the rebel buttons from his coat, as well as his regimental insignia. His mouth twisted at those humiliating memories. He was back to being plain Jesse Bainbridge, and that suited him fine. He was a planter—he'd never liked soldiering. He forced a smile. "What's your name?"

She glanced at him, smiling shyly back. "Willa Freeman."

"I'm happy to make your acquaintance, Miss Freeman," Jesse said.

Her eyes widened at his formality, but she bobbed her head in acknowledgment. "I'm real pleased to meet you, too," she said. "Are you lost, mister? We don't git many strangers up on the ridge."

This girl no doubt knew the location of the Clayborne cabin. He should ask her where it was, but he didn't feel up to it right now. And he certainly didn't feel up to talking to the widow. He'd wait until tomorrow. "No, I'm not lost," he told her. "I—have to take care of some business."

She nodded, asking no more questions. Staying close to him, she pushed aside the rank, tangled growth of laurel, sassafras, and sumac and held it back while he passed as they slowly made their way through a patch of woods.

They pressed through one more patch of underbrush and were in a clearing. A log cabin rose in the middle, behind it Jesse glimpsed outbuildings. A tall, black-haired woman stood on the cabin's small front porch, her hand shading her eyes against the sun as she looked toward them.

Jesse's muscles tightened. He dreaded the next few minutes. He didn't feel up to explaining why he was here to this woman, to anyone. He only wanted to get off his feet as quickly as possible. He forced a smile for the girl, then stepped forward again. Might as well get it over with.

Eden Clayborne's dark brows drew together as she watched the approaching pair. She'd heard a horse's whinny while inside the cabin, but saw none with Willa and the stranger who walked beside her. Who was he?

Willa and the man came closer, and she saw he was limping. Blood trickled down his leg from a gaping hole in his faded, worn gray trousers. A butternut-colored coat was slung over his arm. Tension easing, she decided he posed no threat. He was only a soldier returning to his home, like thousands of others.

Her mouth tightened. *Her* husband wouldn't come back.

The soldier reminded her of the mountain lions she'd occasionally seen during her four years here on this ridge. His thick, shaggy hair was a sunstreaked dark blond, and the sun caught glints off the hair on his well-muscled arms, below the rolled-up sleeves of his coarse white shirt. His eyes, beneath blond brows, were another, deeper shade of yellow-brown. His nose was straight, his mustache and beard a slightly darker shade than his hair. His beard didn't conceal his well-molded facial bones.

Even though he limped, even though he wore only the sad, battered remnants of a Confederate uniform, she knew he'd been an officer. He still had an air of command showing clearly through his exhaustion.

As did his inborn pride and arrogance. He was one of the planters. She lifted her head, her face tightening. Men such as he had started this senseless war which had destroyed so many lives. What was he doing here?

He and Willa had almost reached the porch. And he looked as if he'd never make it up the steps without more help. Eden swallowed, hurrying off the porch. It was possible her assumptions about him were wrong. Even if they weren't, no matter how she felt she couldn't turn away anyone sick or injured.

"This here is Mr. Bainbridge, Miz Eden. He's hurt right bad," Willa said. "I thought I'd better bring him here 'cause it's closer than Mam and Pap's."

Willa called him mister, Eden noted. So he'd not given her his rank. That was fine with her. She'd be glad to call him mister, too. She wanted no more reminders of the just-ended war.

"You did the right thing, Willa."

The woman stopped in front of Jesse. She gave him a tight, forced smile. "Can you make it up the porch steps?"

Surprise snaked through Jesse as he listened to her crisply pronounced words. This was no backwoods mountain woman. Her voice was cultivated and educated—and Northern. A Yankee. He felt his stomach muscles tighten. Her kind had conquered his people. *Defeated.* He hated the word. What in hell was she doing here, on this ridge, in this cabin?

The tall, striking woman wore a faded brown calico dress similar to Willa's. Glossy black braids wrapped around her head. Her skin was tanned a honey-gold shade. But the gypsy-like looks were broken by her deep blue eyes fringed with thick black lashes and topped with arching black brows. As her dress moved with her steps, Jesse saw something else. She was pregnant.

He nodded, his face holding no return smile. "Of course. It's kind of you to offer your hospitality."

His voice was formal and cool, no friendlier than her own, Eden noted. The years she'd spent in these hills hadn't softened her speech, and he liked a Yankee woman no more than she did a Southern gentleman. Good. That made things easier. No pretense would be necessary between them.

Jesse straightened his back and by sheer force of will limped up the steps. He wasn't at all sure he could make it to the cabin door, but he'd die trying. The two females hovered at his side, stopping before the open door. His leg throbbed like hell, and the dizziness had come back.

"Iffen you don't need me anymore, I'll go fetch yore horse," Willa told him.

He nodded. "Thank you. He could use some water." He could hear his voice soften when he spoke to the girl. He had no quarrel with her. He'd fought alongside many a brave hill man, including the one whose family he was here to find. He set his face in rigid lines to keep from showing pain, but knew he had to get off his feet soon or collapse.

Another female voice called from inside the cabin. "Eden, who you got out there? Bring him in."

The woman led the way. In a moment, Jesse's eyes

adjusted to the dimness after the sun-washed day outside. Light shone through gaps in the chinking between the logs, revealing one large room with a ladder to a sleeping loft at the far end. Two corners held beds. In one, an old woman lay, propped on pillows. Even though his vision was wavering, he could see the deep sadness in her dark eyes, in the down-turned lines of her wrinkled face.

"Mother Clayborne, this is Mr. Bainbridge. He has an injured leg, and a fever if I'm not mistaken," the younger woman said in her clear tones. "You may have this bed," she told him, indicating the empty one, neatly covered with a bright patchwork quilt.

Clayborne. Shock spiraled through Jesse's tired body. He jerked his head up and stared at the tall woman. She stared back, dislike, almost hatred, blazing from her blue eyes. Was this Corporal Clayborne's wife? The other woman his mother? One of them pregnant and the other sick or bed-fast?

Jesus, he hoped not. Maybe they were just related to the Claybornes he sought. He closed his eyes as weakness spread through him. He couldn't find out anything more now. He was at the end of his endurance—he had to get off his feet, rest a while.

"Thank you, ma'am," he muttered. He managed to get to the bed, then everything went black.

"Oh, my land!" the older woman said, her voice trembling as Jesse sprawled across the bed. "He didn't up and die on us, did he?"

Eden pressed her hand against his forehead, and her heart sank. As she'd thought, he burned with fever. And her mother-in-law sounded well on the way to a bad spell. "No, of course not. He only fainted. He'll be all right."

Tugging at his scuffed, worn-out boots, Eden hoped that was true. The sooner he was well and on his way, the better. Her instinctive feeling that he wasn't a hill man had been proven when he'd spoken. Her lips thinned. No, as she'd thought, he was a Southern aristocrat.

She finally got the boots off. Both wool stockings had huge holes in the toes. She took them off, too, and carefully tugged up his ripped trouser leg to inspect the wound. At least it had stopped bleeding. It was a gunshot wound, she guessed, although she'd never seen one before. As she'd feared, the wound looked infected, pus oozing out from several places. It also looked as if it had been re-injured recently.

"He don't look all right to me," Hannah said. "Reckon you need to git the smellin' salts?"

Eden pulled a quilt that had been folded at the foot of the bed over him rather than try to get his dead weight under the covers. The infected wound was probably causing the fever, she hoped, because he wasn't coughing and didn't sound hoarse as if he had a respiratory ailment. Of course, any number of things could cause it. She wouldn't think about that possibility.

Turning to her mother-in-law, she forced a smile so the other woman wouldn't see her worry. She might despise his kind, but she didn't want him to die on her bed.

"I think he needs sleep and rest more than anything. But I'm going to make a poultice for his wound. What kind would be best?"

Hannah gave her a sad smile. "Gal, you know as well as I do. Better, now you and Willa are gatherin' all them wild plants to sell."

Eden didn't mind being caught out in her small deception to draw Hannah into a discussion about remedies, because her mother-in-law had perked up and looked interested.

"I believe I'll use slippery elm bark. Comfrey tea later, when he wakes up." Without warning, nausea attacked, and she pressed a hand to her softly rounded abdomen.

The older woman hadn't missed her quick movement. "You need a cup o' peppermint tea, yoreself. You work too hard fer a woman in the fambly way."

And who would do the work if she didn't? "I'm all right. Pennyroyal or crawley root for the fever?" she asked, hoping to distract Hannah.

Hannah frowned in thought. "Crawley root works faster," she finally pronounced.

Eden nodded. "I have plenty on hand."

Her dark eyes clouding, Hannah sighed deeply. "I wisht I was able to hep you."

Eden did, too, but knew urging her mother-in-law to get up and move about wouldn't get her out of bed. Only time could accomplish that. And maybe nothing would.

How they would manage later, when Eden grew heavy with this child and after it came ... no, she wouldn't think about that. She'd take one day at a time. At least a little money was coming in now from the sale of the herbs and plants, especially the ginseng.

"I takened the horse to the barn, Miz Eden. Was that all right?" Willa's light, lilting voice asked from the doorway.

Eden flashed her a quick smile. "It's fine. I'm going to make up some medicines for Mr. Bainbridge." He looked to be in his middle thirties. Again she wondered where he was going, why he was here on the ridge.

Willa glanced at the still figure in the bed, and her eyes widened. "Is he real sick?"

"I don't think so," Eden reassured her, again hoping she was right.

"Reckon I better go on home. Mam will git me with a switch iffen I'm late doin' my evenin' chores." Willa grinned at Eden. "*Get* me, I mean," she corrected herself. "Will you have time to give me a lesson tomorrow?"

Eden hated the way Willa's mother treated her, hated even more the casual way the girl accepted it. She forced a smile. "We'll find time. Come over in the afternoon. Goodbye, Willa."

She watched the girl walk down the steps with a natural grace, and her lips tightened. In the boisterous Freeman household, Willa wasn't much valued. At thirteen, she was considered almost a woman. Eden knew in another year or two, her parents would be finding her a husband.

"Not if I can help it," Eden muttered, searching through jars of dried herbs on a wall shelf. Of course, men might be scarce now. The damnable war had taken a lot of them. Willa's two brothers had all miraculously escaped death, although the older one had lost a leg at Shiloh.

Eden shuddered. She even hated the names of the cursed battles! Hated remembering how she'd brought the newspapers from the settlement in the valley, read the rolls of dead and missing to Hannah and the Freemans.

Finally, the day she'd dreaded had come. Alston's name leaped up at her from the newsprint. He'd died a few days before General Johnston surrendered to Sherman. That was what she couldn't forget, couldn't stop blaming herself for. Last fall he'd come home to recuperate from pneumonia and in January gone back to the war. If only she'd told him about her suspected pregnancy and persuaded him to stay here, he'd be alive today. But her pride hadn't allowed her to beg.

Another, darker guilt gnawed at her. Her grief for Alston was only that for a friend. Not the bitter anguish of a wife who deeply loved her husband. She didn't know when her love had died, but die it had. Long before Alston's physical death.

She found what she needed on the shelf and soon had the poultice ready to apply. Again approaching the bed where the man lay, she was relieved to see he'd regained consciousness.

His tawny lion's eyes stared straight at her. No, she thought, drawing a quick breath, *into* her. For a long moment, she felt as if her heart and soul were bared to this man, this stranger she'd never seen until a few minutes ago.

She stared back at him, realizing something even more startling. She felt, for a moment, as if she knew him, too. Could read the pain behind his disturbing eyes, that bracketed his well-shaped mouth.

His gaze shifted away and he asked, his voice weak, "May I have a drink of water?"

Eden laid her medical supplies down on the chest of drawers near the bed. "Of course." She turned back toward the kitchen area. Hannah was right—she needed more rest. Her mind was playing tricks on her.

"Well, I'm shore glad to hear you a-talkin'," Hannah said. "Didn't know but what you might have left us fer good."

"Oh, I'll be around a while. I'm a tough bird. Take more than a wounded leg to do me in."

Eden, dipping water into a glass, spilled a little. He sounded so bitter, almost as if he were sorry he was still alive. Unbidden, compassion filled her. He'd no doubt fought hard and bravely. Probably from the start, four long, agonizing years ago.

A vision of Alston lying somewhere under the North Carolina ground came to her. She also had no doubt her husband had been a brave soldier.

She finished filling the glass and took it to the man in the bed. She steadied his hand with her own as he drank thirstily. His hand was much too warm; she'd better get the crawley root into him. He drained the glass, then lay back on the pillow, closing his eyes. His long lashes swept his cheeks. Dark circles surrounded his eyes. He looked completely exhausted.

Eden fought another wave of pity. The sooner she could get him well enough to travel, the better. If his class of people had been willing to be reasonable on the slavery issue, there would have been no war for anyone to fight, to be wounded in. To die.

He didn't deserve her sympathy, no matter how bravely he'd fought.

ABOUT THE AUTHOR

Elizabeth Graham grew up in Missouri's Ozark region. She and her husband love to travel and have lived in Germany, Hawaii, Maryland and Pennsylvania—where they owned a pre-Civil War farmhouse. They now make their home in the country near Pensacola, Florida.

With four children and seven grandchildren, family get-togethers are always lively and exciting!

Although Elizabeth has also published several contemporary romance novels, as well as short stories, historical romances are a special and continuing delight to her.